# DAN VINING

"Eerie . . . supernatural noir."
                                        —*Los Angeles Times*

"Dan Vining has reinvented the hard-boiled detective genre and given it a supernatural twist . . . A hip, high-octane plunge through L.A. noir."
                                        —Jeff Long, author of *The Descent*

"Strange, haunting, cool—and very hard to put down."
                —Michael Marshall, author of *The Straw Men* and *Blood of Angels*

"Such a breath of fresh night air. An extremely cool story rendered by a guy who really knows how to sling the language to maximum effect."
                                —Rockne S. O'Bannon, creator of *Alien Nation*

"A great, cynical, hard-boiled L.A. PI novel featuring a fun cast of sleaze monkeys and a great view of the city. Then about halfway through came a curve, no, a knuckling slider—the most surprising plot twist I've ever read maybe anywhere . . . And it worked. From there, [it] went somewhere I never expected. And when it was over, it felt like it was still going somewhere else. Very cool."          —Flint Dille, screenwriter, *Constantine*

"Deft, dazzling, and mercurial. The high concept aside, it's the characters who linger long after the last page is turned: vivid and real if not exactly alive."                —Davin Seay, author of *Take Me to the River*

"Fans of Jim Butcher's supernatural noir Dresden Files series will enjoy this unusual work. A great read."                —*Library Journal*

*continued . . .*

"[A] Chandleresque style and atmosphere [and] . . . a great twist. Smart, fast-paced, entertaining. I didn't want it to end."

—Kevin Jones, screenwriter

"Different, quirky, and scary." —*Midwest Book Review*

"The book has a real voice, style, a graceful blend of caustic observation, nostalgia, humor, and, yes, poetry . . . Revelatory. Readers of mysteries . . . are certainly going to get more than they bargained for."

—William Mickelberry, screenwriter, *Black Dog*

"Vining successfully weaves together two very different stories . . . [His] neo-noir prose sports a refreshing twenty-first-century hipness."

—*Publishers Weekly*

"A private eye book with a supernatural twist . . . fascinating characters and a really cool woo woo element . . . A noirish, haunting mystery."

—*Spinetingler Magazine*

"Dark, surreal . . . If this were a movie, it'd probably be shot in black and white . . . [but] this isn't your ordinary murder mystery. It demands that you think, that you become involved. A final word or two of advice: be wary of Sailors. And stay home on the night of a blue moon."

—*Round Table Reviews*

"Dan Vining is one of the few authors who can consistently write great urban noir with a supernatural twist . . . So very entertaining."

—*Futures Anthology Mystery Magazine*

# AMONG THE LIVING

## DAN VINING

BERKLEY BOOKS, NEW YORK

**THE BERKLEY PUBLISHING GROUP**
**Published by the Penguin Group**
**Penguin Group (USA) Inc.**
**375 Hudson Street, New York, New York 10014, USA**
Penguin Group (Canada), 90 Eglinton Avenue East, Suite 700, Toronto, Ontario M4P 2Y3, Canada
(a division of Pearson Penguin Canada Inc.)
Penguin Books Ltd., 80 Strand, London WC2R 0RL, England
Penguin Group Ireland, 25 St. Stephen's Green, Dublin 2, Ireland (a division of Penguin Books Ltd.)
Penguin Group (Australia), 250 Camberwell Road, Camberwell, Victoria 3124, Australia
(a division of Pearson Australia Group Pty. Ltd.)
Penguin Books India Pvt. Ltd., 11 Community Centre, Panchsheel Park, New Delhi—110 017, India
Penguin Group (NZ), 67 Apollo Drive, Rosedale, North Shore 0632, New Zealand
(a division of Pearson New Zealand Ltd.)
Penguin Books (South Africa) (Pty.) Ltd., 24 Sturdee Avenue, Rosebank, Johannesburg 2196,
South Africa

Penguin Books Ltd., Registered Offices: 80 Strand, London WC2R 0RL, England

This book is an original publication of The Berkley Publishing Group.

This is a work of fiction. Names, characters, places, and incidents either are the product of the author's imagination or are used fictitiously, and any resemblance to actual persons, living or dead, business establishments, events, or locales is entirely coincidental. The publisher does not have any control over and does not assume any responsibility for author or third-party websites or their content.

PRINTING HISTORY
Berkley trade paperback edition / December 2009

Library of Congress Cataloging-in-Publication Data

Vining, Dan.
  Among the living / Dan Vining.—Berkley trade paperback ed.
    p.  cm.
  ISBN 978-0-425-23010-7
 1. Private investigators—Fiction.   2.  Los Angeles (Calif.)—Fiction.   I.  Title.
  PS3622.I56A83 2009
  813'.6—dc22

                                                              2009036407

PRINTED IN THE UNITED STATES OF AMERICA

10  9  8  7  6  5  4  3  2  1

# CONTENTS

## THE QUICK

## THE NEXT

# THE QUICK

# ONE

A rugged malibu canyon, a clear night. The smooth black road ahead, unstriped, wound through slow turns, the headlights igniting the underbrush. There was a song on the radio over the low rumble of the engine. The windows were down, the air sweet with something that picked that night to bloom. For now, Jimmy Miles was just eyes in the mirror. The half-moon came into the corner of the frame, dancing with the vibration of the motor, full of intent, hung up there like a spotlight over the scene. Jimmy watched it until it slid away again.

A few more turns and there was an iron gate flanked by a pair of fifty-foot-tall jacarandas, like purple fireworks against the night sky. On up the canyon there was a dome of glow and noise, but the house wasn't even visible from here.

A guard stood next to a fat white plain-wrap Chevy.

Jimmy was ready for him. "What's the square root of eighty-eight?" he said.

The guard didn't have an answer, just waited, keeping whatever he thought off his face.

Jimmy held up his engraved invitation.

"Thank you, sir," the rented cop said and stepped back, and the Porsche—it was a '64 Cabriolet, a ragtop, black—passed through the gates, nice and slow, behaving itself, and up the drive. The guard watched until it went around the next bend then leaned back against the door of the Chevy. The moon flushed, the shadows changed. The guard looked up at the half-round light high out over the water, but didn't think a thing about it. After a minute, a raggedy coyote crept out of the manzanita. There was a plate of chicken *sate,* or what was left of it, on the dash of the Chevy. The dog lifted his nose at it from twenty yards out. The guard squatted, picked through the gravel until he found just the right-sized rock and sent it back into the night.

The big house was all glass and steel and hard edges, like a cruise ship rammed into the back of the canyon, the bridge facing the Pacific, all the lights burning as if there was some enormous emergency. Tall black doors stood open. Music and laughter. Jimmy got out of the car, said something in Spanish to one of the valet car parkers that got an honest laugh and went aboard.

In the foyer, he tossed the invitation onto a side table and walked toward the noise. The card read:

*Mensa: A Night of Mystery*

Joel Kinser's
June 13th
8 p.m.
12122 Corpo Grosso Road, Malibu

The party was two hours in. Here was a crowd of fairly ordinary people wearing the best clothes they owned, except maybe for the guy in Bermuda shorts, flip-flops, and a Cuban guayabera. They all had drinks in their hands, trying to hold them the right way, and they were a little loud, as if they felt out of place in the big rich house, which inside looked more like a Beverly Hills bank than a ship. Money trumped smarts, at least when you were in the middle of it, even smart people knew that.

Everyone turned as Jimmy stepped down into the main room. There was an Oscar on the piano so there was always the chance a movie star would show. Jimmy was a bit of a clotheshorse. Tonight it was a charcoal suit, a white shirt, a black tie—and pastel suede shoes he somehow made work. There was something about him that was pre-acid sixties, a little Peter Gunn, smoky jazz, cool. He was nice to look at but he wasn't a movie star so the party people went back to their smart conversations.

The host, Joel Kinser, who produced movies, sat on the arm of a white couch, his finger to his chin as he listened to a woman a foot taller than he was.

Jimmy caught his eye. Kinser winked at him.

A waiter came past with a silver tray of martinis, an actor *playing* a waiter actually, in black and white, more waiter than any real waiter. It was the way with movie people, they rewrote their lives to look like movies, cast them like movies, spoke dialogue, saw their houses as sets, their clothes wardrobe, their bodies things to be reworked perpetually by backstage craftsmen. Jimmy went along with the gag, took a martini, let the waiter bow at the waist, didn't giggle. He waded into the crowd. He walked past the guayabera guy just as he was delivering the punch line to his story.

*"And it had already been calibrated!"*

It got a big laugh.

A woman stood at the bar along the far wall under a Ruscha, her face turned away, quarter profile, talking with someone, maybe watching herself in the plateglass window beyond the man. There was something Old School about her look, too, black hair over the eyes, a silk dress that caught the light, shoes taller than they needed to be. In another time, or at least another *movie,* she would have had a cigarette smoldering and a little chrome .25 automatic in her clutch bag. And a hurt in her heart.

Jimmy was watching her when Joel Kinser came up.

"Maybe I could see some I.D.," the host said.

Kinser was just over five feet. He wore a suit the color of raw clay, a black silken V-neck tee underneath, thin-soled slip-ons, no socks, a belt that picked up the hardware on the tops of the shoes. He had his hands in his pants pockets, pockets which were always empty. He hated bulges.

"Look who's talking," Jimmy said. "It takes an I.Q. of one-twenty to get into Mensa. What'd you do, have one of your story editors take the test for you?"

Joel Kinser loved talking about how very intelligent he was. It was almost his favorite subject. He smiled in an oddly feminine way.

"Don't hate me because I'm perspicacious," he said.

Jimmy couldn't look away from the beauty.

"Who's she?"

"Jean Kantke. Go talk to her. We don't bite."

"Oh, I could never *talk* to one of you."

"Funny."

"What would I *say?*"

"Right."

A television star, a comic, came in from the foyer, even later to the do than Jimmy. He stopped on the steps, looking for Kinser, or making an entrance, letting them all get a good look at him. He had a face that made you smile or at least think of smiling. He had a can of beer in his hand and wore a black Hugo Boss suit over a Day-Glo Dale Earnhardt Jr. T-shirt.

*"He's* not Mensa is he?" Jimmy said.

"Just a friend. Like you, Jimmy." Kinser turned up the wattage in his smile and started toward the comic.

"Have fun," he looked back and said. "And, by the way, it's one thirty-two."

Jimmy went over to the bar, stepped behind it, poured out the martini and started making a shaker of something of his own. The black-haired beauty, Jean Kantke, was still there, alone now, her back to him.

Jimmy said, "Just as I pulled up, this great song started on the radio. I was going to hang a U-ey, keep on going. You ever do that?"

She turned. From across the room, she was pretty. From here, she was stunning. She brushed her hair away from her face. Up close, her black hair had a blue shine to it. She had green eyes, a bit sad. Her lipstick was some shade of fifties red, edged in black in a way you couldn't exactly see when you looked for it. Her arms were bare. And long. She laid a hand on the bar, struck a pose, but with her it looked natural. A line of little pink pearls followed each other around her pretty wrist.

As he took her in, in that long second, Jimmy had a thought he'd never say aloud, how a beautiful woman was like a classic car, the bold lines, the unexpected color, the *speed* of it, standing still. And the sense that its time was gone already, even as you stood there in front of it.

"I guess not," he said.

"I might," she said.

"I don't think so."

"Why not?"

"You're not the radio type."

"What was the song?" she said.

"It doesn't matter," he said.

She was drinking a martini, too. Jimmy took her glass, dumped it, poured her one from whatever he'd made in the pitcher and one for himself. It was pink. He dropped a thin green curve of lime peel onto the surface, like a professional, or an actor playing a bartender.

She started to taste it.

"Wait," he said. The lime twist was still turning in a circle on the surface.

She waited.

"OK."

She tasted her drink. "Wow," she said.

"Yep."

"What is it?"

"Manna."

"Manna."

"That's what *manna* means," he said. "In Hebrew. *Mannah. What is it.*"

He heard himself. *I'm trying to impress her,* he thought. It had been a while for that.

He came around the bar. "So, how smart are you?" he said.

"Pretty smart," she said.

She tilted her head to one side a few degrees, a look that was meant to be friendly, open the door a little further, better than a smile. Her skin was perfect, her face full of light. He wondered why he'd thought she looked sad before.

"I'm just here on a day pass," Jimmy said. "I know Joel."

They both took sips of their drinks. She was about to say something when he said, "So, how many languages do you speak?"

"Three or four," she said.

"English, French, Spanish, German . . ."

"English, French, Italian, German, a little Japanese. And I read Russian."

"Yeah," Jimmy said, "but do you know what you call that little thing on the tip of a shoelace, where it's wrapped?"

"In English?" she said.

She was at least as good at this as he was. He smiled, waited.

"Yeah, English."

"*Aglet,*" she said.

He touched his finger to the indentation below his nose, over the lip.

"OK, what's this called, the little dent?"

"The *philtrum.*"

"And the little thing that hangs down at the back of your throat?"

"The *uvula.*"

"This is kind of exciting," Jimmy said. "I had no idea."

She touched the lower part of the opening into her ear, above the lobe. It was as pretty and as perfect, at least tonight, in this light, as the rest of her.

"The *intertragic notch,*" he answered. And then, "Why do they call it that?"

"I have no idea," she said.

He offered his hand. "I'm Jimmy Miles."

"I know," she said.

But then, before the next line, before he found out how she knew who he was, there were two gunshots. There was a beat and then a third shot, all from an adjacent room, too loud for the house, wrong for the scene. Everyone jumped, a few people screamed, but unconvincingly. Others laughed.

And they all moved off to investigate.

Jimmy stayed at the bar. Jean followed the others.

She looked back at him. There was a moment and then he followed her.

In the blond-paneled study there were floor to ceiling books—leather-bound, color-coded, looted from some Old Money family or bankrupt junior college—club chairs and ottomans, green shade lights and ashtrays big as hubcaps, for the cigars. Joel Kinser liked to tell people it was his favorite room in the house. The body on the floor had an effective bloody chest wound, still spreading. She was a woman in her twenties, brown hair, tight low jeans, black Gap shoes, one of those skimpy, navel-baring tees the kids called "a wife beater." If she was breathing it was very shallow. Here was another actor thinking this would do her some good. Her eyes were closed. She was cute dead.

Jimmy and Jean stepped in at the back of the crowd.

The man in the guayabera plopped down in the wingback chair directly over the body. He was an engineer at the Jet Propulsion Lab in Pasadena.

"Don't touch anything, Ben," a woman said.

"I wouldn't think of it, Deborah," JPL Ben said.

Joel was up front playing host. He stepped up onto the first rung of the library ladder.

"Well? Anyone?"

"She looks *dead*," the TV comic said. They all laughed like it was the funniest thing.

"I talked to her," a young man said. He was tall, red-haired, still in his teens. He wore corduroy shorts down over his knees, Birkenstocks with white socks, a T-shirt with a word on it that made no sense. He had a squat brown bottle of Bohemia by the throat, propped against his leg.

"What did she say?" the woman asked.

The young man hesitated.

"Wouldn't you like to know," someone else said.

"What happened to the third shot?" Deborah said. "Give us *something* to start with, Joel."

Kinser was enjoying himself more than he should have been. "I will tell you this," he said. "She's a screenwriter."

"What's her name?"

"Rosie Scenario," the red-headed teenager said, very dry.

Ben bounded up out of the wingback chair. He had already made a discovery behind the couch, was just waiting to reveal it.

"So this would be her agent . . ."

The amateur sleuths gathered around the half-hidden second body, a young Latino in khakis and a white short-sleeved shirt, new running shoes on his feet, stage blood on his temple.

The gore was threatening to drip onto the off-white carpet. Joel lifted the lifeless head and put an *Architectural Digest* under it.

"What's in his hand?" one of the women said.

Someone opened the dead fingers. A computer disk.

"*Datum!*" Ben said.

The air was mock electric.

Joel stepped up another rung. "OK, listen, everyone, tonight we have with us a *professional* investigator, my friend, Jimmy Miles."

Everyone turned to look, but Jimmy was gone.

---

The cue ball struck the five ball, which clipped the eight, sending it into the side pocket.

"I meant to do that," Jimmy said.

Jean had stepped in. It was the game room. They were alone. He retrieved the eight ball and lined up another shot.

She waited, expecting him to speak. He didn't.

"We were hoping you might give us a fresh perspective," she said. "Some original ideas."

"The butler did it."

"Joel said—"

Jimmy took his shot, sank the ball. "I used to have original ideas," he said. "Then time and the world conspired to beat them out of me. Now I think the same thing as everybody else, only a little later."

He was still trying to impress her. He sank the three. It made a nice click.

"Kantke," Jimmy said. "Is that German?"

"Yes."

"Nice to meet you." He gave her a smile and offered her the cue.

She didn't take it.

"I asked Joel to invite you," she said.

In a beat, he changed, went cold, pulled inside. A familiar sadness overtook him, the way a cloud slides over the moon.

He went back to his game.

"I knew you and Joel were friends," she said, as he closed down. "I'd like for you to look into something for me. Joel said—"

Jimmy sank a shot and cut her off. "I helped Joel with something a while back and he's had the wrong idea about me ever since," he said. "I gotta talk to him about that."

"Please," she said. "I know all about you."

Now he gave her a challenging look.

"You only take cases every once in a while," she said.

He waited. He wasn't going to make it any easier for her.

"Nobody seems to know why you take the cases you take," she said, putting one word after another. "Money doesn't seem to be a factor—but I have money."

He already knew that. And he knew that she was used to people listening to her, doing what she said.

He put the cue in the rack.

"Are you in business?" he said.

"I own a company."

"I'm sure you know some investigators, security companies. There are some good ones."

"This isn't about my business," she said. "It's about something that happened a long time ago."

Each one of the words of that second sentence came hard for her. But he still just looked at her and smiled and left her standing there.

A Mexican maid was watching a little TV on the counter in the kitchen. On screen was a school picture of a Latino boy ten or eleven, an image that has come to mean "missing child" or "dead boy." The story was being told in Spanish. The picture of the boy gave way to a family crying in front of a little house, then an angle on a relative arriving, caught in the first moment he stepped from the car and got the news. On the L.A. Spanish stations the crime coverage was always more explicit, more theatrical, more frightening: *Monsters walk among us!* was the theme.

Jimmy came in. The maid tensed, but smiled. He opened a couple of cabinets until he found a glass. She watched as he filled it at the sink and drank it down.

She had a Band-Aid on her finger. He asked her about it. "*Te cortaste el dedo? Penso que era un* hot dog?"

She laughed and shook her head.

Then Jean came in.

She stopped under a bright recessed ceiling light, stood under its glare like a defendant in a sci-fi scene.

"In 1977," she said, "my father, Jack Kantke, was convicted of killing my mother and a friend of hers. In Long Beach. I was five."

*There.*

Jean looked at the maid. The maid looked at the TV.

Jimmy drew another glass of water and looked out at the backyard. A fog was filling the back of the canyon, rolling down from on high like a very slow waterfall. It was always sad when you heard what it was.

"My father was Assistant D.A.," Jean continued. "Mother was a dress designer. It was in all the papers, even *Time* magazine. There were appeals. He was executed in 1992. The gas chamber."

It was so matter-of-fact. So *repeated*.

"I know people say you shouldn't go back into the past," she said.

"I never say that," Jimmy turned and said.

"I just—"

"Were you there? When it happened?"

"No. I was at my grandmother's."

She'd lost some of her *force* from before. He liked her this way. This was the big hurt in her life. Most people, you'd have to know them for months or years to find out what it was. Maybe it was why he did this, *looked into things*. He liked knowing, even when in the end sometimes it tore him up.

"So what do you want to know?"

"If he really killed her," Jean said. "Killed *them*. He swore he didn't."

Jimmy said, "You know, innocent people don't get executed." He watched for some reaction to the word *innocent*. She didn't have one. "You would think it would happen and people like to talk about it all the time, but it really doesn't happen."

He looked at her until she nodded.

"It would be an enormous surprise if he didn't kill them," he said.

There was a long moment. She nodded again.

"So you just want to know how much to hate him?" Jimmy said.

"No."

"What then? What difference would it make? Everybody's dead."

He waited for some reaction to that word, too. To *dead*.

"I just think it would be better to know," she said.

Jimmy put his glass in the sink. "We could have a long conversation about that sometime," he said. "Sorry."

And he left her again.

Jean looked over at the maid, who was still pretending she didn't speak much English. Now on the TV there was a picture of the missing boy in a Cub Scout uniform. And then they were on to some other story.

---

At the end of the night, Jimmy waited out front surrounded by his new best friends, a circle that included Ben the JPL engineer and both murder victims, still in their bloodstained clothes. The fog had them all wrapped up. The TV comic was just hauling himself up into a caution-sign-yellow Hummer.

After Joel and the comic told each other they'd call, the Hummer pulled out and rumbled off to war down the drive. Joel came over to Jimmy's circle. He put his arm around the murder girl and kissed her on the cheek.

"Wasn't she good?" Joel said to everyone.

The actress smiled.

"You broke my heart," Joel said.

"I'm going to go get cleaned up," the girl said and started away. Joel looked hurt. She came back and kissed him on the forehead.

"She's going to be big," Joel said, once she was gone.

"You mean when she grows up?" Jimmy said.

"Funny."

"*Don't hate me because I'm promiscuous,*" Jimmy said.

"She loves me."

The valet brought up the Porsche, left the driver's door open. The engine growled low, warm and friendly, like a dog waiting for its master.

"Thanks for inviting me, Joel," Jimmy said.

"I never know when you're screwing with me," Joel said.

"I just said thanks."

"See?"

Jimmy got into the Porsche, closed the door, punched the gas a couple of times because he liked the sound. "You ever think maybe you were *too* smart?"

"Now I *know* you're screwing with me," Joel said.

Jimmy sped away. The radio came up, loud.

Jean Kantke stepped out of the house just in time to see the taillights disappear down the smooth curving drive.

# TWO

In the belfry of the Hollywood United Methodist Church above Highland and Franklin, an owl with luminous eyes scanned the scene below: the river of taillights coming down from the Bowl, cop cars and an ambulance, their red lights slicing up the night, a body under a sheet, a cop drawing chalk rings around spent shells. In the hills to the right was the Magic Castle. Down from that, the façade of the Chinese Theater, seen from behind. This was inland and there was none of the Malibu fog. The night was especially clear. The lights of the city south seemed to crackle.

The owl took off. Hung on the side of the church's tower was a fifty-foot AIDS ribbon. All the way down below, a signboard announced this week's sermon:

"THE LAST MINUTE OF ETERNITY"

Jimmy drove the Strip with the radio loud, the top down, past famous haunts, rolling eastbound. It was a Friday night so things were happening but everyone seemed to be headed in the opposite direction, headed west. From the looks on their faces they were happy.

He stopped on a yellow at Sunset and Crescent Heights. In the side mirror, the red neon sign for the Chateau Marmont shimmered. Jimmy looked back over his shoulder at the hotel on the rise above the Strip, its turrets and towers, the awnings on the penthouse patio, the roofs of the bungalows behind for the long-termers and New York actors and French directors. They'd just hauled down the tall Marlboro Man billboard who'd stood over the hotel for years, replaced him with a state-sponsored rant about secondhand smoke, a dolled up couple close enough to kiss.

"Mind if I smoke?" the guy was saying.

"Care if I die?" says the girl.

Then Jimmy saw him, a man in a Navy peacoat and watch cap. And this a warm night, too. He leaned against a wall next to a turquoise night-club. This one was young, in his twenties. He drank from a bottle of water, his eyes on Jimmy, a sour expression on his face, a sour smile, as though remembering a sick joke.

They were called *Sailors*.

A trio of Valley teenagers walked past him, stopped to read the names of the bands on the club marquee. The man in the peacoat ignored them, took another drink of water, kept his eyes on Jimmy.

There was an edge of blue light around him, at least to Jimmy's eyes.

"*I know you, Brother,*" he looked at Jimmy and mouthed.

Suddenly the passenger door opened and a girl plopped into the seat beside him, a very young girl in a very short skirt. She yanked the door closed, as if that settled something, closed the deal.

"Hi, what's your name?" she said, like she was thirteen.

Jimmy looked over at the turquoise nightclub. The man in the peacoat and watch cap raised his bottle of water in salute.

The light turned green.

"You'd better get out," Jimmy said to the girl.

"Let's just ride around," she said. "Just until it stops raining."

"It's not going to rain for four months," Jimmy said.

"It rained earlier."

"Bullshit."

"You're not very friendly," she said with a pout someone must have told her was sexy. The car behind the Porsche flicked its lights. Jimmy pulled out.

"I'll take you to the All American Burger," he said.

"Cool." She tugged at the hem of the skirt under her and changed the station on the radio.

"I hate this song," she said.

"I mean, I'll drop you off there," Jimmy said.

She ignored him, fumbled in her bag, found her cigarettes.

"Don't," he said. "Please."

She pouted another half second then closed her bag and turned in the seat to face him, to let him see her legs, if he wanted to look.

Jimmy looked up at the crossroads behind him in the mirror. The Sailor had turned away to walk back up Sunset. On the prowl.

"So. What do you do, Mr. No Names Please?" she said.

"Just drive around."

"Looking for trouble."

"No, I know where that is," Jimmy said.

She bit her lip and said, "I bet."

"You've been watching too much TV," Jimmy said.

He drove two more blocks, looking ahead. It was after midnight now and the night was coming into its own, shaking itself awake like a dog, the whores and their men, the hyper teens, pierced runaways on bus benches, their legs jumping, laughing and hitting each other, all of it looking like fun, for about the first ten seconds. The All American Burger was ahead, red, white, and blue and way too bright.

"This car is cool but it's like older than you are, right?"

"It's a '64."

"And that's like older than you are, right?"

He laughed. "Yeah."

"I have a '99 Corvette back home in Ohio up on blocks with only a hundred miles on it. I was a Gerber baby." She said it all in one breath.

"A *what?*"

"A Corvette."

"No, I mean—"

"A Gerber baby. In ads. In *Good Housekeeping.*"

There was something sweet about her lies, something that made him want to try to pretend he was her brother, take her along with him for a few hours and try to beat back the night.

But before they made it to the All American Burger they came up on a tricked-out pickup on the other side of the wide street. Another girl like this girl leaned in the window, talking to three teenagers wedged into the front seat shoulder to shoulder, El Camino High linebackers.

"Stop!" she said. "I know those guys."

Jimmy pulled to the curb.

She jumped out.

She threw the door closed and leaned all the way in. "You're sweet," she said in that way that doesn't mean anything.

Then she kissed him on the cheek.

She pulled back, *spooked.* She stepped away from the car. She stood on the sidewalk. She touched her lips.

Jimmy drove away, up Sunset.

When he looked up in the mirror, she still stood on the side of the street where he left her, watching him go, holding herself as if from a sudden chill.

Angel's house was halfway down an impossibly steep hill in Silver Lake in a neighborhood of Craftsman bungalows, some restored and almost *too* neat, the rest of them peeling under all the sun the hill took. Jimmy parked the Porsche, wheels canted to the curb. You could hear the music from here. The moon was still up. A couple made out against the fender of a cherry Camaro. They ignored him.

The partiers spilled out of the house onto the terraced backyard. Angel's place was never closed, his friends and wards mostly Latinos with a few Cal Arts types. Three people danced to ska under a string of chili pepper lights hung in a grapefruit tree, its trunk painted white. Somebody on the steps recognized Jimmy as he came down around the side of the house and threw him a beer.

Angel Figueroa huddled at a picnic table with a skinny kid. Angel was in his forties, muscular, "cut," clear-eyed, un-tattooed. He wore starched wide-leg jeans, stiff as cardboard, and a white T-shirt, a look they called California Penal. He spoke Spanish to the kid, fervent. The kid looked at the ground, nodding. In Angel's lap was an open Bible with a homemade leather cover.

Angel looked up.

"Ask Jimmy," Angel said. "Jimmy knows all about Jesus but he won't accept the grace either."

Jimmy nodded hello to the kid, who looked embarrassed.

"I've been working on Jimmy Miles for years," Angel said. "Ask him. I don't go away. Jesus don't go away, I don't go away."

The kid's name was Luis.

"This is Luis."

Jimmy nodded at the kid again.

"Gimme some money," Angel said to Jimmy.

Jimmy dug in his pocket and took out a folded sheaf of bills. He handed it all to Angel.

Angel peeled off two fives and gave them to the kid. "Go ask that *chica* over there why she's been looking over here at you," Angel said. There was a pretty girl on the steps, drinking a Coke, as young as the hooker on Sunset. "Take her up to Tommy's. We all run out of food. Take my truck."

Luis went away to talk to the girl.

"I'm trying to get him in an Art Magnet," Angel said to Jimmy.

Angel shook Jimmy's hand and pulled him down onto the bench beside him.

"Tell me something good."

"I made the run to Tecate the other night," Jimmy said.

"You shoulda called."

"Stopped at that little fish fry place."

"I was probably busy."

"Next time," Jimmy said, to hit the ball back over the net.

"Yeah, *next* time."

Angel stood and put his arm around him. "I got something sweet to show you."

In the garage, a half dozen young men dressed like Angel and with beers in their hands gazed reverently upon a chopped and lowered '56 Mercury, a work in progress ground down to shiny steel.

Angel came in singing, "*Baby loves a Mercury, crazy 'bout a Mercury . . .*" He snatched a handkerchief out of the back pocket of one of the men, mimicked wiping off the hood. The men laughed. Maybe it was a joke about working in a car wash. Jimmy liked the people Angel drew to him, kids struggling to stay in school and men in their twenties and thirties and even forties struggling to stay in or out of any number of things. They looked like killers, but they weren't.

"What's the mill?" Jimmy said and ran a hand along the smooth fender.

"You don't want to know," Angel said.

Jimmy reached into the downturned mouth of the chrome grill and found the latch and opened the hood. There was no chrome on the engine. It was functionality writ large, wedged in its space like an iron fist.

The men stepped closer. Nobody said anything.

"A 427," Angel said. "Holman-Moody built it for Freddie Lorenzen in '66. Come by in the daytime, I'll light it up for you. It doesn't have very good manners."

One of the kids repeated the last in Spanish for the man next to him.

Jimmy lowered the hood, pushed gently until the latch clicked.

"You all right?" Angel said. "You seem a little down."

Jimmy didn't answer. He stared at the bare metal curve of the car, old and new at the same time.

"Come on," Angel said. "Say it out loud."

"You know how sometimes you forget about it?" Jimmy said.

Angel nodded.

"And then you *remember.*"

"What happened?"

"A girl kissed me on the cheek," Jimmy said. "And she *knew.*"

"What girl?"

"Girl on Sunset. A hooker. Jumped in my car."

Angel waited a minute and then he said, "They see a lot of dark shit. They get tuned in to it."

"Maybe she saw what's really there. You ever think about that?"

"Not about *you*," Angel said.

A few hours later, the moon had set, the women were gone, the men were lifting weights. Angel stood over the bench press spotting a fearsome man grinding out a last rep. Jimmy was up on the deck. The Hollywood Freeway was a half mile away and the traffic, even late, threw up a sound like the ocean. When you first heard it, it was exciting in a way, the sound of energy, of motion, of *intention*. But, like the kids out wild on Sunset, ten seconds later it felt like something else, something to turn away from before it pulled you down. He watched Angel and the men for a minute, listened to them teasing each other in Spanish, and then put down his beer, went down the steps to go.

He waved to Angel, started up the side of the house.

"Let's make a run to Tecate some night," Angel called after him. "Eat at that fish fry place."

Jimmy walked up the sidewalk alongside the white house. He brushed aside a branch of trumpet vine that arched overhead. He looked at his fingers.

*Wet, from the leaves.*

————

A little TV offered up the first newscast of the morning. The sound was down but the visuals said enough: the school picture of the missing boy giving way to a live shot of helicopters combing brown hills somewhere in the Inland Empire, Verdugo or San Bernardino or Riverside. Jimmy sat at one end of the long table in the big dining room, eating toast, wearing the same clothes from last night.

The weather came on. Jimmy turned up the sound in time to hear, "A surprise trace of rain last night in parts of Hollywood . . ."

He left it on, walked away from it.

The bedroom was stark, a large room with expensive furnishings out of the past, huge pieces carved from some rain forest hardwood, dark, almost black. Jimmy stood at the tall windows, looking down at the backyard as the daylight burned off the dew. He yanked closed the blackout drapes and lay back on the bed, still in his clothes.

# THREE

Jean Kantke's office was in an industrial building just east of downtown on a street of rag trade shops, down where they made bathing suits and neckties, kiddy backpacks and knockoff men's jeans and underwear. The office was on the third floor, the top floor, and it was crisp and clean and high style, metal frame windows, old-style wide silver Venetian blinds dicing the morning light, and a desk that was silver, too, all curvy, looking like it came out of the purser's office of an ocean liner.

An assistant showed Jimmy in.

Jean kept her eyes down, busied herself with some papers on the desk. She wore a light blue suit, a blue the color of iceberg ice.

"What changed your mind?" she said, still not looking up. She was treating him like an employee. He was used to it. He understood it. People hated to need help, especially in daylight.

"My mind is in a constant state of change," Jimmy said. "Is that an oxymoron?" He was still trying to impress her. And still noticing it.

He looked around. "Nice office," he said.

"Perfume," she said. "I do very well."

"And you smell good, too."

Jimmy inspected a collection of perfume bottles from the past in a tall glass case, all the shapes and colors, cut glass and crystal. On the highest shelf, all by itself, was a black cat. Down low there was a shelf of goofy Avon cologne bottles, VW bugs and banjos and little businessmen with briefcases and black plastic stingy brim hats that unscrewed, a riff on the ordinary people and what they splashed behind their ordinary ears.

Jean was used to getting answers to her questions. "What made you change your mind?" she said again.

Jimmy picked up the black cat bottle. "It rained the other night," he said. "Somebody told me it did, and I didn't believe her."

Now she looked at him. "I don't understand."

"Me either."

Jean pushed back from the desk and stepped to a file cabinet. She found a folder, opened it, glanced at it, closed it. She offered it to Jimmy.

He didn't take it.

"You were five."

"Yes."

"Where'd they send you?" he said.

"What do you mean?"

"You were five. They sent you somewhere."

"I grew up in my grandmother's house."

"In L.A.?"

"San Francisco. Tiberon, actually."

"Is she still alive?"

"No."

"You said you had money. Did it start with her?"

"She had money. But I have my own."

"Any brothers or sisters?" he said.

"A brother, Carey. He lives in Arizona."

Jimmy didn't say anything else. Sometimes when you let silence rise up, people will fill it and some people will say things, sometimes more than they meant to say.

"I left my grandmother's as soon as I could," she said. "A boarding school in Atherton and then Stanford. When I was sixteen." She added the last with an impossible combination of pride and embarrassment.

"That doesn't sound like much fun," Jimmy said.

"I never thought it was supposed to be," she said.

"I didn't exactly make it to college," he said.

She didn't have anything to say about that.

"Can you tell?" he said.

"I don't really know what to think about you," she said.

"But that could be a *good* thing, right?" he said.

They both listened as "La Cucaracha" was played on the horn of a truck in the parking lot below. Jimmy went over to the window and spread the blinds. It was a lunch truck, chromed up, fancy. When you started your shift at five in the morning, you had lunch at ten-thirty. A Mexican man with a coin belt around his waist set up a folding table as the workers came out, all women as far as Jimmy could see. At least now she was talking to him like a person and not like a servant. Or a doctor. Or a priest. But he could tell she wanted this to be over, maybe was wishing she hadn't even thought of this, had never had these questions about her father and murder and a time out of time, or at least had not given in to them.

"Why me? Why do you want me to do this?" he said.

"I asked a few people to recommend someone. I asked Joel—"

He turned away from the window and looked at her. "Joel said he didn't put me up for this. He said you came to him, asking about me. Not about investigators. About *me*."

She just stood there. Whatever it was, she didn't want to say it.

He held out his hand. She gave him the file.

"Do you need a retainer or—"

"Kiss me on the cheek," Jimmy said.

She just waited.

"At the party at Joel's," he said, "before you revealed your ulterior motive, I thought you liked me a little. It'd be nice if it all wasn't just a smart girl's trap."

The phone buzzed. She didn't look at it.

"I don't see—"

"You have to kiss me," Jimmy said.

She kissed him on the cheek. There was a kind of defiance in it, as if she'd made herself believe that it was her idea.

She didn't recoil like the girl on Sunset.

Jimmy opened the file.

"One Ten Rivo Alto Canal," he said aloud.

———

There was a gunshot stretched over a long second and the flash that came with it, flaring in the white bedroom like lightning from a little localized storm. Elaine Kantke, late twenties, as pretty as a model, fell back onto the satin sheets on a circular bed, blood already leaking from the hole in her jaw.

Her silk pajama top fell open. She wore nothing else.

In the same second, a meaty blue-collar man named Bill Danko crumpled where he stood beside the bed as the same bullet which had passed through her tore away his cheek. He wore baggy suit pants and a loud shirt. There was a hi-fi on the nightstand, playing an LP.

Elaine Kantke was already dead. A second shot finished Bill Danko off, caught him in the V just above the bridge of his nose.

Jimmy wondered if they had a name for that.

He stood in front of the microfiche machine in the library at the *Long Beach Press-Telegram*. The killings were played up big, a four-column story and two sidebars. There were pictures of the two-story Spanish style house on Rivo Alto Canal and interior shots of the bedroom, the covered bodies, the bed, the hi-fi. There were arrows and dotted lines and X's and hyperventilated text in the cutlines, all of it under a thirty-six point head-line full wide:

## TWO SLAIN IN NAPLES

Jimmy put in a quarter, hit the button, pulled a copy.

On the inside slop-over page, beside the rest of the story, there was an ad for a VW bug at $1,995. He smiled as he looked at it, that old familiar shape. He pulled a copy of that, too. He rolled through another week of microfiche. Time whipped past like a dramatic effect in an old movie.

He stopped on:

## D.A. ARRESTED,
## DENIES SLAYING WIFE, MAN

After a week or two, the evidence had been assembled. You took your time when your murderer was an assistant district attorney. The case they had against Jack Kantke was only sketchy at this point, at least what was in the papers, but it was enough to arrest, enough for another banner headline.

And enough for most people to make up their minds about Jack Kantke. There he was, if you needed something more, in a shot on the steps of the downtown Criminal Courts Building, his hands cuffed in front of him, an odd half smile on his face. One side of his mouth was grinning, the other wasn't. It was like those tragedy and comedy masks in one man.

He had short hair, shiny, combed left, a white tab collar shirt, a skinny black tie, a style more sixties than seventies. He looked a little like Jack Webb, not the face, just the gray suit and the ramrod backbone.

Or maybe Rod Serling.

They had arrested him at his office. Of course they knew where he lived—he was still living there, in the murder house on Rivo Alto Canal—and they could have done it yesterday, Sunday, when he was home, proba-bly sitting in the sun out front, but they showed up downtown on Monday morning, came right in and walked past his secretary and opened the frosted glass door with his name in gold on it. They would have yanked him right up out of his swivel chair if he wasn't standing already, waiting for them, for *it*. Everybody knew this was high drama.

On down the page were the first pictures of Jack and Elaine Kantke in, as they say, *better days,* alive, smiling, chic, attractive. Party people, yacht clubbers. The shots were from what used to be called the *Soc* section of the paper, Society. *Where were the piña coladas?* One shot was from some official function, the assistant D.A. and his designer wife, Jack in a tux, Elaine Kantke in a black shoulderless gown wearing a loose watch with diamonds on it and diamonds at her ears. This being Southern California, they were probably overdressed.

And then there was a pretty picture of Elaine Kantke they hadn't used in the first go-around, a glamorous headshot with highlights in her hair and angled lighting, maybe a George Hurrell shot. It made Jimmy wonder if she'd been an actress, or had tried to be. When she smiled, at least for this, she smiled with everything. She looked young and happy and healthy. But she wasn't anybody's girl-next-door. She had what used to be called *sophistication,* not always meant as a compliment. She looked a little French. She looked like she smoked.

Jimmy tried to find something of Jean in her mother's face but didn't see it.

He didn't look for Jean in Jack Kantke's face. Jimmy didn't like him. *That didn't take long.* It wasn't the murder so much as the hurt he'd caused a little girl.

And that he couldn't seem to wipe the other half of that smile off his face.

Jimmy sped through to December, a year-end wrap-up, another banner headline:

1977 . . .
## A MERGER   A MURDERER   A MONARCH

Cute.

---

Jimmy looked over at the *Queen Mary* across the harbor as he drove down Ocean Boulevard. He was in his Mustang, a dark green 1968 GT 390 fastback. It was a big sky day, all blue except for a few clouds trying to build into something out over the shipping channel. The Catalina boat cruised toward the end of the breakwater, white as a wedding cake in the clear light.

Long Beach changed block by block, sometimes cleaned-up and rich and then the next street tired, sad, sorry. In one block, it'd be bright white BMW convertibles with blue tops, like they were little ski boats. The next block, left-behind grocery carts. Jimmy couldn't get the pictures of the murders out of his head. It was always like this. It always came to life right in front of him and stayed there until it was over. *Death came to life.* Funny. He tried to find something on the radio to splash a little light his way but it was all talk, talk about money and violence. When he was working, the world seemed made up of nothing but grief and greed and malice. Maybe it set him up to do the job, to see what he had to see, to go where he always had to go. He didn't like it, but when he wasn't on a case, there was something in him that missed it, wanted it. It put him at risk, body and soul, and there was something in him that wanted that because it made him feel more alive.

A narrow thirties-era concrete bridge humped up and over a twenty-foot-wide canal into the "Naples" area of Long Beach. That was what the real estate people called it, since the thirties when it was thought up and built, ten or twelve short blocks of big houses on narrow lots on finger canals, sailboats and harbor cruisers tied up in their "front yards." No abandoned grocery carts here.

Jimmy cruised down a skinny one-way lane. The houses had garages opening in the back onto the alley. It was a Monday but the neighborhood had more signs of life than most moneyed L.A. neighborhoods in the middle of the afternoon on a weekday. The people who lived here now were retired people or widows or people married to widows. You got a coffee and went by the broker's office in the village around ten, read the *Times* outside somewhere and then killed a couple hours before a late lunch. If you had a wife, she laid out your clothes on the bed in the morning, the bright slacks, the knit shirts, and sometimes they matched hers. You stayed away or out in the yard cutting back the bougainvillea long enough to keep her happy. The first drink of the day usually came at about four, unless you counted lunch.

There wasn't a 110 Rivo Alto Canal anymore. The ceramic plaques on the garages skipped from one oh eight to one twelve, probably more out of respect for property values than for the dead.

But there was the house.

Spanish-style, two-story, fading pink. It looked abandoned. *Could it have sat empty all these years?* Jimmy parked where the intersecting street dead-ended at the canal. Across the lane of water, a man hosed off a twenty-two-foot day-sailer. He was close enough to say something friendly, but didn't. A gull wheeled and dropped, threatening to land. The man flicked the hose in its direction.

An arica palm next to the house had a full head of brown fronds ready to crack off with the next real wind, but the hedges and a bird-of-paradise were hacked back and the little patch of grass out front was green so the house wasn't abandoned exactly. Someone was dealing with it.

Jimmy stood before it a long moment and then sat on the seawall. Spanish-style houses always had a nice balance. There was a big picture window to the left, an archway, a little portico, a heavy door behind it, a door with black iron strap hinges and black iron nailheads and a "speakeasy grill" to look out at the Fuller Brush Man through, iron, too, heavy and lacy at the same time. That was Spanish. The walkway and steps were painted red to look like tile or clay.

Jimmy looked up at the second-floor window, another picture window curved at the top to match the arcs below. That was the front bedroom, where it happened. One of the pictures in the paper had a uniformed cop standing at the window, looking out, looking *up* for some reason, as if the murderer had somehow flown out across the canal.

Jimmy walked to the picture window and looked in. Dark drapes faded to green/gray stood open a foot. It was the living room. There were a few pieces of old furniture, what they used to call a divan, *Look* and *Life* magazines on the coffee table, a couple of Klee prints on the walls. It was like a museum of the mid-1970s. Untouched. The table lamps were tall and bulbous, glassy gold dripping over aquamarine. The carpet was white shag. The rotary phone was pink. Over the fake fireplace with its dead and dusty electric log "fire" was a pen and ink sketch of the Left Bank.

Off a dark hallway, a staircase stepped up through deep angular shadows to the second floor. If there were any kids in the neighborhood, maybe *grandkids,* they were sure to swap stories about ghosts. You wouldn't think so, but there were houses like this all over L.A., left-behind houses, *dead* houses. Sometimes it was about uncollected taxes. Sometimes it was about crazy. Usually it was about bad blood running through the constricted veins of bitter heirs. *If I can't have it, you can't have it.*

A spider stepped across the sill. Time meant nothing to it.

Jimmy stepped back. There was music from somewhere close, Abba's "Dancing Queen," more of the past pushing into the present. It was coming from the house two doors down, out an open upstairs window. The song ended and another Abba song started. It was an album. *Who listens to Abba albums?*

There was a sound from across the canal, a sound Jimmy was meant to hear, the sailboat man slapping the hose into coils on the dock. Jimmy looked over. The neighborhood watchman tested the valve again to make sure the water was off and then walked up the short walk into the house, stepped out of his Topsiders outside the door and went in. After a few seconds the white shutters in the upstairs window tipped open a crack.

Jimmy suppressed the urge to wave.

He walked down alongside the canal to the Abba house. A low stucco wall surrounded a small porch, a patio with Adirondack chairs and a little table for the drinks. He knocked on the door. He waited but nobody came. After a minute, the side ended. It was a record player. The needle lifted—you could hear it—and then a click.

"She was there a minute ago."

A young workman with his shirt off was sanding the dock in front of the next house down. He had KROQ on the box, the Chili Peppers.

"Try again."

"That's all right," Jimmy said.

"She was there a minute ago. She likes the sun," the workman said. He made it sound a little nasty.

"Is there still a Yacht Club around here?" Jimmy said.

The workman pointed down the walk.

Jimmy walked away from 110 Rivo Alto Canal but it stayed with him. He couldn't shake it. Instead of the sweet little walk under the trees beside the canal, he might just as well have been walking down that upstairs hallway toward that front room where it had happened, where the lightning had flashed.

He was already inside.

# FOUR

Through the tinted glass of the tall windows of the bar Jimmy watched the Hunters and Catalinas and Ericsons motoring out toward the bight. He drank his beer and swiped a few olives from the tray.

The bartender was on a cell phone to his girlfriend.

"I know," he said every once in a while.

He was too young to know anything about the Kantkes. *Star Wars* was 1977. *Hotel California*. Elvis dying in August. *Car Wash*. *Saturday Night Fever*. *Roots*. *Laverne & Shirley*. Foreigner's "Feels Like the First Time" and K.C. & the Sunshine Band's "I'm Your Boogie Man."

And *Abba*.

Jimmy got up, took his beer with him, and looked at the pictures along one wall, the Long Beach Yacht Club over the years. In the old days, what you had was Old Money enjoying itself. The men wore yachting caps with a straight face, only nobody had a straight face. Then New Money started elbowing in. There went the dress code. The fifties were very black and white and the sixties were . . .

*What were they?*

The seventies and eighties looked even more confused and even drunker. The nineties saw a bit of a return to the old order, at least a stab at it, more contained hair, better clothes, straighter lines, a serious, unblinking *White* look, particularly on the two or three Black members who'd made their way in.

The current crowd in the latest pictures made no sense at all, like the rest of L.A. now, the only center being a lack of center. There were South Americans with ponytails like movie coke dealers shoulder to shoulder, drinks in hand, with USC frat boys and their old men, next to real life hippies in tie-dye next to leathery world-cruisers next to a lesbian couple all in white, she a little taller than *she*. Old salts, new salts, Russians, Armenians,

Redondo car dealers, Indian ophthalmologists. And a dignified-looking Mexican man in a blue double-breasted jacket with gold buttons.

And Ernest Borgnine.

There was a picture labeled "Officers 1975–1976" but no Jack or Elaine Kantke.

A white-haired man and his wife came through the bar, dressed up. Jimmy smiled. They smiled back. A second couple followed the first. The second man wore a pink sports coat, the woman a dress the color of poppies with shoes to match and a pair of sunglasses that remembered the arched-eyebrow tail of a 1959 Chevrolet.

They said hello, too, and seemed to mean it.

"Something going on?" Jimmy said.

"Crabby Lewis," the white-haired man said.

Jimmy followed them into the banquet room.

Up front was a three-foot-tall picture of a tanned ancient mariner in blazer and turtleneck and yacht cap. Jimmy hung around in back. There were only ten or twelve of them, with four waiters.

When they'd finished their salmon and salads, the pink coat man got up and stood next to the picture.

"I remember when my boy Spence went sailing with Crabby the first time," the pink coat man began, his eyes on the big picture. "Spence was twelve or thirteen."

Everyone started nodding their heads. They knew the story. They weren't unhappy. They were too old. Too much had happened. Too many sailors had sailed off to Happy Harbor.

"When they were coming in, Crabby gave Spence a loose ten-foot coiled line, told him to stand in the bow, told him to get ready." *Here it was.* "Twenty feet out from the dock, Crabby said, 'OK . . . *Jump!*' Spence jumped in, still holding the loose line."

It got its laugh.

"That was Crabby. If you jumped when he said to, you were all right."

The people nodded. That was Crabby.

"Spence wouldn't ever do what *I* said," the pink coat man said. "Still won't."

One of the women daubed at the corner of her eye, but she might have been crying about Spence. Or her own Spence.

When it was over, Jimmy bought a round in the bar.

"Everybody liked Jack and Elaine," the pink coat man said.

Everyone nodded.

"His lawyer proved he was in Las Vegas," the white-haired man said. "At the Rotary convention." He and his wife were drinking tall club sodas. He'd sent the first ones back when they came without limes. "The prosecution had to admit there wasn't enough time to drive there from Long Beach after the murders were committed." He sounded like he was still mad about it. Or mad about something.

"The desk clerk testified," another man said. This one looked as if he'd literally stepped off the deck of a boat to be there, sawdust in his eyebrows and in the hair on the back of his hands. Teak. You could smell it on him. "There wasn't enough time."

The pink coat man shook his head. They all shook their heads. Everybody knew all the same things.

"Even with the time change," the sawdust man added.

"We're in the same time zone as Vegas, Ted," the white-haired man said. He was still mad.

"I don't believe so," the sawdust man said.

"Yes. Same. All of Nevada," the white-haired man said. "Including Las Vegas," he added.

"Well, I don't gamble," the sawdust man said.

"You probably *shouldn't,* Ted," the white-haired man said.

The sawdust man *could* have said, "Well, at least my boat isn't made out of *plastic,*" but he didn't. He just filed it away. And took a sip of his free beer.

"And there was the guy in the gas station in Barstow," a fourth man said, to bring it back around. "The gas station guy also verified the time line. Tell him about that."

"I believe you just did, Ev," the pink coat man said and traded a look with the white-haired man.

"What was his lawyer like?" Jimmy said.

"Harry Turner," the white-haired man said.

Jimmy waited.

"You don't know Harry Turner?"

"He's too young," the pink coat man said.

"I've heard of him," Jimmy said. "I didn't think he—"

"He *didn't.*" It was the white-haired man. "Harry Turner was behind the scenes. But everybody who knew anything knew Harry Turner was running Jack's defense. Well, *Jack* was running it but he had sense enough to know to go to Harry. But up front was . . . The guy at the table in the courtroom was . . . What was his name?"

"Upland. Or Overland," the sawdust man said.

"Harry Turner never lost a case," the pink coat man said.

"Still hasn't," the white-haired man said with a harsh little laugh.

"He's retired now," one of them said.

"Yeah, *retired*," the white-haired man said.

A silence rose up. They all knew something that Jimmy didn't know. Maybe someone would say it out loud.

"Up*church*," one of the women said. None of the wives had said anything until now, just sipped their G&Ts and traded looks while the men talked.

The men nodded. Up*church*.

And then things got too quiet again.

"None of you thought Jack Kantke did it," Jimmy said.

"Not then," the pink coat man said. "Nobody could believe it."

"And now?"

There was a long moment.

"Well, there's a system, isn't there?" the white-haired man said.

The woman in the poppy-colored dress took her sunglasses off. She smiled at Jimmy, a smile not connected to anything in the scene but which now made it about her. Her hair still had life to it and whoever had done the work around her eyes had The Touch. She knew what he was thinking and enjoyed it.

"So," Jimmy said, with a look that included all three women, "any of you in The Jolly Girls?"

On the microfiche at the newspaper library there was a sidebar on Elaine Kantke and her best friends. More importantly, *a picture*. Four vivacious, frisky babes at the selfsame Yacht Club bar, four of them on four stools, their hips stuck out.

That was what they called themselves, "The Jolly Girls."

The woman in the poppy dress was quick and apparently spoke for all of them.

"No."

––––––––

Jimmy stood looking down into the water beside a black-bottom pool in a spectacular backyard in Palos Verdes, a bluff overlooking the battered green Pacific.

"You're early," a voice behind him said.

Jimmy turned.

Vivian Goreck approached with a professional smile. She was another striking woman in her fifties. She didn't offer her hand, was from a time just before that. She wore a print dress, bright, tropical.

"You're the same color as the wall behind you," Jimmy said.

"All part of the plan," she said brightly. "Like a spider. Did you look inside?"

"Nope," Jimmy said.

She stepped back slightly and put a new smile on her face and he went where she wanted him to go.

The house was empty, high ceilings, blond floors, a lot of glass, Moderne. A man had lived here, alone, Jimmy could tell that right away. If a woman had lived here anything more than overnight she would have found something to take away at least some of the *edge,* to get the willful solitariness out of the air. A woman who cared about you, if you wanted her, alone was enough to do it.

There was an open kitchen with a pair of chrome sinks sunk in granite. Jimmy turned on the water, cupped his hand, bent and drank.

Vivian watched him. *You see it all.* Besides, she could tell he had money.

"The stove's a commercial Wolf," she said. "The fridge is Subzero. There are double Blankenship disposals, double Nero trash compactors."

Jimmy turned off the water. "Was there a murder or divorce in the house? I always heard people ask that."

She handed him a black dish towel. "They do. No, the house was owned by the builder and—"

Jimmy stopped the pretense. "My name is Jimmy Miles," he said. "I'm not your buyer, I just wanted to talk to you. Your office told me where you were."

She didn't even blink. She was solid. Secure. Jimmy wondered what had made her that way. It was something else you didn't see much anymore.

"Talk to me about what?" she said.

"The Jolly Girls."

She stood up straighter, almost laughed. "Really. Why?"

"I'm an investigator."

"I'm sure there's a statute of limitations on public drunkenness . . ." she said. Here was another beauty who still had her looks but kept reminding you of what had been, the way the fire must have flared once and how everybody, or at least the men, had gathered round to watch it. Jimmy liked her, wanted the time back when she was young.

"Gee, I sure hope so," he said.

"So what is it?" she said.

"The Kantkes."

"Really?"

Jimmy nodded. And waited.

"Who wants to know about that? Why now?"

Jimmy didn't answer.

She leaned back against the counter and crossed her still pretty legs at the ankle. "I used to always say I don't talk about those days," she said. "And now it's been ten years since anybody asked."

"We all used to be jolly," Jimmy said.

"You're a little young to be world-weary, aren't you?" she said in a voice, a *Mrs. Robinson* voice he could hear her using in a bar. "I have a daughter your age."

Then somehow she guessed it. Her mind had been working though she hadn't let him see it.

"Jean," she said.

Jimmy didn't say yes, didn't say no.

"I saw her picture in the *Times* a few years ago. The business section. She's very pretty."

He didn't deny that either.

"What does she want to know?" she said.

"*Who.* It's *who* she wants to know. Her mother," Jimmy said. "Or maybe her father." He hadn't thought of that angle until just that moment, that Jean was doing this to get closer to her father. Or close enough to never come close to him again.

Jimmy walked away from her and into the living room. It was big enough for jai alai. Except for a planter with a ficus in it, which looked brought in for the sale, there was no furniture, no coverings on the windows, nothing but a brass telescope on a mahogany tripod in front of floor-to-ceiling glass tinted the merest green.

The gas fireplace was lit, though it was summer and even here along the coastline there was no chill in the air. Jimmy stared at the stone logs, burning yet not consumed, like something in the Bible. *Like me,* was what he was thinking. He heard her follow him into the room, heels clicking on the wood floors.

"So," Jimmy said without turning from the fire, "did Jack Kantke kill them?"

"No."

Now he turned to look at her. If there was any pain in her memory of those days, of those people, she had found a way not to betray it.

"How do you know?"

"I knew him," she said. "Very well. We all knew each other very well." She gave the last line room to breathe, opened up a space for speculation. "Jack didn't care about Elaine and Bill."

"So he knew about the affair?"

"Of course."

"And he didn't care?"

"I don't think so," she said. "Does that shock you? Sometimes I shock my daughter."

Jimmy wasn't shocked.

"I think Jack thought Bill Danko was rather . . . *below* all of us," she said. "But Elaine enjoyed him. And Jack had other fish to fry, as we used to say."

"He had a girlfriend, too?"

She smiled a quick, complicated little smile Jimmy would think about later. "Actually," she said, "I wasn't referring to his love life. Jack was very ambitious. Ten years after the fact, he was still out on the New Frontier. I think he would have been governor eventually. Or he thought so."

She sat on the corner of the planter with her hip out. Jimmy thought again of the picture of the four of them, posing, full of themselves, at the bar.

"Was the Yacht Club The Jolly Girls' clubhouse?"

"Only in an emergency."

"Where then? Where did you hang out?"

"It's embarrassing to say."

"Where?"

"A place called Big Daddy's."

Jimmy remembered it. Marina Del Rey. A good forty-five-minute drive up the coastline, far enough away to see and be seen by a whole new crowd, and not be seen by people who knew your husband.

"That's where Elaine met Bill actually," she said.

"How close were you to her, to Elaine?"

"Not the closest of the group, but we were all close."

Jimmy said, "So who killed them?"

She said, "I have no idea."

There was a sound from the front of the empty house.

"It came out of nowhere, as so many things do," she said.

A man and a woman stepped in. The man had a phone to his ear.

It was Jimmy's cue. He touched Vivian's arm. "Thanks, the house is perfect," he said, loud enough for the prospective buyers to hear. "We'll talk."

She appreciated the gesture. "I'll be in the office until six, Dr. Miles," she said.

Nice touch.

Jimmy nodded to the couple and saw himself to the door.

Out front in the circular driveway was a cream-colored Rolls-Royce Corniche convertible with plates that read: "BUY BUY."

The potential buyers' Jag was parked behind it.

# FIVE

Jimmy drank a Cel-Ray soda in a booth at the window under a sign that said, "We Never Close." Canter's was where John Belushi had spent some of the last hours of his life. There was the deli and then the bar in the other room, The Kibitz Room. There had been a time when Jimmy collected *last hours* facts, Belushi downing a pastrami at Canter's then going out to Westwood for a chocolate-dipped doughnut at Dupar's, Janis Joplin shooting pool at Barney's Beanery on Santa Monica before the drive up Highland to the hotel, James Dean stopping for a burger at the diner in Saugus before the run to Paso Robles. But the fun had gone out of it in time, after the list of the famous dead got a little too long, or death a little less of a gag.

The waitress came. She was young and Israeli. He didn't want anything else but he ordered a bowl of soup and another Cel-Ray. The place was empty for some reason and he liked her and it wasn't going to be much of a night for her.

He'd picked up a couple of tails, pale men in matching cheap suits, one tall enough to joke about, the other with a shock of bleached hair black at the roots in the style that had passed through the club scene two summers ago. *Sailors.* They were at a table for two in the middle of the room. They'd been down in Long Beach, on the bridge just as he was leaving Naples to go out to meet Vivian Goreck. After he'd left the house for sale, he'd stayed up on the cliffs at Palos Verdes until the sun dropped and then gone by Ike's, his hangout. They were parked on the street in a white Escort when he came out.

They weren't any good at this. Jimmy gave the tall one a look and made him knock over his water.

The second soda came and the soup, a pair of bagel chips speared by the handle of the spoon. The tails decided to pretend they were finished and they got up and left, pretending not to look over at him.

Jimmy slid a *Time* magazine out of a cellophane wrapper. He'd bought

it at a collectibles store down in Long Beach. The cover was black with one
little dim light, a candle, a hand cupped around it. It was from the week in
July of the New York City blackout. He turned over the pages, stepped in.
Here was another time capsule, images of 1977, the worries and frivolities
of the day. Watergate hearings were grinding on. Miss America Phyllis
George married producer Robert Evans "under a four-hundred-year-old
sycamore" in Beverly Hills. War between Ethiopia and Somalia. The Sex
Pistols arrived in America, in New York, sneering in their *Wild One* black
leather jackets, looking scary and silly, like something New Yorkers had
found when the lights came back on.

The story on the murders was halfway through. This was just the kind
of California story the East Coast loved. There were pictures of the house
front and back and a smiling Elaine Kantke and a half-smiling Jack Kantke
and a potato-faced Bill Danko.

The picture of Danko was a mugshot.

The overline read:

### LA DOLCE VITA, RIVO ALTO STYLE

"Did I wake you?"

It was a hot night and Jean Kantke had the lights off. She wore a sports
bra and three-stripe Adidas silks. She was in the living room in her apartment, the penthouse of a four-story building on a curving street in the hills
above Sunset, above the Strip. She pushed aside the sliding glass doors—
the apartment had a fifties feel to it—and walked out onto the deck with
the portable phone. It was a killer view, the Strip below, the orange and
yellow lights of the city stretching all the way down to Compton.

"I never know when people sleep," Jimmy continued. "I mean, regular
people."

"Is that what I am?" Jean said into the phone.

"You have a job," Jimmy said. "An office. Hours."

She stepped to the south end of the wraparound terrace, went to the
railing. It wasn't that late, a little before midnight. She could hear laughter
every once in a while from the open-air cafés on the boulevard with their
tables on the sidewalks.

"Are you alone?" she said.

"Yeah."

"I thought I heard something."

"I'm in the car," he said.

Jimmy was headed east on Sunset, past restaurants and bars with limos stacked up, even on a Monday. He'd lost the tails. They weren't around when he came out of Canter's. Or maybe they'd gotten better. He kind of missed them. The light ahead turned yellow. He gunned the Mustang and it leapt forward.

He turned left onto Miller Drive, up into Sunset Plaza, a neighborhood of houses and apartment buildings built like steps up the hills. Modest entrances, pricey vistas. On a quiet side street he parked in the shadows, turned off the engine.

He got out with his phone, leaned against the fender. There were old-fashioned bulbous streetlights on Corinthian stalks, *white* light, not the crime-fighter orange that colored most of L.A. Three or four houses up the hill, a dog nosed around a trashcan, looked in his direction, then plopped down in the middle of the street.

Jean looked south toward Long Beach, miles and years away.

"Was it cooler down there?" she said.

"Not much."

"At least it's clear."

She was full of longing, vague, undefined. She wondered if he could hear it in her voice.

"The house is empty," Jimmy said. "It looks like nobody's touched it since the murders. Inside, anyway. Is that possible?"

There was a hollow wind down the line a second or two.

"People keep telling me anything is possible," Jean said.

She had a water somewhere. She went looking for it, into the living room, then on into the kitchen.

"What do you know about The Jolly Girls?" Jimmy said.

"They were just Mother's friends," Jean said. "The papers made a lot out of it. They all covered for each other. That's what the papers said anyway."

"It's a funny name," Jimmy said.

Jean found her water bottle in the kitchen, but poured herself a drink instead. Vodka. She opened the fridge for some juice and some ice, left it open, standing for a moment in the cool wedge of white light.

"What was Bill Danko's story?" Jimmy said.

"He was teaching her to fly," she said.

She came back out onto the deck with her vodka and cranberry juice.

"I know, it's a bad joke." She watched the line of jumbo jets descending into LAX, the dimmest ones twenty miles out, almost to the desert, it was that clear.

"A couple weeks before the murders, he was arrested for 'drunken flying.' A police helicopter caught them strafing the house, looping around. The cops followed them back to Clover Field. My father kept it out of the papers, but everybody knew."

That would be Bill Danko's mugshot.

"I guess it was a wild time," Jean said. "Nineteen seventy-seven. Things were coming apart, getting a little crazy. Clubs and . . . polyester. And platform shoes. My father drove a Karmen Ghia. The papers called it a 'European sports car.' They all drank a lot, played around, I don't know what else. Loose but not yet *too* crazy. Just so it didn't get in the papers. Jerry Brown was governor. My father was about to be named to a judgeship."

She swirled her drink, took out an ice cube and touched it to her lips. Jimmy didn't say anything, let her walk around in her memories.

"I remember the seawall in front of the house," she said. "Trying to climb up onto it. But afraid."

"It's about two feet tall," Jimmy said.

"Daddy nervous, Mother laughing . . ."

A moment passed. Noise from down on the boulevard floated up again. Her longing had turned, as it does, to tiredness.

"I guess I'll go to sleep," she said. "Do you have anything for me?"

Jimmy looked up at the four-story apartment building across the narrow street from where he'd parked, the one with the terrace around two sides of the penthouse.

"You mean like a glass of warm milk?" He opened the door of the Mustang, got behind the wheel.

"I mean, can you tell anything yet?" she said. "I don't know how you work."

Jimmy started the engine. "This is pretty much it," he said. He put it in gear.

"Watch out for the dog," Jean said, over the phone.

Jimmy looked up at her. She was at the railing of the penthouse, looking down at him.

"That's Roscoe. He's blind."

"I'll call you tomorrow," Jimmy said into his phone, looking at her.

She stayed at the railing, watched as he pulled out of the shadows. He waited for the dog to move out of the way, drove up the hill, pulled into a stub of a driveway, turned around, came down past her, pulled onto Sunset, headed west, never looking up at her again.

She wondered how many cars he had.

She hadn't told him where she lived. She wondered about that, too.

---

The Mustang was parked in front of a tiki bar on Pacific Coast Highway in Long Beach. There wasn't much traffic. The front door of the bar was propped open with a five-gallon can filled with sand and cigarette butts. The cleanup lights were on. You could smell the beer in the carpet from twenty feet away.

Jimmy opened the hatchback and lifted out the frame of a bike, minus the wheels. He put it together, tightened the hardware, gave the wheels a turn. He was wearing a light-colored zip-up jacket. He took it off, folded it, put it over the rear seat and pulled on a black hooded sweatshirt. The moon was bright in the clear sky but ready to set. He closed the hatchback. He'd kept looking for the tails, the pale men, but they never caught back up with him. He was feeling all alone, so alone even some trouble would have cheered him up a little.

He rode the bike up and over the bridge into the Naples area, rode along the lane, along the backs of the houses, the row of garages, almost silent, almost invisible when he was between the streetlights. The cars in the alley were tucked into their covers. No one was out. A possum crossed the alleyway. There weren't even any free dogs to give chase.

Jimmy stowed the bike behind a hedge and came down the walkway alongside Rivo Alto Canal. He stood in front of the murder house, letting his eyes dilate all the way, now that he was away from the streetlights. A wind came up, rustling the dry, brown palm. The surrounding neighborhood was dark except for the dancing blue light of a television in one house across the lane of water.

Jimmy went to the backdoor, clicked on a penlight with a red cap lens. He read the lock in the knob. It wasn't much of a challenge, so old a good twist would probably open it. He shined the light on a ring of keys, the head of each wrapped in black tape to silence it. He made the match, put the key in and the knob turned. He wondered who the last person to touch it had been.

The door stuck, then gave way. He was in.

A few ancient dirt-crusted plates sat in the sink in the kitchen, a broken saucer on top. The faucet dripped into the center of an iron-stain circle. There was a single clouded water glass on the counter.

There was movement, a shape that turned out to be a cat darting away. Jimmy shined his red light on the window over the sink. There was a cracked-out pane, a tear in the screen.

In the living room, he crossed to the front window, looked out where he had looked in that afternoon. The blue light of the TV across the way was gone now. He turned, took in the room. On the wall by the front door was a picture of Jack and Elaine on a sailboat tied up out front. On the coffee table were *Reader's Digest*s, five or six of them spread out in a semicircle like a hand of cards. There was a *Life*. A chevron-shaped ceramic ashtray matched the lamps. All of it was covered with dust. The living room was unchanged from the newspaper photo taken the morning after the killings. All that was missing was the black-haired cop who'd stood beside the "fireplace" pointing at something that had nothing to do with the carnage upstairs. The wind drawn down the canal came up again. A bougainvillea scratched against the glass, like something wanting in.

There was a small bedroom downstairs. A boy's room.

Jimmy went upstairs. On the walls down the hall were pictures of the family, pictures of Jean, a baby propped onto a silk pillow, a very little girl with a balloon, a four-year-old and her mother on the steps out front, Elaine in a light-colored sundress with a full skirt, a cigarette between her fingers. There was one picture of Jean's brother, a sulking twelve-year-old in a suit that matched his dad's.

He shined the light into the bathroom: pink and green tile, a pedestal sink, dirty, a dimmed mirror. The plastic shower curtain was hard, cracked, brown. There was water in the toilet, which was iron-stained, too.

The door to the bedroom on the front of the house was closed. Jimmy tried the knob. It was unlocked. He stepped in.

It was full dark, shades pulled down over the windows. He swept the room with his light. There was the round bed, the black lacquered "Oriental" bedside table, the funny, overstyled clock radio. Somebody had cleaned the room and pulled the door closed and walked away. Jimmy knelt where Bill Danko fell. He unclipped the red filter from the penlight, scanned the white carpet for some trace of the bloodstain. Clean. He looked over at the floor-to-ceiling silver curtains where, the theory went, the killer had waited.

Jimmy stepped closer, reached out. The cloth had lost all of its life, turned to powder. His fingers went right through it. He touched the shade on the window. It rolled up, clattering and flapping like a window shade in a cartoon. He pulled it back down into place.

He came out, leaving the bedroom door open behind him.

At the other end of the hallway, a door stood open, a third bedroom. Jimmy hesitated. There was something bad still in the air in the house, riding in the molecules. He knew he was built to deal with the past, to walk though rooms most people couldn't bear, but this was creeping him out and he didn't know why.

At the end of the hall he clipped the red filter onto the light again and shined it at his feet, at the frayed carpet, worn in a path in the center. The dim red circle of light crossed the jamb, into the back bedroom. There was clutter just inside the doorway, stacks of magazines, folded grocery bags, a couple of empty flat cans.

*Cat food.*

He stepped in. There was quick movement somewhere, something the same color as the room.

*Where was the wash from the streetlights in the alley?*

Jimmy stepped to the bay windows that faced the back. There were heavy drapes, closed together, and lowered shades behind the drapes. He ran his fingers along the edge of the shade, felt something. He shined the red light: the shades were taped tight against the window with duct tape, blocking any light from outside.

*Or maybe it was the other way around.*

Jimmy was trying to make sense of it when a woman coughed and, in the same moment, a black-and-white TV flashed on.

He jumped half out of his skin, fell back against the windows.

The woman—she had stringy gray hair cut straight across the bangs and wore a faded dress and a sweater and slippers—had turned on the television manually. She now just stood there before it, blue/gray, dead-looking in its light.

She watched it a moment, stepped back, sat in a worn chair.

Jimmy was caught. There was no place to hide. He stood stock still in the pulsing light of the television.

*Was it possible she hadn't seen him?*

No, now she looked right at him, as if he had said that last thought out loud. A cat jumped onto the arm of her chair. Then a second cat and a third and a fourth came out from somewhere to rub against her. She still looked directly at Jimmy where he stood, eight feet away, against the windows, in the wash of TV light.

The red cap to his penlight fell to the floor. He bent to pick it up. She watched him. He looked into her eyes and she looked into his.

He took a step toward the doorway. She followed him with her eyes, her expression unchanged.

And then she looked back at the TV.

# SIX

On the office wall was a colored print of Jesus sitting in his robes across the desk from a businessman in a gray suit.

Jimmy was across the desk from Angel.

"You didn't even see her, man?" Angel said.

"Not until she turned on the TV."

"And she didn't see you?"

"She looked right at me," Jimmy said. "She saw me, but I guess seeing someone standing there wasn't that out of the ordinary to her."

"So who was she?"

"I don't know. Nobody. A street person. Maybe just someone who comes in to feed the stray cats. It was easy enough to get in."

"Sad," Angel said.

Angel's body shop was downtown ten blocks south of the City Center. Through the windows in the walls in the inner office you could see men at work on expensive cars. It was a beautiful old wooden building, once a Packard dealership, with a high arched roof. The floors were slick white. This wasn't an insurance shop. You had to care about cars the way they cared about cars before they even let you through the door. *Clean* was about the highest compliment the men working here paid each other's work.

Luis, the skinny kid from Angel's backyard, worked alone in one corner of the shop, airbrushing a scene onto the tailgate of a chopped and lowered, scooped and stretched Ford F-150 pickup, an artful expressionistic rendering of the L.A. skyline, a pair of woman's eyes emerging from the night clouds, and a blue moon.

Jimmy got up from the chair. There was a picture on one wall in a black wood frame, a World War II–era bomber rolled out in front of a hangar. Huge block letters white across the roof said: STEADMAN. There were palm trees behind it in the picture, Santa Monica behind the palms and an ocean beyond that, suitably gray, since it was wartime.

"You know anybody at Clover Field anymore?"

Angel shook his head. "Nah, it's nothing but general aviation now, Wayne Newton flying in in his Gulfstar."

"I like Wayne Newton," Jimmy said.

"I think we all do," Angel said. "It's not Clover Field anymore."

"Yeah, I know. Everything changes."

Jimmy kept his eyes on the picture.

"So, you gonna tell me?" Angel said.

"Tell you what?"

"Tell me what you're working on."

"A couple of the dead," Jimmy said.

"Lucky stiffs."

Jimmy looked at another picture on the wall, next to the first, as he gave him the short version. "Double murder, 1977, guy killed his wife and her boyfriend down in Long Beach. He was convicted, executed."

"Kantke. I remember it."

"I'm working for the daughter. She wants to know if he really did it."

"What's the point?"

"I believe I asked her that."

"What's the connection to Clover Field?"

"The dead guy worked out of there. A pilot."

In the other picture, Angel Figueroa stood alone next to one of the bomber's fat wheels. The lettering said: "No. 2000 July 16, 1944." He had shorter hair now, a buzz cut, but Angel didn't look much different in the picture than he did here, sitting behind his desk.

"Good-looking guy," Jimmy said.

"I tell people it's Uncle Eduardo," Angel said.

———

"Disco got a bad rap."

Jimmy was buying lunch at Vern's, a red Formica lunch spot out in The Valley on Lankershim Boulevard in North Hollywood, a half-gentrified art and artists' neighborhood they were trying to talk people into calling *NoHo*.

Chris Post drew musical notes on a three-by-five card while they talked. They were at a table in the window with a view to the street. He'd look out the window and then say something else to Jimmy and then draw another note on the card. He had a stack of three-by-five cards with a rubber band around them jammed in the pocket of his pocket tee. He was in his forties. He had bad eyes and long hair thinning on top pulled back into a ponytail. He wore orange jeans. *He was skinny and tall, no ass at all.* That was a line a lyricist friend had put to one of Chris's melody lines once, presumptuously trying to turn it into a *song.*

Chris never spoke to him again.

He was a musician, a real musician, the kind of shack-out-back artist who had twenty thousand dollars' worth of computers and synthesizers and keyboards—and a safety pin holding his glasses together. To pay the rent, he played song demo dates and commercial jingles and the occasional session for a *Touched by an Angel,* but what he really wanted to do was . . . write atonal symphonies and then not play them for anyone. A few years back, Jimmy and Angel had encouraged him to apply for a grant from the National Endowment for the Arts and he did, scrawling, *Go Screw Yourself!* across the application.

Surprisingly, he was turned down.

"Disco got a total bad rap. *Repetitive.* You want repetitive? You ever listen to Vivaldi, or, better yet, Ravel?"

Chris picked up a fork.

"What is this?" he said.

"A fork," Jimmy said.

Chris picked up a spoon. "What is this?"

"A spoon."

Chris started nodding his head. "Which is *better?*" he said.

"I hear you."

"You got a steak, I'll tell you whether a fork is better than a spoon."

"I get what you're saying," Jimmy said.

"Most people don't," the musician said. "Sadly."

Their food came. Chris got a bowl of soup the size of a hubcap, bean soup. Jimmy had just ordered a plate of steamed carrots. Chris picked up his spoon, wiped it off with a napkin.

Jimmy said, "I drove by there. Big Daddy's."

Chris slurped up the first too-hot spoonful of soup. He kept shoveling it in. He *ate* like a musician, like a musician who hadn't eaten in a week.

"How's the soup?" Jimmy said.

"It's all right."

Ten years ago when Chris's mother died, Jimmy had gotten him into an apartment and the first day he'd had to show him how to make canned soup. A week later, he introduced him to SpaghettiOs.

"So, I drove by there, Big Daddy's," Jimmy said. "Where it used to be."

"And it's a Starbucks now," Chris said.

"A Kinko's."

"But you get what I mean . . ."

Jimmy got what he meant.

"I don't get down there to the Marina anymore," Chris said. "It takes four buses." He took out a new three-by-five card and wrote a note to himself. "I'll burn you a CD. The stuff you should be listening to. You ever hear Cerrone?"

"*Love in C Minor.*"

Chris was impressed. "How *old* are you, man?" he said. "I've never been able to tell."

Jimmy let the question go unanswered. "Here's what I need," he said. "You know anybody who spun at Big Daddy's?"

Chris was to the bottom of his bean soup. "Could I get another bowl?"

"Sure."

Chris motioned to the waitress for another bowl, pointed to it like it was a Scotch and soda.

"I knew Slip Tony," he said. "But he spelled it with an *E* instead of a *Y*, like *tone*. Tone Espinosa. He was the best. He wouldn't say a word all night. He had all these imports. He was the first guy I knew of to use three tables. He'd throw something over something with something else underneath and you couldn't believe what you were hearing. Spoken word. He'd lay in a guy saying a poem or narration for a training film for air-conditioning repair. There wasn't anybody in L.A. who was a better DJ—except for maybe about a dozen gay guys in little clubs you never heard of playing tea dances on Sunday afternoons."

"Do you know where he is now?"

"Dead. It's funny," Chris said, then caught himself. "Well, I don't mean being dead . . . He became a cop. He was on a gang unit, right down in there, Venice south. Shot dead. Two years after Big Daddy's, maybe by some slick who two years earlier was out on the floor, thinking how cool Slip was there in the booth, his head over sideways, half a headphone on his shoulder."

"You know anybody else from Big Daddy's? Anybody who's still alive?"

The second bowl of soup came. "I'd also like another one to go," Chris said to the waitress. He looked at Jimmy for approval. Jimmy nodded.

"Lloyd Hart. Lloyd-the-Void. He called himself *Popper* or *Rocker* or something but everybody called him Lloyd-the-Void. He was the DJ in the main room upstairs with the lights in the floor and the *Is-Everybody-Having-A-Good-Time?* jive. Slip Tone was in the *serious* room downstairs." He wrote something else on another three-by-five card and handed it to Jimmy. "I *guess* you could say he's alive."

Chris dug his way down to the bottom of the second bowl of soup and put his spoon aside. He looked out the window again and then drew one last musical note.

He handed the three-by-five card to Jimmy.

"I don't read music," Jimmy said when he looked at it.

Chris whistled an odd little twelve-note tune.

"You just wrote that?"

Chris shook his head, nodded out at the street.

"What?" Jimmy said.

"The palm trees. Other side of the street. Up and down, different heights. If they were notes on a scale, it'd sound like that."

Jimmy held up the card. "Can I keep this?"

"No," Chris said and took it back.

----

*The Love Storm* was the name of the overnight program at KLVV, fifth in the ratings for its time slot. The show had a cosmopolitan L.A. feel to it, slanting noir shadows and cigarette smoke curling out of your radio, but the studios were actually in a squat three-story box of a building on Van Nuys Boulevard in Van Nuys, the transmitter ten miles farther out in the Valley, almost to the mountains in a field of sunflowers. This time of night, the flowers would be closed up tight.

Lloyd Hart was now Darren Price.

He was working alone. There wasn't even a janitor around. Jimmy talked his way in, past the squawk box down at street level. Price had said hello, had said something quick and sharp and funny actually, hope in his voice that it was some young girls out cruising around. When Jimmy said what he wanted to talk about, Price buzzed him up, another case of *"Now it's been years since anyone asked . . ."*

He was still good-looking, in a game show host way, and he had a good, deep, round voice and a way of putting the sound of a warm smile in every word he said. Jimmy thought he recognized the voice from a TV commercial for headache relief, the kind where you got the idea somebody really *cared* about you and your pain. He wore a velveteen running suit,

almost purple, and perfect white shoes, Capezio *dance* shoes. He rocked
back and forth in a chair that didn't squeak. His hand kept reaching for
cigarettes he didn't smoke anymore, hadn't smoked for ten years.

"Hold on a sec," he said and lifted the cans off of his neck and up over
his ears. He leaned to the mic. The song was ending.

Half of the show's audience were love-struck kids dedicating sappy
songs to each other, to break up or to get back together or just to say to
each other, and to the world and to ex-boyfriends and ex-girlfriends, that
*this* love was real and would stand the test of time. The other half was
people at work, at 7-Elevens with a portable on the counter they weren't
supposed to have, people at bakeries and *tortillarias,* in emergency rooms,
in factories where they chromed wheels or assembled meals for airlines,
people cleaning offices, driving cabs, writing screenplays—and cops and
suicide hotline answerers and dope-dealers and whores all waiting around
for something to go down. There was a KISS station in town. Listen-
ers were encouraged to call and repeat the money phrase, that they were
"Kissing at Work . . ." At an hour like this, one other midweek night like
this, Jimmy had heard a listener call in a request to *The Love Storm* saying
he was "Storming at Work . . ."

A jingle played. A saxophone. A woman's voice. The sound of soft, rolling, distant thunder.

It made Jimmy wish it would rain, really rain.

"Andrea is up studying, studying for her nursing finals," Darren Price said,
so close to the mic you could hear the breath going over his teeth. Jimmy felt
like he wasn't there now, that it was just Price and Andrea and . . .

"*Carmen,* she just wants you to know that she's sorry she said what
she said, sorry that it hurt you, and that she didn't mean it. And that the
whole future is ahead for you two and she doesn't want to jeopardize that
because she loves you more than anything. And she wanted to send this
song out to you. She knows you're listening, too."

The song began, a song that didn't seem to connect to words said that
shouldn't have been said or to "the whole future," but the song was good
and the singer sounded as if he really had been hurt somewhere along the
line, had *that* in his voice the way Darren Price had a smile in his.

"I'm union. AFTRA," Price said as he pulled off the headphones and
killed the music in the monitors. "We're all union." It was a way of saying he made good money, more money than he made when he was under
brighter lights, when people knew who he was, when he was right there in
front of them at Big Daddy's when Big Daddy's was the place to be.

*There are all kinds of deaths,* Jimmy thought.

"What was Tone Espinosa like?" he said.

Price squinted as if somebody had turned on the overhead lights. "This is about Tone?" he said.

"No," Jimmy said. "It's not."

"We got along all right," Price said. "He didn't ever really *get* it."

"Get what?"

"He hated it when *Saturday Night Fever* came along. That's just an example. When it got big, he said it was over."

Jimmy didn't say anything.

"Does that make sense to you?" Price said, real perplexity in his voice.

"I guess I know what he meant."

Price shook his head. "Well, I never did. He was about to get fired when he finally quit. They just ran cables downstairs and I played both rooms. I mean, I'm not glad the guy got killed or anything . . ."

The phone never stopped ringing. It was silent, just blinking lights.

Price punched one button.

"Yeah," he said.

"Hey." It was a soft little voice, up past her bedtime. "It's Andrea."

"Hey." Price looked at Jimmy.

"I just wanted to thank you for playing the song," she said.

"Shouldn't you be keeping the line open for . . ." Price looked at a Post-it note stuck on the mic stand. "Carmen?"

"I have call waiting," she said, sexy.

Price was still looking at Jimmy when he said, "I hope things work out for you guys."

"You're so sweet," she said.

"Not really," he said, as a sexy threat.

"Yeah-huh," she said.

"I want you to call me, whatever happens," he said. "On this line, OK?"

She said yes and he said he had to go and cut her off.

"I'm like a priest," Price said as her light went out.

"Yeah, I was just thinking that."

Jimmy told him who he was, what this was, a version that left out murders and executions and little girls orphaned, that almost made it sound like Elaine Kantke had lost her purse or one of her shoes like Cinderella and had hired Jimmy to get it back, all the way back from Disco '77.

"The Jolly Girls," Price said. He used a *slanted* intonation, like a comic. The *Jolly* Girls . . .

"So you remember them."

"There were three of them, *four* of them. They were babes. They were all older than I was. I was, I don't know, twenty-four. They were maybe thirty. It seemed like a real difference at the time, but they were still babes."

"And they always came to the club with their husbands," Jimmy said.

"Yeah, right, I remember that *distinctly.*"

"Who was the leader?"

"Elaine, I guess. I don't know. It's all kind of a blur, if you know what I mean."

Jimmy knew. "Did they do coke?"

"I wouldn't be surprised."

Jimmy had said *they* in a way that meant, "Did they do coke, too?" The DJ wasn't insulted. Lloyd-the-Void had tried to fill the void with one of the things you try to fill the void with. Step One was to accept that you were powerless . . .

"I wouldn't say they were the *biggest* Hoovers among the regulars," Darren said. "But then again, *that* bar would have been pretty high at Big Daddy's at that particular time."

"Did you talk to her much?"

"I talked to all of the regulars. It was part of the job. But I liked doing it. I was kind of a star. I got that kind of response from people, the regulars."

And he began to talk about the nights there. *I love the nightlife, I love to boogie.* He described each one of the lighting effects suspended above the dance floor, how they had been brought in from New York, how there weren't any lights anywhere else in L.A. like those lights. *Turn the beat around, turn it upside down.* He remembered the wattage of the sound system, the size of the big black bass cabinets that sat on the four corners of the dance floor so it came up out of the earth at you, too, how the floor was covered in fog, like a graveyard in a cheap movie. Talking about the past, he had a different kind of energy. He woke up. He had more words at his disposal and they were better words, words that put you there.

He interrupted himself when he needed to change a record or speak some words of encouragement to the heartbroken. An hour passed while he talked and the lovesick went to bed and the requests changed. Now it was more the people at work trying to stay awake, wanting something with a little more heat and a little less hurt.

He remembered what Elaine Kantke drank because he'd buy her and the other Jolly Girls drinks to make them feel special. *Long Island iced teas.*

He remembered that she wasn't the best dancer of the four young women. That would be Michelle. Michelle would also be the biggest Hoover. Elaine would dance every once in a while, but what she really liked was being at the bar, on a stool, facing the dance floor and laughing at her friends.

He remembered Vivian Goreck, a redhead. *Viv.*

He remembered Bill Danko but not by name, just remembered that for a while there was someone Elaine seemed to meet, a blocky guy with his thick torso wedged into the requisite Nik-Nik pointy-collared polyester shirts and beltless, high-waisted flared pants. He remembered his name as *Wayne* or *Dwayne,* which is what you'd think, looking at Bill Danko.

He didn't know that Elaine Kantke was dead. DJs read *Billboard,* not the *Times.* He'd just assumed The Jolly Girls had found a new club or their husbands had finally gotten around to seeing *Saturday Night Fever* and had shortened their leashes.

"I learned two things about the bar business—and about life—when I was at Big Daddy's," Darren Price said.

Jimmy wondered how many times he'd said that line.

"The first thing, Big Daddy Joe Flannigan himself said to me personally. One night after we closed and we were all drinking kamikazes at the bar, he said to all of us, 'What business are we in?' Somebody of course said, the *booze* business, thinking that was what he wanted to hear. He had a white beard, looked kind of like Hemingway and wore these white shorts and a Kelly green shirt and he was big. Joe shook his head. Not the booze business. There were a couple more wrong guesses. He looked at me. I said, 'The *entertainment* business.' Big Daddy shook his head."

Price was going to make Jimmy wait for it.

Jimmy waited for it.

" 'We're in the *loneliness* business.' Not *loneliest,* loneli*ness* . . ."

Jimmy got it. He nodded his head.

"Buying or selling?" he said.

Darren Price didn't get it.

"What was the second thing you learned?" Jimmy said.

"Hats start fights."

They talked another half hour. Lloyd-the-Void looked disappointed when Jimmy stood up to go.

———————

It was almost four. The Kinko's that occupied the space where Big Daddy's used to be was open all night. They'd ripped off the two-story front and put in glass all the way up. It was a box of light in front of the empty parking lot. There were six or eight people in there under the ghastly bright lights, two guys behind the counter and one running the big machine that wasn't self-serve. They probably kept the reams of paper down below in what had been the *serious* room, Tone Espinosa's room.

They'd left the entrance the same, six steps up to what had been the main room of the club. Elaine Kantke and Bill Danko had climbed those steps, looking to do something about their loneliness, if you believed Big Daddy.

Jimmy sat on the front fender of the Porsche, the car he'd picked that morning from the line in the garage.

"Why do people need to make copies in the middle of the night?" he said, out loud, to no one. "What are they copying?"

A coughing VW bug came in, fast. A man with a belly and a colorless T-shirt the size that maybe fit him when he was twenty got out and charged in, taking two steps at a time, his fist clutching a thick sheaf of papers. There was one answer: it was open for the people up all night grinding their teeth at some grievance, consumer or governmental, assembling their cases, ready to by God *fire off* some papers in the morning.

It had been a long day. The days got longer when Jimmy was working, felt that way anyway. This story was at that early stage where everything was incomplete, sketchy, self-contradictory—and he had done this enough to know that a big part of what he was "learning" was just simply wrong.

A seagull landed on a light stanchion. Jimmy turned around and looked toward Marina Del Rey, the immense condominiums which stood over the wide channels and the hundreds of slips. The tops of the tallest masts were visible between the towers.

The light was odd, noncommittal. He wished the sun would come up, right now.

An LAPD sergeant's cruiser pulled in beside him. The cop was alone. The window was down.

"Saint Thomas," Jimmy said.

The patrol cars all had computer monitors hung on the dash now and a full-size keyboard where you used to put your coffee. The radio spoke, the voice female and not very friendly. You could tell the cop was a sergeant by the extra antennas on the roof.

Saint Thomas's last name was Connor. He got out. He looked to be in his fifties, handsome in that cops and firemen way, self-assured good looks, clear eyes, skin wrinkled not from worry but from being on the boat on the lake on days off, or on the sidelines coaching kids.

"You called?"

Jimmy nodded toward the Kinko's and asked if Connor had known the DJ who'd turned into a cop. And then a dead cop. It wasn't that Jimmy thought it had anything to do with the case, he was just curious. It was a good story, in that Movie of the Week way. Or maybe as a pilot for a cop show. Connor didn't know much about Tone Espinosa except that he'd been killed. Cops all knew who'd been killed, almost all the way back to the beginnings of LAPD.

"*Perversito,*" he said.

"What's that?"

"*Little Evil,*" the cop said. "That's who killed him, a gangbanger. He went away for it."

Jimmy told him what he was working on, a version that left out almost everything *but* the murders and the execution and kids orphaned. Connor nodded.

They both looked at the nightclub-turned-Kinko's.

"Disco sucks," Jimmy said, but he was just quoting.

"I just remember getting laid a lot less for a year or so there," Connor said.

"You couldn't dance?"

"I guess not. Whatever it was, what I was didn't work for a while there."

Sergeant Connor gave Jimmy a name or two, people who knew about the club scene back then, the drugs, the money. The bar business was a cash business and tended to have bad people around its borders, but Big Daddy's had been a safer, tamer, *brighter* version of the seventies club scene than some of the others.

Jimmy told him about the woman in the Rivo Alto house, asked the cop if he'd run a check on her, see if she had a history in the Naples neighborhood, in Long Beach. Maybe somebody had spotted her coming and going.

"You want her chased out?"

"No," Jimmy said, and then wondered why he'd said it.

And that was it. A ground fog started to come in around them. It wasn't cold but it *looked* cold.

Connor asked Jimmy how he was doing. Jimmy answered the question for real and asked the cop the same and listened to what he said. They both knew each other's story. When the radio called the sergeant off to something somewhere out there in what was left of the night, the two men stood up and embraced and held the embrace for a long moment.

*Where was that sun?*

# SEVEN

A Cessna landed. Badly. The right wheel touched first, the plane bucked, then the left wheel hit hard. On the grass between the runway and the taxiway, four old men sat in white plastic lawn chairs. They took a minute then held up handmade cardboard squares with numbers, grading the landing as if this was the Olympics. They had all been fliers or had built planes. It was all very unofficial but the understanding was that the old guys had earned the right to rag on the youngsters. Every pilot who landed tried not to look over but all of them did.

This time the scoring fell somewhere between a four and a five.

Jimmy walked up.

"You look like an undertaker," one of the old men, Kirk, said. Jimmy wore a black suit.

He stuck out his hand.

"How are you?"

Angel had called Jimmy from his shop downtown at noon. He had come up with a name for him, somebody who might know about Bill Danko and what had been called Clover Field.

Kirk pumped the hand once. "I told Angel I'd come in to your office."

"Don't have one," Jimmy said.

"Well, let's do it," Kirk said, and then looked at his friends as he made a joke, "I don't have all day."

They walked down the taxiway. They were on the B-side of the airport, businesses in old wooden buildings and World War II Quonset huts, every third or fourth one vacant, airplane maintenance, radio repair, aerial photography, a skywriting company with one plane. Vines covered half the buildings. Most had peeling paint, gloriously neglected. Somehow, here in the middle of L.A. was a sizable section of the *unimproved*. There was probably an old person somewhere who'd so long ignored the men in suits with their Big Plans for the property that they'd stopped coming, now just waiting her out—it was usually a woman—waiting for her to die and get out of the way.

"Angel wouldn't tell me what this was about," Kirk said. "He said you were a private investigator. I guess one of my girlfriends' husbands is onto us."

They weren't headed anywhere in particular but the old man walked at a good steady pace as if getting from here to there was something he'd be judged on.

"I told Angel, I got a photograph of your mother somewhere," Kirk said. "Autographed. I didn't understand those pictures she made over in Europe, but I sure liked *her*."

It made Jimmy smile.

"Where do you know Angel from?"

"Big Brothers," Kirk said. "I ran a unit until I got too old to stand up to all the bullshit." He held up his hand as if testifying. "I mean, I'm not gay, but I can't prove it."

A sleek corporate jet took off behind them, screaming. The 10 freeway was less than a mile away to the north and the 405 almost as close to the east. The roars merged.

When it quieted, Jimmy said, "Angel said you were the guy to ask about the old days here."

Kirk said, "He said it was about the seventies. You call that the old days?"

"It's all relative, I guess."

"I was on the line for Steadman twenty-eight years," Kirk said. "I put Pitot tubes in ST-10s. Before the war, it was ST-3s. The 10s were built right over there"—he pointed to a massive hump-roof hangar, the biggest building at the airport—"and the 3s built in Hangar Nine that got torn down in September of '73."

Jimmy stopped to admire one falling-down building. They had walked almost to the end of the taxiway.

"So what's this about?" Kirk said.

"You remember the Kantke murders?" Jimmy said.

"Sure."

"Bill Danko."

Kirk nodded.

"You knew him?"

"I saw him around," Kirk said. "His outfit was up here behind what used to be the old Clipper Hangar. Everybody said he was an all right guy. That's what you're looking into?"

Jimmy nodded.

"I saw her once, the woman," Kirk said. "She showed up, waiting for Danko to come back from a photo job, a flyover. He had a Cessna 152. Red over white, mortgaged up. She had an old-fashioned hat on her head, tied under her chin with a ribbon, like as if they were going to fly off together in an open-cockpit Waco. She looked like a barrel of laughs."

The old man set out walking again and Jimmy followed him. Kirk talked fast and asked the usual questions, what they *all* wanted to know: what other cases Jimmy had investigated, the stories behind the stories, the moments when the flashbulbs flashed. Jimmy didn't offer much. He never did. He'd long ago figured out that nobody wanted to hear the truth. Death and sex, that's what most of it was about, sometimes money, but he didn't take those cases. A case was never what it looked like from the outside and when it was over, what was important was never the big plot points, the flashbulb moments. It was what was going on unnoticed in the corner of the frame, the ambulance guys rolling out a woman on a gurney, the cops talking to the people in the next bungalow—and a boy steps up across the street into a clot of strangers, just coming home from school. Maybe it was why he did it, to notice the unnoticed, to find meaning there. Or try.

They'd reached the last of the buildings off on a side taxiway. "There," the old man said.

It was a decrepit building, vacant, standing alone, barely standing, a faded Plexiglas sign on the end of it announcing Sunshine Air, a charter company. The sign hung half off. What was left of a painted sign was underneath: *Danko "Flying School"*—just like that, quotation marks and all, like it was a pretend flying school.

"He never could make a go of it, as far as anybody could tell," Kirk said, as if the look of the building didn't get that idea across. "And then Steadman Industries bought him out. For a good price, some said." The old man shrugged. He had lived long enough to see a thousand things he didn't get. "And then Danko was dead, before he could enjoy the money. Well, he bought himself a new plane right off, I guess he enjoyed that. And her."

Everybody seemed to understand how you could enjoy Elaine Kantke.

"You want to look around, go ahead," Kirk said. "Nobody'll hassle you. There's nothing back here now. Now in the old days, on the other side of Hangar Six was—" Another jet roared into the sky, drowning out the last of it.

Jimmy stood there thinking of her, Elaine Kantke in her hat, maybe standing right where he was standing now. He thought again about the detail he'd learned, how the bullet that had killed her, went *through* her, had creased Bill Danko's cheek. It had probably carried some of her to him, a last kiss.

Maybe Jimmy did this for the poetry.

Kirk walked away, leaving Jimmy there to knock around in the past. The front door was locked. He looked in through the dirty windows. The room was bare, cleared of everything but the old newspapers on the floor, a bed for somebody from the way they were shaped, and faded posters of Cabo and La Paz on the walls. On the back wall was an open rectangle where an air conditioner had been. Jimmy went around to the weedy lot behind the building and crawled in through the hole.

There was a small room off the main room. In it, a desk and a pair of chairs and a water cooler with a dusty glass bottle were stacked at odd angles up to the ceiling. There was a file cabinet. Jimmy opened it. It was empty except for rat droppings and a book of matches from a cocktail lounge.

The desk was on its end against the wall. It was as old as the building. He pulled it down, set it back on its feet, rolled over the wheeled office chair. The drawers were empty. There was a phone number written in pencil on the bottom of one, a number with a two letter prefix, from some business in the forties or fifties. Geologists had the right idea about history: it was just layers of sediment, one on top of the other. And, given enough time, any sad piece of shit becomes precious.

Jimmy ran his hands along the underside of the wide center drawer and found a manila envelope wedged into a hiding place. He opened it. It was a bodybuilder magazine from the sixties, big-chested men preening on So Cal beaches.

In the ceiling was an access hatch. Jimmy arranged the desk and the chair, climbed up and pushed the square door up and over and stuck his head through to the crawl space. Screened vents at the two ends of the roof let in enough light to see. There were two cardboard boxes. He took off his suit jacket, folded it and put it over the chair back, climbed through the hatch and crawled toward them.

Both boxes were empty, but scattered among the ceiling joists were a few dozen pale green cancelled checks. With his head against the roof, Jimmy went through them. Ten or twelve were made out to "Beachside Market," each for five dollars, spending money, Danko's allowance. One paid the phone bill. There were rent checks. Steadman Industries owned the building. There were four to an aviation fuel company, three of them with notations about "Late Penalty ($10) Included."

And two to "Chip's Fashion House" for those Nik-Niks.

---

The museum of flight was across the main runway in a cavernous metal building, a new building. A yellow biplane hung from wires from the ceiling, suspended over three open decks of displays, models and full-sized airplanes. Through the floor-to-ceiling glass on the backside of it you could watch takeoffs and landings, listen in on the radio traffic on a bank of headphones. It was the modern opposite of the old men in their lawn chairs on the other side of the runway.

Jimmy was in a sea of Cub Scouts surrounding a restored ST-10, the bomber in the picture on Angel's office wall. The boys jumped up and down below the wings, swatting at the undercarriage, trying to touch the teardrop tanks that hung down.

He went up to the top level.

*Clover Field forty years ago.* There was a wall of photos: the hangars, the workmen like Angel, the bombers coming off the assembly line.

It was also a history of Steadman Industries. As you walked along, the company moved into the fifties and sixties and then the seventies, props disappearing, wings angling back, nothing ahead but a bright, high-flying future. Or so said the PR.

There was a commotion behind Jimmy as half of the Cubs arrived. They pressed their faces against the glass of a display, the re-created Steadman boardroom of the sixties. Jimmy crossed the hallway and looked over their shoulders. It was complete: the original furniture—a great oblong mahogany table and leather chairs—Coke bottles, coffee cups, pads and pens, pictures on the walls, an ST-10 taking off outside a "window"—and ten wax figures seated around the table, their glass eyes fixed on the big man standing before them.

The plaque read:

WALTER E. C. "RED" STEADMAN
FOUNDER
1911–1973

He looked like the kind of man who could get his name painted in fifty-foot letters across the top of a hangar.

Jimmy thought he saw the old guy blink.

When he came back down to the first floor, his tails were back, the pale men who'd been at Canter's. Today, the short one even had on a pea-coat and watch cap. It was easy to make fun of them, but there wasn't any fun in it today for Jimmy. Maybe it was all the scouts, all the innocents. He tried to make it through to the front door without them spotting him, but the tall one saw him and shot a look up at the second man on the higher floor. The two-tone blonde came down the staircase fast and joined the other, the two of them "hiding" behind a stacked rack of bombs, a pyramid of dummies.

Jimmy went after them. *Why were Sailors interested in this?* Maybe he could shake it out of one of them. The two of them tried to get lost in the crowd. They looked bewildered. When you were tailing someone, he wasn't supposed to come after you. They ducked behind planes, pretended to look at the shiny models of 747s and then at the mannequins of stews in pastel seventies uniforms. The Cubs had all descended from the top floor and made the two stand out all the more. Even the short one stood tall over them.

Jimmy kept coming. There was a flight simulator in one corner on the ground floor, a twenty-seater big as a bus mounted on hydraulic lifters. The two pale men cut in line, just making it through the simulator doors before they whooshed closed.

He got close enough to see the name of the ride: "Turbulence Over Tucson." The hydraulics sighed and then went to work.

Jimmy's '70 Dodge Challenger, painted school bus yellow, eight coats, hand-rubbed, was parked all by itself in the last row in the lot. He got in, buckled himself in, lit it up. It had a Hemi 454 V-8 under the bulge in the hood. At idle it made a sound a little like a tiger at the zoo in the middle of the afternoon, sleepy, not all that happy. There was a four speed on the floor. Jimmy backed around, pulled out. He eased up and over three speed bumps and moved onto the street, never spinning the tires once.

Westbound on Pico, he looked up in the mirror. Here they were, two heads in a white Ford Escort a quarter mile back. He slowed, let them close the gap. As they drew near, he pulled it down into second, punched it and hung a right.

They *tried* to keep up. Three blocks into a neighborhood of pastel Mediterranean houses with tender little yards, they stopped in the middle of the street. They'd lost him. The short one slapped the dash.

The tall one, who was driving, looked in the mirror.

The yellow Challenger was right behind them.

Jimmy pulled around the dinky Escort, looked over as he came along-side, then gunned it, leaving a perfect pair of wide black streaks.

---

But they came back and they caught him that night.

It started on Hollywood Boulevard. They were still in the Escort so for a minute it was still a joke. The traffic was light and Jimmy was a little down and almost glad for the company. He wasn't going anywhere, he was just *out*, knocking around in the present, or trying to.

He let them stay close behind him for a mile or so and then took a quick right.

Where, it turned out, they *wanted* him to take a right.

When he came around the corner, the side street was blocked by a pair of black Chevys, nose to nose.

And four more Sailors. All of them had the blue edge of light around them, what you'd call *halos* if they were angels, which they decidedly weren't. The Escort came in behind Jimmy and closed the backdoor.

The new men got out of the Chevys and started toward him at the same moment the tall pale man and the one with the bad blond hair got out of the Escort.

Jimmy turned off the engine. He opened the door, but before he could get out, they pulled him from the Dodge, rough, even though he wasn't resisting and they knew it.

Now he resisted. He tried to break away from them but there were too many of them and they were too sure of what they were supposed to do. When Sailors were involved in anything in L.A., it wasn't personal. They didn't act alone. A stray single one might throw a foot out to trip you going down the sidewalk of a night, say something sour behind your back, but when three or four came after you, got in your face, it was because they *meant* something by it. It was because they'd been told to. It was because you were in violation, *busted* in the part of dark things they ran. Jimmy assumed that it was about the Kantke murders, but maybe he was wrong. Maybe this was about the last one. The last case. Or the one before. Unfinished business. He upset people all the time.

But not ever *Sailors*, until now. They dragged him the half block down to the Roosevelt Hotel, nobody saying anything, right into the underground parking. There was an elevator there, and nobody to stop them from going where they wanted to go.

And then they were all on the roof. Sailors had a thing about roofs. High places, lookouts.

One of the four new ones was a foot taller than the tall pale man Jimmy had made fun of and weighed twenty pounds less. This one was like a tall stick in a suit, though his suit was a better suit than what the Escort boys wore. He had red hair. He had long, long fingers. He pointed one at Jimmy. And said nothing.

"I get it," Jimmy said. "You want me to stop."

Two of the other new ones, big ones who wore peacoats and watch caps, took turns pushing Jimmy backwards. There was an ugly rhythm to it, almost like the three of them were dancing across the roof. They slammed him backwards into the base of an iron radio tower left over from what now seemed like a whole other age.

"You're the Disco Antidefamation League."

One of the big ones hit him in the face.

Long-Fingers came a few steps closer. On his cue, the two big men yanked Jimmy up off his feet and carried him over to the parapet and stood him up there and turned him around and then leaned him out over the drop, holding him by the back of his black undertaker's suitcoat like a puppet. A wind blew up the side of the hotel, almost strong enough to hold him up if they let go. Almost.

Jimmy looked down, way down on the street, the people walking, the tour buses parked in front of the Chinese, a few cruisers out on the wrong night in their perfect lowriders, the lights. He thought of the line, from the Bible, *Cast yourself down*. But this wasn't the pinnacle of the temple and he sure wasn't Christ and Long-Fingers wasn't exactly Satan.

"Look down there," Long-Fingers said. "Can you see them?"

He didn't mean the tourists or the cruisers. He meant what was in the shadows, in the alleyways, behind the buildings. *Who*.

"Can you see them?"

"Yeah, I see them," Jimmy said.

"*You* want to walk around forever?" He said it again, the same words, as if he'd been told to say them, this time so loud the people down on the boulevard could have heard him. "You want to walk around forever?"

There was another kind of Sailor. *Walkers*. You've seen them on your streets, or at least in parts of your town. You've thought it was drugs or alcohol and maybe it *began* there. You've wondered why they keep moving, shuffling, how they went dead in the eye, where they could be going, where they sleep, where they go in the daytime. You wonder that, until the light changes, until your husband says something and you go back to your life, or you think of your wife and what's for dinner in the regular world, leaving them behind, like on the street below the Roosevelt Hotel in Hollywood.

"What do you want me not to do?" Jimmy said. "Give me a clue . . ."

The two big men received another silent signal from the tall bony one and they shoved their charge out over the abyss and then yanked him back, like this was a school bully's prank.

Jimmy didn't let them see the fear they wanted to see. But they saw something and the very tall one turned his back and started away, which meant they were finished, that *it* was finished. The two lifted him down. They didn't look at Jimmy again, just fell in behind the red-haired one with the long, long fingers.

# EIGHT

It was late afternoon but the light wasn't golden, just yellow, as it angled through the high windows of the lab at Jean's perfume company. It was a long room with black-topped tables and real-life blue flame Bunsen burners. Technicians in white smocks worked over chemical analyzers and beakers of liquids, swirling them, holding them up to the light, making notations, conferring with too-serious looks, like scientists in TV commercials.

Jimmy sneezed. One of the white coats looked over, annoyed. Jimmy waved his apology.

Jean stepped toward him from the end of the room.

They took his car, left hers in the lot. They went first to Ike's for a drink. It was Jimmy's hangout, a nouveau-*something* cave on a Hollywood street called Argyle. The light was blue light from the flying saucer fixtures suspended over the bar. There was a Rockola jukebox and it was playing Marvin Gaye, "Come Get to This," the dead man's song still rocking, somehow *new* again, like the light of a burned-out star just reaching earth. It was early yet.

The bartender, Scott, brought Jean a cosmopolitan and then set *two* drinks in front of Jimmy, a martini and a manhattan. The drinks waited, spotlighted, on the bar, like something about to be beamed up into the UFO light fixtures.

Jimmy picked up the martini, took a sip.

"Has Krisha been in?"

Scott shook his head. He looked like he could have been an actor waiting for his break, too, tall enough and still young enough and good-looking in an obvious, immediate way, but Scott didn't want to act. He hadn't come to California for its show business.

"I guess you're still looking for her."

"I just haven't seen her lately," Jimmy said.

Jean wondered who she was, tried not to show it.

Scott stepped away to talk to a customer at the end of the bar.

Jean smiled at Jimmy. She didn't ask him about the case, his work. He wondered why. She had another cosmo and he had another martini and they talked about nothing, about the music and a solitary dancer on the floor.

And then they got up to go. She picked up her little purse on the bar. The manhattan was still there, untouched in its perfect circle of light.

It was almost nine by the time they got to the Long Beach Yacht Club. They'd driven by another place closer to downtown where her car was but the restaurant parking lot was too crowded for Jimmy and he changed his mind and waved to the valet parkers and made a loop through the lot and drove south. There wasn't any boat traffic in and out of the marina so the lights were left to reflect clean and still on the black water. The club was quiet. The early crowd had finished and left. The late crowd was still drinking somewhere else.

Jean ordered a steak. The waiter took her menu.

Jimmy handed him his. "I'd just like a plate of tomatoes," he said. "Bring it when you bring her steak. And another bottle of water."

The waiter nodded and stepped away.

"I don't think I know any women who still eat steaks," Jimmy said.

"Yeah, I'm strange all right," Jean said. She was making fun of him. She took a sip of her drink.

"What happened to your eye?" she said. He had a cut over his right eye from the business with the men on the roof on the Roosevelt Hotel, a little bandage.

"I got falling down drunk last night," he said.

An older couple was shown to the next table. The man held his wife's chair and she smiled at him as he sat down to her right instead of across from her.

Jean watched them. She wondered what her parents would look like if they were still alive. *What would be left of the young faces in the old pictures?* She looked around, the yacht clubbers, the polished brass ship's fittings, the photos on the walls, the hurricane flags hung over the long bar.

She wondered how much like her mother she was.

"Is it all right, being here?" Jimmy said.

"Of course," Jean said. "I'm not sentimental . . . and I don't believe in ghosts."

"Your parents aren't in any of the pictures."

She wondered if he knew *everything* she was thinking.

"You've already been here," she said, not as a question. She moved her drink so the light from the candle floating in the bowl lit it up, made it even prettier.

"You wanted to know how I worked. This is how I work."

"Tell me what that means," she said.

"Everything carries its own history with it," he said. "You do. I do. Objects do. Places. Whatever happened in this room is still here in a way. If you want to see it. If you let yourself see it."

He didn't look away from her. "So there *are* ghosts," he said.

"Are they sentimental?" she said and smiled.

"Some of them," he said.

She didn't want to talk about ghosts.

"Have you ever been here before?" he said.

"There are pictures of me with my parents here."

"But you haven't been here since?"

She shook her head. "Why would I?"

"You must have always wondered the things you wonder now, whether he did it, who she really was."

"No."

"So what makes you want to know now?"

"I don't know," she said, but it wasn't true.

Someone dimmed the lights. It was nine o'clock.

The linen of the tablecloth was so white, the marigolds in the clear vase so bright and perfect. He breathed in her scent. It filled his head. Starting from when they were at Ike's he was saying more than he usually said, letting her see more. *I'm falling for her,* he thought, and thought again how good a word for it it was, *falling,* wherever it led, whatever happened now.

"What are you wearing?"

"It doesn't have a name," she said.

"Your own concoction?"

"Do you like it?" she said.

"I don't know if that's the word," Jimmy said.

She smiled again and looked away. Maybe she was falling, too.

"What is perfume made out of?"

"Oils, mostly. And alcohol."

"How did you get into this?" he said.

"A woman taught me the business."

"How does it work?"

"The business or the perfume?"

"Perfume."

"The molecules of the scent activate receptors in the nose and the mouth, which excite certain areas of the brain."

She drew her drink across the table closer to her, turning it in her fingers. "That's the simple explanation," she said, as a way of teasing him.

"A minute ago," Jimmy said, "I remembered a day with my mother. On Point Lobos. Carmel and Monterey. Out of nowhere. I thought maybe it was your perfume."

"Were there flowers?" Jean said.

"I don't think so. I don't know. I remember the cypress trees." He knew he was telling her more than he should.

"It's not supposed to work that way," she said. "That's called 'a headache.' It's when a scent—" She broke off. "How much of this do you really want to know?"

"More," he said.

"A basic, low-quality scent acts directly on the limbic system in the temporal lobe of the brain. It calls up what are called 'moment memories.' It's better for a scent to be more general. The smell of cotton candy reminds you of a trip to the carnival when you were six. A good perfume reminds you . . ." And here she paused, because she knew how it would sound. "Of being in love."

The ghosts in the room leaned closer.

"Mixing memory and desire . . ." Jimmy said.

She knew the line, but didn't remember what it was from. "What is that?"

"Freshman English. T. S. Eliot," Jimmy said. "'April is the cruelest month, breeding lilacs out of the dead land, mixing memory and desire, stirring dull roots with spring rain . . .' *The Wasteland*. I read it—and quit school."

She laughed. "You just stood up and walked out?"

"I waited until the end of the day," he said.

Even when he lied he was telling her too much.

---

They walked along the canal, past the houses. Jean had taken off her shoes. It usually cooled down at night in L.A., particularly on the water, but this night was as warm as the afternoon had been and the canal stank a little. Every once in a while there would be a flash of white over their heads, a gull reeling. Maybe they fed at night. Most of the living rooms were open to the walkway, drapes drawn back, shutters open. People read in chairs or watched TV. They would look up at the movement outside, unconcerned when they saw that it was a young man and a young woman. Some of the houses flew their own bright flags on angled poles, pictographic statements about the people within, crests and flowers and boats and too many rainbows. One banner brushed across their heads as they walked under it, like a magician's scarf.

"When I was a little girl," Jean said, "I used to wonder what it would be like if your footprints could be seen everywhere you'd ever gone. A path of them. My little footprints would be up and down this walk, I guess. It's almost too much to bear."

They passed three more houses. The wind changed direction suddenly and the temperature dropped ten degrees, a gift.

Somewhere along the way, she took his hand.

A rat watched them from under a painted cement mushroom.

"This is odd," she said, "letting someone into your life so quickly. You already know things about me no one else knows. And you're strange."

"I think you said that already."

"What did you think when you first saw me?"

"That you were beautiful."

He thought better than to tell her his idea about a beautiful woman and a beautiful car, how its time was gone already even as you looked at it.

At this moment, she seemed very *present*.

"That's what men always say," she said. "I guess it gets the desired response."

"I also thought you looked sad," Jimmy said. "In the eyes. Maybe from thinking the same sad thing over and over."

He thought she would let go of his hand but she didn't and they walked on without either of them saying anything. Steps climbed up and over the haunches of a bridge and there was just another short block.

And then they were in front of 110 Rivo Alto Canal.

Now Jean let go of his hand and held herself, like the girl on Sunset after she'd kissed Jimmy and felt a chill run through her. The watchful neighbor across the canal was away or asleep and the house of the Abba neighbor was dark, too. They were alone, or at least as alone as Jimmy's worldview allowed.

She was about to say something, to fill the silence.

"There's a woman living in the back bedroom," Jimmy said.

Jean didn't look away from the house. Even in the dim light he could tell she was trying not to react, or at least not to show it.

Jimmy said, "I don't know if she lives there all the time or just comes and goes."

Jean turned away from the house.

"Have any idea who she is?" Jimmy said.

"No." Then she said, to try to put a period on it, "It doesn't matter."

Jimmy wasn't going to let it go. "Gee, it seems like it would," he said. "Maybe she bought it after—"

Jean looked at him.

"I own the house."

He really hadn't thought of that.

"It sat empty while my father was in prison during the years of appeals. Then it went to my brother Carey and he didn't want to have anything to do with it and needed the money, so I bought it from him."

"Why?"

"He needed money."

"Why did you want it?"

"I don't know. I guess I thought the answers were there. *Here.*"

"When was this?"

"When I was at Stanford."

She made herself turn and look at it again, or to let him know she wasn't afraid to.

"What's it like inside?"

"You've never been back?" Jimmy said.

She shook her head. "My business manager pays the gardeners, the electricity."

"It's like a museum, like a World's Fair exhibit from 1977."

Another chill ran through her.

"A little creepy," Jimmy said. "So who is the woman?"

"I said I don't know. I guess a transient. I should sell it, tear it down."

Jean stared at the dark face of the house for a long moment.

"Are your parents alive?" she said.

The question knocked him off balance.

"No," he said.

Her eyes were fixed on the house, as if waiting for the front door to open, as if she'd knocked.

"If I could see my mother's face, at the moment it happened," she said, "I'd know everything."

"Or your *father's* face," Jimmy said.

Jean turned her back on the house again. This time he took *her* hand.

He drew her to him, held her like a dancer. The wind came up again and it made the tackle on the mast of the sailboat across the canal clang, like a signal that something should be starting or ending.

She touched his forehead, where he'd been cut, knew somehow that it was part of this, that he had already given up something for her.

After a moment, she said, "I have trouble getting close to people."

"I don't know anybody who doesn't anymore," Jimmy said. "Maybe my friend Angel."

"Why is that?" she said. "Do you know?"

"No."

"We should go," Jean said.

They were next to the seawall.

"Stand up on the wall," Jimmy said.

She took his hand and stepped up onto the low wall, like the little girl who had lived in that house and been afraid. She walked along, balancing dramatically, happy again for a second, and when she stepped down she went into his arms and kissed him, both of them out of the reach of the past for another second, even though they were this close to it.

# NINE

They pulled up to her apartment. The radio was on low.

"Can we just keep on going?" Jean said.

He looked at her.

"I like this song," she said.

So that was how they came to drive up through Benedict Canyon to Mulholland and then along the crest of the mountains, the lights spread out first on the right, the Valley, then on the left, Hollywood and West Hollywood. They came all the way out to Bel Air, over the 405, dove right down onto Sepulveda, on through the tunnel. Now the hills were dark, the road winding, and the grid of Valley lights only occasionally flashed through gaps in the trees, or the half-moon.

Jimmy steered right into a wide curve where the two lanes became four, just past the first cluster of houses, moving from one pool of orange streetlight onto another.

The radius of the curve opened and then eased into a left. They had the road to themselves and, it seemed for at least a few more seconds, the night.

The windows were down. "I love that smell," Jean said.

"Manzanita," Jimmy said.

They were just another man and a woman, falling. Out on a date on a weeknight, all the time in the world.

*"You know how sometimes you forget about it?" Jimmy said.*

*Angel nodded.*

*"Then you remember."*

And then there was a kid covered in blood right in the road in front of them. Jean called out a wordless sound like a frightened sleeper. Jimmy saw the boy and braked hard and skidded off the road.

He was sixteen or seventeen, in a bright blue snowboarder's knit cap. He seemed oddly calm, flat, somewhere else already, gone. The blood was from a cut at his hairline and it was still coming, covering his face and now the neck of his Notre Dame High School T-shirt. He just stood in the middle of the street, oblivious to the threat of traffic, slack, careless, as if the worst thing had already happened.

The white Honda Accord was on its roof on the shoulder in a sparkling bed of broken glass, the wheels still turning. Jimmy and Jean got out and Jimmy walked purposefully toward it, left Jean behind beside the Dodge.

She stepped toward the kid still standing in the road.

"Don't touch him," Jimmy turned and said to her, calm. "He's all right."

She didn't understand but she did as she was told. There was something about the way he said it that froze her in place.

"Call," Jimmy said.

The driver was crushed in the frame of the window, hanging half out of the overturned car. Jimmy knelt, put fingers to the boy's neck, felt for the carotid. He stood. On the passenger side in the front seat another teenager hung upside down in his shoulder belt, covered in blood, too, but moving, alive.

The bloodied kid still standing in the road came out of his daze. He looked at Jean as she got her phone out of the Dodge. He started to say something, but then shook his head and turned away from her.

He walked stiff-legged toward Jimmy and the Accord.

He saw the boy crushed in the window, the dead driver.

"Whoa. Sean? Shit, man, I hit my head . . ."

He saw the front seat passenger, moving, alive.

"Oh, shit, man, Sean and Calley . . ."

Before Jimmy got to him, the boy knelt in the broken glass to look into the backseat where there was a third body, another face covered in blood.

Jimmy yanked him to his feet.

"What's your name?"

"I was—"

"What's your name?" Jimmy said again.

"Drew."

Jimmy started walking him away from the wreck.

"We were just—" the kid began.

"The driver is dead," Jimmy said. "The other guy is hurt. An ambulance is coming."

He wrapped his arms around the teenager as if he was nine years old.

"I'm messed up . . ." the kid said. He stared at the half sphere of the moon through the trees, looking like the blade of a Gothic ax.

"I . . ."

Jimmy now put a tender hand to the side of the boy's head and spoke into his ear. Anyone close enough to hear would have understood even less by knowing more, would have said later that the words sounded like Latin, like a liturgy from another country or another century. And then that person would have shrugged.

Jean came closer, stopped a few feet away.

"They're coming," she said. "There's a fire station at the top of the hill."

Jimmy spoke a last line to Drew and then turned him and walked him past Jean, toward the car.

"They're coming," Jean said again.

"I know," Jimmy said to her. "Get in the car."

Jimmy opened the passenger door, put Drew in the backseat. The siren could be heard now, coming down from Mulholland, howling as it passed through the tunnel.

Jean said, "I don't understand—"

"They'll take care of the others," Jimmy said. "I have to take care of him."

"Were they—"

"One's dead, one's hurt. Get in the car." Jimmy got behind the wheel and the engine roared up.

Jean got in. She looked at Drew in the seat behind her.

"My head is messed up," Drew said.

"It's not as bad as it looks," Jimmy said, just eyes in the rearview mirror.

"No, I want the ambulance," Drew said. "This is wack. I'm not—"

Jimmy turned and fixed him with a look.

"I'll get you to a doctor."

There was something in the look or in the words or in Jimmy's voice that made the kid relent, lean back against the seat. With balled fists, like a little boy, he wiped the blood out of his eyes. He looked at it on his hands as if embarrassed by it.

"I'm messed up," he said.

Jimmy steered around the wreckage, the Challenger's tires cracking on the glass frags, and drove on down the hill as the red lights of the ambulance pulsed through the trees above them, behind them.

Jean looked straight ahead through the windshield.

----------

They were in the kitchen. Jimmy stood at the sink drinking a glass of water. Behind him, a pair of hands looped the last two stitches in the cut at the kid's hairline. Drew, now dressed in a clean shirt and pants, had his eyes open but wasn't looking at anything.

The doctor daubed at her handiwork, then sorted through her bag for a bandage.

She was Krisha. She had dark brown hair, pulled back, a serious look like a poet in college. She wore a running suit. She'd been running the loop around the Hollywood Reservoir when Jimmy called.

She smiled at Drew.

"All right?"

Drew wouldn't look at her. Maybe he was imagining her, imagining all of this.

Jimmy had taken Jean home, left her standing in the street with a look on her face that was hard to read, more confusing than confused. She hadn't asked any questions on the drive back from the scene of the accident, hadn't said much of anything. Maybe she had put together an explanation for herself that was sufficient for now. Or maybe there wasn't one, ever, and she knew it. She had stood watching as Jimmy backed down the hill to the next intersection, turned around, drove away.

Jimmy walked the doctor to the door.

"He's OK," she said to Jimmy. "I'll come back in a few days. If his ribs keep hurting, you can bring him in to the clinic after hours. We'll X-ray."

"All right."

"What did he see?" she said.

"I don't know. Not everything."

"Are you OK?"

"I wasn't in it," Jimmy said. "I was just driving by."

"I mean, are you OK?" she said.

"Yeah," Jimmy said. "How about you?"

"I'm keeping busy."

It was a line they used. They said good-night and Jimmy thanked her. He watched from the open door until she got into her car and drove away down the long driveway.

Jimmy turned.

Drew was standing in the doorway to the dining room.

"You people are messed up," he said. "This is some weird shit that is happening because—"

In Jimmy's eyes, the boy glowed with the blue edge, like the Sailor on Sunset Boulevard and the men who'd hauled him to the roof of the Roosevelt, but brighter than them. Vibrant, undeniable, otherworldly.

Drew had stopped in midsentence because now, too, that was the way he saw his host.

Jimmy picked up the blue snowboarder's cap from the table in the foyer and tossed it to the kid.

"Let's go for a ride," he said.

───────────

A fog had come in. Down below at least. They were on an overlook off Mulholland, above the city. Jimmy had brought him up here to tell him. They leaned against the hood of the car, the yellow Challenger, pointed out at the sea of white. An ambulance far, far below pushed up La Brea, the light throbbing red under the cloud, looking like a fissure in the surface of the earth.

Drew said, "I don't know why I'm going along with this bullshit."

Jimmy knew the answer to that. "Because almost everything in you is telling you it's true," he said. "It can't be, but it is."

"You're the same as me?"

"Yeah."

"When did it happen to you?"

"A long time ago."

"When?"

"Nineteen sixty-seven."

Drew looked over at him, the youth still in his face. *How could it be?*

"*How* did it happen to you?"

A solitary car came past on Mulholland.

"People get to tell you that when they want to," Jimmy said. "I was about your age. A little older."

"Why were you there, at the wreck?"

"I was just there," Jimmy said. "I was out driving around."

"That woman who was with you, is she—"

"No."

"What would have happened if you weren't there? If you hadn't come by."

He was smart, asked the right questions. Jimmy remembered when *he* had had all the same questions himself, all at once. It was like this was a foreign country and, somehow, here you were, standing in the midst of it.

"You would have walked away," Jimmy told him. "Into the woods. Wandered around for a while. One of us would have found you or you would have found us. Maybe in a hospital. Maybe a cop, a night watchman."

"Are we angels?" Drew said.

"No."

"Ghosts?"

"No."

"What, *vampires*?" Drew said.

Jimmy looked across at him. "You feel like a vampire?"

Drew said, "No, what I feel like is once I got some blunt down in Huntington Beach that was messed up and I was stupid for three days. I *saw* myself in that backseat."

"What you saw was what was left."

"I don't get that."

"Something they can bury."

Drew looked like he was going to be sick.

"I don't get that."

"It's just the way it is. Something's left behind and yet you're here."

"I don't get that."

"I don't either."

"What is the blue shit about?"

"It's how we see each other sometimes," Jimmy said. "Sometimes it's there, sometimes it isn't. It comes and goes." Suddenly Jimmy was tired, tired of this night, tired of all the times it had been repeated.

"This is bullshit," Drew said.

"Yeah, you already said that."

When they came down off the mountain, it was after three. The man in the peacoat and watch cap was back at his post on the corner in front of the turquoise nightclub at Sunset and Crescent Heights, now joined by another Sailor dressed the same. Their eyes tracked the passing Challenger.

Drew looked over. There was the blue flash.

"So they're the same as us?" Drew said.

"No," Jimmy said, a little too abruptly.

"What's the difference? I kinda like the coat—"

"There are two ways to go. That's the other way."

Since they'd come down off the mountain, Jimmy had been thinking about himself, not Drew, and he had gone to a dark place inside. Dark and quiet.

By now they were on Santa Monica. Jimmy looked over as he drove past one square, blockish building. Clover. It was closed up tight now, a row of razor wire around the lip of roof showing silver in the streetlight, like a crown of thorns.

Jimmy thought how it *had* been like his church once. In a twisted, dead-end sixties way.

And then he was driving past Chateau Marmont again. It was something they all did. *Returning.*

*Looking up at the roof again.*

A cop car cruised along beside them. The cops, a shaved head East Islander and a Latina woman, looked them over good but it was mostly the car, the paint job, the clear-coat, the way the reflected lights rolled off the rear deck in perfect *Os*. The two cars, the Challenger and the cop car, stopped side by side at the next corner, at the light.

"Take me home," Drew said. "I want to go home." He had a whole different voice suddenly.

"No," Jimmy said.

"I want to see my mother."

"No."

"I'll get out then. I'll go to them." He was talking about the cops next to them.

"I meant you can't. It won't do any good," Jimmy said.

*"I want to go home."*

———

It was a quiet street in a residential neighborhood in the Valley, an area called Studio City. There were large trees and sidewalks, old-style white streetlamps, cats watching from under parked cars, artificial Ohio. Jimmy killed the headlights, slowed to a stop. A half-block ahead, there was a cluster of cars around a house, the only one with all the lights on. A dog in a fenced yard next to the car barked three or four times, then stopped.

With the windows down, you could hear the soft roar of the 101 freeway a half mile north, that sound like the ocean, but nervous. Jimmy opened the glove compartment. There was a bottle of water. He snapped the top and handed it to Drew.

Drew was staring at the house.

"How long?" Jimmy said.

"My whole life," Drew said. That defiant voice was gone. He was a little brother again.

Jimmy just let the engine idle. The sense of the neighborhood was heavy in the air. The trees leaned over to hold it in. They knew the boy here. Drew had probably learned how to ride a bike on this street. Before that, the joints in the sidewalk had made a beat to sing a song to as his father or mother pushed him in a stroller around the block. Maybe the yard in front of that house had carried a balloon sign, now almost too sentimental to think of, that said, "It's a boy!"

*Everything carried its history.*

Now it's a *dead* boy.

Someone was arriving, a shiny duelie pickup, probably someone who worked at the studios, a gaffer, a grip, a carpenter. They liked duelies. The man got out and rushed toward the house.

"It's Terry," Drew said. "My mother's—" He didn't finish it.

The front door of Drew's house opened, throwing an angle of light onto the lawn, and a man from inside stepped out of the doorway and opened his arms to the man coming up the walk.

The front door closed. Shadows crossed on the drapes.

"You could look in the window," Jimmy said, "but you don't want to carry that around with you, seeing them this way. You could walk in, but they wouldn't know you and it would only add to their pain."

Drew looked at him. "I look the same. How can that be?"

"They wouldn't know you. To their eyes you have a different face. It's something that happens inside their heads, the people you leave behind. They have their boy. They're going to put him in the ground in a day or two."

Jimmy could hear the breath catch in Drew's throat.

"But you're here, in the flesh," Jimmy said. "With us. To be this second version of yourself."

"This is wack," Drew said, his eyes on the house.

"It's just the way it is," Jimmy said. "I didn't design this. I don't know who did."

Now Drew was crying.

"You're here for as long as you're here, until whatever unfinished business you have is finished. You can try to do some good—or you can be one of those people we saw on the street back there, on Sunset, here to do wrong."

He didn't tell the boy that there was a *third* thing you could be. A *Walker*. Dead to the world, this world and the other.

"You have a new family now," Jimmy said, flat and unsentimental, looking straight ahead at the grayed-out trees in the next block.

He heard the door open as Drew bolted from the car.

Jimmy went after him, as once somebody had gone after him.

He caught up to him on the lawn, on the black grass.

"Leave me alone!"

"I'm telling you, there's nothing you can do," Jimmy said, loud enough to wake the neighbors. "I know."

Drew had stopped.

"Come on," Jimmy said.

The door opened. The man, Terry, had heard the noise, the voices. He came out onto the front step. He tried to make sense of two strangers standing there ten feet away.

"Don't say his name," Jimmy said.

Drew turned toward the man. With the door open, there was light on the boy's face.

"Don't," Jimmy said.

"What are you doing?" Terry said.

A woman stepped into view behind him in the doorway.

"Who is it?" she said with the saddest kind of hope.

———

As the sky turned pink, Jimmy yanked close the blackout drapes in the bedroom at the end of the hallway in his house. Behind him Drew was on his back on the black covering on the bed, eyes open.

# TEN

In the morning paper there was an article about last night's accident, a picture of the overturned Honda, a headline:

## TWO DEAD, ONE CRITICAL
## IN CANYON CRASH

There was a school picture of Drew, probably from two or three grades ago, a straight-faced, trying-to-look-older pose. His last name was Hastings. The other dead boy had been a runner, had held some state record so he got more ink. And a *smiling* picture, taken from the sports pages of the Notre Dame High School paper.

An adjacent article showed the same photo they were using of the young Latino boy lost in the brown hills out in what they called the Inland Empire and, now, a picture of a man in handcuffs, a Mexican man who looked as if he'd never smiled.

"The news is always the same," Jimmy said. "It just happens to different people."

Angel came into the dining room from the kitchen with a cup of coffee.

"I almost drove him down to The Pipe last night," Jimmy said. "Maybe he should see that *first*."

"He'll know about it soon enough," Angel said.

Jimmy picked up a phone and dialed the number for Jean's office. She wasn't expected in all day. Jimmy called her apartment. After three rings, the machine picked up. Jimmy hung up.

"She was with you?" Angel said.

Jimmy nodded.

"What's her name?"

"Jean."

"What's her last name?"

"I told you, Kantke."

"What did she see?"

"A car wreck," Jimmy said.

Angel took a sip of his coffee, waited for Jimmy to remember who he was talking to.

"I don't know what she thought," Jimmy said. "She didn't say anything. I took her back to her office to get her car and then followed her home."

Jimmy went into the study. Angel followed him.

"So she's the Long Beach thing. The murders."

"Yeah."

"So it's more than the case. With her. For you."

"I guess it was getting to be. I don't know what it's going to be now."

Jimmy sat behind the desk and pulled the keyboard closer and rewound the digital machines that recorded output from the security cameras that ringed his property. Between midnight and one, the pale men and the big men from the other night on the hotel roof had made an appearance at the back gate, testing the iron bars, hanging out for twenty minutes.

Jimmy put the picture onto a flat screen monitor on the wall.

"You know these guys?"

Angel looked at the screen and shook his head. Jimmy froze the image and clicked a few keys and the printer printed out a hard copy.

"Maybe they were selling magazines," Angel said.

"I played a little road tag with the two on the left the other day. They were in an Escort."

Angel got the joke.

"Lon and Vince," Jimmy said, looking at their pale faces. "And then the other night I met the other two and a leader, a guy close to seven foot. They showed me the view from the Roosevelt."

"And that has to do with *this*?" Angel said.

Jimmy didn't know. Or wasn't ready to say. He shrugged.

Drew was in the game room playing pinball, a bottle of Dos Equis sitting on top of the glass. A TV was on, big screen, street luge skaters ripping down a too steep canyon road somewhere, crisscrossing, losing it, spinning out, crashing into hay bales. Drew apparently didn't get the connection or he would have turned it off.

Jimmy stepped into the doorway.

"I have to go somewhere. You want to go with me?"

"Go where?"

"I'm an investigator. I'm working on something."

"A what?"

"An investigator."

"What's the point?"

"You'll feel better if you do something, if you go out there and try to find some answers to the questions that there are answers for. Like I said, there are two ways to go."

"Yeah, I know," Drew said. "Everybody's gotta believe in something. I believe I'll have another beer . . ."

Jimmy turned to go.

"Let me ask you something," Drew said to stop him, not looking up from his game. "Can I die? I mean, *again*?" Maybe he *did* get the connection between the crashing luge skaters and what had happened to him on the canyon road.

"You can get hurt," Jimmy said, "*bad,* but you won't die." Here was another chance to tell the kid about the *third* thing that could happen, about how your spirit could die and you'd be left with even less, how they could take your spirit away, the thing they'd hauled him up to the roof for, just so he'd remember it. "You're here until it's time for you to go—"

"Yeah, I know . . ."

"But you can't bring it on yourself and nobody else can bring it on you."

Drew threw his weight against the machine to force the steel ball uphill.

"Even if like a bullet went through my head, I wouldn't die."

"No."

"If I was shredding down a mountain and pulled a full-on Sonny Bono, I wouldn't die."

"No. You could get messed up, but you wouldn't die."

The pinball machine clattered wildly. Something had happened.

"The pathetic thing is I don't know if that's good news or bad," Drew said.

Jimmy said, "That's why there are—"

"Yeah, 'two ways to go . . .'" Drew said. "'Use The Force, Luke.'"

———

Jimmy knew most of the story and a phone call to a friend in politics brought the rest. Harry Turner was a "kingmaker," one of the men—or, depending on whom you talked to, *the* man—you went to if you wanted to be governor or a federal judge. Or, if you believed everything you heard, the anchorman on the local news in Santa Barbara where one of Harry Turner's five big houses was. It was one of those stories that over the years got better and better. To run things in California, you had to wait in line.

The man at the head of the line, hand on the gate, for the last twenty years anyway, was Harry Turner. He'd been the real lawyer who ran Jack Kantke's defense, behind the scenes, behind *Upland* or *Overland* or *Upchurch* or whatever his name was, the Long Beach lawyer whose name nobody could remember but who had to sit at the table next to defendant Kantke and take the loss when it came. When Harry Turner stopped practicing law himself, "retired" in the nineties, he still kept his firm open with a half dozen lawyers angling to be his favorite, his heir, the son he never had. He went even further behind the curtain. He was on a dozen boards of directors. He owned car dealerships. He owned a chain of smog inspection stations. He owned billboard companies. He held patents for devices he couldn't point to on a table, for "processes" he couldn't begin to explain. He owned a restaurant. He owned *airports*. He made money while he slept.

And twenty years ago, with a new dogleg in the aqueduct to bring in water from the Colorado, he became one of the "visionaries" turning green the Coachella Valley out past Palm Springs and Indian Wells. Desert into farmland. He had a thousand acres of winter lettuce and another five hundred in table grapes.

He was eleven feet tall, on the back of his horse.

He rode, not that fast but steady, out of a block of date palms planted in rows and then along the edge of a field of something so green it clashed with the sky. He rode without changing his pace right straight at the black pickup with the ranch logo on the door, came up fast enough to make them all turn their heads aside. He wore chinos and short brown Wellington boots and a long-sleeve white shirt. He stayed in the saddle, all eleven feet of him.

Jimmy had been hand-delivered by a pair of robust cowboys who made the Sailors on the roof of the Roosevelt Hotel look anorexic. These men were Basque, real cowboys. They'd stopped Jimmy even before he made it to the gates of the ranch, sixty seconds after a black helicopter had overflown him in the Mustang on the mile-long road in off of the highway. They'd shown him where to leave his car in front of one of the very clean outbuildings. One of them nodded toward the front seat of the black truck and then got behind the wheel and the other man climbed in back and sat against the tailgate and rode that way all the way out into the fields.

They were strong and their suspiciousness was industrial-strength, but they weren't smart. Jimmy had told them he was the mayor of Rancho Cucamonga.

Harry Turner looked him over, looked at his sissy shoes, his Prada suit, and smiled a little sourly.

*"Mr. Mayor,"* he said. He had a walkie-talkie hanging off his wide brown belt. They'd called ahead.

Turner climbed down out of the saddle and took off his hat, a flat-brim Stetson that made him look like a mounted cop. His hand came out and Jimmy thought it might be the start of a handshake but Turner was just reaching for a kerchief he kept tucked up his left sleeve. He wiped off his forehead, even though he wasn't sweating.

Jimmy still hadn't said a word. It was the right thing not to say.

"You had lunch?" Turner said.

He didn't wait for an answer, just walked past Jimmy toward a black flagship Mercedes S600 that hadn't been there thirty seconds ago. Another Basque man now stood beside the pickup. Mexican men in jobs like these always looked at the ground when you weren't talking to them. These men looked at *you.* One of them retrieved an automatic rifle from the trunk of the Mercedes before Turner got behind the wheel and they left.

They drove for a mile between two fields and then turned right and drove another mile. All the roads were paved. They had them to themselves. There were tumbleweeds and burger wrappers blown against the chain-link fences. They came out onto the access road and then onto the highway, Interstate 10, headed east through the brown and the green, all of it as flat as the top of a stove. They drove and drove. The Chocolate Mountains on the other side of the valley were getting bigger in front of them.

Maybe they were going to Phoenix.

The green glass in the window beside Jimmy's head was an inch thick. He tipped his head over to where he could see the side mirror. The black pickup was a half mile back, three of the Basques shoulder to shoulder in the front seat.

Turner didn't say much of anything, beyond naming the crops in the fields alongside the interstate as they passed, three kinds of *summer* lettuce, "baby's breath"—which he sure enough made sound like a *product*—jojoba and sod. The sod farm was out the window for a long minute at eighty miles an hour, an expanse of lawn with no big house behind it, unsettling, *wrong.*

They passed a section of planted date trees, *Medjool* dates, Turner said.

"Dates are too sweet." Which meant they were somebody else's dates.

Jimmy didn't disagree.

Just as he was settling into his seat, thinking they *were* going to Phoenix, or at least Blythe, they came up on a big new gaudy Morongo Indian
casino with a hundred-foot sign out front and a name that didn't say anything about Indians. Turner looked over at it with a long look that made
Jimmy figure he owned that, too, or a piece of it. And he took the brand-
new exit just past it.

But they weren't going to the casino. They took another road, another
*paved* road straight south for five or six miles and then there was a big
white box of an aluminum building, nothing else for miles, with three
Lincoln Town Cars and a pickup and a new Cadillac in the lot in front. It
didn't have a sign.

There was just one long wooden table inside but it was covered with
white linen and the tableware was silver, though a plain pattern. There
weren't any flowers. There weren't any windows either. It was about sixty
degrees, a hundred and nine outside.

A single waiter in a plain-front white shirt and black pants stood next
to the kitchen door. There wasn't any music, just six or seven men talking.
They were all dressed like field hands. In four-hundred-dollar boots. None
of them were young.

"We waited, Harry," one of them said. The plate in front of him had
a pile of bloody bones and a last smear of what looked liked creamed
spinach.

Turner slapped the man on the back.

"Don't get up," he said, since the man wasn't moving.

He shook the hands of two of the other men. One of them introduced
the man beside him he'd brought as a guest. Turner knew the rest of them.
He didn't introduce Jimmy and the other men didn't ask.

"Looks like it's lamb," Turner said as he and Jimmy sat down across the
table from each other at one end, away from the others.

Jimmy nodded.

"It'll be good," Turner said. "Americans don't know how to slaughter
lambs." The way he said *Americans* made Jimmy wonder if maybe Turner
wasn't his real name. A lot of the farmers and ranchers out here were
Armenian. "Most Americans *think* they've eaten lamb and most of them
think they don't like the taste. You butcher it wrong, you let any part of the
meat touch the layer of fat just under the wool and the lanolin turns the
meat, gives it that *lamb* taste."

The waiter came with two plates, put them in front of the men, and
filled their glasses with red wine.

"But maybe you already know all about lamb," Turner said.

"I didn't know that," Jimmy said. "I even thought I liked it." He picked up a lamb chop and chewed off a bite.

It was the best lamb in the world, the lamb of kings.

Or king*makers*.

"Guess I see what you mean," Jimmy said.

"You know how to eat it," Turner said. He picked up a chop with his fingers, too, out of the puddle of blood.

Turner said what Jimmy had already figured out, that a group of them in the Valley had gotten together to make this place, a private dining hall, built it, built the road out to it, hired a chef away from some hotel.

"French," Turner said. "But he's all right."

Jimmy ate his spinach. From that first *Mr. Mayor* out in the fields under the nonstop sun, he knew Turner was onto him. He also knew that was the way to get in to see someone like Harry Turner. You lied to *him* in the right way, in this case the smart-ass way.

You sure didn't come in trying to flatter him. A man like Harry Turner had stood before a line of flatterers stretching away to the horizon. You didn't bow and scrape. Even the waiter knew that.

So Turner was onto him. The question was how much.

The waiter stepped in to top off Turner's wineglass. Turner looked at him.

"We'll do that."

The waiter left the bottle and backed away. The wine was a Jordan Beaujolais.

"I understand you want to know about my brilliant defense of Florence Gilroy in the poisoning death of her third husband," Turner said.

So they'd radioed out to the fields that the mayor of Rancho Cucamonga was there to see him. And Turner had said *bullshit* and told them to call in the plate on the Mustang. Then who knows what other calls he'd made, even before he started riding in from the date palm oasis. Whomever he'd called, Harry Turner knew everything he needed to know. Or thought he did.

"I *do* want to know. Sometime," Jimmy said.

Turner wasn't in a hurry to eat. It made Jimmy know that this was more important to him than it could have been, maybe even than it *should* have been.

"Did you look up Barry Upchurch?"

Jimmy shook his head. "Is he still alive?"

Turner said, "You know, I don't know." It was a lie.

The last three men left together. One of them, the one who'd intro-duced his man to Turner, put a hand on Turner's back as he passed and leaned in close and said something, three or four sentences, into his ear.

Turner nodded. And then shook his head no.

"That's what I said," the man said, loud enough to hear.

Then they were alone. The waiter even disappeared.

Turner said, "Where were we?"

"You were saying Jack Kantke couldn't possibly have done it because he was talking about the Dodgers with the gas station guy in Barstow at eight-fifteen and the time of the murders was determined to be between eight and midnight."

"*Six* and midnight," Turner said. "They couldn't peg it any closer, not then. 1977. Maybe today."

"Six and midnight," Jimmy corrected. "Still . . ."

"He drove fast," Turner said.

"I thought of that," Jimmy said.

"You like to drive fast."

"I just like to drive. I even like to sit in cars in my driveway."

Turner ate a good half of his meal before he said anything else. There were linen napkins. He wiped the blood off of his lips onto one.

"I never understood why the other side didn't say that," he said. *"He drove fast."*

"People hate math," Jimmy said.

Turner nodded. He thought he was being likeable.

Jimmy tried to come at it from another angle, got out a few words of a question, when Turner cut him off.

"We *bought* the guy at the gas station in Barstow. Six hundred dollars, as I recall. And I think he asked for a pair of Dodgers tickets, his idea of a joke. He's dead now."

"But not because he had a bad sense of humor," Jimmy said.

Turner gave a little hint of that sour smile again.

The waiter reappeared without being called, put a cup of black coffee beside Turner's left hand. He was left-handed.

"So what time *did* Kantke stop for gas?" Jimmy asked.

Turner said, "About two hours after he shot and killed his wife and Bill Danko."

Just like that.

There it was.

In case Jimmy didn't get it the first time, Turner said again, "He drove fast."

"It would have been rush hour," Jimmy said.

"It was a Saturday," Turner said. "But you knew that."

Jimmy did know that.

He put his fork and knife on top of his plate.

"So," Jimmy said. "What's for dessert?"

"None of us eat dessert," Turner said, looking straight across the table at him. "Vanity. Young wives."

"Did you see him executed?" Jimmy said, right back to his eyes.

"You make it sound like an obligation."

Jimmy didn't know how he was supposed to take that.

"You lose the case, you have to watch the man die?" Turner said.

"I guess it's a long way up to San Quentin."

"Jack Kantke and I weren't friends," Turner said. "I was just a lawyer trying to help a fellow member of the California Bar."

"'In good standing . . .'"

"All of us," Turner said.

———————

When Jimmy came out of the dining hall into the glare of the sun, into what was now the hundred and *ten* degree heat, his Mustang was sitting there waiting for him.

And Jimmy had the keys in his pocket.

He looked up at the utterly clear sky. There wasn't even a daylight moon. He hadn't seen Turner come out behind him and hadn't heard anything, but now the black Mercedes pulled out of the lot and onto the road, followed by the men in the pickup in their black *txapela* Basque berets.

And then Jimmy was alone out there.

# ELEVEN

When Jimmy stepped out of the farmers' and ranchers' private dining room in the middle of their made-over desert and looked up at the rich blue of the empty sky, for some reason he remembered something he'd heard a NASA scientist say once on a television program, that space wasn't all that far away, *that if you could drive there in a car, you'd be there in an hour.* And he remembered something else from the program, that way way out, a few billion miles past that first edge of space, sometimes they would identify a body by the *negative* evidence, know something was there because everything pointed away from it, because there was a too clear expanse of nothing.

What Harry Turner had said—and what he hadn't—had turned Jimmy's mind. Turner had stated outright that Jack Kantke had killed his wife and Bill Danko, then driven hard and fast out of L.A. to cobble together an alibi. What Turner had said, had *confessed* on behalf of his client, was meant to convey the same message to Jimmy as the trip to the roof of the Roosevelt Hotel with the Sailors. *Nothing to see here, move right along. . . .* Harry Turner had read Jimmy Miles as wrong as the tall bony redheaded Sailor and whoever had sent him. What was meant to drive him away only drew him in closer.

Maybe it was just the look in Harry Turner's eye.

Whatever it was, Jimmy now guessed, just for himself, that Jack Kantke *hadn't* killed his wife and her lover. He didn't know who did, didn't know *why,* but, just for himself, he was all but sure it had been somebody else standing with the gun behind the wisp of a curtain in the white front bedroom in the Rivo Alto house and that they'd gassed the wrong man.

If you still believed in the notion of right and wrong men.

---

California 74 was a winding, climbing two-lane road highlighted in the AAA tourist guides as something special, *the Palms to Pines Highway,* slithering its way up off the desert floor into the San Bernardino Mountains, toward Mount San Jacinto, "from a desert oasis to snow capped mountains." And, though it was June, almost July and the valley behind him was baking, there *would* be snow on the sides of the road when he got to the higher elevations, up to the top, into the evergreens, eight thousand feet.

But he wasn't there yet and he was enjoying the drive. He came to the first of the tall stick trees and pulled off the road and got out. The air smelled cool and green, like the world wouldn't mind if you lived another day or so. That was the way it was in the mountains. Back down behind him in the desert, Nature didn't much care if you were there or not, regarded you the way a tortoise looks at you, *Are you another rock?*

Jimmy opened the hatchback and pulled the soft, worn red plaid Pendleton shirt out of the grocery bag. He was alone on the highway, hadn't seen another soul for twenty minutes. He took off his white silk short-sleeved shirt and then the T-shirt underneath it. It wasn't cold at all but the air made his skin ripple. He pulled on the stretched-out Sears undershirt from the bag and unbuckled his slacks and dropped them and slipped into a pair of faded, patched-at-the-knee Levi's. He folded his suit pants and sat on the rear bumper and changed his socks and put on a pair of black hightop Converse All Stars.

He'd bought the clothes at the Salvation Army in Palm Springs. Everything came to a couple of bucks less than what he'd paid for the socks he walked in wearing. He wasn't in any hurry, knew where he was going next, so he spent some time talking with the woman behind the register. She had that look in her eye, that *recovered* look, a little shaky but she was going to be all right, had managed to get in the present, to just read the page in front of her. Maybe she could tell Jimmy how to do it.

The shirt felt good. He wondered about the man who'd worn it last. Angel had told him about a preacher who made a thing of only wearing the clothes of men in his congregation who'd died, clothes bundled up and handed over by widows and grown children, after they'd buried their faces in the shirts one last time. Jimmy buttoned up the plaid shirt and closed the hatchback. Clothes with a history, it fit.

In Idyllwild, he bought ten dollars' worth of gas and paid cash. The attendant, a high school kid, looked him over good, though he didn't get up out of his plastic chair to do it. The Mustang was a little too cherry to really match the driver in the knockaround clothes, but the kid and the locals walking by didn't seem to notice, didn't seem to be thinking much of anything when they looked at Jimmy. Which was the idea.

Idyllwild was a collection of log buildings on both sides of the highway on the flat part of the summit. A pair of Alpine A-frame gift shops, almost identical, stood across the road from each other, each with an eight-foot redwood bear out front, chain-saw carved. There was a restaurant. There was an ice cream parlor. There was a bar. There was a little brown wood church up the highway. And a "creekside" motel with cabins.

Jimmy drove across the highway from the gas station to the restaurant and parked the Mustang and got out. A slice of a giant sequoia, taller than he was, was leaned against the wall on its edge, like a big coin. It was polished, the rings clear. Events in History were marked with little flags on pins, nine hundred years of history, if they had it right, fires by blackened rings, droughts by thin rings, Columbus setting sail, Lincoln dead, Kennedy dead, a man on the moon.

It was late enough in the day that Jimmy decided he'd stay over, go at it in the morning. This was where Barry Upchurch had retired, probably moved into what had been a weekend place before. Jimmy had found the lawyer's name listed in a "Mountain Areas" city directory in the library down in Palm Springs. Then he'd found an article in the microfiche about an Idyllwild *No Growth!* committee Upchurch had served on when he first came up the mountain ten years ago. Retired So-Cal lawyers seemed either to go to the mountains or the beach, the size of the house and the acreage determined by just who you kept out of jail or bankruptcy. The lawyers who put people *into* jail, when they retired probably just stayed in their houses in the Valley or out in Santa Monica, grandfathered in.

Upchurch wasn't a government lawyer but from what Jimmy had heard and read he hadn't had a big client practice either. His house was likely a cabin on one of the roads heading up into the low hills above town, nothing fancy, a couple of bedrooms, or maybe a glass-fronted A-frame, if the seventies had made a bit too much of an impression on him. Jimmy had an address but he wasn't just going to walk up to the door, at least not yet.

There was snow on the shady side of the cabin, a short foot of it banked up against the stone foundation. Each cabin had a cute wildflower name. The key to "Star Lily" had a green plastic fob, old style. Jimmy opened the door. There was red carpet, fairly new but an old-fashioned pattern.

There was no TV, no phone. An empty fireplace, gingham curtains somebody had made by hand, a bedspread picking up the same reds and greens. There was a kitchenette. Jimmy tried the faucet. There were two jelly glasses in the cabinet. The water was cold and sweet, better than anything in a bottle with "mountain" in the name.

But the cabin was too lonely to stay in, with the light dying and all in among the tall trees, and Jimmy turned around and walked out. Better to be out with people, even strangers, than in with himself.

He went next door to the Evergreen Club. It was dark, but in a good way. There were antlers on the wall and pictures of "Early Idyllwild" and an oversized electric train running on a track up just under the rafters.

And Barry Upchurch was at the bar.

Probably.

Twenty years, not ten, were added to the face from the picture in the microfiche of the *No Growth!* Committee. Maybe there had been too many nights here drinking what looked like bourbon in a rocks glass. He had a *mad* look to him, in his eye, in the way he sat hunched over, protecting the space in front of him. And he smoked, too.

Everybody Jimmy had been meeting lately looked like they were trying to get over something.

The barstools didn't swivel so Upchurch and the three or four regulars beside him were using the mirror over the bar to watch the young woman shooting pool behind them.

She was traveling, alone. She had a backpack, a real backpack, not an *accessory,* stowed against the knotty pine-paneled wall, worn hiking shoes, a tan that wasn't from a UV lamp. She was German or maybe Swiss, tall enough to be a model. Short, dark red hair, cut different lengths, like a Beatle, good for the trail. She was laughing at herself between missed shots and drinking a dark beer. The kid from the gas station was her partner.

He put his stick back in the rack, shaking his head. "I gotta go," he said.

"Sorry," she said, heavy accent. "I'm terrible! Please not to be giving up on me, I am *trying.*" She laughed between every other word and touched his arm.

"No, it's all right," the kid said. "I just gotta go. You're OK. Really. It was nice to meet you . . ."

He held out his hand.

"Greta," she said.

He shook her hand. "Enjoy." He left.

She racked up the balls again while the regulars at the bar poked each other in the ribs. Your turn. But it was too early and they were all too sober, or too old, to make a move.

Jimmy took a stool. The bartender was a woman past sixty, maybe past seventy. She had a cigarette going, too, lying in an ashtray swiped from a fancier place than this.

Jimmy ordered a dark beer. A *German* beer.

"Good luck," the barmaid said.

But Jimmy wasn't going to make a play for the girl. Now he was there to watch Upchurch, maybe close the distance of the three stools between them, talk to him before he *talked* to him. He hadn't meant to get into this tonight but sometimes *The Case* had other ideas, its own sense of timing.

It turned out one of the other men was a lawyer, too, and still had a practice going down in Palm Desert. This one was twenty years younger than Upchurch. Upchurch listened to him go on and on about a case, more detail than anybody wanted or needed, another murder but this one more immediate than the Long Beach murders long ago, this one about a meth lab in a double-wide too many miles up an unpaved road.

Upchurch just nursed his drink and nodded every once in a while. This gang had probably all heard *his* murder story too many times. Or maybe he wasn't a talker.

When the beer clock said *seven,* Upchurch got up and stepped back, steady, not the least bit drunk. His pants leg was hiked up. He slid it down, over the little Colt Detective Special .38 in an ankle holster stuck in the top of his black socks.

Upchurch picked up the change that had been sitting there all along and pushed two singles across to the trough. The barmaid palmed them straight into the pocket of her jeans and somehow made the whistle on the chugging electric train toot.

Jimmy waited a minute and followed him out.

Upchurch came out of the town store across the highway with what looked liked a thick steak wrapped in pink butcher paper. Jimmy was in the shadows alongside the gas station. It closed at nightfall, lights out. Upchurch walked back across the empty blacktop, not in any hurry at all, apparently not having any idea someone was watching him. He glanced at a Jeep CJ-7, old style, open on the sides, parked in front of the bar, walked past it, started up the easy hill, walking in the middle of the gravel road.

Jimmy waited, followed him.

A woman in her fifties came out to poke at a charcoal fire in a steel drum smoker out behind an A-frame all by itself next to a dry creekbed in among a good stand of trees. There was an owl somewhere, hooting. She searched for it with her eyes. Then she went back inside. Jimmy watched.

And then the barrel of the tidy .38 was behind his ear.

Upchurch didn't say anything smart or sarcastic or even nasty, just had Jimmy walk the rest of the way up toward the house, toward the light so he could get a better look at him, his gun now down at his side.

When they got into the light, Jimmy told him who he was, what he was there for.

Upchurch dropped the .38 into the pocket of his chinos but didn't shake Jimmy's hand or anything.

The woman, Ellie Upchurch, stepped out onto the deck, surprised to see anybody, her hand going to her breast.

"He's here about Barry," Upchurch said.

*Maybe he was schizophrenic.*

But then they went inside the house and the first thing Jimmy saw was a portrait of the *real* Barry Upchurch, under a brass-plated tube light. Maybe a client had painted it, "in partial payment for services rendered." The Upchurch in the painting was older than he would have been at the time of the Kantke trial and he was better looking than his big brother, probably always had been. But the eyes, the face had the same *slapped* look.

The other Upchurch, whose name was D. L., stepped past Jimmy without looking at him and took the pistol out of his pants pocket and put it in a drawer in a table with a Tiffany-style lamp on it and a vase of pretty purple mountain wildflowers called nightshade. Ellie Upchurch came over and took D. L.'s hand and kissed him on the cheek, something Jimmy guessed she always did when someone was looking at the portrait of her first husband.

D. L. grunted something that could have been, *I love you, too.*

The A-frame was nicely furnished without a lot of references to the past, his or hers or *his,* except for the portrait. There was an oval "rag rug," on top of pine flooring, a Kennedy rocking chair, an over-and-under shotgun on pins on the wall, nothing too fancy, a Browning. There was a big leather chair in front of the stand-alone black Swedish fireplace, a healthy fire, a *National Geographic* bright yellow on the ottoman. It was all one big room, with a bedroom upstairs, a loft.

"You can go on," D. L. Upchurch said and walked toward the open kitchen. He meant that his wife could talk to this stranger about her first husband, his brother. He took the wrapped steaks from the counter and put them in the fridge. He got himself a Bud Light in a can and then dug around in the back of the icebox until he came out with a bottle of beer, dark German beer. He handed the Beck's to Jimmy after he wrenched off the cap with his bare hand—it may or may not have been a twist-off—and then he went outside, left them alone.

She sat in the leather chair and Jimmy stood beside the fire and she gave him a version of the intervening years. Barry Upchurch had practiced law in Long Beach another twelve years after the Kantke trial and then he retired and they moved up the mountain and he died two years after that.

The short version was he'd never gotten over it.

"*Doctors* are like that, some of them," Jimmy said. "They keep it to themselves but it rips them up when they lose one."

She sat with her legs crossed, her hands in her lap. "That wasn't Barry's problem," she said. "He had no problem losing a case."

She probably didn't mean the twist of bitterness in the way she said the line.

"It wasn't that," she said.

And then she went into it in great detail, the days and weeks of that time, of 1977, starting even before the trial began. She never referred directly or even indirectly to Harry Turner setting things up, running things from behind the curtain, but he was as *present* in the story as if she had named his name or he was standing there in the room with them. They'd disagreed from the start, Barry Upchurch and "the others," until Upchurch finally got the message and shut up and stopped having ideas, or at least stopped saying them out loud.

And then came the verdict. And then the appeals. And then the execution.

"His practice picked up after the Kantke case," she said, this time intending every bit of the bitterness she laid onto the words. "It was quite remarkable. Some of the finest criminals in Long Beach were suddenly Barry's."

Jimmy asked her the question he already knew the answer to.

"No," she said. "Jack Kantke was innocent. Completely. And Barry knew it. And knew how to prove it."

She laid it all out. It had to do with the killer behind the wispy curtains in that front bedroom, waiting, and the angle of the barrel of the .45 in that hand, the trajectory of the two bullets, the *height* of the shooter.

And the fact that Jack Kantke was an inch over six feet.

"They wouldn't use it," she said. "Barry went to the mat but they wouldn't use it. And it killed him."

She heard what she had just said.

"Killed *both* of them I guess."

"You never knew why," Jimmy said. "Why they wouldn't use it."

She shook her head and then looked at him as if maybe, now, *he* was going to tell her. When he didn't, she said, "So I guess losing *did* take its toll. Or maybe it was seeing the ways things really are."

Jimmy would remember that last line.

She invited him to stay for the steaks but he just shook her hand again and looked again at the portrait and went out the way he'd come in.

D. L. Upchurch was watching the fading charcoal fire.

"You can stay," he said. "Eat."

Jimmy looked at that face in the red and orange light. What would come to him in a minute was starting to come now.

"No, that's all right," he said.

"Up to you."

Jimmy said, "Sorry about the creeping around. I really meant to come out here in the morning."

"Old habits," D. L. said. Maybe it was an apology, too.

Then Jimmy got it.

He stayed put in front of the man.

"She tell you about the trajectory?" D. L. said.

"Yeah."

"The angle. The shooter behind the curtain."

"Yes."

"Bill Danko's *wife* killed them," D. L. said, straight ahead, eyes down. "She was five-foot-one."

D. L. Upchurch *was a cop*. One brother's a lawyer and his big brother's a cop, like something out of an old Warner Bros. movie.

And not just *any* cop, a Long Beach cop, the Long Beach uniformed cop in the newspaper picture looking out of the murder bedroom. Looking *up*.

---

Jimmy went back to the Evergreen and drank dark beer until they closed and then he was in his cabin with the tall German girl. They kissed and that's all they did and only that because the day and the work with its tricks and surprises and reversals had gotten to him.

And because they were both so far from home.

# TWELVE

A cat rubbed against his leg as Jimmy stood in the middle of the back bedroom in the murder house. It was late afternoon. Needles of light shot through pinholes in the shades taped against the windows. There was a second bathroom off the bedroom. He hadn't noticed it the first time. She was in there. The water was running.

She came out, saw him. She was startled, but again accepted the apparition before her, even as she tried to ignore it. He did see her hands shaking a little this time.

She walked past him and sat in her chair, looking at the TV, which wasn't on, *not* looking at him.

"My name is Jimmy Miles."

"Not funny," she said.

"I didn't mean to scare you. I knocked. On the backdoor."

"OK, I'm not going to talk to you," she said. "I'm not going to talk to you because then it'll be you *and* the others."

She was only in her forties, maybe even her thirties. The other night, Jimmy thought she was older. She wore the same worn dress, faded roses, a sweater over it, slippers on her feet. He made a harsh judgment: she'd never been pretty, except maybe to her daddy.

"I know you see people," Jimmy said gently, "but I'm really here. I'm real."

"The beat goes on," she said to the blank TV.

"I just want to ask you about this house."

She still wouldn't look at him. Jimmy took an apple from his pocket. He took a noisy bite. She didn't look at him but the smell of it suddenly filled the room.

"Any of them ever eat an apple before?" he said.

She glanced at him. He took another bite. From his pocket he produced another apple. He put it on the TV tray beside her chair, the way you put down food for a dog you just rescued and then step back.

She watched the action, then tried to shake it off.

"The beat goes on," she said, staring ahead again.

Jimmy sang a line of "The Beat Goes On."

"Any of them ever *sing* before?"

She gave him a quick look, a flash of impatience.

"Yes . . ."

"Take a bite," Jimmy said.

She hesitated, then reached for the apple on the TV tray. She took a bite.

"It's one of those new Fuji apples," he said. "How do you think they did it? How do you get a brand-new apple?"

She took another bite. "You didn't knock," she said. "You said you did."

"I knew you wouldn't answer. What's your name?"

"I can be here," she said. "I've got a right."

"I have nothing to do with that. What's your name?"

She looked at him. "Rosemary. Rosemary Danko."

Jimmy already knew it, before she said it.

"You look like your dad," he said.

"I've got a right to be here. This is where they killed him. I'm not leaving."

He stepped back, leaned against the wall.

"Where do you get your food?"

She straightened herself in her chair. "Two a.m., I go to the Ralph's. It used to be a Hughes. They cash my checks and they take my stamps."

"Are you on medication?"

"They think I live at the other place, over in Garden Grove," she said. "Sometimes I have to go over there on the Six Bus, to keep them thinking that."

A cat jumped into her lap. She looked at it a moment, as if she wasn't sure what it was. Then she relaxed.

"They won't kill me here," she said, as much to the cat as to Jimmy.

"Who wants to kill you?"

She said something that he couldn't understand, something mumbled, swallowed up.

"Say it again," he said.

She suddenly looked at his feet. "I like your shoes. Most people don't wear those."

"Who wants to kill you?" he said again.

She looked at him hard, suddenly angry. "Who are you? What does this have to do with apples?"

"Who killed your father?"

"I know what I know. That's why I don't live over in Garden Grove."

Jimmy nodded as if he understood.

"They knew his weakness," she said. "They were waiting in the closet."

Maybe it was *the pretty people*—maybe that was what she had said.

Jimmy asked her again who *they* were but she just ate her apple. Every bit of it, stem and seed.

"I've never seen a picture of your mother," Jimmy said.

"She comes on Sundays."

Jimmy waited.

"And I go there Mondays. When she comes here, I know the next day is Monday."

"What does she say about you being here?"

"We don't talk," Rosemary said.

"What does she say about you being here where they killed him?"

"That's what she doesn't talk about."

"What day is today?" Jimmy asked.

She got up out of her chair.

"Did you ever hear the record they were playing?" she asked, her face opening up a little, "Daddy and that woman?" She didn't wait for an answer, opened the front of a nightstand, an old humidor cabinet, and took out a 45 record in its original sleeve. She stepped over and put it on a turntable with a fat center post, a teenager's record player. It clicked, the arm moved over, it began.

It was Streisand's "People (Who Need People)."

"It was still playing, again and again, when the police looked in the window. They left it here. They had no idea how it fit in . . ."

They both listened to it. When it ended, it started again and Jimmy left her there.

---

After dark, about nine, when the neighbors would all be inside with their prime-time TV or their murder books and their third or fourth drinks, she came out. The streetlight over the alleyway behind the house was out. She pulled the door closed behind her and started away, nothing in her hands. One of the cats came out of the broken kitchen window and watched her go from the sill.

The Number Six bus was crowded with domestics headed home from the beach neighborhoods, a funny name for the cleaning women since most of them were illegals. They carried plastic bags of the supplies they preferred, pungent disinfectants, Day-Glo green. Since it was the end of the day, they didn't talk to each other.

Rosemary Danko was in the sideways seat behind the driver. Jimmy sat in the last row, against the window. When she'd sat down, one of the cleaning women moved away. Rosemary knew Jimmy was there, had turned to see him at a stop where a man with no shirt had gotten off the bus. She had looked right at him. He thought for a second she was going to lift her hand to wave.

The bus took her all the way into Garden Grove, a twenty-minute trip straight east on Westminster. Away from the water, it got hotter by the mile. Jimmy could feel it coming through the glass of the closed window. Inland, it hadn't gotten any cooler when the sun went down. It was another reason the women didn't talk.

She got off at a big cross street and walked north two blocks and then over a block. When she passed through a section with the streetlight shot out or burned out, she quickened her pace.

It was a ground-floor unit in a building of ten apartments. She knocked at the door and waited for almost a minute before she knocked again. Then, impatient, sighing, she took the key from the black mailbox beside the door. She wiped her feet on the mat.

Estella Danko had died fourteen months ago.

Jimmy stood in the dining room at the round white Formica table and went through the mostly unopened mail. She had died somewhere out of the house. She had died suddenly. There were quarterly dunning letters from a nursing home but Estella Danko hadn't died there. She had worked as a nurse and had left without turning in her uniforms. Died inconsiderately, without giving them notice.

There were government letters referring to Rosemary. She was on disability. Her utilities for the apartment were being paid direct by some agency. With the death of her mother, she'd gotten a bigger check. She had been an L.A. Unified School District teacher, ninth and tenth grade math, a school in Diamond Bar. Her middle name was Marialinda. Rosemary Marialinda Danko.

Jimmy looked in on her. She had gone straight into one of the bedrooms, her mother's bedroom. She was watching television, sitting on the end of the stripped mattress. It was one of those dating shows. She looked over at Jimmy, waved him away.

In the living room he found a cabinet full of old pictures, the next best thing to living witnesses. He turned on a floor lamp and pulled it closer and sat on the end of the coffee table. There were boxes of photos, loose and in leather albums. The Dankos liked cameras.

There had just been the three of them. They'd had a house somewhere for most of the time, had lived in other apartments in the early years after a wedding in what looked like Rosarito Beach, down over the border on the way to Ensenada. Estella was Mexican. She had been a beauty but she was the size of a child.

Every picture except the wedding had the baby in it. And then the baby grew. There was one of Rosemary at four or five on a pony at the rides in Griffith Park, her smiling father sitting on the rail as she passed behind him staring straight ahead, a scared look on her little face.

Jimmy slipped it into the pocket of his shirt.

Almost every other picture of Danko had him beside one plane or another. There was a framed photo in fading colors of a four-place Cessna, red over white, Danko standing with his hand on the tip of the wing, the world head-quarters of the Danko "Flying School" in half-focus in the background.

"Dancing Queen" was painted on the engine cowling.

Jimmy took that one, too.

And he found the picture of Estella Danko to take. It was from an open-air bar somewhere, sand on the floor and the beach in the background, probably down in Baja. Three blond girls, probably college kids, more *pretty people,* were grouped behind Bill Danko who sat on a silver beer keg, his legs open, wearing shorts and *hurraches,* his elbows on his knees, aviator glasses, a big grin on his face, a bottle of beer in his hand. Estella was off to one side, away from the others, not happy, as if the girls had waved her into the shot.

It was hard to imagine a .45 in the empty little hand at her side but not so hard to picture a murderous look in her eye.

There was a sound from the kitchen.

Rosemary stood in front of the microwave.

"Three zero zero," she said, more than once.

It dinged. She opened the door and took out a package of macaroni and cheese. She pulled back the covering and set it on a plate to cool. She held her fork in her hand and waited, like she was counting seconds in her head.

She did all right with numbers. She just didn't know what day it was. She had a broken sense of time and she didn't know who was dead and who wasn't anymore.

Jimmy felt a certain kinship.

It was a rough night on the strip, odd and ugly and edgy for some reason. Young men who'd all stripped off their shirts ganged in front of The Roxy, spilled out onto the sidewalks between a pair of shows for some metal band come round again. They were like natives on the banks of a river. Some of them were trying to get a fire going in a trash barrel to complete the picture. Ninety degrees at eleven o'clock and they're starting fires.

Jimmy rolled past, Streisand's "People" still looping in his head from the weird afternoon, making the scene all the stranger.

He slid in the CD his musician friend had made for him, the collection of disco music Chris thought he should be listening to. The first song was lush, symphonic, with a sexy chorus, women singing the same three words over and over. It was romantic, dramatic. It was soundtrack music, for the movie playing in the heads of twenty-somethings on the dance floor, over-riding, at least for part of a Saturday night, their ordinary lives.

One of the Roxy natives jumped out from the others, slowly and delib-erately flipped him off as he cruised past. Maybe the kid could hear the disco music.

Or maybe he just didn't like Fords. Jimmy was in the Mustang. After spending the early part of the night with Rosemary in the house in Gar-den Grove, he'd taken a cab back to Naples where he'd left the car and then driven up from Long Beach on Pacific Coast Highway, the slow way, trying to sort it out. Estella Danko was dead but that didn't make much difference to him, to the case. Now he'd *met* her. He even had her picture in his pocket. Dead now or not, there was a good chance she was the one who'd done the killing. Jealous, left-out wives pulled triggers in bedrooms all the time. D. L. Upchurch thought she had done it and he had brooded over all this more than Jimmy had or ever would.

*She was five-foot-one.*

And she wasn't her husband's Dancing Queen anymore.

So Jimmy thought he was getting closer to certainty, to an end to it, closing in on something he could take to Jean.

*Your father didn't kill anybody. She did.*

He'd gone by Jean's apartment. There was no answer downstairs, no lights in the penthouse. He still hadn't seen her or talked to her since the night they'd come upon Drew. He wondered how *gone* she was.

Jimmy thought he was closing in on certainty, but what he *didn't* under-stand was what this particular piece of old history had to do with Sailors.

His tails were back, Lon and Vince, still in the subcompact Escort, almost bumping into him when he slowed.

And now there was another one.

At least this one had better taste in cars. He was in a black 745 iL BMW, smart because it blended in in most parts of L.A. better than a basic Ford. And this driver knew what he was doing, stayed two blocks back and turned off onto side streets just a half second before you really noticed he was there, making you think maybe you'd imagined it.

But Jimmy knew how to do this, too, and had caught a good look at the car twice, once on PCH and once when he was coming back down onto Sunset from Jean's.

It was then that he got a look at his face. When the driver knew he'd been seen, he'd turned into the space in front of a restaurant, had even gotten out to meet the valet, very cool. He was tall, skinny, in an expensive black suit, slicked-back hair. He was too far away, but maybe it was Boney M, the tall one with the long fingers from the rooftop of the Roosevelt.

Jimmy figured he'd never see the man again, though that didn't mean he wouldn't be there.

It was their mistake. If they'd stopped following him a week ago, he probably would have ended it by now, told Jean it was over, that there was nothing worth knowing that he could tell her. After the night in the canyon when they'd come upon the overturned Honda, everything in him had wanted to wrap up the case, tell her whatever he could tell her, and then see if there was any way to salvage things with her.

But they hadn't quit. They were back, following him, nosing around, keeping it alive, accomplishing the opposite of what they wanted, making *the black clear space where the answer was* a thing he could never turn away from now.

He looped around and cruised by Jean's a third time.

The lights were still out and this time he didn't go to the door. The song on the CD lasted all the way there and halfway back to his house down Sunset, the singer telling him she loved the nightlife but sounding a little sad, like she was trying to convince herself.

# THIRTEEN

It was an old line producer's office, bad art, big furniture, a slab of chalk for a coffee table. Jean was alone, on the pink couch. She picked up a book, smiled when she read the spine. Behind the couch was a wall of photographs, the *Everybody-Knows-Me-Wall*, pictures spanning twenty years, marked by the changing hairstyles of Joel Kinser, who was in every one, his head an inch too close to the head of each famous actor or politician, Gerald and Betty Ford among them. So Kinser had spent a little time at the Betty Ford Center out in Rancho Mirage. It was a big club.

Jimmy was in one group shot, three or four nobodies, Joel and a star. It was recent. They all looked like themselves. But a few rows over was a picture from the past, Jimmy and Joel and an actress. Joel had a blown-out eighties look, from another time, but Jimmy didn't look much younger than now, much changed, unless you noticed a brightness in his eye then that now was gone, or at least dimmed.

Joel came in. He kissed Jean on the cheek. "I'm sorry," he said. A movie star out of the limelight lately was a step behind him.

"Do you know _____?"

"No." Jean extended her hand.

"This is Jean Kantke," Joel said. "We're in Mensa together."

Jean still had the book in her hand.

"Where did you find that?" Joel said. "I've been looking for it."

Jean handed it to him.

"Catullus," Joel said.

The fading star waited a moment, nodding, and then said, "I gotta roll outta here, Joel." He told Jean it was nice to meet her and left.

"Are you doing something with him?" Jean said when he had cleared the frame.

Joel leafed through his phone messages.

"Hollywood has two speeds," he said. "'Screw you' and 'Yes, Master!' Is the commissary all right?"

There were only ten tables in the Executive Dining Room, blond chairs, skylights, a Hockney on the wall, waiters who *didn't* want to direct.

Joel nodded to a man taking a table alone across the dining room. The man gave back less.

Their food had just come.

"What did Jimmy do for you?" Jean said.

"Found an actress who didn't want to be found," Joel said. He was staring at his fish.

"Where did he find her?"

"Mexico."

"You aren't going to tell me who it was?" Jean said.

"_____. We were in the middle of shooting and suddenly she's gone. Tuesday, she's there. Wednesday, she's not. I put three other guys on it, regular guys on it. Nothing. Then Jimmy found her in like a day. How, I don't know. It took another day for him to go down there and talk her in. Following Monday, we're back rolling."

He stared at his fish.

"The picture never worked. We could never get the third act right. It did all right foreign. I always assumed Jimmy had a thing with her, but he said no."

"Look at this piece of salmon," he said in the same breath. (He pronounced the *L*.) "A little *parsimonious*, isn't it?"

"Try putting some salt on it," Jean said. "What else do you know about him?"

He poked at the piece of fish, as if it could change. "Fairly bright. Locked in a Peter Gunn kind of thing with his clothes, but he has taste."

"Has he ever been married?"

"Don't know. Is he gay? I don't know. So, I assume he's working for you. He took the job."

Jean nodded.

"And you want it to be something else."

"No . . ."

He waved the waiter over. "I'd like a bigger fish," he said and handed him his plate.

He looked at Jean. "That salt thing. Funny."

She waited for him to answer her questions.

"Everybody loves Jimmy," he said. "He works that Little Boy Lost thing. I could never pull that off."

"He's not lost," she said. "He knows exactly where he is. He just isn't telling."

"And this for you is a turn-on?"

Jean didn't answer.

"You know who his mother was, don't you?" Joel said.

———————

Darren Price drove up Jimmy's long gravel driveway in a fifteen-year-old Mercedes convertible with a vandal's cut in the top patched with duct tape.

Jimmy was waiting for him on the steps that led up to the tall dark front door. It was the afternoon but he got the idea that the DJ hadn't been to sleep since his overnight shift. He got out of the Mercedes wearing the same velveteen exercise suit and white Capezio dance shoes from the other night.

Lloyd-the-Void stood with his mouth open, looking at the house. He looked back down the long driveway to the iron gates and then back at the house and the motor court and the four-bay garage. All four garage doors were open. In separate stalls were the black Porsche convertible, the Mustang, the yellow Dodge Challenger, and in the last garage, covered by a tarp, something with high poking fins and bright wide whitewalls.

"Holy shit," Price said. "Your house has a *name*? I'm in the wrong business."

Jimmy took him inside, through the house, past the living room, into the office, the room with the chromed racks of security gear and electronic equipment.

"Holy shit," Price said again.

Jimmy sat behind the desk and put his feet up. He was barefoot. He was waiting for Price to get over the money around him and to say why he was here, why he'd called.

"You want anything?" Jimmy said.

"I want a house like this," Price said. "And four cars." He sat in the leather and chrome chair in front of the desk. He put his feet up, too, like Jimmy, like they were new best friends. "What's the one under the tarp?"

"I'm afraid to look," Jimmy said.

Since Price apparently wasn't going to start, Jimmy decided maybe *he'd* go first. "Did you ever see Bill Danko's wife at Big Daddy's?"

"He was married?"

"Yeah."

Price shook his head.

"Five-foot-one. Spanish."

The Xeroxes, the newspaper articles of the case were spread out on the desk. Jimmy slid a few papers around and found the picture of Estella Danko.

Price looked at it, handed it back. "I never saw her. Or didn't know I was seeing her if I did. I didn't even think about anybody being married. It wasn't about that."

"You said you remembered something," Jimmy said.

The kid Drew came into the room, looking like he just woke up. He stood a foot inside the doorway. He ran his hands through his hair, standing there, and then shook it out. He wore it in a long, shaggy skateboarder's cut.

"My hair stopped growing," Drew said.

Jimmy nodded.

Drew glanced at Darren Price, then walked out again.

Price tried for a second to fit this new piece into the Jimmy Miles puzzle, then gave up.

"Do you want to hear this or not?" Price said.

"Sure."

Price woke up a little more. "OK, I was telling this girl about how I was working with you on something, on the thing," he said.

Jimmy let that pass without comment.

"She wasn't even *born* then, but she said something that made me think of something."

Jimmy just looked at him. He liked him better in the middle of the night. He guessed that almost everyone did.

"Anyway. This girl, I told her about that time, what we talked about, and she said, 'Four girls wouldn't be friends.'"

Jimmy didn't have much of a reaction.

"The Jolly Girls," Price said, said it the same way he'd said it at the radio station, The *Jolly* Girls.

"OK."

"Then I remembered. *Michelle.*"

"The one who did the most drugs."

"Yeah. Did I tell you that?"

"Yes." Jimmy waited. "What about her?"

"Michelle hated Elaine—and, you know, *not* in that way girls are. *'I hate you!' 'I love you!' 'You are so my best friend!'*" He said it in a funny voice-over voice, good enough for a cartoon. "There at the end, Michelle really hated Elaine Kantke. It was real."

"Why?"

Price took a beat, knowing he had something.

"Bill Danko. Michelle liked Danko. I couldn't see what the attraction was with him but, anyway, they both liked him. And, *sorry Elaine,* Michelle saw him first."

"Maybe he was with both of them," Jimmy said.

"I don't think so. He was love-struck by Elaine from what I saw. He stopped dancing with Michelle. That means something, or meant something then."

Jimmy found the copy of the shot of the four Jolly Girls on the stools at the Long Beach Yacht Club.

"Which one was she?" he said.

Before he answered, Price said, "This was before Slip Tone, before they hooked up. You knew they were married, right? Michelle and Tone?"

Jimmy didn't. "When?"

"Right when he quit. To be a cop. And then she died, after like only a year."

"Died how?"

"Swimming. At Mothers' Beach. Right there in the Marina."

Price bounded out of his chair and came around and looked over Jimmy's shoulder at the picture, standing too close.

"The short one. That's why she *loved* platform shoes."

---

There were too many dead.

Coming back from the desert and the mountains, Jimmy thought it was pretty simple. He'd find Bill Danko's short little jealous wife. Maybe she'd be a nurse somewhere, estranged from her daughter, wondering where she was, and Jimmy would be able to tell her, after she'd let him see her guilt about the murders without ever exactly admitting it. But now the Estella Danko story had come and gone, felt like it anyway, like time-lapse film footage of a storm out over the desert, arising out of nowhere, building fast into something dark and big and full of heat lightning, and then dissolving away again to nothing, as quickly as it had come. Estella Danko was dead, past admitting anything, even with her eyes. And now there was

Michelle. He wished he was driving across town to meet *her* now, wished she had a store somewhere or was a decorator or a lawyer or somebody's mother or a school administrator, straight-arrow and proper, even square, giving nobody in her life now any reason to suspect she'd once been a disco dolly in tall shoes with a tingling nose. But she was dead, too. He wasn't going to get the chance to look into her eyes either and ask about those old murders.

Sgt. Tom Connor coached a kids' soccer team. It was late in the day but there was still another hour of daylight left. They were practicing in a city park in Van Nuys. He came over to the sidelines as Jimmy stepped away from the yellow Dodge Challenger.

Walking up to him, Connor said, "What I like about soccer is that most of the fathers don't really know anything about the game." The kids kicking goals behind him were nine or ten. Even the goalie would laugh when they scored on him. "I think that's what they like about it, too. The boys, not the dads."

Connor went right to it. Jimmy had called him, filled him in on what he'd learned about Michelle Espinosa.

"Homicide detectives came in, but they didn't end up with anything," Connor said. "On paper, it was a drowning. She went out, pretty deep, out into the channel, in among the sailboats in the slips. There wasn't anybody around her. It was a little cold. Nobody else was in, all of them up on the beach with their kids, in the shallows or digging in the sand."

Jimmy knew there was something else.

"But . . ."

"But she was a swimmer and diver in school," Connor said. "USC on a scholarship. And it was a *marina*. It's not like there were waves or undertow or anything."

A ball came over. The cop kicked it back.

"What about drugs?"

"Supposedly she had cleaned up her act," Connor said. "She and Espinosa were married by then but he wasn't a cop yet."

And then he was a *dead* cop, Jimmy thought, somebody else he wasn't going to get to look in the eye.

"She was pregnant."

Connor let that hang in the air for a minute.

*Mothers' Beach.*

They both thought about the name.

"Maybe losing her was what made him want to be a cop."

*There were too many dead.*

"Did you check on the Kantke thing?" Jimmy said.

"I did. A guy's still alive who was the second lead detective on it."

"And . . ."

Connor shook his head.

"They had their killer. And they were good cops."

Jimmy thanked him, was ready to go.

"You think what?" Connor said. "This Michelle did it? Shot dead her ex and her ex-friend?"

"I don't know."

"And then, *what?* Someone drowns her for that?"

"I don't know," Jimmy said.

"You're forgetting something."

Jimmy waited.

"Jealousy wasn't that big around then," the cop said. "Remember? *If it feels good, do it.*"

"I think that was the sixties, Tom."

"The sixties was weed. The seventies was blow. But same difference. *'Oops, I screwed your girlfriend. Sorry.' 'No problem.'*"

Jimmy nodded.

Connor said, "I guess there could have been some other motive."

"For which one?" Jimmy said. "For Michelle murdering them, or for someone murdering her?"

# FOURTEEN

Jimmy rang the bell downstairs at Jean's and waited.

Nothing.

Just as he turned to go, it buzzed open.

He rode the elevator up. It was unlocked right into the penthouse, opening onto a foyer, the living room beyond. Jean wasn't there, wasn't in the living room anyway. The sun was just going down and the light looked like tea, made the room look like something out of an old magazine. The elevator doors closed behind him. It was quiet enough to hear the gears and pulleys as it took itself all the way down to the first floor.

"Where are you?" Jimmy said.

She didn't answer.

On the desk were a dozen books about Hollywood, *new* books, open. He got the idea they were meant to be seen. He clicked on a light. There was his mother's face under his fingers, black-and-white, high-glam portrait more shadow than light. The other books were opened to other pictures of Teresa Miles, with a famous French actor, with a famous American director, slant-back wooden chairs on a round rock beach somewhere in the South of France. She had close-cut blond hair, eyes that looked away in every shot, that very commercial, very exploitable look that said *Save me* and *I'm too much for you* in the same moment.

There was a Xerox of a fan magazine article from the late sixties with the headline:

### TERESA MILES' TRAGIC BREAKDOWN

And a paparazzo's photo of the actress coming out of one of the bungalows at the Chateau Marmont, shaken, eyes on the ground.

In the background was a teenager in bellbottoms.

There was a reprint of the newspaper obituary:

## MILES' DEATH REVEALED

Fifties "New Wave" film star Teresa Miles died two weeks ago in Twenty-Nine Palms, Calif., it was revealed Saturday. She was thirty-eight. Cause of death was listed as "emphysema."

Miss Miles' former manager Len Schine confirmed that the actress, star of such films as *Marina* and *Morning at the Window* (*Le Matin a la Fenetre*), was buried at an undisclosed location following a private service.

She had no survivors.

Miss Miles, twice nominated for an Academy Award, two years ago suffered a nervous breakdown and retired from . . .

Jimmy tossed the obit into the desk. It was covered with papers and books. It was like his desk only *he* was the subject under investigation.

He heard something above him.

He stepped out onto the patio. Jean was up on the sloped roof overlooking the deck, sitting with her knees drawn up to her, with a glass of wine, looking out at the pastel haze.

The way up was to step onto the low wall around the patio and then walk along it to where you could step up onto the roof.

Jimmy joined her, silent for a long time.

"I came by a couple times. Called."

"I know," she said.

"I'm sorry. I mean, if I hurt you."

"Is that what you think happened?"

She kept her eyes on the streaked sky. It looked like it had been painted by a child.

"I don't know. I'm only inside *me*," Jimmy said.

She looked at him, for the first time since he sat beside her. And she smiled.

"What happened to that kid?"

"He's staying at my house."

She waited for him to say more.

"He's all right," Jimmy said.

That was all he was going to say about it. An ambulance screamed up Sunset. They listened until it faded.

"Why the books? In the living room."

"Just trying to understand," Jean said.

"Understand what?"

"You. This."

He wondered what all she meant by *this*.

"It isn't supposed to happen, is it?" she said. "Getting involved this way."

"I don't know," he said. "It happened. I'm happy."

"You don't look happy."

"It's my facial structure," Jimmy said.

She stood. She offered him her glass of wine.

"You look like her," Jean said.

He took the glass of wine, took a sip. It was as warm as the air.

"I remember what you told me in my office," she began, "that first day, that maybe it wasn't always better to know everything."

"You *can't* know everything so it doesn't really matter."

"I don't care about the murders anymore," she said firmly. "I don't want to know. I don't need to know."

"The woman in the house is Bill Danko's daughter," Jimmy said. "Her name is Rosemary."

"I don't care."

"She was nine or ten when he was killed. Her mother died a year or so ago. Maybe that pushed her over the edge, sent her looking for the house in Naples."

"I want this to end," Jean said. "This is my choice. I don't need to know any more."

"I don't think your father did it. Your mother was probably just in the wrong place with the wrong guy. There's a woman who may have done it, one of her friends. Actually, there were *two* women who may have done it. Bill Danko had a wife."

"Stop."

"There's some link to now, to today."

"Stop it."

"To the people who run things. But I don't know why."

"*Stop!*" Her fists were clenched.

But he wasn't finished. He wanted to *tell her*. He wanted her to know *all* of it.

But he stopped himself.

————

She wanted to get out, to cool off, to ride somewhere, so they were on the streets of Hollywood in the yellow Challenger. It was after nine and still hot. They rode out Sunset, east, into East L.A. Jimmy pulled up into the corner lot where there was a Tommy's burger stand, the original Tommy's. A *paletero,* a Mexican ice cream man with his *triciclo,* a cart on rubber wheels, was supplying dessert for the crowd sharing the white-painted picnic tables. Jimmy bought Jean a cup of shaved ice doused in bloodred watermelon syrup so sweet it made your teeth hurt.

They doubled back on Sunset Boulevard in East L.A. The traffic was heavy but easy going. A real-life lowrider came past them in the other lane, bass notes thumping, echoing off the faces of the storefronts and second-story apartments that made the street a canyon. Maybe everyone was just trying to cool off, nowhere to go, to forget about what they would have to remember tomorrow.

Jean looked out the side window, a girl on her front steps, reading a book by streetlight. They were on Franklin now, one edge of Hollywood, in a neighborhood of single houses with no yards, sidewalks right up to the windows, rental houses, Russian families in this block, and a few busted actors.

"Who was it?" Jean said, still looking out the window. "Which friend of Mother's?"

Jimmy thought, *No one can look away. Everyone has to* know.

"Michelle. Michelle Simmonds. She became Michelle Espinosa."

"One of The Jolly Girls."

"Yes."

He told her about the *five-foot-one* angle.

"Have you talked to her?"

"She's dead a long time."

Jean nodded, still not looking at him. She thought that was all there was. She felt strong for asking.

"I think someone killed her," Jimmy said. "But it wasn't down as a murder. She drowned. In the Marina."

Jean turned and he saw the sudden hurt on her face, the *world-pain.* Jimmy kept forgetting that most people didn't see the world the way he did, the way he had for most of his years, full of treachery and death and dark motives. Most people thought almost everyone was good.

"Maybe I'm wrong," he said. "I have to watch myself."

"What do you mean?" She didn't feel so strong anymore.

"Always thinking the worst," he said. "People die all the time. Natural causes."

They had passed into Los Feliz, a richer neighborhood of thirties and forties apartment buildings on streets sloping up toward the low hills, the backside of the Hollywood Hills below Griffith Park.

After a ways, Jean said, "You said this was somehow connected to other people. Who?"

Like an answer, there were headlights in the mirror.

They were back. They'd been behind them all the way from before Tommy's, through four or five rights and lefts, a white Taurus, two heads haloed by the lights behind them.

Lon and Vince had traded in the Escort for a Taurus.

Now they were closing. Fast.

Jean looked over at him, saw him with his eyes on the mirror.

"Put on your seatbelt," Jimmy said.

She turned around to look. "What?"

On the next side street, a second car, the black BMW 745 iL, waited at a stop sign—with a man in a peacoat and watch cap standing beside it.

"What's the matter?" Jean said. "Who are they?"

Jimmy gunned it and the Challenger streaked away, blowing past the BMW on the side street, leaving the Taurus to try to catch up.

She put her seatbelt on.

The man in the peacoat next to the BMW stepped back and the driver pulled it into gear and spun into a U-turn and roared up the hill.

Jimmy was already two blocks away. He'd taken a hard left off of Franklin, onto Vermont, rolling up the rising straight street with the Taurus closing on him.

"Who is it?" Jean said.

"They've been following us."

"What do they want?"

He was very cool. "We'll lose them up here," he said, as if it was an answer.

The speedometer popped up to seventy. Jimmy went through a red light at a cross street called Ambrose and the Taurus stayed with him.

But didn't make it.

A Jeep coming fast through the intersection tagged the left rear panel of Lon and Vince's Taurus and sent it spinning, a pair of quick 360s in the middle of the X.

Jimmy watched it in the mirror, the hit and the spinout. He was already at the next corner. This time the light was green.

But then the black BMW came at him from the intersecting street,

Los Feliz Boulevard, trying to T-bone him, or at least be there when somebody else did.

Jimmy stood on it and cranked the wheel, sliding sideways to avoid
him, then sped up the hill as the BMW skidded to a stop inches away
from the nose of a fat beige Lexus.

The two Sailors in the Taurus recovered and went after Jimmy, front
wheels smoking.

The BMW had stalled out. The driver lit it up again, backed it into a
hard J and went after them, fishtailing for a second before the big powerful
car got into the groove.

The three cars—Challenger, Taurus, BMW—blew into Griffith Park
on a straightaway on a boulevard through a canopy of trees, blew *one, two,
three* past a sign nobody had time to read:

OBSERVATORY   GOLFCOURSE   ZOO   MERRY-GO-ROUND

The Taurus was falling back, outgunned. Jimmy was at eighty, leading
the thing. Jean sat with her hands on the dash in front of her, like it was
a roller coaster.

The first climbing left into the higher parklands was coming up fast.
Just as they went into the hard curve, the BMW came up on their right,
door to door. Jimmy dropped down a gear and the Challenger and the
BMW took it together, mirror to mirror.

Jimmy looked over to see the driver. The BMW eased off and fell back
in behind him, then rolled over onto Jimmy's left, moving up. They went
like that through a pair of *esses,* a chicane. Jimmy would surge ahead for a
moment, but the BMW would gain in the corners.

"I might have brought the wrong car," he said.

Jean was wide-eyed.

*"Stop, please,"* she said.

The two cars banged fenders as the BMW driver tried to shove them
into the outside rail. Jimmy got his first good look at him, but didn't have
time to process it.

The Taurus was back.

The three cars came around a corner, three wide, and there was the
Griffith Observatory, lit up, green-domed, as sudden as an explosion. The
turn was a hairpin and the screeching tires made people look, tourists and
teenagers crossing over from the parking lot.

The BMW sideswiped a van and spun into the parking lot and the Taurus rear-ended it. They were stopped.

Jimmy pulled away.

It was all downhill now, a straightaway down the backside of the low mountains. He wasn't slowing.

Jean looked back.

"*Stop*," she said. "*They're gone.*"

But as soon as she'd said it, she saw the two pairs of headlights coming after them. She looked at him, at the look in his eyes. He was all the way into it, given over to it. It was frightening.

They roared past two men standing close by a tree. Ahead was a cluster of cars, lights out, pairs of men leaning against the fenders, others sitting atop picnic tables, eyes bright dots in the Challenger's headlights.

Jimmy braked hard and stopped. Stopped dead.

"What are you doing?" Jean said.

"Get out. I'll come back for you."

She didn't want to get out.

"*Get out.*"

Jean opened her door.

"It's all right," Jimmy said, but he was still that same man, changed and frightening and too full of purpose.

She got out and he sped away, the power slamming the passenger door closed.

Jimmy looked up in the mirror at the paired men and Jean, a couple of them stepping toward her.

Ahead he had a clean straight run through a corridor of tall, dusted eucalyptus, a bridle path on one side. The speedometer, dim and green, touched a hundred. The Challenger was made for this.

He smiled.

In the moment he thought *he* was made for this, too. He shifted up a gear. The engine sucked in boost. Ahead, the mouth of a gentle curve. Jimmy barely slowed as he steered into it.

Horses. *Horses.*

Suddenly there were *horses* alongside the road, six horses, empty saddles, tied together and led by a mounted cowboy. All in the same second, the cowboy turned two silver reflecting eyes toward the car howling down the straightaway at him and the last animal in the line reared and leapt sideways into the road, and then the next in front of it followed.

Jimmy yanked the wheel. The Challenger skidded and smoked and screeched and then slammed against the stout trunk of a eucalyptus.

He was thrown against the window, knocked out.

The first minute passed.

The Hemi engine raced, roaring, then died.

The horses whinnied wildly, all of them rearing now, shredding the air with their front hooves in the wash of the Challenger's headlights still burning through the stirred up dust.

The BMW was first to arrive. The driver got out.

The cowboy fought to gather and control the six horses and himself.

"He was—"

"Yeah," the BMW driver said, cool and calm. "Go to the phone. Get some help." She had an accent.

The cowboy did as he was told and let go of the spooked horses and pulled himself into the saddle of his own horse and rode away down the path. The trail horses tried to scatter but were still lashed together and pulled in different directions so that none of them escaped.

The wrecked, smoking Taurus arrived. Lon and Vince. They got out, pumped up, ready to hurt someone but Jimmy was bloodied and looked dead.

Another minute passed.

A black Lincoln Town Car pulled up. Lon and Vince straightened, almost came to attention.

The backdoor opened.

Jimmy had started to come around. He was bleeding from a cut on the side of his face. He tried to focus, the headlights, the images through the shattered glass, through his own blood which streaked the window: the cars, one white, two black, *figures moving*.

He saw the red-haired man with the long fingers, Boney M, get out of the back of the Lincoln Town Car. And, with the door open, another man in the backseat, under the spot of the reading light, a big man, familiar.

*Then someone was walking toward him.*

It was the BMW driver, the man in the expensive suit, slicked-back hair.

*But it was a woman in a dark expensive suit.*

It was the German girl from the Evergreen Club, from the dark beer, from the kisses in his cabin. He even heard her voice, her accent, as she said something to Lon and Vince.

But then things got darker and faded out.

# FIFTEEN

The sun was just up, the air smoky with a warm fog.

Jimmy was backed against a tree, sitting in the eucalyptus leaves and brown grass. It looked like deep woods. You couldn't see the road from here, or anything else. It was like he was in Australia, or wherever it was that eucalyptus trees came from.

There was blood, dry and almost black, all around him, so much of it that he wondered how it could all be his.

*He thought of Jean.* He got to his feet.

Everything ached. One eye was sealed shut some way he didn't want to see. A finger was broken. A few teeth felt loose.

*"Let me ask you something,"* Drew said. *"Can I die? I mean, again?"*

*"You can get hurt,"* Jimmy said, *"bad, but you won't die."*

*"Even if like a bullet went through my head, I wouldn't die."*

*"No."*

*"If I was shredding down a mountain and pulled a full-on Sonny Bono, I wouldn't die."*

*"No. You could get messed up, bad, but you wouldn't die."*

They'd pulled him out of the car and dragged him away and worked him over, Lon and Vince and maybe even the German woman, hoping for maximum mayhem, hoping to mess him up good, to try to make their point another way.

Or maybe they did it just because they enjoyed it.

He came out of the trees and found the straightaway road and then the scarred trunk that told him where he'd crashed, the skidmarks on the pavement and the furrows in the leaf-covered ground of the bridle path.

The yellow Dodge was long gone, but his shoe was there.

And the scars from the hooves of the trail horses.

He thought maybe he'd dreamed them.

He found the tracks where the black Lincoln had stopped and then turned around to go back up the straightaway. Somewhere in the fog, he'd decided the big familiar man glimpsed in the backseat had to be Harry Turner.

But maybe he'd dreamed him.

---

Jimmy and Angel went first to Jean's apartment.

Angel waited behind the wheel of his truck, the one with the blue moon over the city and the woman's eyes airbrushed on the tailgate.

There was no answer. Jimmy came back and got in.

"She wasn't there?" Angel said.

Jimmy shook his head. Angel pulled out.

"She had a phone," Jimmy said after a minute. "She probably had somebody come get her."

He called her office. She was in a meeting.

Jimmy tossed the phone onto the seat between them. Angel looked at him.

"She's all right."

Angel stopped at the bottom of the hill. "Where do you want to go?"

"Home. I'll get a car."

They rode along in silence another four or five blocks, then Jimmy said, "Maybe you can run down the Dodge, take it to the shop, see if you can put it right. I guess the cops towed it."

Angel nodded. "How bad is it?"

"Bad."

Angel turned right. "You might want to get cleaned up a little, too."

Jimmy dropped the visor on his side and got his first look at himself in the mirror. He flipped the visor back up. It was better not to know.

"So what's happening with this lady?" Angel said.

"I hadn't talked to her since that night we picked up the kid," he said. "She was spooked then. I don't know what she's thinking now. Maybe she's figured it out."

"I doubt that," Angel said. "She's still around."

Jimmy fell silent.

"It was the same Sailors?" Angel said.

"The goofy guys and the leader from the thing up on the roof of the Roosevelt. And there's something else going on. There's a man in the middle of it, too, not a Sailor but maybe a kindred spirit."

"Who?"

"His name is Harry Turner. The lawyer behind the scenes in the murder trial. He put a tail on me. He might have been there last night."

Jimmy wished again he'd gotten a better look at him, at the big man in the backseat of the Lincoln. *If I could be sure.* It was how Jimmy knew he had passed over into the land of the secret, the territory of the unknown that always came in the middle of the case, when he heard himself saying, again and again, *If I could be sure.*

"She was there, the tail. In a 745 BMW. She's German. She's not a Sailor either. Neither of them are."

"She's the one ran you into a tree?"

"No, I did that all by myself."

"How do you know this guy hired her?"

"I saw him in the morning and she was there the same night. Up in Idyllwild."

"Tailing you?"

After a moment, Jimmy said, "Yeah, very close."

Jimmy thought about her lips, about the way she'd put her hands over his eyes when she kissed him. He didn't have to wonder what he'd said to her, what he might have revealed. He hadn't said much of anything. And neither had she. She was good. In that bad kind of way.

Harry Turner had read him right. Jimmy remembered Rosemary Danko's line, *They knew his weakness.*

"Why does this guy still care about some old settled murder case?"

"That I don't know," Jimmy said.

They rode along another block.

"God had his hand on you," Angel said.

Jimmy nodded, never looking at him. They were on Sunset now, going past Tower Records yellow and red and then The Whisky and then the Hustler store full of tourist shoppers. In daylight. *Was there any more secular place on the face of the earth?*

Jimmy had a decision to make, to go toward it or away from it.

"So what are you going to do now?" Angel said, just as Jimmy was wondering the same thing.

# SIXTEEN

Some things look like what they are. Jimmy and Jean were heading north on California 1, the coast road, approaching the southern end of Big Sur. This was the edge of a continent and it looked it. The road was just now climbing into the high section, coming up off of the grasslands and cattle ranches past Hearst Castle and Cambria. The massive mountains, long and brown and only crowned with evergreens at the highest reaches where the fog was, broke off jagged into the ocean, ending big.

It had cooled off as soon as they'd rolled over the mountain from Thousand Oaks into Camarillo, Oxnard, and then Ventura. They had the windows down. If you knew what to listen for, what to separate out, you could hear the wind off the ocean, singing, constant, blowing through the dull leaves and the slick red trunks of the manzanita covering the foothills.

Jimmy dropped it down into second as he steered into the first tight climbing curve. They were in the Mustang. He went in hotter than he could have, the C-force snugging him into the bucket seat. At the first switchback, there was already a hundred-foot drop-off to the rocks below and the very blue water.

Jean looked over at him for a long moment, as if the look and the time were needed before she said something, but she didn't say anything, she just studied him. When he'd come to her office just before noon, he'd told her that she should get away, that she should go off to hide someplace. She'd said no. Then he called it something else and she'd said yes. In the end, it turned into this, going north with no set destination, no time frame, the two of them. She'd come straight from the office. She was wearing a suit.

He was wearing a clean white shirt and a clean white splint over his ring finger on his right hand, the hand resting on the gearshift. He was bruised and butterfly-bandaged, now with two cuts on his head, over his eyes.

She was still looking at him. Anyone else would have turned to look at her.

"It's good to get out of the city," she said.

"What do you want me to tell you?" Jimmy said.

Now he looked over at her.

He kept surprising her. Being with him meant things moving at odd speeds, sometimes coming out of nowhere, sometimes *not* coming when they were expected. And only now was she beginning to be able to read his tone. His abruptness meant only that he was ahead of her.

She could have asked him what she really wanted to know, what she *suspected* about him, about this, but she didn't. The answer, if he'd given it, would have brought her all the way into it, into an idea she thought she might not be able to accept. Not yet. Do you ask a question when the answer might be that the world is not what you've always thought it to be, that everyone else thinks it to be? That there is something in between what you believed were two absolutes, *the* two absolutes, that the dead, some of them, are somehow here?

"What happened after you put me out of the car?"

"I crashed, went home." He enjoyed his joke even if she couldn't.

The two-lane road was rising so steeply Jimmy double-clutched and downshifted into first. The engine and the gearbox sang a warm low note. On the shoulder on the opposite lane was the first of the Big Sur hikers, shorts, tanned legs with braided calf muscles, a day pack, a wide floppy hat. He was in his sixties. He carried a gnarled walking stick that came up to his chest and he kept his pace even as the path angled up under him.

"I came by, where the car was," Jean said. "My assistant came and got me. We drove on down. I saw your car smashed against the tree. There was a police car there and a tow truck and a man on a horse, but nobody else."

He didn't say anything.

"The men in the two cars came right past me. They must have been there when you crashed."

"They pulled me out."

"What'd they do?"

"Dumped me in another part of the park."

"Who were they?" she said.

He looked at her. "It's probably about another case, something out of the past."

He wasn't going to say anything else about who they were. Jean rolled up her window. It was almost cold.

She waited a beat.

"Why didn't they kill you?" she said.

Jimmy looked at her. Maybe she *was* going to ask it. She'd seen Drew walking away from the turned-over Accord. Maybe she'd also seen his bloodied crushed body in the backseat as they drove away on down the hill. Maybe she'd read the papers the next day. That night and afterward she hadn't asked the right questions.

And she was afraid, but not as afraid as she should be.

*Why was that?*

She knew more than she was letting on.

"They were just trying to scare me off," Jimmy said.

"Did they?" she asked.

It was a good question.

"I think *I* know enough right now," he said.

It was a good answer.

After a minute, she said, "We seem to take turns trying to talk each other out of this."

He didn't say anything for another five minutes as the road climbed higher and then leveled off, tracing with every turn and switchback the fingers of land that broke off above the ocean.

That was another way he was different. He could say nothing.

———

There was a gas station, a pull-off right after a blind turn. The gas was thirty cents a gallon more than it had been twenty miles behind them but everyone stopped anyway. It was the first place to get out, stretch, and let the full view fill your head. There was a sleek tour bus four shades of purple, with a glass front, top to bottom. Germans. All of them were out of the bus, smoking. Gulls floated overhead, facing out to sea, staying in the same spot by riding the updraft off the cliff face, angled heads watching the tourists below, occasionally calling with a cry that sounded unsettlingly like screeching tires.

Jimmy topped off the tank and cleaned the windshield. He kept an overnight bag in the back, one in every car. He unzipped it and took out a soft Patagonia shell, a pullover. He put it on. The heat of L.A. was far behind.

One of the Germans came over to admire the Mustang. He walked around it, careful to keep a respectful distance. He nodded at the hatchback vents high on the rear quarter panel, the "gills," then went to the front and squatted before the shark's mouth grill, as if to see what it would look like swallowing you whole.

He stood up. *"Bullitt,"* he said.

Jimmy nodded.

The man smiled and made an up and down motion with his hand, like a porpoise diving and surfacing in the surf, the "Bullitt" Mustang flying up and over the streets of San Francisco.

Jimmy nodded. *"Ich versuche zu, zu mein Mustang auf dem Boden behalten,"* he said. *"I try to keep my Mustang on the ground."*

Jean was in the little store. She took a Martinelli's sparkling apple juice from the cooler, twisted it open and drank it while she walked the aisles. She picked up a bag of trail mix called "Big Sur Sunshine" and a candy bar, looked through the rack of T-shirts and sweats and found a hooded sweatshirt with a minimum of decoration. She got a few more things and went to the register. On a shelf behind the clerk was a flock of souvenir ceramic seagulls floating over redwood blocks on wire stalks. When the door opened, the draft made them dance.

Jimmy came in to pay for the gas.

"Do you want anything?" Jean said.

Jimmy saw her things on the counter. There was a toothbrush and toothpaste.

"No."

"And the gas," Jean said to the woman behind the register and handed her a credit card.

"And this," Jimmy said. He took an atomic fireball from the bowl on the counter.

They drove on through the afternoon. Another fifty miles and they passed into the first of the massive trees the drive was also famous for. Orange poppies flashed in bright sunny patches where the road cuts were. A rocky creek ran alongside the road, glimpsed now and then through breaks in the green. The air had that evergreen smell that made the whole day seem like morning. The trees grew taller, closing in on the swath of bright blue overhead.

Then the light began to change, and quickly.

Just in time, the road broke back out into the open, to the coastline, and they stopped at the first motel.

The room was paneled with redwood, diagonal. Jimmy came in alone, left the door open behind him. He tossed the overnight bag onto the bed. He opened the drapes, slid open the sliding glass door. The wing of rooms was on a pad high above the surf, a hundred yards above the rocks and the water, but the glass door was still grayed with ocean spray. There was an hour or so of daylight left.

In among the trees, it would already be dark.

Jimmy cracked the seal on a bottle of water and lay on the bed with his head against the bag. He looked at the redwood ceiling, the redwood beams, the redwood walls. People came here for the big, tall, indomitable redwoods, to literally put their arms around them, put their cheeks against them, and they also wanted their rooms and their restaurants paneled with rough-sawn dead redwood.

He looked out the open sliding door. There was a patch of grass and a pair of white plastic chairs and then a row of cypresses at the cliff's edge.

*Cypresses.*

Jean came in. She carried a paper bag, another raid on a gas station store. She emptied it of bottles of juice and sunblock, a bag of sunflower seeds, sweatpants to match her sweatshirt, and a pair of pink canvas shoes she'd never wear at home.

"Look," she said. She lifted out a cheap tape player. And a cassette tape. "Reggae." She said it with an exclamation point.

Jimmy sat up against the headboard, watched her as she fit the C batteries into the machine and then went to work on the stretch-wrap around the cassette.

She said, "In the gift shop they had tapes of 'Sounds of the Sea' and 'Sounds of the Big Trees.' *Relaxation* tapes." She slotted the cassette into the machine.

"*No Woman No Cry*," she half sang, before it began.

"It bothered you that I said you weren't the type who drives around the block to hear a song on the radio," Jimmy said.

"I hardly ever think about it," Jean said.

She smiled and the music started, a crack of a high hat and then a rolling rhythm. It wasn't "No Woman No Cry," but a song that began:

*I don't want to wait in vain for your love . . .*

But neither of them thought the song was about them, or at least about this. She turned it up and fiddled with the bass.

*From the very first time I rest my eyes on you, my heart says follow through . . .*

"I got two rooms," Jimmy said.

She didn't say anything, went into the bathroom and changed into her new sweatpants and cheap pink shoes. When she came out, she smiled at him and walked past him out the sliding door to see if she could see the water.

She went all the way out to the edge. She turned and looked back at him through the open door, happy.

———————

She talked him into taking the ragged path zigzagging down the cliff-face to the rocks and the water. It took thirty minutes down, from the warning sign at the top to the sweet little cove and improbable beach below perfectly littered with driftwood, and almost an hour back up, the last half in the dark with Jimmy going ahead and Jean holding his shirttail and laughing.

They drank a bottle of Liebfraumilch over dinner at the seafood place next to the motel and then another. They took what was left in their glasses out to the cliff's edge and listened to the wind and the surf far below that they couldn't see except when the biggest waves blew out white against the rocks.

Jimmy pulled back the cover on the bed.

"Can we leave the sliding glass door open?" he asked.

It was chilly, but she nodded.

The lights were out. The moonlight lit the walls. He realized what the bias-cut paneling on the walls had reminded him of when he'd first come into the room: recording studios. There was a time when they all had walls that looked like this, diagonal redwood paneling. He'd spent hours in those rooms.

"People come to look at the trees and then sleep in redwood-paneled rooms," Jimmy said.

"And come to the ocean and eat seafood," Jean said. She was drunker than he was. She put on a funny voice. "'Let's go someplace beautiful— and eat it!'"

There was a silence. She kissed him. He touched her neck. Her breath in his face was sweet and warm, the last drink of the night.

"*You proceed at your own risk,*" she said, laughing too much.

———————

He was up early, before there was light. He sat in a chair and watched her sleeping. It had been a while since he'd been with a woman. As he watched her, as he listened to her breathe, he felt sorry for himself. It had been a while for that, too.

He showered. After he shaved, he dried his face and looked at himself in the mirror. The sunblock Jean bought was on the counter, a pink bottle, sunblock for kids, *no more tears*. He squeezed a white circle of it into his palm, rubbed his hands together, spread it across his forehead, nose and cheeks. The smell of it hit him, summers on the beach or on a sailboat, way back. That smell and the memories it brought with it, the Liebfraumilch last night, *Mother's Milk,* the cypresses, this road into Carmel and Monterey—he knew already what the day was going to be about.

And wished he'd gone south instead of north.

Two hours later, he was on Point Lobos. There was a thin fog. Jimmy stepped out onto the point. Here the cypresses were gnarled, arthritic, almost bare but still alive, their roots reaching down to find unlikely nourishment in cracks and crevices in the rock. Lace lichen bearded the branches of understory trees. Cypress Cove and Pinnacle Cove were to his right, Bluefish Cove beyond. There were prettier places all around him, where the trees were fuller, where there was more color, but this was where he'd stood with his mother all those years ago.

He was sixteen. An hour earlier, in the car, after she'd gotten out, as he sat listening to the radio, he'd laid a tab of acid on his tongue.

"It's a shame to shoot color," Teresa Miles had said.

She had a Leica on a leather strap around her neck. On her, it looked like jewelry. Her hair had just been cut short and she kept running her fingers through it, what was left of it. She was flying away in a week for a movie. She wore a thin sweater that buttoned up the middle, buttons made of abalone. She had perfect breasts, full for a woman as thin as she was, and always wore French bras that offered them up with a little less self-consciousness than Playtex or Maidenform. It was another thing Jimmy resented about her, the way his friends looked her over when she stepped into the room, and the way she pretended not to notice.

"It doesn't matter," Jimmy said. He leaned against a cypress. His mother was out in the open. It was overcast, a world of grays. "It's going to look like black and white anyway."

"No, it won't," she said. "It won't have the *drama* of black and white!"

"Drama." Jimmy repeated her word.

"Why don't you play your guitar?" she said. "Get it out of the car. Play me one of your songs."

*No. Because you asked me to.*

Nothing was happening. Jimmy wondered if the acid was bad, or not acid at all, a trick played on a rich kid in the lot behind The Troubadour.

But then a rock flared at his feet and then another.

She brushed his hair out of his eyes. It was 1967. His hair was long, as long as The Beatles' and The Beatles' was getting longer with each LP.

She walked away across the rocks.

He'd been up all night and she didn't know it, had come back at four or five from hanging out at Clover. It was the recording studio on Santa Monica Boulevard in Hollywood, a low-cost place, one main room and a booth for vocals, the control room, an "artists' lounge" with a pinball machine, which was just the first skinny room you came into off the dirty street. A singer/songwriter had worked all night on one track. Nobody. Jimmy knew the producer, who was older than sixteen but just a kid, too. It was that time when hits could come out of anyplace, any*body*, so almost everyone was cutting tracks and getting paid for it.

And The Beatles were on Blue Jay Way.

"Come here!" his mother said, her voice bright and theatrical.

Below the point, in a small cove that had no name, out past the shore-break where the water rose and fell predictably, gently, four or five sea otters rafted among the swirling canopies of giant kelp, on their backs.

"See what they're doing?"

*They're beating their chests.*

"They swim down under the kelp and find a perfect flat rock and then a clam or an oyster or even an abalone and then they come back up to the surface and roll over and then pound away on their little rock until the shellfish cracks open and they can eat it."

She held his hand, like he was six. "They used to say, until just a few years ago, that what separated Man and the lower animals was that only Man used *tools*. They don't say that anymore, but that's what they taught us in school, probably you, too. But I always knew it was wrong because I knew about this."

*Tools. Could this get any more stupid?*

She pulled him to her, put their hands behind her back. Her breast was against him. Her perfume had its hands around his throat. He loved her so much and, even now, he felt like she was already gone.

He let go, pulled away from her.

"So what do they say separates us now?" Jimmy said.

"I don't know," she had said.

A cormorant screeched overhead and Jimmy looked over at Jean, a hundred yards away, kneeling next to a rock in her pink canvas shoes.

Jimmy looked back down at the cove. The *selfsame* cove.

Back at the motel, the sign warning guests of the liabilities of the trail down to the beach had said more than, *You proceed at your own risk.* It also said, with an odd stiffness, as if the owners were Swiss or Austrian, *Be advised that the return is more difficult than the descent.*

————————

They went into Carmel for a late lunch. There was more wine. For some reason, Jean was under a cloud and not saying much.

Jimmy didn't really know her but he blamed it on Carmel. He'd never liked the town. It was too relaxed, or relaxed for the wrong reasons. There was too much money here, or too much money too far removed from the labor that produced it. Carmel always seemed to him to have too many retired airline captains and their flight attendant wives, too many personal injury lawyers in their forties who'd had a wonderful tragedy walk into the office one day, the kind that meant more than just another Porsche, that meant *freedom* money. But, as it turned out, here it was only the freedom to fret over the lightness of the pasta or the year of the wine or the elasticity of the skin of the person across the table from you. Most of them didn't even play golf. They just "lived well" and repeated too often that line about revenge.

Jean put her knife and fork across her plate. She ran her fingers through her hair, fluffed it out, like his mother had in his memory, and leaned back, her legs crossed at the ankles under the table. She smiled at him, the way you have to the day after you make love in a motel, if you haven't split already. She had bought clothes at a shop a few doors down from the restaurant, had changed in the dressing room, a silk dress the color of the tarnish on a bell, or the lace lichen they'd just left on Point Lobos. Whether it was the dress or the light filtered through the oaks on the patio, her green eyes looked blue. Blue and sad.

Or maybe she was just hungover.

"Was that where you and your mother were, the memory you told me about when we were talking about perfume?"

"Yes."

"How old were you?"

Of course he couldn't tell her.

"I don't know," he said.

*Fifteen or sixteen.* Sixteen. *It was early in the summer, 1967. The Doors'
first album had just come out.*

"I looked at *City of Light* the other night," she said.

*City of Light* was the movie Teresa Miles went off to shoot the week
after the day on Point Lobos.

Jimmy wondered again what she knew, how much she knew.

"How many of her movies have you seen?" he said.

"I think they were called *films.*"

Jean smiled. Her eyes had gone back to green again.

"All of them," Jean said. "I'm a fan. Now."

A waiter came, asked if they wanted coffee. They didn't. Jimmy ordered
a crème brulee.

"We'll share it."

It was another thing you did the day after the night in the motel.

"Most of the books said she had no children," Jean said.

"She tried to keep me out of it," Jimmy said. He was telling her more
than he should again.

"One said there was a son. Another that there were *two* boys, one who
came along much later in her life. I guess that was—"

"Lies."

"Who was your father?"

"He was a director. Married to someone else."

A bird snapped down onto their table, a finch. It eyed a crust of bread,
looked at Jimmy as if waiting for permission. Jimmy kept still. It pecked
at the crumb then flew away as quickly as it had come when someone
coughed at a table across the way.

"One of the books," Jean began, "one of them said there was a rumor
that your mother didn't die, that she was still alive somewhere."

Jimmy looked at her.

"No."

When they finished, Jimmy gave the waiter cash and Jean crossed the
patio into the restaurant to go to the ladies' room. A man paused in his
attention to his wife's lines of dialogue to follow Jean with his eyes.

Jimmy stared at him, wanted to yank him out of his chair, shove him
until he backed up with his hands in front of him.

He wondered where *that* came from.

They started up the sidewalk. The collectors' car show was on in
Monterey. A convoy of restored Corvairs came past in the tunnel of trees,

eight or ten of them nose to tail, half of them turquoise. Coming along behind was an enormous old Packard with the spare on the running board and a Klaxon horn that the locals—were they called *Carmelites?*—probably didn't appreciate.

Jean went into a hat store. Jimmy ducked into another shop to buy something for her. When he came out, she was across the street and down in the next short block. She waved happily and called out to him.

She was in front of a tiny redwood chapel, an Episcopal church wedged between the shops and restaurants. Once she knew that he had seen her, she went inside.

Jimmy crossed the street.

He stepped into the dark cave of the chapel. Candles burned in red cups, dozens of them, a decorating touch more California Mission Catholic than Episcopal. Or maybe Jimmy was just in a sour mood. It was warm and pleasant in the tiny sanctuary, smaller than a candle store, and they were alone.

Jean was in the second pew, kneeling on the drop down pads. She straightened, crossed herself and sat back with her hands in her lap. There was a "good little girl" rigidity to her posture. It was sweet.

Jimmy sat beside her.

She was reading from the *Book of Common Prayer.*

"It's the *old* book of prayer," she said. "Before the revision. Look. You can tell."

She passed him the book, her finger on a line in what was called The Apostles' Creed. As his eyes crossed the page, she said the line aloud in a soft voice.

*"And sitteth on the right hand of God the Father Almighty; from thence He shall come to judge the quick and the dead—"*

"Now it says, 'the *living* and the dead'," Jean said.

*The Quick and The Dead.*

Jimmy looked at the altar. All the wood was red. The light of the votives was red, warm, pulsing. It was like being inside a beating heart. He brushed his hair back. He could smell her on his hands. Last night, after they'd made love, when everything was still quiet, before anyone broke the charm, she'd touched his face.

"Tell me your secret," she had said.

# SEVENTEEN

"The kid is gone," Angel said.

Jimmy stripped off his shirt, took a clean shirt from the stack in the closet. Angel had come over to be with Drew at Jimmy's house while he was gone with Jean. When they'd come back, Jimmy had tried to talk her into staying with him for a few days but she'd said no. Angel had sent two of his friends to go home with her, to stand watch over her, to stand between her and *Them.*

"First night you left." Angel waited a beat to deliver the rest of the bad news. "He took the Porsche."

Jimmy buttoned the shirt.

He went into the office, stood over the desk, looking at all the papers and the pictures. The dead, the living. The case. He found the canceled checks from the rafters of the Danko flying school.

Angel came in after him.

"Did you tell him about the moon?"

"I told him the rest," Jimmy said, "but not that."

"Somebody should tell him."

"Somebody probably has."

"What are you going to do about him?"

"Nothing, for as long as I can," Jimmy said.

---

There was a silvery path across the water to the fat moon. Jimmy found Kirk, the old Clover Field expert, at the end of the Malibu Pier, a pole over the side, his fishing license in a vellum envelope pinned to his funky hat. Something flapped in a white lard bucket next to the old man's beat-up tacklebox.

Jimmy leaned over for a look in the bucket.

"You don't want to see that," Kirk said. "I don't even know what it is. I'm going to take it back to this science teacher I know."

Jimmy leaned against the rail, turned his back on the moon.

"What do you need?" Kirk said. "You aren't dressed to fish."

He *was* fishing. The checks were for overdue aviation fuel bill payments and rent checks made out to Steadman Industries. They had made him rethink the thing Rosemary Danko had said that he didn't quite hear, when he'd thought she'd said her father's killers were *the pretty people*.

Maybe it was the *airplane people*.

"I found rent checks Bill Danko paid to Steadman Industries."

Kirk nodded. "The old man owned everything at Clover. The airport was the city's but all the buildings belonged to Steadman."

"You ever hear of any run-ins between Danko and him or his people?" Jimmy said.

Kirk shook his head. "Red Steadman wouldn't have anything to do with a small fry like Danko."

"Did you ever meet him, Steadman?"

"Sure, he was there all the time in the war days. He'd pick up a rivet gun, come in over your shoulder, put one in to show you how it was done. He was all right, but he'd definitely tear you a new one if you looked at him wrong."

Jimmy had also come back to the year-end wrap-up:

### 1977 . . .
### A MERGER   A MURDERER   A MONARCH

"When was the merger with Rath Aircraft?"

"I guess seventy-six or -seven. Steadman died Christmas Day, 1973. Three, four years after that. It never could have happened when Red was alive."

"You were still there? After the merger?"

"A year. I finished out my time. It wasn't the same."

"Why?"

"I was out of the old days, when it was 'Steadman and his boys.' The companies may have ended up merging but Red Steadman and Vasek Rath sure as hell never did, never would have. They hated each other. Since we worked for Red we hated Rath, too, even with Red dead and gone. Who'd want to work for that bastard Rath?"

Kirk filled a cup from a thermos. He'd not touched the pole over the side and apparently nothing had touched his bait either.

"I make it sound like I *liked* Red Steadman," he said. "Once he was dead, he got larger than life. You know what I mean?"

Kirk shook his head, shook off the past.

He looked at the moon, startling each time it caught your eye.

"Look at that," he said, "best moon for Pacific seawater fish, fat, almost full."

Jimmy thanked him and started back up the pier. A little boy and his mother came toward him carrying their tackle, a couple of old poles and a battered box. The woman wore a crisp shirt tucked into a long white skirt that caught the light, low heels. Jimmy wondered what their story was. She was too young, too together-looking to have a boy that age, but she did. And it was too late for them to be out here like this, too, but they were.

The boy looked at him the way boys without fathers look at young men, hard and soft at the same time, trying to connect.

Jimmy knew it too well. He pointed a finger at the boy.

"Good luck," he said.

---

The headquarters for Rath-Steadman was three identical mirrored boxes with greenbelt all around, standing alone in an industrial park, inland and south almost to Orange County. Jimmy looped the perimeter of the empty parking lot and parked the Mustang in the front row, just as if he belonged there, and settled in to wait out the rest of the night. Dawn came in an hour or two, the orange parking lot lights overcome by a sky flushed an embarrassed pink.

They unlocked the doors at nine. The receptionist was dressed like a pilot, all the way up to her angular cap. Jimmy paused over a glass-tombed model of a passenger jet labeled, "RS-20," Rath-Steadman's latest, and came up to her desk, which was tall and which she stood behind.

"Good morning," she said.

On the wall behind her were portraits of the founders, Vasek Rath and Red Steadman. For two men who hated each other, they looked a lot alike, big-chested, clear-eyed.

"I'd just like an annual report," Jimmy said.

She seemed a little disappointed for some reason.

"Public Relations, Tenth Floor. Your name?"

He told her. *Harry Turner.*

She tapped on a keyboard and a pass popped up out of a slot in the stainless steel.

He was alone in the elevator until it stopped at the third floor and three men in suits got in. Matching suits. As they rode up, the three men traded looks and nodded at each other, wordlessly continuing whatever they'd been in the middle of before. Then, at about the sixth floor, one of them said, darkly, "*Tim,*" and the other two nodded. Nobody said anything else and they got out on nine. They never looked directly at Jimmy.

He had punched the button for the top floor, eighteen.

When the doors parted it was the boardroom and it was empty. The drapes were open. There was a view almost to the ocean, over the planted greenery and then the San Diego freeway and, beyond that, the spires of a refinery with its flaring burn-off stacks. The table was forty feet long, oblong, perfectly smooth, any claw marks buffed out.

There were pictures of the directors in a row across one wall, meat-eaters one and all, including the two women. It was the usual mix of yesterday's politicians and sports statesmen. None of them looked as if they could have stood up to Red Steadman or Vasek Rath in the old days.

Maybe one man.

Jimmy was going through a trashcan when a side door opened and a fruit tray as tall and comic as a Carmen Miranda headpiece came through the door. It was on a cart, wheeled in by a young assistant something or other.

Jimmy excused himself and stepped back into the waiting elevator.

"No problem," the kid said.

Jimmy stopped at Public Relations on the way down.

In the lobby he nodded and smiled at the receptionist on his way to the door and waved his annual report.

She looked disappointed again.

He looked back at her.

"What'd it close at yesterday?"

"Seventy-seven and an eighth," she said. "Up a quarter today, Mr. Turner."

He half expected her to salute.

"Outstanding!" Jimmy said.

He took the corporate report out to the parking lot, sat on the hood of the Mustang and opened it. There were the same pictures of the founders and the directors. Kurt Rath, Vasek Rath's son, had a page of his own as CEO. He was in his thirties, looked like a Luftwaffe pilot. Jimmy ran the math. Rath-the-Younger was just a few years old when Bill Danko and Elaine Kantke died. Vasek Rath had died twenty years ago, five years after the merger, leaving his son enough stock to take control when he came of age.

In the picture, Kurt Rath was trying to manage a bit of a smile but knew not to give away much.

A look that made Jimmy want to buy a hundred shares.

---

Alone on the putting green at the most exclusive country club on the Westside, Jimmy sank a twenty-footer, clean, straight, no suspense.

"I meant to do that," he said.

He dropped another ball and lined up his shot. Behind him, Kurt Rath, CEO, strode toward him followed by a nervous younger man, the club's starter.

"Is this him?" Rath said.

The starter nodded.

Jimmy turned. *Who me?*

"This idiot jammed us *both* up," Rath said.

Jimmy still stood over his putt.

"Yeah? How'd he do that?"

"I have a standing twelve noon tee-time Thursdays. I've had it for six years. Everybody knows it. And this moke says someone in my office blanked it this morning, which is impossible, and now you've got it."

Rath's partner stepped up. He looked like a nice guy, nice smile, good build, nice tan. He looked like the kind of guy you could beat every Thursday.

"Hey, how's it goin'?" Jimmy said to the beatable man.

The man nodded back. He was already embarrassed by what he knew was coming next from Rath.

"Look," the CEO began again.

"Take it," Jimmy said.

Rath had expected a fight. It took a moment for him to regroup.

"I own a little R-S stock," Jimmy said. "I wouldn't want to be responsible for you having a bad day."

Rath nodded four or five times, started away.

Jimmy dropped his head to concentrate on the long putt.

He sank it. Rath looked back about the time the ball snapped into the cup.

"You want to join us?" Rath said.

*Who me?*

Jimmy walked after them and caught up and shook Rath's partner's hand.

"Sonny Ball," Rath said.

Jimmy shook Sonny Ball's hand. Rath never offered his.

After the round, they had a drink.

Rath was going back to work so for him it was just a grapefruit juice with a splash of cranberry juice on top, like a dash of blood.

He wasn't talking. And Jimmy hadn't learned anything from Rath on the greens, except that he lifted his head and he was better at long putts than short. Jimmy didn't really know what he was looking for. He'd long ago stopped being restrained by that, by what somebody else would see as a lack of purpose. He just went where it seemed he should go, heard what he heard, saw what he saw.

And thought about it at night instead of sleeping.

Rath drained his drink and spit a cube of ice back into the glass and stood up.

"Enjoyed it," he said. "People never kick my ass, even when they can."

Sonny Ball looked into the Scotch he was having.

"It was only a couple of strokes," Jimmy said.

"Yeah, I remember," Rath said.

Rath patted Ball on the back as he left. When he was ten feet away, he half turned.

"Call my office. We'll get you over for lunch."

He meant Jimmy.

"Outstanding," Jimmy said.

For a while, he chatted with Ball, a retired United pilot with a good long story about Bangkok, but he didn't learn anything about Rath-Steadman there either, the old days or the new. Then the rich old men started filling the place, bright clothes, bright colors on men you knew had terrorized and ball-busted "their people" yet had survived it, the company life, the dictator's life, the acid in the mouth and the unsatisfied knot in the gut that usually killed off these guys long before now.

Jimmy finished his martini, stood to go, leaving the two fat olives on the spear.

---

A pair of moons hung in a jet black sky.

Below, a tracked rover the size of a suitcase hustled over the surface of Mars.

Or at least that's the way it looked.

Behind the glass, Ben, the Jet Propulsion Lab engineer from the Mensa murder mystery night at Joel Kinser's, wiggled the rover's controls, spun it around in a circle.

The name "Rath-Steadman" was stenciled on the side.

Ben offered the controls to Jimmy. Jimmy declined.

"When we were ready to put out the first pictures from the surface of Mars," Ben said, "I downloaded a fuzzy image of Elvis and superimposed it over an up-slope, very dimly, *perfect*. But somebody caught it before it went out."

Ben flicked the stick.

"Watch this."

The multimillion dollar toy popped a wheelie.

In the JPL employee's dining room, Jimmy drank a bottle of water and watched as Ben attacked his five o'clock "lunch," a can of sardines with a pull-top lid and two slices of dark rye wrapped in wax paper.

"I'm not going to eat that pear," he said.

Jimmy took the pear.

"Rath-Steadman. Past, present, or future?" Ben said.

"Whatever you know."

"I know everything," Ben said, a simple statement of fact.

"Start with the past."

"When Rath and Steadman merged in 1977, two rather interesting companies were lost and one rather uninteresting company was born, producing a particularly undistinguished series of spectacularly successful airplanes."

Jimmy took the first bite of the pear. Ben eyed him, as if he now regretted giving it up.

"Presently," Ben said, "R-S is in a becalmed patch of sea, captained by Kurt Rath, who is a real son of a bitch, to use the technical term. As for the future, all eyes are on the sky . . ."

It was a joke. Jimmy didn't get it.

"The war with the birds . . ."

Jimmy still didn't get it.

They took Ben's car, a dust-white twenty-year-old Honda Civic. Ben cut across Pasadena and then up through La Canada/Flintridge. He was a shortcut kind of guy, a surface street guy. He made fifty right and left turns in the twenty-mile trip, maximizing the torque in each gear, sometimes violently downshifting as he yanked the car around a turn, all while *Persian* music squeaked out of the Honda's cheap speakers, snake charmer's music to the untuned ear, and too loud to talk over.

Jimmy held on, his head under the lowered cloud of the torn headliner. They came down Sepulveda from the north, faster than the cars on the adjacent freeway, right and left and right and left down into Van Nuys to an industrial park.

One last turn and they were on the tarmac of Van Nuys Airport.

"You have a plane?" Jimmy said.

Ben threw open the doors of a hangar. There was an experimental plane hardly longer than the Civic with an odd wing configuration, two place, prop aft.

"I built it. In my garage," Ben said as he yanked away the blocks and shoved it toward the doorway.

The light plane had power. There was some chatter on the radio as they came up the runway, fast.

"It's the same model as John Denver's," Ben yelled to Jimmy as he pulled back on the stick and the plane leapt into the sky. "That seems to impress some people."

They crossed the city. What would have taken an hour and a half down below took ten minutes. They flew over the Rath-Steadman headquarters, the parking lot where Jimmy had burned up the last hours of last night. It was late afternoon and the light and the distance and the angle made everything look good, the shining buildings and rolling, green manmade hills around them, even the refinery, Oz in this light.

Ben banked right, a steep turn, and they were facing the dropping sun. As they approached the coastline, Ben looked down, shouting over the noise.

"See any B-One-RD's?"

"What?"

"B-1-RDs."

"What?"

"Birds."

Jimmy looked over the side.

Below was a grim expanse of what once were wetlands, a broad section that fed, in a few flashing waterways, into the Pacific. It was a landscape dotted with abandoned tuna boats and decaying pleasure craft and a few figures too far off to read.

Jimmy's eyes darkened.

"Last wetlands in the South Bay," Ben yelled. "Rath-Steadman wants to build RS-20s here. Buddy of mine has been doing a little stealth air-mapping for them. Immense plant, no more wetlands. Look for the PR campaign to start soon. *'Birds for Jobs!'"*

Ben pushed the plane into a wild, diving turn.

"I like birds," he shouted, "but I'd bet on Rath-Steadman . . ."

The little aircraft spiraled down over the cluttered wetlands for an up-close view.

A man in a peacoat and watch cap looked up, a gasoline rainbow at his feet.

# EIGHTEEN

It was on Western the block above Third, a storefront church with services in Spanish and Korean depending on the night, formerly an adult book-store, next to a new adult bookstore. Through the open doorway, twenty folding metal chairs, a low stage, a plywood pulpit. A Fender Stratocaster leaned against an amp. It was the end of the day and hot and the Wednes-day night services wouldn't begin for another hour but a few people were already in place. A seven-year-old girl in a dress the color of cotton candy played scales on the upright piano.

Jimmy and Angel were out front on the sidewalk.

Jimmy started by telling him about *The Airplane People*.

"Red Steadman owned the building the murdered boyfriend's business was in, a flight school. I think somehow Danko got mixed up in some Steadman business and they killed him and Elaine Kantke for it."

"I thought it was about disco," Angel said. "What? Mixed up in what?"

"I don't know."

"It's all a long time ago," Angel said. "I don't see how any of it matters now."

Jimmy had an answer for that.

"Rath-Steadman wants to build a new plant down in South Bay," he said. "On some wetlands. That's the link to today."

He waited before he said the next.

"It's down at The Pipe."

Jimmy let it sink in. Angel's eyes darkened the same way his had when he'd looked over the side of the little plane.

A skinny preacher got off a bus and walked toward them up the side-walk carrying a white-cover Bible the size of a cake box. He rolled his hand across Angel's back as he passed, not wanting to interrupt what might be a witnessing.

"So that's the link with Sailors," Angel said.

"I guess."

"They want it to happen or *don't* want it to?"

"I don't know," Jimmy said.

Angel shook his head. "Are you still seeing them?"

"Not since the chase in the park."

"What about the German woman?"

Jimmy shook his head.

Inside the church, someone played a brash chord on the guitar. "What about Jean?" Angel said as it blew on down the sidewalk.

"I still haven't seen her."

"Why is that?"

"I stopped calling her, stopped going by."

"Why?"

There was a billboard down the street behind Angel for some movie that had opened and closed a month ago. Now it was peeling in the weather. The stars, man and woman, beamed toothy grins out at Jimmy, in their confidence just about the most pathetic faces on the street.

"I knew your guys were watching out for her."

"Go to her," Angel said. "Tell her her daddy didn't do it and whoever did is probably long since dead. Whoever did it and for whatever reason."

Jimmy nodded.

"Get her in the *now*," Angel said.

"I'm trying."

"Get *yourself* in the now."

Jimmy smiled. "I've never had much luck at that."

"Then you can maybe see what there could be with her. You could use some *love* in your life."

"I already got you," Jimmy said.

The music inside started, drums, piano and guitar.

"You wanna come in?" Angel said.

Jimmy shook his head.

Angel pulled him close for an embrace, then pushed him away.

"*Con dios.*"

Jimmy started toward the Mustang down the street.

"'*Someday this wall shall crumble, tumble and fall . . .*'" Angel called after him.

Jimmy turned. "What book of the Bible is that from?"

"Los Lobos," Angel said.

---

Ike's was dead and Scott wasn't behind the bar.

Jimmy drank a beer. The handful of people who were there all had the same guilty look, embarrassed that they'd not known what everyone else apparently had known, that tonight you didn't go to Ike's.

The cop Connor came in. He was out of uniform, wearing his out-of-uniform uniform, a starched Brooks Brothers button-down shirt with the tail out over ironed, creased jeans.

"Nobody's seen him," Connor said. "His neighbor said he didn't come back last night, after his shift."

They were talking about Scott.

Jimmy turned around on the stool to face the bar, but avoided the image of himself in the mirror that was waiting there.

"What the hell is going on?"

"It's getting close," Connor said. "People are getting stressed. Let's go look for him."

Jimmy put some money on the bar and got up.

Then Jean came in. Angel and two of his men were behind her. The bodyguards were Hispanic. Big arms. Angel saw Jimmy and Connor, tipped his chin up to say hello. He and his men took a table out of the way as Jean came to the bar.

Connor stepped away to leave them alone. He went over to the jukebox. After a minute a saxophone piece started, so sentimental and blue the few people in the place turned to look, wondering if it was meant to be a joke.

"I was thinking about you all day," Jimmy said to Jean. The way he said it didn't have all that much romance in it.

She nodded in a way that meant she'd been thinking about him, too, and maybe the other way.

"I called," she said. "Then I thought you might be here."

"I came by a few times," Jimmy said. He came by *once*.

"I've been staying in a hotel. I found myself leaving all the lights on at home," she said.

"Come stay with me."

He didn't say anything else.

She nodded.

He was still standing. He looked over at Connor.

"We have to go see about a friend of ours," Jimmy said. "We'll come back for you here."

"Can I come with you?"

*Maybe it was time.*

They left Angel's truck and Connor's red Corvette in the lot behind Ike's and the four of them took the Mustang, Jean and Connor in the tight backseat. The traffic was light, even down the Strip. Angel's friends followed closely in a low-slung Chevy for a block or two then flashed their lights and peeled off.

Scott's apartment was on Doheny Drive at the corner of Elevado three or four short blocks up from Santa Monica Boulevard in West Hollywood, a cool white tower ten stories tall, lights in the landscaping shining on its face.

Jimmy stayed behind the wheel while Angel and Connor got out. Connor rang the bell downstairs and waited. Angel looked over at Jimmy, then got out a ring of keys and unlocked the outer door and went in. They all had each other's keys.

Jean took this in, put it with the other things she'd learned that deepened the mystery.

"Scott is the bartender at Ike's. He didn't come in today." Jimmy didn't turn around when he spoke to her, didn't even look at her in the mirror. "Nobody's seen him since he left work last night. A neighbor said he'd looked a little shaky the last few days."

Jean just looked at the back of Jimmy's head.

Angel and Connor came out. Connor stepped into the backseat again, Angel got in front.

Angel shook his head.

"Maybe we'd better—"

"Yeah, I know," Jimmy said and put it in gear.

He made a U-turn on Doheny and then a left on Santa Monica Boulevard, drove past The Troubadour, then across West Hollywood into Hollywood.

To the foot of the Roosevelt Hotel.

And the *Walkers.*

This time there were dozens of them in clusters in the alleyways in the three blocks around the hotel, the men (and a few women) Boney M had wanted Jimmy to be reminded of from that perch up on the roof.

They never stopped moving, Sailors ashore forever. They wore whatever they wanted, whatever they had. They lived on the street or in a few hotels the other Sailors kept open in an act of kindness. And *fear,* fear that any Sailor could end up with the same dead look in his eyes, the same lack

of purpose—either for good or for bad—that was in their shuffling move-
ments. This was the worst the worst Sailors could wish on you, what they
could threaten you with, what they could hold you out over a precipice and
make you see, what they could drive you toward, what they could hand
you instead of death. It was a mystery how it happened but some Sailors
saw something that made them fold, made them shuffle like this, made
them *walk*. Death would be a step up.

Jimmy drove slowly past one knot of men.

"Did the kid come back?" Angel said to Jimmy.

"No," Jimmy said, knowing Angel was thinking maybe Drew was down
here, too.

"Stop," Connor said. "*There*."

"Scott's not here," Jimmy said.

There was a man apart from the others who was probably Scott's age,
who at least looked up at the Mustang. He was dark with filth. He didn't
look like anybody anyone could recognize anymore.

"That's not him," Jimmy said.

"Let me check," Connor said.

Jimmy stopped and they let him out and the cop walked over to the
blackened man.

"He couldn't have fallen that far in a day," Jimmy said.

Then he remembered Jean in the backseat.

Jimmy turned to look her in the face. She had that *world-hurt* face
again, but brave, taking her medicine. He felt ashamed of himself for not
having the courage to tell her a better, *easier* version of the truth of who
he was.

Connor came back. He got into the backseat beside Jean. She could
smell the men on him.

Connor shook his head.

"He's not with them," Angel said.

"I believe I just said that," Jimmy said.

He sped away from the men, faster than he meant to.

"What about his old place?" Connor said.

Jimmy nodded.

---

When you were one of them, you knew everyone's story, how *It* had happened. Five years before this night, Scott had put a bullet in his head. His
boyfriend had died exactly a year earlier.

And now here was the apartment building where they'd lived together. It was a twenty-unit four-story box of a design duplicated all over L.A., screaming *seventies!* The front was all glass, the foyer two stories tall. A long light fixture hung from the ceiling looking like an protoplasmic explosion. It was on a street called North Rossmore, a *transitional* street, also duplicated all over L.A. A block north was a golf course edged with million-dollar houses, a block south the last funky half mile of Hollywood.

Jimmy tried a key in the glass door of the entryway. They'd changed the locks. Angel came around from the side of the building. "Over here, door into the garage."

Jean came with them this time. They all went down some steps and in through the garage. They came out into the entryway where the mailboxes were and the elevator.

Angel hit the button. They rode up, not talking.

Jimmy knocked on the door to the apartment. There wasn't any sound from inside. A stereo thumped somewhere down the hall, or maybe it was just someone thudding a fist against the common wall.

Jimmy was about to try his key when the door in front of him was yanked open.

A man with bugged out eyes.

"Just *leave* it!" He was what they used to call a *hype*. "Just *leave* it, man!"

Jimmy asked the wired man if anyone out of the past had been by the apartment that night. He got the door slammed in his face. The pounding down the hall stopped, took a breath or two, started again.

Angel was ready to go but Connor, who had cop instincts, who remembered things other people didn't, looked at Jimmy and shot his eyes up toward the ceiling, the roof. They were on the fourth floor. There were stairs up.

The door at the top was jammed. Angel put a shoulder against it and it opened and the four of them came out onto the roof.

The building wasn't deluxe enough for any decking or patio furniture or umbrellas, or tall enough to offer much of a view.

While Angel and Connor stepped off in different directions, Jimmy went over to the edge and looked down at the traffic on Melrose. There was a car double-parked in front of a restaurant, five cars behind it, honking, nobody willing to give in and pull around it in the open inside lane. Across Rossmore and down a ways was the Ravenswood with its neon rooftop sign, where Mae West had lived out her life. Next to that, the El Royale, where George Raft had kept a bachelor's pad.

Jean came up behind Jimmy, put her arms around him.

He didn't expect it. Later, when he thought about it, maybe when he thought about it too much, he remembered it feeling in the moment like she was holding someone else.

"Jimmy," Connor said.

Angel had found Scott at the other edge of the roof, sitting cross-legged, his back against a TV antenna.

Jimmy left Jean and went to him. She stayed where she was.

The three men stood over their friend a moment and Jimmy said something and Scott nodded. Angel squatted beside him. Jimmy crouched down and offered his hand. Scott took it and they held hands that way a moment. Connor seemed to stand guard, though against *what* wasn't clear.

Jimmy pulled Scott to him and said things into his ear in a voice so low Jean couldn't hear any of it, just as it had been with the kid Drew standing in the middle of the canyon road, trying to put it together, eyes on the moon.

*More questions than answers.*

There was a fuzz around the green letters on the El Royale sign and, up Vine, the Hollywood Hills were wrapped in something. Maybe it was going to rain overnight. But the weather had gone a little haywire. No one was predicting anything with much confidence.

*What was going on?*

Even she felt it, that everything was lurching toward something, not out of control exactly, just out of *our* control, in the control of something very very basic, like a car coming down out of the hills on a rain-slicked street.

# NINETEEN

It was morning and raining. Jean brought a cup of coffee into the living room in Jimmy's house. She looked out the tall window. Two more of the weight lifters from Angel's backyard stood guard under the dripping overhang of the four-bay garage. The garage doors were up. There was the Mustang and empty spaces for the wrecked Dodge Challenger and the Porsche Drew had taken. In the last bay was the tarp-covered car with the high fins. Jean watched as one of the iron men lifted the corner of the cover for a look.

The rain helped, made her feel safer. She'd lived years in Northern California and so she liked the rain. Here, when it rained everything fell apart. The weathermen apologized, the freeways clogged with spun-out cars, mudslides slopped across the curvy foothill roads. Everybody either drove too fast or too slow and everyone bitched. People walking their dogs looked out from under their umbrellas and rolled their eyes instead of saying *Good morning,* if they looked at you at all.

Jean cranked open a window an inch or two so she could hear it and smell it. It reminded her of San Francisco, of Tiberon, of Atherton, of the hills above Stanford, brown today and green tomorrow, as the drops ticked into the gravel under the eaves. In California, the rain was usually like this, flat, steady, without drama.

Maybe that was what the locals hated about it.

It was a huge room. A child could stand in the fireplace. Everyone knew the history of the house. It had been built by one of Los Angeles's first oil barons in the twenties. A movie star had owned it in the forties, put in the pool in back, the motor court and the garage. The star had sold off a half acre in the fifties but there were four and a half acres left. It became a museum in the sixties, restored more or less to the look of the oil baron's home, paid for by the family out of their great wealth. Out of vanity. No one ever toured it except elementary school kids coming in buses for field trips. The grounds were good for picnics.

Then Jimmy had bought it.

But his name wasn't on the deed. Jean had checked. It was owned by a trust. *Blue Moon*. She wondered what the name meant.

There was a grand piano, the wood as black as the black keys and so shiny you didn't want to touch it. Next to it was a tall glass case with a beautiful white dress in it. And a picture of Teresa Miles, in her prime, in the fifties, wearing the same dress in a scene from a movie. *Morning at the Window*. Jean opened the case and felt the fabric. She lifted her fingertips to her nose and breathed in the scent on the cloth.

They'd made love again last night. After that first night in Big Sur, they'd slept in the same bed two more nights in a small hotel in Pacific Grove with a view across Monterey Bay, but had not made love again. It was a comfortable avoidance. Neither of them thought it meant anything worrisome, only that what had happened the first night could stand on its own.

And she had not asked again what his secret was.

He wasn't in bed when she awoke at seven that morning. He'd stayed beside her all night, curled against her. She awoke several times, pulled out of sleep by the strangeness of the bed and the room, needing a moment to realize where she was. Then she would close her eyes again as she felt him against her. She knew he was awake. (She'd not yet seen him asleep.) She thought of him as a restless man, an unsettled man, but he wasn't restless in the middle in the night, with her. He was the kind of man who held you while you slept.

Jean closed the glass cabinet.

She went into Jimmy's study. The bank of security monitors was lit, color images, cameras panning automatically across a half dozen sections of the brick and iron wall that surrounded the property. Another of Angel's men stood in the rain just inside the gate below the house down a slow hill. And another patrolled a back gate.

*Was this really now that dangerous? What had changed?*

On the desk, spread out, was the case. Jean stood before it, picked up the old *Time* magazine. She looked at the pictures, at a photocopy of a one-inch story about Bill Danko's arrest for "drunken flying" she'd never seen before. It mentioned "a female companion." She'd thought her father had managed to keep all of it out of the papers. She looked through the cancelled checks.

There was a clip from the business section of *The Times*:

The aviation industry was stunned in early June when directors of Steadman Aircraft and The Rath Corp., former bitter rivals, announced the two companies had agreed to merge.

And there was the year-end wrap-up.

1977 . . .
## A MERGER   A MURDERER   A MONARCH

Cut into the copy was a picture of her father being led into the courthouse in handcuffs, Jack Kantke in a gray suit, three-button, buttoned up, a narrow black tie. Jean had seen the picture before but this time she noticed what a bright day it had been, everything almost washed out, and the pathetic smile on her father's face.

She looked into his eyes and felt embarrassed for him.

*What had changed?*

She'd never felt embarrassed for him before. She wondered what of him was carried on in her. It was every child's question if you waited long enough or if circumstances exploded in your face.

At least the picture of the *Queen Mary* was simple enough. *The Monarch.* Nineteen seventy-seven had seen the "gala" tenth anniversary of the arrival of the ship to Long Beach Harbor as a tourist attraction.

Scott stepped into the doorway.

"Sorry," he said when she jumped.

They considered each other a moment.

"I was looking for Jimmy," he said.

It was awkward. Jean had the thought that it was as if the bartender and Jimmy were lovers, which wasn't true and made no sense, like they were both Jimmy's lover.

*It's just that they share such a secret,* she thought.

"I don't know where he is," Jean said.

"He just went for a walk in the rain," Scott said. "We spoke. I thought maybe he had come back."

It stayed awkward. He looked at the bank of monitors, points of view like eyes moving from side to side, like heads saying *no* very slowly. He looked at her again and then looked away. He felt ashamed about what she'd seen on the roof the night before.

"I made some coffee," Jean said. She held up her coffee mug. "In the kitchen."

She sat down behind the desk to make it seem as if she belonged there, that she wasn't snooping, that she had permission. Or, maybe *that she knew*.

Scott looked at the clippings, upside down.

"This is about you?"

She nodded. "My father. And mother. It started out simpler."

"Yeah, things get complicated."

There was another silence.

"How long have you known Jimmy?" she said.

"Years."

Jean realized she couldn't tell how old he was. A week ago, behind the bar, he looked liked he was in his twenties. Now, here, before her, he looked fifty.

"Can I ask you something?"

She saw him flinch slightly. He waited to hear what it was.

"Why does he order a second drink when he comes in Ike's and then just leaves it on the bar?" she said.

"A manhattan."

She waited.

"It was what his mother drank."

"What do you do with it when he leaves?"

Scott smiled. "Give it to someone who looks like they need it. Tell them it's from a secret admirer."

Jimmy came in, drying his hair with a towel. He'd heard the last of what Scott said.

"Do they believe it?" Jimmy said.

Scott turned. "Every time." He left them alone. Jimmy patted his back as he went past.

Jean was still behind the desk, the case in front of her.

Jimmy tried to read what was on her face.

"Now you know everything," he said.

Jean stood. "Sorry."

"It's all right, stay there."

Jimmy smiled. "You put everything in piles."

Jean looked down at the neatened desk. She'd hadn't remembered doing it.

"That's a little embarrassing," she said.

He put a different look on his face. "What do you want to know?"

"Nothing," she said.

"My turn to talk you into it," he said.

"No."

He stood in the same place, across the desk from her, with all of *It* between them. She knew he was going to wait for her to say something.

"Who's this?" She took a photo from the desk, Harry Turner.

He told her his name. "A lawyer. Or at least he started out as one. He was behind the scenes in your father's defense. He runs things. That's what he does. Who he is."

She dropped the picture, careful *not* to put it atop one of her piles.

Jimmy wasn't finished.

"And he's on the board of directors of Rath-Steadman."

Harry Turner's was the face Jimmy had recognized from the wall in the boardroom on the top floor of Rath-Steadman as maybe the one man who could have stood up to the old men, to Vasek Rath and Red Steadman.

"The merger in 1977 is connected to the murders?"

He nodded. "Rath-Steadman is ready to build a new assembly plant down in Long Beach. Somehow that's connected to this."

Jean came around the desk to him. She thought she was going to go into his arms but he didn't want that. Without pushing her away, he pushed her away. Maybe *he'd* decided something. There was an anger in him this morning she didn't understand.

"Are you going to stop now?"

"No."

"I told you I don't care about this anymore," she said.

"It's taken on its own life."

"Why are you doing this?" she said. "Pushing my face into it?"

"I want you to know everything I know."

"I don't care about Rath-Steadman. I'm at peace with the idea of my father, what he did or didn't do. I don't *want* to know everything. Not anymore. I want . . ."

And she waited before she said it.

"*You.*"

"Your brother Carey is on the board, too," Jimmy said.

Something broke inside her, like a support, something that held up part of the façade. He saw her crumble.

He heard himself, the way he'd said it, wondered if some part of him meant to break her. Or even drive her away.

"He doesn't have any hand in the day-to-day operation of the company," Jimmy said. "He's just on the board."

She sat in the chair.

He waited. "And he has three million dollars' worth of R-S stock."

"Where does he live?" she said, suddenly smaller.

"He has a house in Palos Verdes. And a penthouse in a high-rise on the harbor in Long Beach."

He could see her pulling herself together again.

"Have you talked to him?" she said.

"No. Have *you*?"

She didn't understand the accusation in it. She said, "Carey called me on some anniversary of the execution. I was at Stanford. That was the last time I talked to him. I heard seven or eight years ago that he was a lawyer, that he was living in Arizona."

"He practiced four years," Jimmy said, "private practice, then filed for bankruptcy. He's had inactive status with the Arizona Bar ever since."

She wanted out of there.

"Was there bad blood between the two of you?"

"No," Jean said. "There wasn't anything. There *isn't* anything."

"Where did he go to live after the murders?"

"He was eight. A boarding school in Scottsdale."

"Why didn't he live with you and your grandmother?"

"I don't know," she said. She got out of the chair.

"You never asked?"

"Why are you being this way?" she said.

He didn't tell her, he didn't know.

"I'm sorry," he said.

She knew he'd hold her now but now she didn't want it.

------------

There was a full daylight moon over the high-rise Deco apartment building on Long Beach Harbor. It was a pretty building, twenty stories high with ornate bas-relief detail over the black frames of the windows. It was from the twenties, recently refurbished, reconfigured into condominiums for young professionals and widows with a sense of style. The rain had ended at noon and left behind the brightest kind of sky, a few round white clouds and a view all the way to Catalina.

The gate on the subterranean parking lifted. After a moment, a white Porsche Cabriolet came out. It stopped. The top folded back.

It was Carey Kantke.

He looked like his father, wore his hair in the same crew cut though there was probably a different name for it now. He was in his late thirties, the same age as his father at the time of the murders, the trial. He ran his hand through his short hair, checked it in the mirror and pulled out of the parking garage and onto West Shoreline Drive, turning right.

Jimmy waited and then fell in behind.

Jean had gone in to her office after they'd talked in the study. Jimmy had told her to stay there at the house behind its high walls, that things were getting weird, but she'd had other ideas. Angel's men went with her. Jimmy thought that if they could get through these next days, with all they would hold, he and Jean might be together for a while, might have a chance. But he didn't tell her that.

There was a stop for lunch, a sidewalk café on East Second Street, a street of gentrified shops and galleries with only a few taco stands and tiki bars left over from the old days. Carey Kantke ate alone, got up once to collapse the green umbrella that shaded his table. Jimmy watched from across the street on a stool at a sidewalk Mexican juice bar splashed with orange and yellow paint. Carey had a coffee and a refill and then paid for his lunch with cash, standing beside the table, talking with the young waitress, all the time in the world.

The valet pulled up with the white Porsche. Jimmy drank the rest of his milky, too sweet *horchada,* left two bucks for the man behind the counter. Carey never saw him, never looked around as he dropped behind the wheel. This wasn't a wary man.

The white Porsche humped up and over the concrete bridge on East Street, into Naples, then right onto the perimeter loop called The Toledo.

And then right again, onto Rivo Alto Canal.

Maybe Carey Kantke had his own version of *returning.*

Jimmy dropped back and parked the Mustang and jumped out and followed the Porsche on foot. The lanes behind the houses were narrow and the pace was slow, slower even than the three-mile-per-hour speed limit posted on funny hand-painted signs.

Carey drove past the house at One-Ten, the murder house, and parked behind the garage of the two-story house two doors down. He got out and went up the walkway between the houses leading to the front, to the canal and the waterfront sidewalk.

It was the house where Jimmy had heard Abba's "Dancing Queen" drifting out of the upstairs window.

———————

Jimmy watched the house from a rental boat, cruising in the canal. Carey Kantke had been inside forty-five minutes. Jimmy cut the engine and let it coast until it thunked into an empty dock. He took the housing off the little outboard and pretended to adjust the carb while he kept his eyes on the house.

In time, Carey came out onto the porch with a Coke. He unbuttoned his shirt and dropped into a pink Adirondack chair, lifting his face into the sun.

Right at home. *Why?* What was Carey Kantke doing there, two doors down from the house where his young life and his sister's had been blown apart with a pair of gunshots in the middle of a summer night?

Then the answer, at least part of it, came out the front door. A young woman. She was in her early twenties but with this kind of good looks it was hard to tell. She could have been sixteen. Or thirty. She wore white shorts and a short top that tied up high enough to show her stomach. She handed Carey a portable phone with someone on the line. Carey said hello, listened, said a few words and handed it back to her. She sat in a second matching Adirondack chair, a long tan leg over the armrest. There was something very familiar about her.

Then the next part of the answer came out.

Vivian Goreck.

The real estate lady Jimmy had talked with at the empty Palos Verdes house. Former Jolly Girl.

She was the young woman's mother. It was obvious when they were next to each other. Vivian stood over her daughter and brushed her fingers through her blond hair until the young woman pushed her mother's hand away.

Jimmy would learn that her name was Lynne.

Vivian sat on the low wall that edged the porch and joined in the conversation between the young people. No one was in much of a hurry. A seagull landed on the neighbor's fountain, atop a *cement* seagull, balancing on the other gull's back. They all watched it, enjoying the joke. It drank. It flew.

After a few more minutes the young woman and Carey got up. He kissed Vivian Goreck on her cheek and they left. The Jolly Girl stayed seated on the low wall. She looked down, pulled out a dandelion growing from a crack in the concrete.

Jimmy got the boat to a dock and then ran between the two closest houses.

He came out onto the alleyway just as Lynne and Carey got into the white Porsche and drove off.

The garage was open. There was Vivian's Rolls, with its BUY BUY license plates.

---

On a bluff above the ocean at Palos Verdes was a glass and steel house with an angular face like the prow of a ship. Jimmy was above it on the adjacent point, an empty lot muddied from the overnight rain. He scanned the scene with binoculars. The white Porsche was in the driveway.

This was Carey's other address.

He stepped into view in the glass living room. He went to the tall window, looked out at the expanse of ocean with his hands behind his back like a captain of a ship.

But wait.

*Was it Carey?*

Lynne Goreck came into the room. She went to him at the window, went into his arms. They kissed. She stepped away. He turned again to look out at the Pacific, then followed her, moving out of view.

A minute passed. Jimmy heard an engine start. The white Porsche curled around the circle drive and sped away up to the coast road, Carey behind the wheel, alone now.

Jimmy looked back at the living room. The room was empty.

But then they were back, the man and Lynne Goreck.

The phone in Jimmy's pocket rang.

It was Jean.

He listened for a long time.

"I'll meet you there," he said.

# TWENTY

The back of the house at one-ten Rivo Alto Canal was blackened but not burned out. A fireman kneeled just inside the backdoor, beside the water heater.

"What was it?" Jimmy said.

The fireman looked the two of them over.

"I own the house," Jean said.

"Oily rags under the water heater," the fireman said.

"Was anybody—"

Jimmy pushed past him and headed upstairs.

"No. They got out," the fireman told Jean.

Jean followed Jimmy. She slowed as she moved through the living room. It hadn't been burned but the smoke had crawled across the ceiling and stained it. Her eyes went over the pictures on the walls, the coffee table, the divan. She'd never been back.

Jimmy was already at the door of the back bedroom upstairs. The door-frame was blackened and some of the dirty carpet had been burned over to the doorway.

Jean came up behind him.

"They said she got out."

They stepped into the room together. The fire had burned the shades off the windows so there was light. The TV was melted, the recliner singed and blackened and its plastic melted, too.

A voice startled them. "You the owners?"

A fire marshal, a handsome man in a perfectly white shirt with a badge on the pocket, stepped out of the second bathroom. He wore rubber gloves.

"I am," Jean said.

"Who was she?"

Jean said, "No one. No one was supposed to be living here."

"It was a woman. I guess a transient," the fire marshal said. "Living here." He looked around the room. "And six or seven cats. So far."

Jean turned and walked out.

"It burned itself out up here," the fire marshal said to Jimmy. "There's not much structural damage. It came straight up from the water heater below, rode up the stack."

"Was the backdoor locked when you got here?" Jimmy asked.

"Yeah, it was. Pulled tight."

Jimmy looked into the bathroom. It was smoke-damaged but not burned. A yellowed shower curtain with flamingos on it still hung on its rings. The mirror above the sink over the years had lost most of its silvering. There was a splotchy black hole in its center where your face would be.

The fire marshal squatted next to the carcasses of two cats at the base of the bay window, trying to decide what to do with them.

"Her name was Rosemary Danko," Jimmy said.

The fire marshal stood.

"You knew her?"

"I talked to her once."

"You want to tell me why?"

Jimmy told him. Some of it.

Jean was in the car when he came down. He got in without saying anything, started the engine and pulled away.

He looked in the mirror. Vivian Goreck was standing with the other neighbors in the middle of the lane.

"Where are we going?" Jean said.

"She had another place," Jimmy said.

———

And another fire.

A red L.A.F.D. Suburban was parked in front of the apartment building in Garden Grove Jimmy had followed her to, crossing town on a hot bus.

Jean stayed in the car.

Jimmy walked around the side of the building. On the service porch of the corner ground-floor unit another fire marshal stood beside another water heater.

"Who are you?"

"I knew the woman who lived here."

"Where is she? We thought it was vacant."

Every time Jimmy heard that word *vacant*, he thought of the look in Rosemary's eyes.

He came in off of the service porch through the kitchen and into the living room. It was gutted, burned to the studs, and the cabinet that had been full of pictures was now a collapsed, empty box.

It would have been neater if there was a body in one of the two places— *If I just could be sure*—but whatever threat in her madness Rosemary Danko had been to them, it was gone, as gone as she was. They'd cut her out of the story. And the traces of her mother with her.

*Five-foot-one.*

Jimmy stood in the warm sun out front for a moment. It was good to breathe the open air.

He got in the Mustang. Jean looked at him and he shook his head, though it wasn't clear what he meant by that.

It just meant *no*.

---

Nine o'clock at night and the traffic on the 405 north was still clogged. It should have opened up hours ago. They were stopped cold in the fast lane at the top of Sepulveda Pass, up where Mulholland crossed overhead with a high bridge. The line of cars ahead of them stretched for two miles down across the San Fernando Valley, the spaces between the sets of red taillights never expanding beyond a car length.

Jean had a beach house north of Malibu at Point Dume. Jimmy was taking her there the back way over Kanan Dume Road, *the fast way* he had thought, until a half hour ago. This time she hadn't said no when he told her what to do, when he told her she had to leave town because they'd kill her, too, if they thought she knew something, if they thought she was in their way, cut *her* out of the story, too. He had said she should go to San Francisco, had said something that made no sense to her—*They won't follow you out of the city*—but she told him about her house at the beach.

Both of them could still smell the smoke on their clothes.

"That was my room," Jean said.

There was nothing to say to that.

"How old was she?" Jean asked.

"In her forties."

"What was she like?"

"Crazy."

It wasn't enough for Jean. She looked at him.

"Lost," he said. "Haunted."

He had plenty more words where those came from. His life had been filled with Rosemary Dankos.

"What was the other place?"

"It was her mother's."

"I'd like to think she lived there most of the time. At her mother's."

"She probably did," Jimmy said.

"Are you sure she's dead?"

"No. Not sure. But I don't know where she'd be if she wasn't, where they would have taken her, why."

"So she's dead."

"I would guess she is."

"What do you think caused her to come to my house?"

"I don't know. Maybe it was when her mother died. She had nowhere else to go for family. Her father had 'lived' there in a way, had history there. She sat around thinking about it. Sometimes you have an idea in your head about something like that—and then it just starts growing, like a potato under the sink."

A car edged up beside them. The man looked over at them, at Jean, liked her looks, kept his eyes on her as if they were in a bar.

"So you think they killed her?"

"I don't know."

"Is my brother involved in this?"

"Rath-Steadman is," Jimmy said. "I don't know."

"Yes, you do. Tell me."

They had inched up over the crest of the mountain to where they could look down on the scene ahead, the shimmering valley lights and the traffic stilled in both directions, red taillights down, white headlights up in the opposite lane.

Now they could see what it was. A mile down the steep run of the freeway where the 405 met the 101 there were clustered spinning lights, red and blue, an accident.

Her hand was on the seat beside her. He took it.

"You'll be all right at the beach," he said. That was all he would tell her. For now.

"This could all be over in a few days," he said.

She wondered what difference a day or two made now but she didn't ask and the two of them said nothing for a long time, watching the dead traffic in front of them, the accident far below, the TV news helicopters that floated, turning, high above the scene, red lights blinking, like sparks above a fire.

# TWENTY-ONE

He felt like running, as if this was something he could outrun. After he left Jean at her Malibu house, Jimmy drove *north*, not south, up California 1, then back inland through the mountains to Thousand Oaks and the 101 East, a great loop onto the 210 to cross the base of the Angeles Forest and the mountains above Glendale.

Now it was way after midnight.

When he turned back down into it, when he was riding down out of the foothills, it was like L.A. was on the bottom of a dark ocean, the spikes of downtown still a half mile below the surface, the green copper dome of Griffith Observatory a decorative toy on the floor of a midnight aquarium. And the air was bad, even in the middle of the night. The air was heavy. He felt *compressed*. The feeling was so real it was hard to breathe. He had to fight the panic, the urge to jump from the car and swim frantically for the surface.

He tried to drive it out. He cruised the streets of Hollywood until the whores were gone, down through the canyon of billboards on the Strip, past the all night newsstand.

He didn't go home.

He drove all the way out through the winding turns of Sunset Boulevard, all the way back out to Malibu, to the beach at Point Dume, almost where he'd started. He parked on the access road. He found at the edge of the dial a drifting Mexican pirate rock station with old music. When morning came, an offshore wind came with it and stood the waves up straight and tall. Jimmy watched at the water's edge. The wind came up stronger until there was a wave that rose and rose and rose and wouldn't break.

# TWENTY-TWO

There was one last set of checks.

In the study, standing at his desk, Jimmy shuffled the deck until he came to one made out to somebody named Roy Pool with the notation "Payroll." He turned it over. On the back was an endorsement by Mr. Pool, notably florid, and a deposit stamp that said, "Ringside Liquor."

It was still there. It was in Hawaiian Gardens, south and inland, straight in from Long Beach. Everyone said there was no *heritage* in L.A., but some things survived the perpetual reinvention, like red sauce Italian restaurants and old-style Mexican places with dusty sombreros on the walls. And corner liquor stores. Most of them had come right after the war with names that meant more then than now, names like Full House, Victory Liquor, and Ringside.

The clerk was in his sixties. He came out the front door with Jimmy and squinted in the sun on the sidewalk and pointed down the block and then over.

Jimmy set out walking, drinking the bottle of water he'd felt obliged to buy. The heat wave had broken, but it was still hot. Hawaiian Gardens didn't have much to do with either Hawaii or gardens, block after block of apartment buildings and strip malls, a few dead cars on every block painted with dirt and plastered with Day-Glo *Notice to Remove* stickers. A bus smoked past, covered top to bottom and front to back with an ad for a movie, a grinning black man with a .9 millimeter that stretched ten feet.

The clerk at Ringside Liquors had given Jimmy a number from his files, three-by-five cards in a green shoebox, but Roy Pool's house was gone. Now a big ugly apartment building covered the space of four numbers.

But there was a neighbor, a sole survivor in a Spanish bungalow—they liked to call it *Mediterranean*—with peeling pink paint and a few yard-birds in even greater need of a touch-up. Jimmy knocked on the steel security door that ruined the look of the little house.

It took a long time, then an old lady answered. She never opened the steel mesh door, even after she saw that he was a nice young man, but she told him where to find Roy Pool, that he was "still kicking" as she said, though his house was long gone.

Capri Retirement Villa wasn't as grim as it could have been. The sidewalk out front was clean, the paint was fresh, and a pair of fluffy Boston ferns hung from hooks in the overhang out front. Somebody cared. Jimmy stopped by the desk, then came down the corridor and found the room.

At least he was awake. Everyone else was sleeping.

Roy Pool, who looked to be in his sixties but was probably older, sat in a wheelchair looking out the sliding glass door at the concrete "garden" in the middle of the four-sided nursing home. He wore silk pajamas with a scarf at the neck. The vintage bodybuilder magazine hidden under the desk at the Danko flight school was his.

"Hi."

He turned. "Hello."

"I'm Jimmy Miles. You're Mr. Pool?"

"Yes, I am."

"I'm an investigator. Can I ask you about Bill Danko?"

"What kind of investigator?"

"Private."

"My," Pool said.

He wheeled around to face his guest and looked him over, his eyes lingering on Jimmy's shoes, black suede loafers with silver diamond shapes across the top.

"This isn't for one of those television shows, is it? I detest television."

"I'll watch a ballgame every once in awhile," Jimmy said. "That's about it."

There were three or four old movie star pictures on the walls and a one-sheet for *Now, Voyager*. A magnolia blossom floated in fresh water in a globe that used to be a fishbowl. On the desk in a plain black frame was an eight-by-ten of a much younger Roy Pool, a dramatic, side-lit pose.

Pool saw Jimmy looking at it. "The older I get, the better-looking I was," he said.

At Pool's feet was a small oxygen bottle. He lifted the pale green mask to his mouth and inhaled, held it delicately with two fingers like the cigarettes he once smoked, which made this necessary now.

He took the mask away and exhaled. "So, who's your patron?"

"Elaine Kantke's daughter."

"Who apparently has never been told that The Past doesn't care what we think about it."

"What about the future?" Jimmy said.

"Cares even less," Pool said.

Jimmy straightened the photo on the desk. "You were Bill Danko's—"

"*Secretary.* There's nothing wrong with the word."

"I want to know if there was some connection to Rath-Steadman."

Roy Pool looked at Jimmy levelly for a long moment, then got out of the wheelchair and stepped over and closed the door.

"Not that anyone in this place can *hear* . . ."

He moved gracefully. Jimmy thought the word *queen* wasn't really such a pejorative. Pool dropped into the chair by the desk and crossed his legs at the knees and then lifted his face into the light angling in from the patio, as if he wanted Jimmy to remember exactly how he had looked when he told him what he was about to tell him.

"So, there was a connection between—"

Pool held up his hand.

Jimmy gave him his moment.

"One week before he was murdered, Mr. Danko—I always called him that although he would repeatedly ask me to call him 'Bill'—Mr. Danko took several important persons up one night to fly over the proposed site for an industrial park in the Inland Empire."

"At night?"

"There was a full moon." He gave Jimmy a look meant to squelch any further interruptions. "Among those passengers was Vasek Rath of Rath Aircraft and . . ."

He allowed a ridiculously long pause.

"*Red Steadman* of Steadman Industries . . ."

Pool let his wild revelation hang in the air a moment. He'd waited years to give this speech.

"Though, of course, Red Steadman had died some four years *previous* to that time, so how could that be?"

He looked Jimmy in the eye, ready for a challenge.

He wasn't going to get it.

"Mr. Steadman was wearing a disguise, but not a very good disguise," Pool concluded. "My point being that Mr. Danko that night saw something or realized something that he was not meant to, namely that the two companies were about to merge—and that Mr. Red Steadman had apparently *faked* his own death some years earlier."

He took another drag of bottled oxygen.

"Did *you* actually see them?" Jimmy asked.

"They left at midnight. Mr. Danko told me about it in great detail the next morning." Pool picked at something on the knee of his pajamas. "I should have bought some stock."

"Who else do you think he told?"

"The events that followed would suggest Mrs. Kantke." There was another theatrical pause. "And perhaps Michelle."

Pool waited to see if Jimmy knew the name.

"Espinosa," Jimmy said.

"Yes, eventually that would be her last name."

"They were still in touch? Michelle and Danko. Or was there something more?"

"Mr. Danko had a weakness for her."

"There was some evidence the actual killer was short," Jimmy said, just to see what would happen.

"Michelle *was* short."

"And so was Estella Danko."

Pool went a bit sad and sentimental. "And neither of them wanted anything other than Bill alive and loving them."

He corrected himself. "*Mr. Danko.*"

"You never testified?"

"No."

"Why?"

"No one asked. And, for a long time, I was quite peeved at that."

Here was another soul who wanted Jimmy to stay a little longer. Pool took a thick manila envelope from his bedside table, unwound the string closure and handed it over. Jimmy knew everything he needed to know, enough to pull him down further, make him feel that weight, that *compression* again, but he took the folder.

It was a file of clippings and pictures, like Jean's, which now had become his. There was a two-inch article about the drowning at Mothers' Beach in Marina del Ray. There was no clip about Tone Espinosa shot dead. The newspaper picture of Red Steadman in his prime was almost brown but time hadn't taken the hardness out of the boss's eye, that look the old man on the pier had remembered. That same look, softened only a little, had been in the eyes in the wax figure presiding over the boardroom at the Museum of Flight. Red Steadman.

And somewhere else. *In the now.*

---

Jean was out past the shore break. It was afternoon. She pulled hard on a concluding stroke and rolled onto her back with the last of the energy, gliding like a seal.

She watched her hands describing figure eights as she treaded water. The waves, from this far out, seen from behind, looked like hands pushing something away.

She looked skyward. There was a daylight moon, just risen.

White.

A perfect circle.

A communion wafer.

*Where did that come from?* She hadn't taken communion in ten years. She thought of the little church in Carmel, that afternoon, the way the candles weighted the air. *The Quick and The Dead.* That memory led her to another from long ago, a little girl—*four?*—with her mother in an Episcopal church in Long Beach in a straight wool coat, pink with pink buttons in a style like the one John John Kennedy had worn in the famous picture, and the hat, too, which she held in her hands because her mother was kneeling beside her. Suddenly there was a bird, a brown wren probably, something small and common, flying around the airy vault above the altar. There were a few other children and they began to laugh and Jean began to laugh with them until the adults got up from their knees.

Jean didn't remember what happened next. How odd that she wouldn't remember the ending.

A swell lifted her and she saw Jimmy on the beach.

She washed the salt out of her hair over the kitchen sink with a round striped pitcher.

"Have you been all right up here?" Jimmy said.

"I'm fine," she said.

She squeezed the water out of her hair with a kitchen towel and stepped closer to him.

She kissed him.

He wondered if she could feel the change in him.

He found a blue bottle of vodka in the freezer and poured an inch of it into a green glass and walked with it to the windows that tried to frame the ocean. He stood with his back to her. Far away, almost at the horizon, a sloop was passing, so far out it was flying a spinnaker. He waited. He felt himself going back to his life, back to *before,* back into himself, from wherever he had been with her. It felt like falling backwards. It felt like a plug being pulled. It hurt and was sad. If he wasn't a man, he would have howled like a dog.

There was a TV on the countertop, the first of the afternoon news shows, a brushfire somewhere, tanker helos dropping showers of red water. Jean watched it. The sound was low.

Jimmy still was looking out at the sea.

"One of The Jolly Girls, Vivian Goreck, still lives two doors down from your house," he said. "With her daughter, Lynne."

Jean remembered the picture, the four of them at the Yacht Club bar, starched white blouses and round pearlesque earrings the size of quarters.

"I remember her."

Something had changed in Jean, too, and he felt it. She had decided something. He didn't know what it was.

"She was pretty."

"Vivian Goreck bought ten thousand dollars' worth of Steadman stock in July of 1977, three weeks before the merger of Rath and Steadman. It was worth a hundred grand six months later. Today, it's two or three million."

"She's the one who ties this to the past?"

"One of the ones. Also her daughter. She's seeing your brother."

Jean nodded. She accepted it.

He was surprised that she *wasn't* surprised.

"My mother was killed because of stock?"

Jimmy told her about Roy Pool and the midnight flight of Vasek Rath and Red Steadman. He told it just the way Pool had told it, Bill Danko and some big shots, a man thought to be dead wearing a disguise, a famous man who'd apparently faked his own death for some reason.

"They needed a pilot too dumb to know what it meant. But Danko wasn't *that* dumb, or your mother wasn't. Danko probably told your mother. I don't know who she told. After the drunk flying thing, I guess Rath and Steadman knew Danko was a problem."

"Maybe Vivian and my father were having a thing."

"Maybe." It was something he'd thought of, too, something cued by one of Vivian Goreck's smiles. "Maybe *she's* the one who put that half smile on his face," Jimmy said.

"So who killed my mother and Bill Danko?" Jean said, too coolly.

"Nobody. Somebody in the shadows. Somebody who's probably dead now, too. Somebody short."

He kept his eyes on the water.

"So there it is. It's over. That's everything there is to know."

She nodded, whether she believed that lie or not.

"My father had a stroke, a small one," Jean said. "Half of his face was slightly paralyzed. Carey told me that, when I was at Stanford. I never knew. The jury thought he was smirking at them, too."

*There was always something else to learn.*

He still wasn't looking at her.

"Where is Carey's house?" she said. "You said he had a house and an apartment."

"Out on the point. Crown Road. It looks like a ship."

She went to him. She put her head against his back as he stood at the window.

"I have to go," he said.

"Why? Where are you going? Stay here."

Jimmy turned to face her. "I can't. But you should still stay here," he said.

She remembered his line, *this could all be over soon.*

"When are you coming back?" she said.

He told her he'd call her in the morning. She pulled him to her but he was somewhere else already.

"I'll call you," he said.

As he walked away, she looked at the television. A shimmering live shot of the daylight moon filled the frame, icy. The newscaster was saying, "Tonight Southlanders will witness a rare conjunction of folklore and science, a real live 'blue moon.'"

She heard Jimmy's voice out front, speaking to the guards, Angel's men.

"A blue moon—I'll bet you didn't know this Trish—a blue moon is two full moons in one month," the voice-over said. "It only happens once every eight or ten years. It looks like any other moon but this one seems to be bringing with it unusually high tides along our coastline."

She heard the Mustang start.

"Once in a blue moon . . ." the newscaster said.

# TWENTY-THREE

Angel was standing in the driveway in front of the garages when Jimmy came back from Malibu. It was dark already, the moon through the trees.

"Your Porsche is downtown," he said before Jimmy got out.

They both knew what all it meant.

Jimmy went in and took a long shower, changed clothes. He sat in the dining room and drank a glass of water. He'd looked at the blue revolver in the desk drawer in the office but closed it without taking it. *Who was he going to shoot?*

They drove out Sunset in Angel's pickup. It was a Thursday night but there was traffic, a rattle and hum in the air, people either driving fast or way too slow, sudden screeching U-turns in front of you, cars double-parked, as if everyone was off on his own trip.

Angel went south on Highland.

"Where'd you spend last night?"

Jimmy just shook his head.

"I called, came by," Angel said.

"I just rode around."

"Rode around."

"I ended up out at the beach."

"A sailor watching the sea."

"I'm all right," Jimmy said.

"Good," Angel said. "We'll see about *tomorrow.*"

They came south six more blocks.

The wave was breaking.

*Returning* . . .

Jimmy looked over as they passed the recording studio. *Clover.* The past was knocking him on his ass, had been for days now, since Big Sur. Old music kept going through his head. On every other street corner he saw a memory in bright relief, a piece of a scene, in daylight or dark, played at double speed, or half.

There was the razor wire around the roof. They used to go up there, on the roof, smoke and look out over low Hollywood.

He was on the roof with _____ one night at the end of a session and the singer said he'd give Jimmy a ride back to the Chateau Marmont. Jimmy didn't have a car but in those days you didn't need one if you looked right, if you were in on the joke, in on the big idea they'd all just that summer discovered. 1969. You stood by the side of the road looking the way you looked and someone would stop and you'd get where you wanted to go, particularly if you didn't much care where you went.

This night it was _____.

But they hadn't gone back to the Chateau Marmont but to three or four houses instead, up in Laurel Canyon and, even though it was four in the morning by then, all the way out to Topanga. There was downstairs cocaine for everybody who came by and upstairs coke for the famous people and their friends, even their new friends. His mother was gone, off on location again. No one was waiting up for him.

The singer came through the room, said some of them were leaving for the desert, to ride horses. And peyote.

Jimmy told him he'd see him tomorrow night at Clover.

He had talked for hours with a girl who'd been to Morocco but he was alone on the deck when the new sun broke over the ridgeline and lit up the head of a royal palm across the canyon, as suddenly as if fire was involved.

Angel drove, low in the seat, his arm on the armrest between them. Now they were down in South Central. Angel wasn't afraid of any part of L.A. so they were on surface streets. Black men sat on the fenders of cars parked in front of houses with barred windows but nice little yards, one of those TV news neighborhoods where the mothers put their children to bed in the bathtubs some nights in fear of gunfire.

Jimmy dropped his window. Angel reached over and turned off the A.C.

"I used to live down here, block west of Normandie," Angel said.

There was vague music from multiple sources. Angel drove slowly, out of respect for the people who lived there. The streets were concrete with a bead of black tar in the expansion joints. The truck's tires thumped rhythmically, like a heartbeat, another kind of music. They slipped past one bungalow, all blue-lit inside, just as the front door came open, letting out an explosion of television laughter. A woman stepped onto the porch and called out something to the men. Two of them had a pit bull spread-legged on the hood of a Buick Regal, slapping it in the face every time it thought to move.

"Her father is a Sailor," Jimmy said.

He hadn't said anything since Highland, since Angel had asked him where he spent the night.

"I thought maybe it was headed that way," Angel said. "How did you find out?"

"I saw him. Palos Verdes. A house his son owns. I saw him kiss a young woman, the daughter of one of The Jolly Girls. She looks just like the mother did then."

Angel nodded.

It was a Sailor thing, you drove the car you drove then or would like to have driven. You lived in the house you lived in then, if you could. And you tried to find a new version of the girl you loved then.

"How much are you going to tell her?" Angel said.

"Not much. There's not much I can tell her without telling her everything."

"Maybe she already knows."

Jimmy shook his head.

"I don't think so."

"He was living here all along, ten miles away? And you think she didn't know? She just happened to find an investigator who was a Sailor, too?"

Jimmy didn't answer it. He'd asked himself the question enough. None of it was important to him anymore. None of it would make any difference.

He would just let the wave break.

"How much longer did you think you could wait before you told her what was up with you?"

"Longer," Jimmy said.

They rode another block. An ice truck came past. *Hollywood Ice.* Angel turned left on Exposition to head downtown. His rough leather-bound Bible on the dash started to slide sideways.

Angel put a hand on it to stop it.

"I wish I had what you have," Jimmy said.

"What's that?"

"Believing that everything is part of the plan."

"Me or you believing it isn't what makes it true," Angel said.

They drove under the Harbor Freeway toward downtown and something else came to Jimmy, something else he should have seen before. That he was the same age as the kid Drew that daybreak in Topanga Canyon, the morning of the last day of his life.

---

The alley was a dead end. Jimmy's black Porsche sat, top down, dead center in the circle of light an old-fashioned incandescent streetlight threw.

It looked like what it was, bait in a trap.

They got out of the truck. The key was in the ignition. The Porsche was clean. There weren't even any fingerprints on the glass. It was as if someone had wiped it down just minutes before they arrived.

It was almost eleven o'clock. There were a few homeless people but no Sailors. And this wasn't where the Walkers lived. Downtown was *real* Sailor territory, too hardcore for anybody but the strong ones.

Drew had come right down into the middle of the darkest version of the Sailor world.

Or been *brought* to it.

There was shuffling in the shadows. A man in a peacoat and watch cap. He said nothing and barely looked at Jimmy. He finished his cigarette and dropped it at his feet and stepped back into the deeper darkness without lifting his eyes again.

Jimmy turned to look at Angel, who stood beside his truck.

"Why not?" Jimmy said.

# TWENTY-FOUR

"Hello, sweetheart," Jack Kantke said.

The wind off the water stirred the flame-vine over the door. The night air was cool. He stood in the doorway in a white short-sleeve shirt over black beltless slacks and black oxfords. There was a cigarette in his hand. The smoke curled up his arm.

He had aged. But not enough.

"Hello," Jean said.

"Come in."

The view through the floor-to-ceiling windows in the living room was of the ocean crossed by the light of the full moon. The large room was sparsely furnished with a nautical theme. There was a loud ticking from an unseen clock.

And a real live Jolly Girl stood in the middle of the room. Or so it seemed. The hair, the eyes, the heels, the sawed off pants they used to call *Capri*. Lynn Goreck smiled politely at Jean, her hands clasped in front of her.

Jean sat in a chair.

Her father sat across from her.

Lynne leaned on the arm of Jack Kantke's chair, her hand on his shoulder, a possessive.

"Would you like anything?" he said.

Jean shook her head.

"Could you get me some water," he said to Lynne.

The girl gave him a flip look and stepped away.

Jean couldn't stop staring at her father.

"You saw me someplace, didn't you?" he said.

She realized for the first time that he was very moved at seeing her. He looked as if he was about to cry.

"A year ago," Jean said. "I was down at Balboa Island. I saw Carey. I thought he was still living in Arizona. I followed him. I was about to go up to him—"

"And you saw me."

Lynne came back with a glass of water, no ice. She set it down on the arm of his chair. Kantke looked at her, a look meant to send her away. She turned and left the room.

"She's Vivian's daughter?" Jean said when she was gone.

Kantke nodded.

"I've been waiting for you to come see me," he said.

"So Vivian knows? About you?"

He shook his head. "She wouldn't understand," he said. "She thinks Lynne is involved with your brother. Vivian's never seen me." Kantke looked over at the doorway Lynne had stepped through. "I've found people of your generation more accepting of something like this," he said.

He smiled that half smile.

"Or maybe she just thinks I'm insane."

The ticking continued. Kantke looked at the source, a large ship's clock on the wall, then back at Jean.

"I didn't kill your mother," he said.

They both listened to the clock. Jean didn't let him off, offered nothing to help him.

"You look so much like her," he said and it caught in his throat. "It's not easy, seeing you."

She said nothing.

He stood, stood over her for a moment. He seemed as tall, for a moment, as a father seems to a child.

"I don't know what your investigator has told you . . ."

She waited.

He stepped over to the windows, walked toward his reflection, considering it from head to toe. It would not have surprised Jean if he had walked through the glass into the night, leaving the reflection to come forward to speak to her.

He stopped at the glass.

"How'd you find a detective who was a Sailor?"

"What does that mean?"

"It's what we call ourselves."

"How long have you known I had someone looking into this?"

The way he smiled—she could see his face in the glass—made her wonder what powers he might have, how much he knew, what he could do, what *they* could do.

"I saw him on the bluff, yesterday, watching the house," he said.

"How did you know that he was—"

"We can spot each other. What has he told you?"

"Not very much. Nothing about *this*."

"How could he, once he was in love with you?"

He still looked out at the water, like Jimmy in Malibu.

"Maybe you should explain it to me."

He took a cigarette from one pocket and a gold lighter from the other and lit it.

"Death," he said, with the tone of voice fathers use to explain things to their children, "doesn't end everything. Not always. Sometimes something is unfinished in a life and this happens. Someone is left behind until the unfinished thing is finished."

He turned to look at her.

"I was executed. They buried my body. A few days later, I was walking the streets again."

She could walk out the door, but she didn't. She met him where he was, continued in the scene as if he'd just said he'd been sick, been treated, rose up off his sickbed, healed. In that way she surprised herself more than he'd surprised her. She felt very strong. *So this was the kind of knowledge that made you stronger.*

"Is that what's been left unfinished," Jean asked, "this business about Mother?"

"I don't know," he said. "We never know what it is."

He blew out smoke. "It's not like we hear voices from the clouds, telling us what to do. There are rules. We just don't know what they are."

He smiled. But then it was gone. He walked back to his chair and picked up the glass and drank the water, all of it. He looked at the big clock again, seemed as if he had things to do, places to go. He put down the glass and stepped closer and stood over her again, casting a shadow over her, as he meant.

"You've inadvertently threatened some powerful people," he said. "I'm worried about you."

"They were responsible for Mother's murder."

"It was a long time ago. It doesn't matter anymore."

"But it's true, isn't it?"

"It was a long time ago, Jeanie."

"They killed a woman who was living in the house," Jean said. "Bill Danko's daughter. They're killing people *now*."

Kantke lifted a hand to stop her.

"There are killings every day, every week, every year for a thousand years in all directions. You have to stop this, sweetheart."

He looked at the clock again. "You should go. Go back to the house at Point Dume. You'll be safe there. They won't follow you out of the city. This all will be over soon."

Jean stood, but not to leave.

"Why? What do you mean? What happens now?"

He held out his hand to her, pulled her close to him. With his touch, the *reality* of it hit her, unreal as it was. She felt as if someone had pulled the plug on her power source. She was in free fall. Maybe now the floor beneath her would open up and she'd fall through to some other unthinkable *other* world. Long seconds passed to the ticking of the ship's clock.

"I remember your aftershave," she said in his arms.

"Aqua Velva," he said. "Your mother always hated it."

Kantke held her tightly, as if he would never see her again, breathing in her scent, his eyes on the round moon out the window, which looked like the head of a hammer.

Now *she* had a secret.

# TWENTY-FIVE

The shadows where the man in the peacoat and watch cap had been led to a canyon between buildings, a grid of alleyways, unpeopled. Jimmy and Angel walked straight ahead, not following the man, who was out of sight, but just going the only way there was to go. As they stepped past one intersecting alley suddenly there was light from above, like a spotlight, the full moon in a wedge of sky.

Ahead was an abandoned building, an old factory from the looks of it with a loading dock ramp and painted-out windows. A sliding iron door stood open.

"I guess all this is part of the plan," Jimmy said. "*Somebody's* plan."

Inside the shell of the factory, five Sailors stood in a rhombus of moonlight cast onto the floor from a skylight, all of them pulsing blue, more strongly than before.

They parted.

There was Drew in his blue snowboarder's cap, sitting on the floor. The Sailors seemed to enjoy the drama of the reveal. Others of them appeared behind Jimmy and Angel to block their exit.

It wasn't necessary, Jimmy and Angel were already resigned to what would come next. The Sailors surrounded them and Drew, took them by the upper arms and they set out.

They went down ten steps into an underground passageway, a corridor lined on three sides with asbestos-covered pipes. As they walked—it could have been a half mile—the passageway shuddered sometimes, probably trucks passing overhead. You would have expected to see rats but there weren't any. They would have been welcome.

"I gotta say, man," Drew said to Jimmy as they were hustled along, "I thought you and your people were messed up, but these people are *really* messed up."

One of the Sailors shoved him forward.

Drew yanked his arm away. "Back off! We're going!"

He looked at Jimmy. "*Where* are we going?"

Jimmy knew but there was no reason to tell him.

They came to an elevator. Old, brass. They rode up, eight of them crammed into the space.

Drew said, "Everybody's getting real jumpy. Something's about to happen, right?"

Jimmy just watched the numbers.

"Yes, but not here," he said. "This is something else."

The elevator doors opened onto a landing. They were pushed through a pair of heavy doors.

It was a courtroom.

Jimmy and Angel had never been here but they knew about it. They were on the top floor of the old Hall of Justice, a Gothic granite block on Spring Street across West First from the modern Criminal Justice Building that replaced it. Everywhere across L.A. Sailors were in control of abandoned places, of spaces like this, for whatever purposes. A part of the night was theirs and there were enough of them to assure its continuance.

The courtroom echoed with the sound of a dog barking incessantly, sharp, regular. Clocks covered the tall paneled walls, clocks of all sizes and shapes, *named* clocks from banks and long-closed businesses: square, round, octagonal, all running at different speeds, some backwards, some very slow, like clocks in hell, and some too fast to watch, hands spinning like knives.

Drew was scared, or just creeped out.

"Anybody know what time it is?"

Jimmy seized him by the front of his shirt. "They can't do anything to us," he said. "Nothing that really matters. Remember that."

He let the kid go.

"Whoa," Drew said.

The barking continued, unbroken, like a metronome. Drew narrowed his eyes to look into the shadows. The hanging lights high above them were dim, half of the bulbs burned out. Shutters covered the tall windows on the west wall, keeping the light in. The wooden seats had been ripped out, stacked in the back, but the high bench remained at the front of the courtroom.

A collection of Sailors, twenty or thirty of them, milled about the room or leaned against the walls. Here there were some women, too, though they wore the same clothes as the men and most of their sex had been taken from them, or let go. Their eyes bore the same open yet dead look as the men, a look that might come to the rest of us from staring at great distances for long hours.

They all pulsed blue, as blue as blue could be.

"Somebody oughta do something about that dog," Drew said.

"It ain't a dog," Angel told him.

Jimmy's eyes were on something else, *someone*. A woman, the only woman in the room in a dress, though it was a shabby one with faded roses.

*Rosemary Danko.* Alive.

She stood before the high bench, looking up at it.

Jimmy started off across the room toward her.

"Who is she?" Drew said.

Angel said, "I think somebody from one of Jimmy's cases. But she was supposed to be dead, killed a few days ago."

"She's one of us?"

"No. Look at her." She *wasn't* wrapped in the blue.

Rosemary was still staring at the judge's bench, a smile on her face, when Jimmy touched her on the shoulder.

She turned to look at him. "I knew you'd be in on this, sooner or later," she said. She turned her attention back to the bench and the big clock behind it, the only one in the room that showed the real time.

It was a quarter to midnight.

"Tell me what happened," Jimmy said.

"I looked up and they were there, just like you," she said, "a short one and a tall one. They had a lot of questions, just like you, and then they took me out of there. The tall one with red hair started that fire on our way out. We rode in a car over to Garden Grove. It was dark, after the news."

She was still looking at the high bench. It was the old style of courtroom, the kind that still ends up in movies, though the justice system has moved on to blond Formica and low tables and "theater seating."

There was a wooden chair beside the bench. Maybe there'd be a last-minute witness in the case, a quick wrap-up, surprising, yet the only thing that could have happened.

"What did they do to you?" Jimmy said.

"They could have killed me quick but they just kept asking questions."

The big hand on the big clock jumped, a minute.

"I guess *now* is when they're going to kill me," Rosemary said.

"Nobody's going to kill you," Jimmy said. But he wasn't so sure.

She stepped up and sat in the witness chair. She leaned over to look at her feet on the footrest, ran her hands over the dark worn wood of the arms.

She raised her right hand.

The barking stopped.

Rosemary laughed, thinking she'd caused it.

There was silence in the room now, only the whirring of the clocks. The peacoats as one had turned toward her but it was not because of her.

A door had opened behind her, the door beneath the biggest clock, the only one that told the right time.

Angel and Drew came up to stand behind Jimmy.

Los Angeles still existed, the *regular* world, wrapped in its regularity and regulations, laws and principalities. It was just outside, down at street level. A cab on Alameda, street people in doorways, Salvadorans a block over getting off a Greyhound, Japanese tourists lifting food to their mouths in the glass restaurant atop the Otani five blocks away, laughter in The Jonathan Club, Dodger Stadium a half mile away.

The regular world was still out there, *alive.*

But this, starting *now,* starting here, was something else.

The first through the door was Boney M, tall, red hair.

Next was a very short man built like a boxer, a prison boxer, a man in his fifties, gang-tattooed, Mexican.

Angel looked at Jimmy.

"You know him?" Jimmy said.

"*Perversito,*" was the answer. Little Evil.

There was a moment when the doorway was empty and then Red Steadman stepped in. He wore a brown suit, white shirt, tie, very chairman of the board. He was a huge man, six-five, barrel-chested and heavy in that way men used to be.

Here was the familiar big man in the back of the Lincoln at the end of the chase in Griffith Park.

He stepped to the front so they could all see him.

He filled his bull chest with air. His blue aura was faded, old, but intense in its own way.

He seemed, in this moment, their king.

Rosemary Danko, still in the witness chair, the only wholly live person in the room, trembled pitifully at the sight of Red Steadman and the others. She knew who they were. Here were her *airplane people,* in the flesh. Or some version of it.

She stepped down off the stand.

She got as far away from them as she could in the room.

Steadman fixed his eyes on Jimmy. Jimmy remembered old man Kirk's line about his former boss: *He'd definitely tear you a new one if you looked at him wrong.* What unfinished business had cast *him* here? He was such a ruler it was hard to imagine him in a personal way, to picture his family, a naked moment, a love in his life beyond the things he built.

He stared at Jimmy. It was hard not to shake.

"There's a price for defiance," Steadman said.

There was an ugly sound from the Sailors.

"Tie their legs," Steadman ordered.

The closest peacoats seized Jimmy and Angel and Drew.

"Not him," Steadman said. He meant Drew.

"He's with us," Jimmy said. The men were already wrapping duct tape around his ankles, around Angel's ankles.

"We'll see," Steadman said.

It was called *Clocking.* Ropes came out from somewhere and the peacoats threw them over the light fixtures and knotted them and took the ends and threaded them through Jimmy's and Angel's ankles.

"Tight, so they won't get loose," Steadman said. "Let them spend the night *here.*" It sounded like the worst kind of threat.

They strung them up upside down.

The ghouls now started shoving Jimmy and Angel, hanging that way, until they were swinging from one end of the courtroom to the other, in separate arcs, hung from separate light fixtures.

Drew watched.

Rosemary cowered in the farthest corner.

Jimmy and Angel bent at the waist to keep their heads from dragging on the floor. The peacoats would shove hard each time a man came by until Jimmy and Angel were crashing into the walls.

Jimmy slammed into the big clock over the bench. It fell, shattered, but the scattered pieces kept spinning.

*Then the clocks stopped.*

All of them.

As Jimmy and Angel still swung back and forth, the peacoats all turned to watch the dozens of clock faces on the walls as now, slowly, they synchronized, zeroing, going to midnight.

Out the open window, the moon had just turned full, a specific moment none of us could see or sense, but they could.

The room began to empty.

"Take the boy," Steadman shouted.

Sailors surrounded Drew and dragged him away toward the elevator.

Steadman exited through the door behind the bench with his men and then they were alone in the hollow room, Jimmy and Angel, the pendulums centering.

No one had touched Rosemary. They were going to let her live. When she realized that, she made her own way toward an exit.

As Jimmy and Angel pulled themselves up, grasping at their ropes . . .

*Tick.*

The clocks as one recorded a minute lost, a minute after midnight, the beginning of what was called *The Day.*

The last day for some of them.

# TWENTY-SIX

A crab, just a pair of ragged claws, scuttled across the surface of the moon reflected in an oily pool.

Rats scurried over broken glass. The air stank.

You came in this way: There was a pipe, on its side, an immense section of pipe tall enough to walk through standing up—and three peacoats now walked through it—a gateway through the sawgrass that rimmed the last remaining acres of wetlands of Long Beach.

It was after one.

"I hate these last hours," Jimmy said.

Angel, in spite of himself, felt his own spirit dropping. It was all converging, and it was all about death. He spoke a prayer in his head, the words echoing there as if he'd said them aloud: *Lord, just let me see Your face.* He wanted to be strong. Clear. Sure. The one the others depended upon. They all hated this time, when it came round again, *the blue moon,* for all the pressure, the insecurity it brought, the questions it threw at them. They even hated it for what was at its core, the promise or the *threat* of resolution.

The tide was coming in. Before them was a wasteland of flotsam and jetsam, of abandoned boats, of bleached logs, of weather-battered and sea-battered squares of plywood, of hundreds of big and little chunks of Styrofoam reflecting white in the light of all that moon, looking like bones strewn across a cemetery after a flood.

"There's a fire up there," Angel said.

They were closing in on the hull of a rusted tuna boat, big as a gas station, at a wrong angle, listing in a sea of mud and grass. Fire flickered in the broken-out windows.

They were looking for Drew.

"I don't get this," Angel said. "Why'd they do this?"

"They just want to mess with us."

As they slogged forward, they came upon a body floating face down, a peacoat, arms outstretched, the dead man float. Angel lifted him by the collar. He was alive. Angel yanked him out of the muck, holding him by the collar like something foul.

The man coughed his thanks.

"I know you, Brother," he said, like a punch line.

Angel deposited him in a derelict turquoise speedboat. The man sputtered and then grasped the wheel, as if heading out for a day on the lake.

"*Get me out of here,*" Jimmy said.

A few faces appeared. Fifty or more of them lived down here, who feared the downtown, not Walkers, but who didn't have it together enough to be of use to the powerful Sailors. Or maybe they were just waiting like everybody else and liked the water, even this brackish swamp. They lived in houses made of boat wreckage, cabins from cruisers stripped of their hulls or shacks of plywood built in where the grass was tallest, to hide them. Some had put a few boats seaworthy enough to cruise out to fish in the dark. Some of them now stood in front of their shacks, watching without much feeling as Jimmy and Angel passed.

They reached the stern of the tuna boat where the fire burned. There were crude steps made out of oil drums stuck into the mud. Jimmy and Angel stepped up them, though the bow of the boat was almost afloat with the rising tide, shifting, moving underfoot.

They crossed the canted deck and went down into the hold. Below, the fire burned in another oil drum, black smoke rising through a rusted out gap in the overhead. The space was empty but there were rough sounds, men's voices, from the next chamber.

The boat shifted. The oil drum fire slid sideways. Angel danced out of its way.

In that next chamber they found three men beating a kid. Jimmy saw a flash of blue, Drew's snowboarder's cap. He pulled away one of the men as Angel slammed another against the bulkhead. The third man struck the kid two more times and then stood up.

The kid said, "OK. All right."

It was some other kid.

Jimmy yanked him to his feet.

"Where did you get the cap? Where is he?"

"I don't know, man," the kid said. "What difference does it make? He was here. Now he's gone. Who are you?"

Jimmy snatched the snowboarder's cap off the kid's head. The boat shifted again. Angel fell against the steel wall. Something crashed down behind them.

"Let's get out of here," Angel said.

The tuna boat was fully afloat though still heeled over onto its side when they came back out onto the deck into the stinking air.

"Maybe they already took him on board," Jimmy said.

There were people all around the tuna boat now, wading up to their chests some of them, others trying to make use of the wrecked boats that still floated. A pregnant woman, full and round in her rags, sat in a Zodiac as a man waded beside her, hand on the gunwale, hauling the boat tenderly, as if she were Mary on the donkey.

They all moved in the same direction across the wetlands.

"What time is it?" Jimmy said.

"*There*," Angel said. "Your guys."

Across the watery grasslands, the bad-joke Sailors Lon and Vince slogged through, dragging Drew with them.

They were in water up to their knees and easy to catch.

Jimmy pulled Drew away from Vince, the shorter one, and knocked down Lon, the tall one.

Drew wore a peacoat and watch cap now. Jimmy yanked at the lapel of Drew's coat.

"They put this on you?"

"We didn't do nothing," Vince said.

"He did it," Lon said.

"They said if I was with them I could go home," Drew said.

Jimmy dragged him away.

"They lied," he said.

Lon came back after him. Jimmy grabbed him by the back of the neck and shoved him facedown into the tide and held him there until his legs stopped kicking.

Angel pulled Jimmy's hand away.

Lon surfaced, sucking in air again.

Vince half thought of coming after Angel. Angel hit him in the face for it, three quick blows, dropping him backwards into the water beside Lon.

"So this is where—" Drew began. It was like he was stoned.

"No," Jimmy said.

"Come on," Angel said.

And so Jimmy and Angel and Drew fell in with the others, moving like an arrow, all of them, in the landscape of refuse and nature, men and women, the moon reflected a hundred times in scattered shards of water. A wider, higher view would show their destination five-miles distant across the wetlands and then across the sculpted landscaping and empty parking lots of the Long Beach harbor.

There, lit like a cathedral, *The Queen Mary*.

# TWENTY-SEVEN

Angel looked at the sky as they moved up the gangway. There was a little breeze. It was cool in that off-the-water way. A few clouds were crossing the moon.

Tonight it almost was blue.

"Beautiful night," Angel said. He looked at Jimmy. "And it'll be a good day tomorrow, whatever comes."

Jimmy nodded, but didn't look like a believer.

Not everything in the Sailor world had a name but this was called *The Hour*. It came—it was not an hour but a *moment*, a click of the clock— when the blue moon was at its zenith.

It would come tonight at forty-seven minutes after three.

The Hour had a certain formality to it, a ceremonial air, nothing handed down from on high but a man-designed affair which had become this over time. Or so the older Sailors said. They could have been lying or simply had it wrong. Theirs was not a *holy* order. A few Sailors were on the decks, leaning over the railing as people will do, smoking, watching the others. Some strolled the promenade deck, arm in arm. Others were just arriving. Everyone knew not to come too early so they all tended to appear at once, when the hour changed, when the last hour came.

The long iron gangway that during the day carried tourists onto the haunted black and white ship now carried the wetlands people, the people from The Pipe, the moody Sailors from downtown, regular citizens, the powerful from on high and the weakest of the weak.

All but the Walkers, who no longer knew to come, to hope.

As they stepped onto the gangway, some removed their peacoats and watch caps, threw them in a pile as if they'd never need them again. Underneath, some wore period clothes, clothes from their specific time, polyester from the seventies, denim from the sixties, a few ancient Sailors in wool suits who at least looked like they belonged on the *Queen*

*Mary.* Some, like the people from the wetlands, walked in in that stunned, doomed way, but others were treating it like a holiday. Inside there would even be Sailors in festive costume as if putting on some other guise would better prepare them for what was to come.

At the end of the gangway, an officer greeted them, or at least a man in an officer's uniform. He nodded to each man or woman as they stepped aboard and checked his watch from time to time, a large gold pocket watch.

The pregnant woman from The Pipe stepped forward on the arm of her man. A gentleman in a cutaway tuxedo, vest, and striped trousers, certainly the oldest among them all, tipped his hat and gave a little bow. The woman blushed at the attention. The night had already become unreal and otherworldly, even for them.

The welcoming officer stopped the pregnant woman.

She wasn't a Sailor.

The man with her protested but without much conviction because he knew the rules. She waited where she was and her "husband" went aboard without her, looking back once. She picked up his watch cap where he had dropped it.

More cars were pulling into the parking lot. Some were big, expensive. The custom was to leave the keys in the ignitions, the doors unlocked. Whoever was left when it was over could take what they wanted.

A security car arrived. An excited guard jumped out almost before the car stopped rolling. He pushed his way into the middle of the Sailors, wide-eyed at the improbability of it all.

"Who are you? What is this?"

What did he expect to hear? A *prom*?

A hand touched the excited guard's shoulder.

It was Connor. In uniform.

"It's a private party," the cop said.

The security guard started to protest.

"It's all right," Connor said calmly. "We're here."

The guard went away.

Jimmy and Angel were about to board when Jimmy saw Jean.

She was at the mouth of the gangway. Waiting, watching.

Jimmy went down the ramp to her, against the stream of Sailors boarding.

"You have to go," he said.

"What is this?"

The clouds passed off the moon. The light brightened.

"I can't explain it," Jimmy said. "And you can't see it."

He started away.

"Is my father here?" Jean said.

He stopped. He was ten steps past her. He looked at her.

"I talked to him," she said. "Tonight."

"What did he tell you?"

Jimmy didn't want to know, but it was the next thing to say.

"That he didn't kill my mother." She waited a moment. "And *what this is.*"

He felt as if she was suddenly across the widest ocean.

"Go back to the beach house," he said.

"I'm coming aboard."

"No."

Angel stepped up. "It's time," he said.

"You can't be here," Jimmy said to Jean.

"*Tell her,*" he said to Angel and walked away from her.

"Go home," Angel said. "He doesn't want you hurt."

Angel went after Jimmy.

She followed after them.

"I'm coming aboard," she said. She caught up. "I'm coming aboard," she said again.

The officer on deck put out a hand to stop Jean.

"You know she can't come aboard," he said.

Jimmy shoved him back out of the way. *Let her see it.*

---

The three of them entered the grand ballroom, a tall Deco space with funereal elegance. There were multiple levels where once there had been cocktail tables or roulette wheels. An enormous crystal chandelier hung over their heads.

The room was filled with Sailors. They stood in clusters, among friends, waiting. Scott the bartender was there, Krisha, the woman doctor who treated Drew, one of Angel's bodybuilder friends, Connor.

*And Perversito.*

*And Boney M.*

*And Lon and Vince.*

The old man in the tuxedo played an out-of-tune grand piano, the bad notes giving the scene the feel of a cheap dance hall somewhere or a wake.

The room was ablaze in blue light.

Jimmy held Jean's arm. She pulled away from him and set off on her own to find her father.

Jimmy just watched her go.

"Three minutes," Angel said.

There was an ornate clock. *Very English.* It ticked loudly enough to be heard over the voices and the music.

"Just stay with us," Jimmy said to Drew as they moved back through the crowd. "Just do what we do and watch." He remembered the first blue moon, when *he* was a kid and went from knowing everything to knowing nothing.

Drew did as he was told, fell in behind Jimmy and Angel as they moved through the clusters of Sailors. The room was almost howling now in anticipation, pulsing like a blue cloud somehow captured in a room, like a storm in a box. The tuxedo man played louder and louder to be heard over the growing din, lifting his curled fingers in great dramatic gestures with each chord.

"Does this just keep getting weirder and weirder?" Drew said as they moved through it.

Jimmy looked at him. "It's beautiful."

Jimmy kept going.

Angel put an arm around the boy. "It's a *little* weird," he said.

Jimmy saw Jean with her father, talking, close. So there he was, just like the picture from the *Press Telegram,* the narrow black tie, the white shirt, the gray suit. *The half smile.*

Before he thought about what he was doing, Jimmy charged up to them and threw Jack Kantke against the wall. Jimmy's anger wasn't at Kantke and Kantke's anger wasn't at him but neither man cared in the moment, they both just wanted to tear something apart.

Kantke threw a punch. Jimmy avoided it and shoved him back into a glass cabinet, shattering it. Kantke recovered and came after him and Jimmy knocked him down onto the bed of broken glass.

Jimmy ripped the leg off of a table. He stood over Kantke. He raised the club.

The ticking grew louder and louder as the piano fought it.

Angel seized Jimmy's arm. Jean screamed.

Peacoats arrived and pulled Jimmy away from Kantke.

Red Steadman was behind them, dressed as an admiral. With him were Boney M and Little Evil, but it was Steadman himself who seized Jimmy by the neck, lifted him off his feet.

*"Not here!"* he yelled into Jimmy's face.

But then the ornate clock chimed.

The ship's bells began to sound.

Steadman released Jimmy.

Kantke got to his feet.

Jean stepped back.

*The men and women on the floor lifted their hands.*

Angel took Drew's hand in his and lifted it.

"What?" Drew said.

The piano player stood, lifted his hands.

*Was it praise or surrender?*

Jimmy looked at Jean. She was terrified.

He closed his eyes and raised his hands.

Steadman raised his hands.

The ship's bells ceased.

There was stunning silence, the silence at the end of the world.

Someone started crying.

The blue pulsed so brightly it hurt the eyes.

And then, as one, as if there was no time in the world, as if there was no *Now,* only *Always,* all in the room *spoke a line,* as one . . .

*"Come The Flood, we will say goodbye to flesh and blood . . ."*

Jimmy's voice could be heard.

Angel's voice, loud and prayerful.

Steadman, rough, impatient, chafing at obedience.

Drew, repeating the line a half beat late.

The room hummed with expectation.

There was a long, hollow moment . . .

## THE LAST MINUTE OF ETERNITY

And then a man collapsed where he stood.

And then another.

And then the man who had brought the pregnant woman, falling dead away.

*All in, twenty or more of them.*

Drew watched them fall.

And then there were no more. "Whoa," he said.

Jimmy opened his eyes.

*It was over.*

He scanned the room. There was Angel, still on his feet, tears in his eyes. Scott. Krisha. Connor.

Steadman.

Behind him, Jean knelt over her father's body. *He was gone.*

Jimmy went to her, leaned over and put a hand on her back. She looked up at him.

She shook her head. Sometimes what you have to do is walk away. She got up. He didn't try to stop her as she pushed through the others, left them all behind.

The piano man began again, a tune that started out sad, and those who remained began to tend to the bodies around them, crumpled forms in the clothes they last wore living.

# TWENTY-EIGHT

As first light came, a fishing boat with no name rode the swells of the gray water off Long Beach, well out from the shipping lanes. Jimmy and Angel and Drew were at the rails, steadying themselves as the boat climbed and fell. The engines idled and the captain tried to keep it headed into the wind but the ride was rough.

Steadman was forward, directing several peacoats bearing the first of the bodies, strapped with weights, wrapped for sea burial in unbleached cloth. As the bearers carried a body by, every man on deck reached out a hand to touch it. Drew did as the others did. He was back in his blue cap. Then the body was lowered over the side, sucked down feetfirst with hardly a sound.

As the peacoats went forward for the next, Angel and Drew went with them to help. There was a truce now, for this.

Steadman came to Jimmy.

"You know you won't stop me," he said. "Even with everything you know, you still don't understand, do you?"

Jimmy didn't answer him.

"We'll win," Steadman said. "We will win."

"You probably already have," Jimmy said.

Angel and Drew and the peacoats came back with another wrapped body. Jimmy reached out to touch it.

Steadman blessed it, too, but left his eyes on the breathing man before him.

# TWENTY-NINE

Jimmy was on the rooftop patio of Jean's apartment. It was clear with one of those once- or twice- or three-times-a-year views, all the way to Catalina. The traffic below on Sunset was heavy but the sound was reassuring, people in motion, full of purpose, everything shiny and bright and clean.

Jean came out with a bottle of water. Jimmy cracked the seal and took a drink.

"Do you believe in heaven?" she said.

He took another drink.

"No," he said, "but I believe in a whole bunch of places they've never given a name to."

She smiled and walked to the railing.

"It really is over with your father," Jimmy said behind her.

She nodded.

She turned to face him.

"When you said that you can't know everything, I guess this was what you meant."

He looked at her. "At the time I think just meant . . . *generally.*"

She wasn't close to him.

"So you just wait . . . for the next blue moon?"

*Their* story was over. At least for now. They both knew it.

"Nah, we were just kidding about all that," he said and tried a smile.

"I'm moving," she said. "To San Francisco."

He nodded.

"Maybe, after awhile . . ." She trailed off. He didn't help her finish the sentence.

"I have something for you," she said.

She went into the apartment and came back with something closed in her hand. She stood in front of him. She opened her hand.

It was a glass bottle, perfume in a functional but elegant glass bottle. He took it. It was a beautiful color.

"It's what your mother wore," Jean said. "They don't make it anymore. I had it synthesized. The scent was still on her dress in the case."

He took her hand.

"Maybe this will help you remember her," she said.

# THIRTY

Jimmy whipped away the cover—like a magician!—On the last car in the garage. It was a snow white 1969 Chrysler 400 convertible with white leather interior, with three-foot fins and what the lowriders called monster whitewalls, though his mother certainly never called them that.

It was her last car and Jimmy rode with the top down and good music on the radio over to Hollywood and then down to the 10 past Parker Center and Union Station, the sky still full on blue, and holding, in daylight, the diminishing moon.

Some days people are happy. There wasn't any explaining it but today people were happy. They waved at the sight of the huge white car, big as a boat. Jimmy wore a light green jacket that looked like '69, like a college man in '69, and they were happy with him, too.

He waved back.

The traffic broke open, as it always did, just past San Bernardino, the long hill up to the wide-place-in-the-road town called Beaumont. Jimmy stopped for a Coke at a drive-in. He always stopped at the same place. It was usually only twice a month but the high school girl there knew him and the Mexican boys who did the cooking knew the car.

He sat on the red-enameled picnic bench out front. It was over a hundred and yet there was snow on the mountains behind them.

*California*.

The desert road, Highway 62, curved away from the Interstate just past Palm Springs, four-lane but wide open, the exit curving and canted so perfectly that at high speed it was like banking in a plane. Ahead, a pass through the mountains, into the high desert, through valleys named for Indians and spiked trees, past copper-colored hills and the Marine base.

Teresa Miles sat in the sun in a wooden chair being read to by a nurse who looked up and smiled as Jimmy walked across the grass toward them. The rest home—now they called it *Extended Care*—was very private and very pretty, three low adobe-style buildings the same color as the desert mountains around them. There was an oasis in the center of it, a few palms around a pond. It was restful. It was constant.

It was the kind of place that could keep a secret.

The nurse bent over and told Teresa Miles her son was there. She had her eyes closed. Her expression didn't change.

It would be polite to say that the movie star still had the same magic in her skin, in the bones of her famous face, but it was gone, or almost gone. She was very white and her skin seemed much too thin, almost like the shell of an insect when the shell is left behind.

Like a woman who when her only son dies, steps off the roof of a hotel above Sunset, and she is left behind.

The nurse walked away.

Jimmy bent over and kissed his mother.

"I saw a coyote with two pups," he said.

She opened her eyes but her expression didn't change.

Jimmy sat on the grass next to her chair. A hawk turned circles in the sky over the oasis and then, just as he was noticing the grace of it, dropped onto something unseen in the brush.

He took the perfume bottle from his pocket.

"I brought you something," he said.

Her hands were in her lap. He put the bottle in her hand. Her fingers tightened around it. Jimmy uncapped it. He touched the glass stopper to her cheek and, under the expanse of our sky, a little more life came back to her eyes.

# THE NEXT

# ONE

Would you like a side of *Death* with that?

It was the Saugus Café, thirty miles north of downtown L.A., off Old 99, the Newhall Road, one of three or four spots claiming to have laid the table for James Dean's last meal, a slice of apple pie and a glass of milk if the legend had it right, before he drove his Spyder 550 on north over the Grapevine to Cholame and the Y intersection of the 41 and 46 highways where a Cal Poly kid in a black-and-white Ford turned in front of him. The diner was borderline shrine. There were pictures of Dean all along the wall above the long counter, the one from *Giant* with his arms draped over the rifle across his shoulders like it was the top bar of the cross or something, the other famous one that everybody's seen, Dean's hand at his waist, middle finger and thumb curled to touch, index finger pointing off camera. Above the register was one of Dean leaning against the silver Porsche roadster in front of a gas station down in L.A. where he had picked up his mechanic that morning. That *fateful* morning . . . Isn't that what they say? The two were on their way to a pro-am race up at Salinas when they bought it, when Mr. D waved the black flag. It was like they always said over the PA out at the old Saugus Speedway on hot Saturday nights, "The most dangerous miles driven tonight will be your trip here and home . . ."

But then again, as the racers like to say, it's not the going fast that kills you . . . It's the sudden stop.

The waitress waited. "Would you like a side of beans with that?" she said again.

"What kind of beans?" Jimmy Miles said. The place wasn't crowded. It was early afternoon. He could play with her a little.

"Ranchero beans," she said.

"Pot beans," Jimmy said.

"Uh-huh."

"Maybe cooked with a little bacon."

"Uh-huh."

There was a fly, big and blue and buzzing, the size of a jelly bean, flying in wack circles over the booth, slamming itself into the same spot on the plate glass window every half minute, trying to get out of there but not learning a damn thing from previous experience.

Jimmy knew a thing or two about that.

The waitress snatched it out of the air and snuffed it, dropped it onto the linoleum floor and flipped it under the table with the toe of her waitress shoe all in one seamless little . . . what would you call it? Dance?

"I guess I'd better," Jimmy said. "And a beer. Whatever you drink."

"I drink cherry Cokes," she said.

She was the kind of waitress who didn't write anything down, and he was the kind of customer who hadn't needed a menu, so she just tapped the Formica twice with her short, unpainted nails and stepped away.

"And pie," Jimmy said after her. "Apple. And milk."

"Why not?" she said without turning.

Jimmy looked out the window, across the street, at the old clapboard train station. It used to be across two lanes; now there were four and clotted with traffic. A hundred years ago, it had been a stagecoach trail. Two hundred, a mission trail, friars and priests. Five hundred, five *thousand*, and it would be indigenes with leathery feet, breaking the dirt down to dust.

The girl came back from the bathroom. Her eyes were red, but she wasn't crying anymore. She had a folded brown washroom towel in her hand, too rough to put to your eyes. She was maybe twenty-five, a Latina, but one who'd probably never been south of San Diego. Or maybe even Long Beach. She was wearing a rayon dress, like this was the forties. Or *The Postman Always Rings Twice*.

She hadn't looked at Jimmy once since he'd come in, or at anyone else in the place, off on her own trip. As soon as she sat back down in the banquette, her food came, a tuna melt and a side of fries from what Jimmy could see. She smiled up at the waitress, an open-eyed look that almost asked the woman to sit down and talk about it, femme to femme. Almost. There was a lot of *almost* in the young woman's story, from what Jimmy could already see.

"Anything else, hon?" the waitress said to her, like a nurse.

The girl shook her head. When the waitress was gone, the forced smile fell off the girl's face. She arranged the two plates so it suited her, pushed the ketchup bottle forward an inch, and then picked up half the sandwich and took a bite. A big bite, like a teenager, like a teenager on a date. They usually didn't eat, not like this, when they were sad or shaken and running like this. She reminded Jimmy of someone, though she didn't look anything like the other one, a woman out of his past—a face, a pair of eyes, a mouth, a shape still waiting in a room inside him anytime he opened the door. Maybe it was this girl's appetite. She ate like the date she was on was the tenth date or the twentieth or some number past counting, as if she didn't have to prove she was "ladylike" anymore. Like she loved you and knew you loved her, had seen her all kinds of ways.

Like that other one.

Or maybe it was just that her dress was soft light blue, like the feeling she brought over you.

She never finished her food, stopped after those first big bites. She bothered the fries another minute, then gave up, pushing the oval plate away so she could put her hands on the table in front of her. She wasn't married, or at least didn't wear a ring. She didn't wave for the bill, didn't seem in much of a hurry to get back on the road, just sat looking out the window right past Jimmy at her car, a baby-blue '70s Buick Skylark convertible that had been lowered a bit. A couple of minutes slid by like that, with her looking past Jimmy at the car, then the waitress appeared and pushed the ticket across the table to her. She looked at the slip of paper and took in a breath and slid out of the booth, as if it had been a note from the older woman that said, *Honey, you're just going to have to go on and deal with it.*

Her eyes were leaking again before she reached the door.

Jimmy waited a minute or two and then left a twenty on the table and stepped out into the dust and the truck stink from the highway. The Skylark was already gone out of sight, but it didn't matter. He knew she wasn't going anywhere but north. She wasn't going to turn around and head back to Los Angeles, he knew that. She was *hard*-running and that meant north and there was really only one way to go.

The sun was bright; the light had a kind of aluminum sheen to it. It had been hot the last few days. Hot and dry. Jimmy reached in and opened the glove box and found a pair of beat-up Ray-Bans. Tortoiseshell, almost red. He had brought the Porsche, the '64 Cabriolet, the ragtop, and the top was down. It wasn't the best car for this kind of thing, too showy, too one-of-a-kind, but something had made him pick it. He opened the door and let the wind blow through it a minute, cool off the seats before he got in it. It was September.

Dean died in September, didn't he?

Because he knew he could catch up to her, Jimmy didn't get back on the 5, took a right off Newhall Road instead, and drove out past what was left of the old speedway. A little memory jag. There were the wooden stands, red and white, peeling a little but looking permanent. The track was a dead flat third-of-a-mile asphalt oval, a "bullring" racetrack that had started out as a rodeo arena. A subdivision had built up around it now, plain-Jane two-story stucco houses with saplings staked in the yards, blank-faced houses, sand colored, looking like the boxes real houses would come in. The last races had been run ten years ago, but the owners had kept it up, rented out the facility for Sunday morning swap meets. A couple thousand people would come, even driving up from Los Angeles, church for believers in bargains.

But it was empty now, about as empty as empty gets. Where was the tumbleweed blowing through? Jimmy jumped a low chain-link fence on what they called the back chute and walked out to the center. It was paved from one side to the other, cracking and not as black as it used to be but so hot his shoes smacked.

He looked up at the stands, found the row where he used to like to sit. The top row.

Where *they* used to sit.

It looked bad in the daytime. In the present.

———

So maybe it wasn't about James Dean after all . . .

The Skylark girl (he'd learn in a minute her name was Lucy, *Lucille*) had taken the exit off the 5 onto California 46, headed west toward Lost Hills and Paso Robles, and now she blew right by the intersection where Dean had died and then on past the memorial, a granite marker and a bend of stainless steel wrapped around an oak next to a café six miles along at Cholame.

Jimmy didn't stop either, just hung back a mile. A little two-car caravan traversing central Cal. There was enough rise and fall on the highway to give him a good look down at her every minute or so, to keep her in front of him without her seeing him.

He pulled off after ten or twelve miles of that.

"Did you do the Skylark?"

He was on the shoulder, directly under a whistling cell tower "camouflaged" to look like a spindly evergreen, which was particularly stupid given that this was in the middle of bare brown rolling hills, it the only "tree" for miles. Unless you counted the occasional oil derrick.

But the reception was good.

"I painted it for her," Angel said. "For her boyfriend, actually. He give it to her."

"Is he the problem?"

"You really *are* a detective."

"So he let her keep it when he left?"

"I guess. She kept it."

"I don't know, bud," Jimmy said, "I might be on *his* side, taking a man's car."

"He's dead."

"What's her name?"

When Angel told him, Jimmy sang, "You picked a fine time to leave me, Lucille . . ."

"Loose *wheel*," Angel said.

Back in the day on those Saturday nights at Saugus Speedway, when one of the old clunker stockers would kick loose a wheel, send it bouncing across the infield, the announcer—Jimmy remembered his name, Virgil Kirkpatrick—would wait a beat and then say the line: "You picked a fine time to leave me, loose wheel . . ." And the crowd would laugh, like he was Jay Leno.

"I drove on out there," Jimmy said. "The speedway. Jumped the fence."

"And it was sad," Angel said back to him.

"I can take sad," Jimmy said.

"Not so much as you think," Angel said.

"She's headed toward Paso Robles, unless she just wanted to cut over to the 101 or the coast. Any idea why?"

"That's why I'm paying you the big dollar," Angel said.

"I haven't been out of town in a while," Jimmy said. "It's nice out here." A wind had blown over the hill, and the air smelled good, like the inside of a wooden box.

"Where did you pick her up?"

"She was right where you said she'd be, bright and early."

"Eagle Rock."

"Eagle Rock," Jimmy repeated. "She took a long time to pack the car, like she was waiting for me."

Nothing whistled down the line for a second or two.

"How does she look?" Angel said.

"Like they all do," Jimmy said. "One kind of them."

"Lost."

"Spooked. Alone. Running," Jimmy said. "Trying to get from what was to what's next. Way young to be so hurt. Or maybe I've just seen too many of them."

"Or maybe you're getting old in the soul," Angel said.

"It's about time."

"She's good-looking, huh?"

"She's not a Sailor," Jimmy said, almost a question.

"No."

"Tell me who she is to you," Jimmy said.

"Nobody," Angel lied. "Just a kid I wish wasn't so down."

———————

Lucy in the Skylark stopped in Paso Robles all right, parked on the street, the main street, beside a pay phone. Pas was a pretty little town, out of the way enough to have slept through most of the booster efforts to improve it. There were a lot of Victorian B and Bs, ten thousand oaks, more brown grass hills ringing it. They'd all flush green in another month or so when the rain started. Father Junipero Serra had stopped here, planted the flag a few miles north, Mission San Miguel Archangel.

But nobody was going out by the mission today.

Lucy made a call and then got back behind the wheel and waited.

She seemed a little fidgety. She put the top down, out of nervousness, the way a girl straightens her skirt as the boy is coming back to the car. Or the way girls did when they still wore skirts, when the baby-blue Skylark was new. She kept her eyes straight ahead, except for looking up in the mirror every once in a while.

Jimmy was out of the Porsche, up the street a half block and on the other side. He'd gone into a wood-front store and bought a pack of cigarettes. He hadn't smoked in ten years. A pack cost what it used to cost to go to the movies. He sat on a bus bench, sat up on the back of it like a hawk on a perch, and pulled the red ribbon and opened the pack. He tapped one out and put it between his fingers and struck the match.

*So I'm one of those,* he thought, *a guy a memory makes start smoking again.*

The first drag almost took off the top of his head.

A kid came walking up to the Skylark, walking in from a side street, thirteen, fourteen, on the out end of a growth spurt. (He'd probably been three inches shorter at the beginning of summer, when school let out.) He wore a Cake T-shirt and plaid "old man" polyester pants and red Converse lowboys. And a black porkpie hat. He carried a hard-shell guitar case, a Les Paul from the shape and size of it.

Jimmy liked him right away, pretty much everything about him.

Les put the guitar in the backseat before he even really looked at Lucy behind the wheel. He stood there. She got out from behind the wheel to come around to him. He dropped his head and sent his eyes sideways. She was about to hug and kiss him, standing there beside the car, but thought better of it, just smiled a big, real smile and touched the brim of his little hat with a finger and said something that made him pull his head away and pretend to be irritated.

*Fourteen.*

He had a school backpack over his shoulder, his luggage. He threw it into the backseat with the guitar and got in up front. Lucy started the car and said something to him. He nodded. She threw the Skylark into an incautious U-turn and whipped around and came in right in front of Jimmy on the back of the bus bench and stopped. Big as hell.

She pushed it up into park and got out. She walked right past him without even half a look. She was either on to him or unnaturally oblivious.

Jimmy stayed put, ten feet away from the car. Les Paul fiddled with the radio controls, opened the glove box and dug around in it, but nothing seemed to catch his eye. He put his head back against the headrest, like he was half asleep. Or jazzbo cool.

Lucy came out with the goods, unbagged, a plastic bottle of Dr Pepper for the boy and a bag of Flamin' Cheetos. She had a Diet Coke for herself and a limp length of Red Vines hanging off of her lip. She got back behind the wheel. She snatched one of his Cheetos and popped it in her mouth and started the engine. She seemed, at least for that moment, almost happy. She drove off, still somehow managing never to acknowledge Jimmy's existence, just as the boy never had.

They were brother and sister.

Les Paul and Lucy in the Sky with Diamonds.

Jimmy had found a CD in the glove box he didn't remember ever buying, a double disk of Beatles outtakes and song demos from the time of *The White Album* and a few even back to *Sgt. Pepper's*. It seemed just right for this trip, loose, clean, unpredictable, underproduced, each song stripped down to its essence, sometimes with lyrics that had gotten dropped before the slick, finished versions. Just now, with Paso Robles in the rearview mirror and the Skylark a quarter mile ahead, it was "While My Guitar Gently Weeps," and a new verse . . .

> I look from the wings at the play you are staging,
> While my guitar gently weeps . . .

Jimmy sang out loud, riding along in the wind, sang the verses he knew, that everybody knew, and smiled all the way through the new verse, digging it.

———————

There was no wrong way to come into San Francisco. No wrong time of day. No wrong time of year. Here was one place, changed as it was, that didn't make you wish it was twenty years ago. Or fifty. Or even make you wish that you were that younger version of yourself, before everything happened that had happened, as some places do. As L.A. did.

You were you, now was now.

San Francisco was San Francisco.

It was eight or nine at night when the two-car caravan blew in from SoCal. Since it was just past summer, there was still some light in the blue to the west, Bombay-Sapphire-gin-bottle blue. Of course, it was twenty degrees cooler than it had been down south. Just right. The Skylark was five cars ahead of Jimmy, top up now. The top on the Porsche was still down. There was traffic around him, but Jimmy still heard the pop, the click of the Porsche's lighter and reached for it, turned the orange circle to him and lit another cigarette. He had stopped a ways back and bought a couple of bottles of beer. What was next, torching up a joint? He was enjoying himself a little too much, like that early part of a night (that later turns out bad) when you first taste that first drink in the first place you stop and she for a minute lets down her resistance and looks at you, just in the moment, forgetting for a moment what you both know, that you were both there to talk the other out of or into something.

So Jimmy was still thinking about *her*. And they'd never even been to San Francisco together.

Lucy and Les had come all the way up the Central Valley on the 101, staying at the limit. The sister and brother had talked a little, then had fallen silent, at least from what Jimmy could see ten car lengths back. A bit below San Jose, in the last stretch of farmland, as the sun was dropping, Lucy had pulled into a rest area and gone to the ladies' room, leaving the boy in the car. She stayed long enough to make Jimmy wonder if she'd fallen back into her gloom. Or something worse. Maybe she'd just made a call from the pay phone. She didn't seem to have a cell. When she came back to the car, that's when she'd put up the top. And she drove faster after that. She'd remembered *something*, something her brother had let her forget for a little while there.

Jimmy followed the Skylark down off the Bayshore and into the city, the dropping left turn down into the Fillmore, heading west on Fell. For a quick flash, there was the skyline to his right, a clutter of blocks dropped in the foreground.

Lucy had the use of a third-floor flat in a Victorian in the regentrified Haight, on Central, a block up from Haight Street next to little Buena Vista Park angling up the hill. Jimmy slowed at the corner where she'd turned, saw where she'd parked, halfway up the hill on the right.

He looped a block and came back on the intersecting side street. There was a lucky parking spot in the dim space between two streetlights. He parked, reached back, and hoisted up the top and snapped it down. It was cool. There was *moisture* in the air. Imagine that.

He watched. And waited. She just sat there, motor idling. Then she got something out of the glove compartment, maybe a white envelope, read something off the face of it, and looked over at the number on the corner building, the Victorian. She turned around in the intersection, put the car right in front, the nose pointed downhill now.

She sat there some more. The boy kept looking over at her.

A man with a white ponytail, a man in his sixties, came past on the sidewalk across the street, came down the hill from Buena Vista Park walking a dog, a chow with a loose black tongue and a tail curling up and over. The man seemed to Jimmy to make a point of *not* staring at the new-comers sitting in the Skylark under the circle of streetlight, kept on going down the hill. He lived over the wine shop at the lower corner, at Central and Haight. The chow waited, looking down at the ground like an old man, while his owner unlocked a black lacquered door. The man looked once back up the hill before he went in and the dog followed.

Across from the corner Victorian was a four-story building, a little too neat, too perfectly painted, with Catholic trappings, a cross on the crown of the roof and a flash of gold here and there. A nun in a blue habit was framed in a tall second-floor window with the white globe of a ceiling light over her head. Two girls played a board game framed in another window a floor above her, teenage girls in light blue smocks . . . What were they called? *Shifts.* On one girl, the cloth was stretched tight across her belly. Then Jimmy realized the other girl was pregnant, too, from the fullness in her face as much as anything. But not so far along. It was a home for unwed mothers.

It was a nice neighborhood. The Haight had been a lot wilder and woollier when he'd lived in San Francisco.

Lucy got out from behind the wheel. She went to the apartment building two doors down the hill on the same side, rang, waited there at the door. The boy got out a beat after she did and stood beside the car, looking up at the navy-gray sky. He looked like he was thinking that it was going to rain, but it was just the way the nights were in San Francisco in September, something else Jimmy remembered afresh. The boy looked over at his sister waiting there at the door, the way she was acting, but he didn't dwell on it. It was just one more thing he didn't get.

A woman answered Lucy's bell, came out onto the sidewalk, out under the streetlight, and the two of them talked for a second, the slanted sidewalk forcing them to stand oddly, a little uncertainly. In time the other woman, who was enough older than Lucy to have a little mother in her manner, a little sympathy (or at least *judgment*, which is a kind of concern), reached into the pocket of the long sweater coat she wore and came out with a key, a loose key, and an index card. She put the key and the card in Lucy's open palm and looked at her with that look again, the neighbor lady's own version of the tough-love look the waitress had given Lucy back at the café in Saugus.

Lucy nodded and thanked her and said something that looked like, "I will." The boy got his guitar and pack out of the backseat.

Five halting, unrhythmic tones sounded. Each of the three apartments in the Victorian had its own door at street level, on a marble stoop. Lucy had opened the center door, stepped just inside, the index card in hand, to punch a code into the alarm. There was another, longer tone, the all clear, and Les followed her in, climbed the stairs behind her carrying his gear, as the door closed itself. After a minute, a light came on in the front room on the third floor.

Jimmy started the Porsche. He pulled forward and turned right, drove up the hill on Central, alongside the Catholic home. He went to the top of the hill, to the park, and turned around and came back down and snugged the car in against the curb. From here he could see straight across into the apartment, from Lucy's top-floor flat on down. There were closed drapes in the living room, but in the bedroom the blinds were raised. The boy Les was in the kitchen, looking up at the light fixture.

It was wide-screen, like a drive-in.

The air had weathered up, gotten heavy with water. Jimmy suddenly felt a little hollow inside but shook it off. So he waited, behind the wheel. He smoked another cigarette, though he was already getting bored with it. Smoking. He spun the dial, found a good station on the radio. They were playing Zeppelin, *Houses of the Holy*, broadcasting from somewhere down on the waterfront.

Act two, Lucy came in and sat on the edge of a stripped bed in the front bedroom, alone, her hands on her knees. Her worries, her sadness, the *heaviness* had sure enough come round again. Big surprise, it was lying in wait for her four hundred miles north. Jimmy wondered if she had any idea that half the neighborhood could see in, could see her sitting there, if they looked.

The boy came into the bedroom. He looked at her but just stood there in the doorway.

"Say something to her," Jimmy said. "She's your sister."

But the boy just stared at her. Jimmy had decided a ways back down the road that they hadn't seen each other much lately, were unused to each other. Lucy lifted her head and said something. The boy nodded and left the room.

After a moment, the downstairs front door opened, and he came out onto the sidewalk. By now the night had that horror film look to it, fog hanging around the streetlights, making each of them look like something *alive* wrapped in a gauzy cocoon. She had given him the keys, to lock up the car. Les got behind the wheel and put the key in. He looked for a second like he was going to take it out for a spin. He canted the wheels to the curb. Maybe he knew more about San Francisco than his sister did. He sat there a minute with his hands on the wheel. Jimmy could see through the back window over the seat backs that the radio had come on when he'd unlocked the steering wheel. Maybe the kid liked Zep.

The kid leaned forward over the steering wheel and looked up at the apartment, at the light in the bedroom. He turned the key, and the radio light went out.

After he'd locked up the car again, he stood for a moment on the sidewalk looking down at the sideways traffic on Haight Street, an electric bus clicking by, rolling toward Ashbury, too fast, rocking, just this side of out of control. Les didn't see it, but the man with the white ponytail was watching him around the edge of the blinds in his second-floor bay window.

The kid went back up.

The overhead light was still on, but she wasn't in the front bedroom anymore.

"She sent you away," Jimmy said.

He watched as the boy went looking for her, worry in his manner, too.

Jimmy found her first. There she was, up on the roof, at the edge. Flat, no railing. She was looking out levelly, not up, not down, a look that said she just might take the next step in front of her, whether there was anything there or not.

So it's going to be *tonight* . . .

Jimmy got out fast, left the car door open.

But then Les came out onto the roof behind his sister.

Jimmy stopped.

When the boy said something, the first thing Lucy did was to take a step back from the edge.

# TWO

Jimmy couldn't sleep, *didn't sleep,* so after he'd checked into a high suite at the Mark Hopkins on Nob Hill, he went back out into the night. He left the Porsche in the hotel garage and took a cab. He went by the house on Central. The lights were still on in the front bedroom, but now the shades were down. There was the blue flare of a television behind the drapes in the living room, and the kitchen was dark.

The cab driver didn't seem to make anything out of Jimmy telling him to just park at the top of the hill, looking down at the house. Ten minutes passed that way. Ten minutes of nothing. There was jazz on the radio, very low. The fog had settled in even thicker. July and August, Jimmy remembered, were the months when the fog really came in. Nobody told September the season was over. An electric bus blew past down on Haight Street. Jimmy motioned for the cabby, the same black man in his forties who always seemed to be driving the cab in San Francisco, schoolteacher's black-rim glasses and a Kangol cap, to roll on down the hill. The cabby rolled on down the hill. To the corner.

Jimmy got out, paid him off through the open window, with an extra twenty to really make him wonder what *that* had been about, and set out walking in the direction of Haight and Ashbury. He turned to watch the cab pull away, waiting to see the cabby's eyes in the rearview mirror, but the cabby never looked back.

It was San Francisco. Maybe he wasn't that weird here.

There was a Gap on the corner of Haight and Ashbury. No Starbucks. Yet. But a wannabe Starbucks a few doors down. There was a good crowd. By now it was almost midnight. It took Jimmy a second to remember what day of the week it was. Thursday. The coffee drinkers were mostly professionals, young, not so young. Dressed nice. Good haircuts. In pairs, most of them.

Jimmy got a tea and a madeleine and brought them outside and sat at one of the little white corporate tables. There was only one other smoker, a self-consciously scruffy man in his late twenties, in a rough-weave unbleached wool sweater, off-white, over dark green cords and what they used to call desert boots. Suede. Probably Tommy Hilfiger. He had one leg angled up into the chair. He was smoking a good cigar. With the gold band still on it. Jimmy wanted to put a fist in his face, but only because of how young he was, how apparently happy he was, and because the woman leaning into him looked a little, in the eyes, in the cheekbones, like Mary.

*Mary.*

A bus came. Jimmy jumped on it. It was the 43. He rode it out Fell along the Panhandle, halfway to the zoo and the ocean and then back again, back along Oak Street, along Market to the Embarcadero and then Fisherman's Wharf.

The night was still very alive down along the waterfront, postmidnight, out-of-towners most of them, honeymooners, lovers on lovers' long weekends, groups of three or four or five or six, more than a few in them in red sweatshirts with somebody's logo, a convention of somebodys.

And *Sailors*.

That didn't surprise Jimmy. This is where they'd be. And when. Was that why he'd come down here, looking for his kind? That felt a little pathetic to him. The bus he'd ridden in was one of the last of the night, five or six other passengers and Jimmy. Maybe there'd be another run, one last loop when the bars closed, whenever that was.

Most of the people were at Pier 41, where the red-and-white boats over to Alcatraz docked. The last Alcatraz boat came back at six or seven, but the ticket windows were still open for tomorrow's runs. It sat out there, Alcatraz, across the night, swathed in the clouds of fog that sat on the Bay. Other nights you'd be able to make it out from here, the lights, even the shape, the edges, but not tonight. Tonight there was only a sweeping light on the highest building, behind the cotton of the fog, and a moon up there somewhere, too, or a piece of one, a dull glow at two o'clock.

There were street entertainers, each with his own little knot of audience. There was a juggler. There was a close-up magician, making things disappear.

There was a man painted silver. Head to toe. In a silver tux and tails, silver spats and silver shoes and a silver top hat that stayed somehow on his silver head. With a boom box. Dancing like a robot.

The Sailors moved among the tourists, bumping into them like pickpockets, knocking into strangers just for the joy of it, for the harshness of it, with a rough laugh whenever a man from Kansas or a woman from Germany would excuse themselves, though it was the Sailor who had run into the innocent. Same as it ever was. Some of the tourists would check their pockets, to make sure.

But it wasn't their wallets that had been taken.

A couple of the crab stands were still open. Five bucks got you a red-and-white square paper tray of shredded Dungeness crab with a quarter lemon and a tear of sourdough baguette. Jimmy sat on the stool, close enough to be getting a facial from the stinking steam that came out of the stainless steel box. He'd already shoveled a forkful into his mouth. It was good.

"What do you want?" the teenager working the stand said. It was a Leone Brothers stand. This kid was likely a Leone grandson, maybe great-grandson.

His tone was a little quick. Jimmy waited.

"You look like you want something else."

"More cocktail sauce, I guess," Jimmy said.

The kid put an open paper cup of red sauce in front of Jimmy, the kind of little cup they put pills in, in a hospital. "You want horseradish, say it."

"I do."

The server spooned an amount of white horseradish that would have been too much for the average person into another paper cup and set it beside the first one.

"That's the way I eat it," the boy said.

"You still eat it?"

"Every day."

"I thought maybe you'd get sick of it."

"Every day. Ask him."

"Who?"

The boy looked over Jimmy's shoulder at a busboy pulling up black rubber mats, hosing off the underneath. The stand was in front of the mother restaurant, closed up at midnight.

"Do I eat crab?" the kid asked.

"Every day," the busboy said.

From twenty feet away, a Sailor was watching them, watching the dumb little play, the tourist getting stroked by the Welcome to San Francisco Committee. This one, this Sailor, sat on the closed lid of a Dumpster, a blond man who'd been a bit overinfluenced by Billy Idol, a little too pretty, lips too full in that pouty Billy Idol way. He wore what a lot of them wore, the ones with that certain attitude, the navy peacoat and watch cap. This one also wore black straight-leg 505s, pegged skintight, and pointy-toed fairy boots like The Beatles used to wear.

Only *red*.

"I know you, Brother," he mouthed to Jimmy. There was just a hint of blue around him, as if he were wrapped in another kind of fog. And he had that look, that Sailor sneer.

Why were they always so sour?

"Nice night for a white wedding," Jimmy said back at him, across the twenty feet between them.

The crab kid gave Jimmy a funny look.

Then everything started to speed up. Another Sailor came over to Red Boots with an *it's-happening-now* look on his face, and Red Boots jumped off the Dumpster. He didn't even look over at Jimmy as he went past. On a mission. None of it surprised Jimmy or made him wonder where they were headed. They were always scurrying around with sudden purpose, this kind, this time of night, like junkies energized by the rumored arrival of dope.

What did surprise Jimmy was that the crab kid was a Sailor, too. When the first two passed, the second Sailor caught the kid's eye, motioned with his head. The crab boy fell in step with them, abandoned his post at the stand. The trio headed off across the last hundred yards between restaurant row and the waterfront, leaving Jimmy to wonder if he was losing his sense of things, getting slow. He'd missed it. There was nothing about the kid that made him think this one was a Sailor. No lost look in the eye, no flare of blue. No fatalism. No bitterness.

He wondered something else, if the kid had read *him*.

Jimmy went after them, took his little twist-off split of Napa Chardonnay and what was left of the crab with him.

The drama was at Pier 35, one of the old World War II–era buildings, with its big, flat, blank face.

A matched pair of perfectly naked girls was on the lip of the two-story facade of the building. Black-haired, with cute helmet haircuts, turned under just below the ears, bangs straight across just above the eyes. They looked a little French, a little Godard. They were holding hands.

*Girls Gone Wild.*

They had a good-sized crowd of their own, five or six banks of people standing before them in concentric half circles, heads back, smiling, entertained.

But then there was a man, whom Jimmy hadn't even seen until just now, who *wasn't* naked, right behind the girls, all in black, hidden by the shadows on the ledge until now, who now leaned into the frame and said something into the space between their two heads, something that only took a second.

Or took half the night, depending on how tuned in you were.

And, next beat, the girls jumped, hand in hand. Dove . . .

They were so pretty, so *French*-seeming, had such beautiful bodies; it was clear the rapt crowd half expected them to arc back up into the air and land on their feet, like Cirque du Soleil. Instead, everybody got to watch as the two crashed into the cement in front of the dock building face-first, shoulders and chests first, one girl somehow slightly ahead of the other and with a sound like hundred-pound sacks of potatoes thrown off a loading dock.

Nobody stepped closer for a closer look. Nobody had to check to see if they were still alive.

Jimmy was in the second row, and he didn't step closer for a closer look, either, but he could *smell* it over the wet-dog musk of the Bay. It was a smell he knew.

When he looked up at the top of the facade again, the man in black was gone.

Crab Boy was behind Jimmy, over a row or two.

He looked at Jimmy. And *smiled*. How inappropriate.

The two Sailors in peacoats and watch caps, Red Boots and the other, didn't waste any time. They jumped on it, were already on the move, working together, doing this thing, Red Boots shoving people back and the other Sailor getting right in their faces for up-close scrutiny, one person at a time, looking each person in the face.

It had a name. It was called, prosaically, *Looking*.

Then Crab Boy split. Something else had caught his eye, movement out at the edge of the crowd. Somebody chasing somebody.

Jimmy went after him. After them.

Three other peacoats chased a man down the alleyway between Pier 45 and the back of Alioto's. Crab Boy jogged after the three new Sailors and the one they chased, but at a pace that said he didn't mean to catch them, just wanted to be there when they all got to the end, when they caught the man.

The *silver* man. It was the silver-painted dancer.

The three overtook him and knocked him down and began a beating that scattered a clot of seabirds hunkered down in the shadow of what looked like a warehouse. Crab Boy came up and stood over the beaters, like a supervisor, like the boss's son who'd been made night shift manager. Not getting his hands dirty. There was an ugly rhythm to it, the way they beat him, taking turns on him, each of them hitting him in the face twice and, at the same time, saying something.

Two words.

Jimmy caught up, jumped right into the middle of it. He seized one Sailor by the back of his blue-black wool coat. (It felt damp, perpetually damp, out in the weather like this.) Jimmy pulled the Sailor away, off the silver man, cast the bigger man aside with a strength that surprised both of them, that even made Jimmy wonder why he was suddenly filled with rage, why he'd gotten into it without a hesitation, without thinking. The other two Sailors didn't miss a beat, kept pummeling the silver man, saying the same two words that Jimmy still couldn't make out.

"All right. Cool," the kid said after a minute. Instead of "Enough" or "Stop."

The other Sailors stepped off.

*"Damn!"* the silver man said, still on the ground. Turned out he was black under the paint.

They all caught their breath. Jimmy turned to stare at the crab kid. The other Sailors were walking away.

"You look like you want something," the kid said to Jimmy's glare.

*Now* the kid flashed blue, but not in a way Jimmy had ever seen. A crackling, electric, staticky way, gone as soon as you noticed it.

Jimmy didn't crack wise back at the boy. He'd only been in town a few hours. It wouldn't get him anything. The kid turned in his very white Nikes and went back up the alley.

They were back behind the restaurants. The smell suddenly hit Jimmy, with his sinuses opened by the adrenaline coursing through his system. It was like ammonia.

*"Damn,"* the silver man said again.

Jimmy held out a hand to him, to pull him up.

The silver paint seemed to filter the man's blue edge, like a gel on a spotlight.

Another Sailor.

His silver top hat had gotten knocked off. He retrieved it, tried to straighten out a crease it had picked up. He stopped to look at it in his hand, as if he'd suddenly realized what an improbable thing he'd become.

"What were they saying, when they were pounding you?" Jimmy asked.

"'Who's next?'" the silver man said in a way that meant that he didn't understand it, either.

# THREE

"Machine Shop."

"What do your friends call you?" Jimmy asked.

"Jus' Shop. Or 'Shine."

"Really?"

"I'm not sensitive."

The lights atop the EMT ambulance were still on, a red pulsing sweep projected ten feet tall against the face of the building at Pier 35, where the girls had jumped, making the scene look like a rave. But with nobody there. Raved out. Most of the crowd had dispersed even before the coroner's van and a couple of news trucks had arrived.

The fog had descended thicker. Jimmy looked away from the death scene, up toward Coit Tower. It wasn't foggy there. Clear. Something else he remembered from his days in San Francisco, how the fog moved around, how you'd be talking about it on the phone to someone across town, making jokes about the doom and gloom (if they were new to what everyone here called The City), and the person on the other end would be just as likely to say, "It's clear here."

He and the silver man were on a bench in front of Pier 39, drinking coffee. Jimmy had said he'd buy the street performer a drink, a last drink before the waterfront bars closed, but they were outside drinking coffee instead. Good coffee. Black. Jimmy got the idea that Mr. Machine Shop here was a program drunk. A Twelve-Stepper.

"Why did they come after you?"

"I said something," Machine Shop said.

"Said what?"

"I yelled up at them. The girls. 'Don't do it! Don't listen to him!'"

Jimmy noticed his silver hand shaking a little as he brought the cup to his silver lips. The paint was wearing thin. He wondered if it was toxic, what the effects were of putting it on night after night.

"I shouldn't say it, but those girls were very sexual."

Jimmy nodded.

"I mean . . ."

"Yeah, they were beautiful," Jimmy said. "Very young."

"I know I shouldn't even be thinking that, but—"

"Did you know them?"

Machine Shop shook his head.

"Know anything about them?"

"I saw them earlier. In the ring."

"The ring."

"The audience."

"Did you know *him*, the guy who gave them the go?"

"Never saw him before tonight," said Shop a little too quickly. "You mean the skinny guy, in the black turtleneck? Maybe wearing a cape?"

Jimmy waited.

"OK, yes, I know him," Shop corrected.

"Who is he?"

"I know him. I don't know his name." There was another momentary delay. "OK, his name is Jeremy. Jeremy."

"He's a Sailor," Jimmy said. Not really a question.

"He's down in here all the time," Machine Shop said. He turned and looked for the big clock on the face of the mall of T-shirt shops. It was two forty. "He's all right."

Jimmy waited.

"I stay out of his way," Shop finished.

"Is he a Sailor?"

"Oh yeah," Machine Shop said. Then he said the same thing again, another way, a way that meant that the caped man was *really* a Sailor.

"Was he with them earlier in the night?"

"Not when I saw them."

"How did the girls look then?"

"All right. Kind of sad in the eyes maybe. They were holding hands then, too. Wore little white silky dresses."

"They were twins," Jimmy said.

Machine Shop nodded. "Don't get that every day. Barefoot, too." You could see him get lost in a thought about them. Then you could see him shake himself out of it. Here was a man trying to do right, be good. To walk the line. *What Would Johnny Cash Do?* He uncrossed his long legs and stood. "I guess that'd be a real bonus for them," he said. "Getting *two*. Twins."

Jimmy put that in his pocket, to think on later.

Machine Shop had retrieved his gear from where he'd stowed it behind a parked car before the trio had chased him down the alleyway. He reached down and snapped out the handle on his roll-away, the wheelie that carried his stuff, a silver-painted boom box and a plastic, silver-painted top hat, for "contributions."

"You make any money at this?" Jimmy said, looking up at him, still on the bench.

"It's a life," Machine Shop said.

Jimmy got the joke. A Sailor joke.

The trolley was coming up around the curve, up the Embarcadero from Pier 29. The night's last train.

"Where you *from,* man?" Machine Shop said. "I know you ain't from here. You ain't even from Oakland."

Jimmy told him.

"You just about the *bluest* man I ever saw," the other said. "You so blue sitting there, even a Norm could pick you out . . ."

———

Jimmy walked "home." Through North Beach, up Columbus. It was just a bit after three, and San Francisco was a late town, so he wasn't alone. Drunks and lovers. And drunk lovers. A cab would come by every thirty seconds. Every other one, the empty ones, would slow to look over at him. He'd just shake his head, headed up that straight, gentle slope. He was wearing a black suit, the black suit he'd had on all day, since six that morning. It was linen, over a white shirt. He turned up the collar. Maybe that would show the cabbies that he *meant* to be here.

*Did* he? Mean to be here? He remembered why he was here. He thought about his friend Angel, thought about Lucy, hoped she was asleep in her borrowed bed over in the Haight.

Then he went back to thinking about himself.

He realized he was looking for the U.S. Restaurant. It was gone. The U.S. had been there for fifty years, in a wedge-shaped building, a 24/7 place where bartenders came after their shifts, cooks and waiters, musicians after gigs, pimps and drug dealers, and *Rolling Stone* writers who counted themselves part of that crowd, somewhere in there. The stromboli-and-cannelloni-for-breakfast crowd.

But it was gone. Well, not gone, exactly: replaced by a new and improved version of itself four or five doors down. And closed at ten.

In the next block he found another open-late place. It was almost full. He ordered a glass of red. It came in a water tumbler, just like at the U.S. (So he wasn't the only sentimental one.) He sat at the bar. Alone.

Not exactly. Halfway up Columbus, he'd noticed the Sailors on the other side of the street climbing the opposite sidewalk, trying not to look over at him, Red Boots and his sidekick. Now they were here, in the corner in the restaurant, drinking espresso. The bad ones always came in pairs, and the good ones were always alone.

It was dogging him, had followed him the four hundred miles north from L.A. the same way Lucy's blues had followed her. It wasn't just the tails he'd picked up, the foreshadowing of trouble, the suggestion of the last act. What was on his shoulders, weighing him down was the reality of his state, of *their* state, even the ones he hated, like the murderer in the black cape. It had followed him. It was there every time he looked for it, every time whatever had distracted him away from it stopped distracting him from it. It was as present as the two tails across the room. It was his heartache. Everybody gets a heartache; this was his. It made every day a hole he had to claw his way out of, just to begin again. It was enough to make you dive off a roof, as if that'd fix anything, end anything.

Had he really thought that phrase, the *reality* of his state? Funny word for it. More like . . . unreality. More like . . . "*death's other Kingdom*." A little T. S. Eliot for the fans.

Jimmy drank the last of the red. And only then noticed there was another full glass waiting beside it. Another Chianti.

He stared at it. The bartender came past.

"What's this?" Jimmy said.

"Somebody bought you a drink," she said. She was in her forties, with longer hair than most women her age. It was something else San Francisco had, bartenders and waiters who weren't just doing this while they were waiting to get famous. Or waiting to find someone to pair off with who was. She smiled the nicest, simplest smile. Jimmy had the instantaneous thought that he'd like to curl up in her arms on whatever quilt-covered Victorian bed she had in whatever vanilla candle–scented apartment in whatever working-class neighborhood she and her cat lived in. Or even just lie there and watch her as she pulled down the lacy shades to keep out the morning, while Mr. Kitty walked the infinity sign in and around her ankles.

"I bet you aren't working on a screenplay," he said.

"Oh no, you're from L.A.," she said with mock sadness.

"What did he look like, my secret admirer?" Jimmy asked, to set her up to correct him, to say *She*.

"Can't tell you," the bartender said instead. "That would violate the Bartenders' Code."

"A regular?"

"Never saw him before," she said. "But then again, I don't usually work Thursdays."

Jimmy turned on his bar stool to follow the bartender's eyes to an empty table, a table near the Sailors. Just looking in the tails' direction was enough to spook them. They left their coffees and headed for the door.

"What's your name?" Jimmy said, looking back.

It was Angelina.

He looked across the bar at her and recited . . .

*Those who have crossed*
*With direct eyes, to death's other Kingdom*
*Remember us—if at all—not as lost*
*Violent souls, but only*
*As the hollow men*
*The stuffed men.*

"What do you think of that, Angelina?" he said after he'd uttered the lines.

"I think it's the Chianti talking," she said.

He said, "No, if it was the Chianti talking, it would be . . .

*Nel mezzo del cammin di nostra vita*
*mi ritrovai per una selva oscura*
*ché la diritta via era smarrita . . .*

"OK, I admit it," she said. "*I* bought you the drink."

Jimmy knew it wasn't true but appreciated the flirtation. "Dante's *Inferno*," he said. "Chicks always dig it."

He stood. The second glass of wine was untouched, catching the light.

The bartender looked sorry to see him go. "Aren't you going to drink it? Maybe she's coming back."

"Chianti makes me sentimental," Jimmy said. "I've had enough. Next thing you know, I'll be quoting poetry . . ."

On his way out, Jimmy went by the empty table. Where his admirer had been? A table in the corner. There was only an empty glass.

And, improbably, a scent still hanging in the air, the scent of a woman.

––––––––

He stood outside, looked up Columbus, the rise up the hill, a bigger hill to the right and the Financial District to the left, the point of the TransAmerica Pyramid piercing the lifting fog.

A bit more of the Dante he'd rattled off inside found its way into his mouth. Standing there looking up Columbus, he translated it . . .

*So did my soul, that still was fleeting onward,*
*Turn itself back to re-behold the pass*
*Which never yet a living person left . . .*

His new best friends were waiting in the shadows across the street. Jimmy set out to walk the rest of the way back to the Mark Hopkins, up and over another hill, Nob Hill, which took up most of two hours and what remained of the night, and left Red Boots and the other Sailor thoroughly winded.

He decided not to think about the dead girls. And he didn't.

# FOUR

The morning broke eternal, bright, and fair.

Or so it looked to Jimmy. He was on the open top deck of the red-and-white ferry that crossed the Bay from Pier 41 to Sausalito. He'd gone back to the hotel to change, to shower, to go from the black linen suit he'd worn yesterday to another linen suit, this one the color of the little spoon of cream on the Irish coffee at the Buena Vista. A cream-colored suit over a black shirt, like today was going to be the opposite of last night. *As if*, as the kids say.

But it *was* a beautiful day; a few clouds pushed all the way back over to Oakland. Tiburon was in front of them, Alcatraz sliding by to the left. On the Rock, another red-and-white boat off-loaded the 10:10 crowd as the first-run-of-the-day people queued up for the trip back across to San Francisco. (Did they still call it that, "the Rock," after the movie, after the wrestler who'd named himself after the movie and then become a movie star?) Jimmy could hear the voices of the kids on the Alcatraz dock, loud, vacation loud.

Down below him a deck, Lucy *almost* looked caught up in the new morning thing herself. She sat out in the open in the middle of the first row of fiberglass benches, ten feet back from the splash zone, the V of the bow. She'd made a friend, a white-haired lady in a spiffy blue-and-white Nautica windbreaker, a happy lady, a talker. Lucy said a few words in reply now and then and nodded every few seconds. Women liked her, Lucy. Jimmy wondered why, what it was that was in her eyes or the shape of her mouth or the way she held herself that made women like her. And want to help her. He hadn't really looked her in the eye. Up close. Maybe it'd move him, too.

The boy Jimmy was calling Les Paul for the shape of his guitar case came out onto the deck with two hot chocolates in his hands and a frosted, sprinkled donut stuck in his mouth. It was a little cool out here on the

water, but he was wearing just a T-shirt. He handed off one of the cocoas
to his sister and sat a few places away on the end of the bench, so as not
to intrude in the back-and-forth between the women. He sat there and
went to work on his donut, eating the way kids do, taking a bite and then
looking at the thing, studying it while he chewed. He looked over at Lucy
and the Nautica lady. Jimmy got the sense that the boy knew his sister was
hurting, off balance, and that he didn't much relish the role of helpmate,
was glad for some help.

*Training for the women ahead for you*, Jimmy thought.

Les only stayed on the bench a minute. Too much energy. Too much
juice running through the lines. He took his breakfast snack up to the
bow, lay forward into the angle of the hull on the port side. A gull found
him immediately, with that bright donut, took up a position in the air two
feet above the boy's head, locked on, even when the boat rose or splashed
to one side, powering through a swell. *This is his job*, Jimmy thought about
the bird, *as much as popping and locking for the tourists is Machine Shop's
job nights down on the waterfront.*

Les broke off a piece of the donut and ate it very deliberately and then
another and then another until it was gone, and then the bird moved on
to the next mark.

Jimmy lifted his gaze to Tiburon, getting bigger in the frame. It was
like another Alcatraz in size and the lift of its hump, but an island of a
whole other order in its hospitality, its richness. And its freedom? It was
green, for one thing, and dotted with houses. Old Money. San Francisco
doctors and lawyers. Second and third generation. Maybe fourth.

He saw that Lucy was looking at it, too, even as the white-haired lady
prattled on.

"Is that Tiburon?" Lucy interrupted her to ask.

"Yes, it is," Jimmy saw the white-haired lady reply.

There was a change in pitch, and the boat slowed. It was a commuter
ferry, with a stop in Tiburon before the turnaround in Sausalito. They were
a good half mile out from Tiburon but, even over the sounds of the water,
the engines, the wind across the decks, they could hear hammering. And
old-school hammering, too, with a hammer, not an air gun. Jimmy scanned
the houses up and down the hill and down to the rocks, the water's edge,
until he found it, the grand old moss-green Craftsman "cottage" with a
scar of new wood on one side of its face and a carpenter, now a third of a
mile away, in khakis and a white sleeveless tee, raising and dropping that
hammer, a half beat off from the sound that crossed the water.

---

Sausalito was Sausalito. You had to look hard to see how it could be a real place to real people, a place to live and not a happy hologram that zapped back into the projector once the last tourist turned his back to go up the ramp to the boat.

Lucy and Les had fish and chips at an H Salt Esquire that faced the waterfront and the marina. It was early yet, right at twelve, and there wasn't much of a line. They brought the food outside, very accommodating for the investigator tailing them. Lucy seemed to fall back into herself over lunch. She stopped eating and pushed away her little newspaper-lined basket of greasy fish.

Jimmy hated to say it, but he was already tired of her here-we-go-again soul-sink act. Les reacted to it immediately. Maybe that was what irritated Jimmy, how the boy scrambled each time to find in himself some sense of what to do to help.

"It's just a piece of fish," Jimmy said aloud.

The panhandler on a break on the bench beside him stirred. "You sure you can't help me out with gas money, man?" he said. "I'm stranded."

Jimmy got up, never even really looked at him.

"God bless you," the panhandler said.

Next, there was some jewelry for Lucy to look through, a rack out under the perfect sun alongside the very clean sidewalk in the bank of stores and bars along Bridgeway, the main drag. Jimmy strolled along across the street, stopping when she stopped, catching the mundane details to pass on to Angel. Lucy fingered a necklace while the bosomy young hippie woman who'd made it told her how good it looked on her. Les stood by, patient, putting on a good show of having no place he'd rather be than with his depressed sister in Disneyland. The boy pointed to another necklace, and the hippie girl took it down and handed it to Lucy. Lucy undid the clasp and held it up around her neck, but it was clear her heart wasn't in it anymore.

A passerby offered an opinion. "It looks good on you," Jimmy saw her say.

She was a real beauty, the passerby. Alone, too. With an expensive, trendy, flat leather bag over her shoulder, matching her expensive, trendy, pointy shoes, Jimmy guessed. The bag and shoes were bold yellow, golden-rod. She took off her sunglasses, shook out her hair. It was women like this with hair like this who made them come up with a new name for *brown*. She wore a white dress, full in the skirt, belted, V-necked, summery, so white it splashed light onto the storefront. She was Lucy's age, maybe a little older. The dress was long and had something of a *Town & Country* classy modesty about it. But it didn't stop Jimmy from imagining her legs pretty much all the way up to the top.

Lucy smiled and thanked the passerby but didn't want to talk. The woman smiled in return and walked on.

Lucy and Les took the bus.

Jimmy took a cab.

Right across the Golden Gate.

There was the city, off to the left. The day was still wonderfully, deceptively beautiful, clear and blue. And that moon. A daylight moon, almost full, sitting atop the point of the TransAmerica Pyramid like a balloon. The window was down, and the air smelled good. Jimmy realized he was happy. Go figure.

It was even a nice taxicab, patchouli and all. The driver was a Mr. Natural with dishwater blond dreads. The picture on his license had him with the same look, five or six years earlier. In the movie playing in Jimmy's head, here was the long-term live-in "husband" of the busty jewelry maker on the street back in Sausalito. He had the Pacifica station on the radio. They were against the war.

Lucy and Les's bus was four car lengths ahead. It was a commuter. With a rainbow running down the side. It changed lanes. The cab driver changed lanes with it.

"You're from L.A.," Mr. Natural said. He had his window down, too, enjoying the sea stink, too, the cool air. The cab was an excellent old Checker, with wing vents, as God intended, so there wasn't a roar that had to be shouted over.

"Yeah," Jimmy admitted.

"I can read people."

"So what was it? What said L.A.?"

"The suit, I guess. The extra button undone on your shirt. Your shoes. A little showbizzy but not executive suite. But not actor, either."

"You've been reading my mail," Jimmy said.

"I used to be a haberdasher. Eleven years."

"Do they really call them haberdashers?"

"They did when I was doing it."

"Here? San Francisco?"

"Right on Union Square," the cabby said.

Jimmy tried to do the math. The driver looked late thirties at the most.

"You ever see that movie *The Conversation*?" the cabby-haberdasher said, taking one hand off the wheel, turning, looking back, getting eye to eye.

"Yeah," Jimmy said. "Gene Hackman." He waited.

"I love that movie," the other said.

The Sausalito bus blew by the toll booths in the far right lane and pulled over. There was a plaza at the head of the bridge and a small commuter parking lot.

There wasn't any chance of the bus pulling out anytime soon, so the cabby just slowed and picked a lane and waited through the minute that it took to come up to the toll booth.

"Be here now!" he said to the toll taker, a gruff-looking 1950s-looking man, probably Italian, as he handed over five bucks.

"Baba Ram Dass," the toll man said. "He's sick, you know. And broke."

Mr. Natural just shook his head sadly.

He held up his right hand so you could see it in the rear window and started across three lanes to the outside. Remarkably, people yielded. He left a car's length between him and the bus, so they had a clear view.

When the bus's door opened, the first one off was a leathery little man in his sixties in a serious bike rider's frog suit. He went around to the front of the bus and started unhitching his lean red-and-green Euro bike off the rack.

"Some don't like to ride across the bridge," the cabby said, narrating. "Guy that size, he might be right."

"When I was here before, they didn't used to let you ride across," Jimmy said.

Mr. Natural shook his head. "You got it wrong," he said. He turned around to look at Jimmy. "Unless you haven't been here in twenty years and you're a whole lot older than you look. They put the bike lane in, in 1992."

Lean Man mounted up, headed on south into the city.

"They used to be worried about jumpers," the cabby said. "Stupid. No bike rider is going to jump. Think about it."

"I was always surprised they let you *walk* across," Jimmy said.

"They couldn't stop people from walking," the cabby said. "It would be admitting something they're unable to admit."

Lucy and Les Paul got off the bus. Jimmy dug into his pocket for his sheaf of bills.

"I heard something on the radio this morning," the cabby said. "They said new figures show that the cost of living now outweighs the benefits."

Lucy and Les just stood in the sunlight a moment next to the bus. They looked like they were coming this way, coming back across the bridge. They'd walk right by him if Jimmy stayed in the cab. He got out.

He leaned in through the open passenger window, handed Mr. Natural two twenties. "Thanks," he said.

"It's a joke. Think about it."

"I'm laughing on the inside," Jimmy said.

----

But Lucy and Les didn't come back across the bridge. Not yet anyway. Instead, they found the stairs that led down to the Golden Gate Bridge observation area and gift shop, a round building with glass sides and an iron skeleton, probably the same iron from the bridge. Below the shop, down through the tops of the dark green trees, was brick Fort Point, built around the massive foot of the southern base of the bridge.

The shop was crowded. The "gifts" were grouped by languages. You couldn't call them trinkets. The "lap throws," whatever they were, were 129 U.S. dollars, which apparently was a sensational bargain if you were Japanese. Lucy and Les Paul stayed by themselves, as much as it was possible in the packed room.

She dug in her purse and came out with coins for Les for one odd hand-cranked vending machine. A penny and three quarters. The low-tech machine smashed an elongated image of the Golden Gate onto the raw stock of the penny—and kept the six bits for the trouble. Les turned the big handle and made one and got so happy he looked about ten. Lucy laughed off a handful of years, too, and then went back to her purse for more quarters and another penny for another go-around. A matching pair. Maybe they'd get the hippie girl back in Sausalito to turn the pennies into earrings.

And then Lucy was sad again.

What happens to happiness? Where does it go when it goes? And how? Out of the throat where the throaty laughter was born, across the tongue, across the teeth? Are there people who can *see* it leaving, drifting out? Is happiness exhaled like breath? Does it float into the clouds? Does it hover over our heads like a departing soul, hanging around to haunt us once we're low again, dead to joy again? *That's my happiness up there . . . It used to be mine.* Because Lucy *was* happy, Jimmy had seen it with his own eyes, as clearly as he could see anything else in the gift shop. And now it was gone, as gone as anything could be gone, sucked out of her, breathed out of her. She'd stepped out into the sunlight in her new jeans and white top. (Out of the wind, off the boat, and away from the water, she'd pulled off the jacket and tied it around her waist by the sleeves.) She'd stepped, still laughing, out of the gift shop, holding the bright flattened pennies up to her ears until Les snatched his away from her. The sun should have lifted her spirits, made her even happier, but the opposite happened.

Or *something* happened. As they came out onto the observation area, she just stopped (it was next to one of the coin-operated telescopes) and went from happy to sad. Jimmy had come out ahead of them, was across the way against the low wall that hemmed in the observation area. It was almost as if she'd seem him standing there and thrown on her depression again, like a wool overcoat, just for him.

But she had a savior. Or at least a friend. The woman in the white dress with the yellow purse and yellow shoes and the highlights in her chestnut hair. She was back, apparently hitting the same tourist spots as Lucy and Les, though she didn't exactly look the tourist. She stood, alone again, just this side of the snack bar on the observation deck. Was she in line? She never turned away once she'd seen Lucy, sad ol' Lucy, once she'd seen what was on her face, coming out of the gift shop.

She started toward her.

"Are you all right?" Jimmy watched the woman in white say, right into Lucy's ear. She touched her arm, just above the wrist, with just her fingertips.

Lucy nodded, but in a way that made it obvious she wasn't. Maybe too obvious.

Les was still standing there beside his sister. The woman in white said something to the boy that Jimmy couldn't read. Maybe it was, *Leave us alone a minute.* Les started away for the concession stand. He only made it a few feet before Lucy called him back and handed him a bill.

Les went to wait in line at the snack bar. For what? A water? Coffee?

Jimmy's impatience with Lucy was back again, too.

*Get her a hankie. Get her a beer to cry in.*

*Get her a blue key light to stand in, to add to the effect. Get her the world's smallest violin.*

The woman with the white dress and yellow purse led Lucy to a bench across the grassy observation area, held her by the arm as if she was eighty and in her vapors. A Japanese woman on the bench rose when she saw the distressed women approaching. She bowed and backed away.

The women sat. The woman in white had those long legs of hers crossed, showing through the inverted V in the skirt, unbuttoned two buttons.

"Sexy Sadie," Jimmy said.

Were they holding hands now? They were hip to hip. They were fifty feet away, as far away as you could get without going over the berm. Had they moved there because of him, out of earshot of any men, even the anonymous L.A. man in the off-white linen suit? Sexy Sadie would ask a quiet question, and Lucy would nod. And then, after the warm bond between them had bonded still warmer, Lucy would offer a question, and the woman would nod.

Where were the steaming cups of chamomile?

But then, when Lucy put her eyes on the ground and said nothing for a long time, the woman leaned close and whispered in her ear.

It made Jimmy remember something. From last night. Another whisper.

Les Paul was still waiting. He wasn't monitoring his sister, didn't even look over that way, seemingly glad to have been assigned a task that involved action and not emotion. At the head of the snack line was a barrel-shaped man, European, with a dictionary in his hand, squinting at the white plastic movable type on the black menu board. This could take awhile.

When Jimmy looked away from Les and back at the pity party on the bench, the two women had been joined by a third. Another woman.

When it came to this supporting cast, each woman was better-looking than the one before, though it was wrong to try to rank them. Each one was better-looking than she had a right to be. Professional-strength beauty. Sexy Sadie was on the tall side, model tall, brunette. This new one was almost short, black-haired, blue-black hair cut close to the head, with ragged bangs, that shake-it-out shaggy boy look. And vibrant blue-green eyes, bright enough to be read a mile away. (Or across the observation area, at any rate.) Maybe they were contacts. She had a killer body, stretch-wrapped in what was probably pleather, a sixties minidress and matching high sixties boots, so far on the other side of self-conscious she couldn't even see us from there, back here in Dullsville.

Polythene Pam. So good-looking she looked like a man.

The woman in the white dress had been alone walking down the street in Sausalito when she'd stopped to offer Lucy advice about the sidewalk jewelry. And she was still alone, or alone again, when she'd spotted Lucy this second time, in front of the gift shop. And now Sexy Sadie had just happened to run into her very best friend in the whole world, and just when another poor sister needed bucking up, too, because these two, Sadie and Pam, were definitely close. Hooked up. Not sisters certainly. Lovers? Welcome to San Francisco. Maybe they were just two very *on* women. Or maybe Jimmy was just lonely. They flanked Lucy, sitting so close the three of them still left room on either end of the bench.

They worked her, poor Lucy. There was no other way to look at it. They were going to console her or die trying. Sadie would say something in one ear, and Lucy would nod or just keep staring at the grass in front of her and then, before Lucy could nod again, Pam would lean in to say something in the other ear, both of them close enough to kiss the downhearted girl.

It was something to behold, and Jimmy beheld it.

He looked over at the snack bar. Les was coming back with a Coke and a bottle of water. He was accompanied now by the stout European man. Jimmy decided on second look he was probably Italian. Homme Italia carried a hot dog and another Coke. He said a few last words to the boy and then waved with the hot dog. He looked a little lonely, too.

Les headed toward the spot where his sister and the stranger had been when he'd left them, out in front of the gift shop, before they moved to the bench across the grass. Les didn't seem to realize they weren't there until he was right on top of the same spot. He looked confused.

"They're on the bench," Jimmy said to himself.

But they weren't.

When Jimmy panned right again, the bench was empty.

He had a hunch, a bad feeling. He tried to talk himself out of it, even as he ran up the metal stairs, back up to the level of the bridge.

Three steps at a time, and there she was.

Lucy was on the bridge, walking away, walking toward the center. She was already a hundred yards gone. Alone. Walking away. She wasn't in any hurry, but there was a kind of scary purposefulness to her gait, almost as if she was counting the steps.

*Ninety-seven, ninety-eight, ninety-nine . . .*

She was still fifty yards ahead of Jimmy when Les blew past him with a concussive blast that almost pushed Jimmy into the rail. The boy still had the two drinks in his hands, but he dropped them now, first the Coke and then the bottle of water. The water bottle skittered across the walk and bounced into the air and then under the railing that separated the walk and bike run from the fast traffic.

The water bottle bounced into the air and was struck by a northbound

Saab, dead in the windshield, bursting. The driver spooked at the splash, the flood, locked the brakes, and crunched the nose of the car into the rail and took the hit from a tailgating Ford Festiva, all in the time it took Jimmy to realize who'd blown past him.

Les never looked back, even as the line of cars in both hot lanes skidded and smoked and banged into each other.

Lucy kept walking. The inverted arc of the main immense suspension cable was beside her to her right, descending as she crossed the lateral plane toward some inevitable point of intersection, the descending curve and the baseline, as if the whole of the Golden Gate were a graph to illustrate the diminution of something. Hope? Promise? A fall from a great height.

But Les caught up to her.

When Jimmy saw that the boy was going to overtake her, or rather when he saw her reaction, when he saw Lucy let go of the dark thing she was holding on to, he stopped, let them have their moment. He had to remind himself that they didn't know who he was.

Lucy tried to cover with a line or two, and her brother offered her the grace of something close to a laugh, though he certainly didn't mean it. His face was flushed from the run. Now he bent over to catch his breath. It occasioned another line from her. The sidewalk was empty around them, had been empty for almost all of the boy's run after her. It was odd.

The two consoling beauties were nowhere to be seen. They'd just disappeared, like a magic trick, like a magician's two lovely assistants.

Now the traffic recovered, rolled past Lucy and Les, except for the cars that had crashed. The drivers were out of them now. From the passing cars, no one looked over.

# FIVE

Jimmy sat with his eyes closed in a club chair by the window in his tenth-floor suite at the Mark.

For three hours.

There was a bedroom and a sitting room. He was in the bedroom, with the drapes open. When he'd first come back from the Golden Gate, from following Lucy and Les, from looking her right in the eye as she'd walked right back past him on the bridge, he had sat there for a long time and watched the light change, the clouds moving in across the Bay, their quick shadows crossing Alcatraz. Then he'd closed his eyes. Now it was five thirty. The day, which had begun so beautifully, was ending that way. At least for those looking at the sky.

Jimmy opened his eyes. He stood and took off the coat of his suit and laid it across the bed. He looked at the clock. He put on some music, the jazz the black cabby had been listening to, old jazz from a station that broadcast from down on the wharf and used Billie Holiday's "I Cover the Waterfront" under its station IDs. He walked back to the window. The low air conditioner under the tall picture window blew right at his groin. It would have been funny, worth a joke, a line, if he'd had anybody in the room with him. He found the little door to look in on the AC controls, fiddled with the knobs and buttons, but couldn't shut it off. You didn't need AC in San Francisco, and the hotel *didn't* have it for years, didn't have it the last time he was here. The windows used to open, even the tall ones. He felt his anger rise, felt it burn out to the surface from whatever tight, dark spot he usually kept it stuffed into.

"*Goddamn it!*" he said, slamming the little lid closed.

The machine wasn't a bit offended, responded only by blowing more cold air at his genitals.

Jimmy snatched up the phone and rang the front desk.

"Yes, Mr. Miles," a man with a young voice said, a beat sooner than you'd get for a regular room in a regular hotel.

"I can't turn off the air-conditioning," Jimmy said, *barked*, like some I'm-paying-a-thousand-dollars-a-day L.A. type. He heard the way he sounded but blew out the rest of it anyway. "I don't want it; I don't need it. I want to open the window. I'm not going to jump. I just want some pure air. I want my goddamn window to open the way it used to open."

"Yessir. Sorry."

The wall behind the bed was mirrored. Jimmy got a look at himself on the phone, the clench of his jaw.

He took what they call in childbirth pain-management classes "a cleansing breath."

"Mr. Miles?"

"Yeah, look, I'm sorry," he said with his normal voice. "Just tell me how to turn this thing off or send someone up."

"They're already on the way, Mr. Miles."

He hung up. There was a trio of water bottles on a smoked green glass tray on the table beside the bed, the Mark Hopkins label. He opened one and drank it down, standing there. He took a second one to the window, cracked the seal on the bottle.

Any time Jimmy cursed in front of his friend Angel, "took the Lord's name in vain," Angel rebuked him. Or thought of it. He should call him. He should have called him already. He hadn't reported in since he'd stood on the brown hillside west of Cholame. Yesterday morning.

What would he report? Lucy had looked all right when he left her a few hours ago. The brother and sister took a cab from the bridge back to the Haight. Jimmy was in a cab right behind them. He blew past them on Masonic, then had the cabby loop around up by the top notch on the park and came back down. He'd waited up the hill that way, like a jealous lover, like a nervous dad, for twenty or thirty minutes before the cabby shifted in his seat one more time, and Jimmy let him roll on. They were home. They were OK. But something *had* changed that morning. Jimmy had looked into her eyes, really looked. On the bridge, the boy had reached her in time, and she had put a look on her face that tried to laugh it off, to say that this couldn't possibly be what it appeared to be, a woman purposefully pacing off the last of her life. Jimmy had the details, if Angel wanted them. Les had made his awkward joke about dropping her Diet Coke and water. "I didn't know what you'd want," Jimmy saw him say. And then, as the traffic came back to speed, blasting past them headed north, as *life* had resumed, Lucy had put her arm in her brother's, very grown-up, and they had turned and started walking back. Jimmy was against the rail. He set out walking, *toward* them. So they wouldn't be suspicious of him. (He couldn't believe they hadn't yet made him, with all the close surveillance. But they weren't criminals. Why would they think anyone would be watching them?) And so, walking toward Marin, with the two of them walking back toward the visitor center, he came face-to-face with Lucille. Up close. Close enough to see into her eyes.

Here's what changed in that moment: Jimmy wasn't impatient with her anymore. He no longer doubted the genuineness of her melancholy.

He drained the second bottle of water. Now night was falling. He'd have to go back out there to her, back to the Haight, wait there at the apartment building until she came out. Or went to the roof again. He had to do what he could do. He had to go to work. It was what he did.

So why did he have this knot in his gut?

Why was he so full of anger?

There was a knock at the door, a little less subservient sounding than he would have expected. Maybe he hadn't intimidated the house staff after all.

It was a black man. Tall. Bony. He looked a little like Al Green, standing there, especially when he smiled, with big, perfect teeth.

He was wearing black-and-white suede shoes. With dice on the toes.

"I maybe got something for you," he said, stepping right on into the room after a quick look down the hallway in one direction. He closed the door behind him. "Little sumpin' sumpin'."

Jimmy looked from the shoes back up at his face.

"Machine Shop," he said.

"How are you, man?"

He looked naked, diminished, out of his silver paint. The face and neck were swollen in places from the beating he'd taken behind Alioto's, but Shop was dark-skinned, and the bruises would be hard to see. One eye had probably been swollen shut when he awoke that morning. It was still puffy, teary. There was a hematoma in one corner of the white of the eye, like a drop of red ink in a teaspoon of milk.

"I called, but . . ." He stopped. With Machine Shop, it was like there were two people in there, engaged in steady, often heated conversation. The other must have said something. "All right," Shop said, "I never called. I just came over."

"How'd you know where to find me?"

"You had matches from the Mark, when you were smoking. You smoke too much, man. The body is a temple."

"I just quit."

"Good. You had two packs of matches. You got to the end of one, and you had another pack. So you had to be staying here, not just using a pack of matches somebody gave you. And then I made some calls."

"Calls."

"I keep my ear to the anvil," Shop said.

"Called who?"

"All right," Machine Shop said, "I didn't call exactly. I just asked around about you. I have my network. Down on the water. Who you were. I knew where you were from, you told me that. I asked people who knew people. I found out, you know, what you do."

Jimmy waited.

"You know, that you're a detective and all. From Down Below."

"You mean hell?"

"L.A., that's what I call L.A. It's one of my trademarks." He heard another inner rebuke. "All right, that's what a friend of mine calls it. Los Angeles, Down Below. Or jus' D.L., short for Down 'Low."

"D.L. instead of L.A.," Jimmy said.

"That's jus' him," Machine Shop said. "Look, like I said, I maybe got something for you . . ."

"Tell me what you think you know about me," Jimmy said, an edge to his voice now.

"That you're a detective. You look into things for people. But not for the money. You work out of your house. That it has to be something that, you know, touches you in your soul."

"That it? Is that who I am?"

"That, you know, you're a Brother. Well, not a *brother*, but, you know, a . . ."

There was a knock at the door.

"That's probably him now," Machine Shop said.

Jimmy reached for the knob, not really hearing the last thing he'd said. "That eye looks bad," he said. "You know any Sailor doctors?"

"Look, before you—"

Jimmy opened the door.

Two people stood there. One was a very short man, built like a bomb. Brown cuffed trousers, a white short-sleeved shirt, tight over the biceps.

Brown wing tips. A full head of straight black hair, oiled, combed back, a once-a-week barbershop haircut.

And a sad, Greek face.

The other guy standing there was a thirty-year-old boy in a Kelly green Mark Hopkins blazer who wondered who the man beside him was.

"Is this him?" the Greek man said to Machine Shop, pointing a finger at Jimmy.

"I said wait," Machine Shop said. "Downstairs."

"Mr. Miles?" the hotel boy started.

Jimmy dismissed the boy. "It's all right," he said, "I'll do it myself."

The green-blazered boy looked at the tiny, strong man and then at the tall black man with the beat-up face.

"You sure?" he said.

"Yeah, thanks," Jimmy said.

The hotel runner gave Machine Shop and the short Greek man another comprehensive look, as if he might be called upon to testify later, and nodded to Jimmy again and padded away.

So then it was just the three of them.

Jimmy let the Greek man come in, even let him close the door behind him. He didn't break five feet, but no doubt he could kick both of their asses.

"Have a seat," Jimmy said to the little guy. The Greek man took a seat.

Jimmy snagged Machine Shop's eye and tipped his head for him to follow him into the bedroom.

Shop came into the bedroom. Jimmy closed the door. He just looked at Shop, asking the obvious.

"It was his daughters who stepped off last night," Shop said.

Jimmy didn't exactly see *that* coming. People were always showing up with "a friend," some old grievance they thought Jimmy could fix, something "that should just take a couple hours." If you were a plumber, after you'd had a burger or hot dog out in the backyard, before the game started, they'd probably ask you if you'd mind taking a quick look under the toilet.

But this came at him from an unexpected angle. Had he forgotten about the beautiful naked girls, the dive off of Pier 35 last night, his first night in town? *It's not the going fast that kills you; it's the sudden stop.* He went over to the window. The city was purple all of a sudden, from one edge to the other. It was like a postcard with the color out of whack.

"The twins," Machine Shop said.

"Yeah, I know. What's he doing here?"

"He doesn't know how to deal with it," Shop said.

"I'm not a counselor," Jimmy said.

"He has all these questions. I thought of you."

"Yeah, I'm the answer man," Jimmy said, with his back still turned.

"He lives across the Bay, El Cerrito," Machine said. "They were just out of high school. They were younger than they looked. I thought they were from some other country, but they were just girls just out of school, come into the city for, I don't know, the nightlife. You see a lot of them down there, more than you'd think."

When Jimmy didn't say anything, didn't even seem to hear him, Machine Shop kept on, "He got the call at one-something in the morning. He came over there to the wharf. He was still there when I came back at dawn, like I always do, after I went home and got out of the paint. He was just walking around, standing there at the place where it happened. I hesitated to talk to him, but it was easy to see who he was."

"What did you tell him?"

"I tried to comfort him. Just that—"

"What did you tell him about me?"

"Just that you were a friend of mine and that you were a detective, that you looked into things."

"That's it?" Jimmy said, turning to look at him, a hard question.

"That's all I said," Shop said. This time there didn't seem to be a second voice in his head calling for a correction. After a second, he said, "They still lived at home."

"You're *playing* me," Jimmy said, looking back down on the bruised city. "Stop it."

Shop held up his hands. "He just needs—"

"He needs somebody else," Jimmy turned and said. "I'm not a shrink. I'm not a minister. How am I going to help him? I don't know shit. I'm not smart. My instincts are lousy. I hear something wise, and I make a joke about it."

"I understand," Shop said. "I fully understand."

"I have something I'm doing already. For a friend of mine. Tell him—"

But then the door opened, and the father stood there. He looked at Jimmy and then at Machine Shop and then back at Jimmy. Maybe he'd heard them through the door.

"He said you were there, too, that you saw it, too," the short man said. Only now did he let them hear the hint of an accent, a little Greek in the voice to match the shape of his face and the color of his eyes.

"Yes, I did," Jimmy said. "I'm sorry."

The man reached into the pocket of his shirt.

"Don't show me pictures," Jimmy said, raising a hand against him.

The man pushed the picture back down into his pocket.

That sad Greek face. It could have been half of the comedy/tragedy emblem. There's no tragedy like Greek tragedy.

"What's your name?" Jimmy said.

"George Leonidas."

Jimmy offered his hand. "Jimmy Miles."

"It means *lion*. My family's name."

"I know," Jimmy said.

"Why do you know?"

"I've been around." Jimmy was still standing at the window. He turned, took a step closer to the man, a sympathetic step. But what he said was, "I can't help you."

Machine Shop lowered his head and closed his eyes, his hands folded in front of him, like an elder standing before the first pew.

"I have to say," Jimmy said, with that same impossible mix of hard and tender, "there probably isn't anyone who *can* help you. What's happened is awful and wrong and impossible, but you have to take it. And probably alone. This time, it's your turn."

"God*damn*," George Leonidas said. It meant three or four things. *Goddamn you* was one of them.

Jimmy just stood there in front of him for a long time. Neither man moved, almost as if Jimmy was ready to take a shot to the mouth if that's what George the Lion needed to do next. But the small man just stood there, eyes on the floor. Jimmy could hear each breath he exhaled over the feathery whisper of the air conditioner.

It could have ended there, but then Leonidas said something, still staring at the muted green carpet in front of him, said it to himself more than to anybody else, or to God, something that flipped it all toward the other world.

"I saw Christina," George Leonidas said. "And she saw me."

———

"There is a place, a position, something, *a state*," Jimmy said, "between being alive and being dead. Not alive, not dead. In between."

There it was, for those who like their reveals cold and hard.

They were down in the Tenderloin. In the Porsche. Jimmy had the gray light of the dash on his face, the shining wood-rimmed wheel in his hands. He was riding in third gear with low revs, and the engine was purring. The Porsche was glad to be up out of the hotel garage, out breathing the night air. Jimmy was half lost but wouldn't admit it. It was a bit after nine, early yet, but the alleyways were already spotted with street people. Early yet, but there would still be a mad yell every once in a while, echoing off the emptied buildings. There wasn't much other traffic, a cab every once in a while or a lost, slightly spooked tourist or a box truck making a night delivery. Not even any cops. They'd roll in later, when the Tenderloin got its full freak on.

A *place*, a *position*, a *state*.

*Something*. He'd never found a noun for it. And as for the verbs . . . well, the verbs only added more confusion. To the uninitiated anyway.

"I know it makes no sense to you," Jimmy said. "How could it? You saw their bodies. But then you saw the one of them, up and walking, hours later. Who can understand that?"

George Leonidas was in the passenger seat, one hand on the grip bar on the dash, the way old people will do, or people unused to sports cars. Staring straight ahead, like he was scared. As if what he was wide-eyed about was the speed and the low-slung car. He didn't say anything.

Jimmy kept up the monologue. It was always a monologue. "They're called *Sailors*," he said, hearing himself pick the pronoun. *They*. "Not alive, not dead exactly. At least, not gone. Not a ghost, but flesh and blood." He thought of the mash of meat and blood where the two had impacted. He had seen the bodies, too, and before the sanitation death techs had cleaned things up.

He steered into the first of the real mysteries. "When this happens, when one of . . . them is born, they take on a new face, but, for the first hour or two, if the loved ones are around, the new might resemble the old, if they saw each other. But just for the first hours. Or, other times, it's not that way at all. It's not set. Each time is . . . each time."

His voice was low and steady, undramatic, like the engine of the car, just cruising through wild territory. He heard himself. It was like listening to his voice on a tape recorder. *Jimmy Miles Explaining It*. He remembered something he hadn't thought of in years, a ride with his father, when he was ten or eleven, when his father told him he and Jimmy's mother were divorcing. Middle of the afternoon, picked up from school. The tone was the same, Jimmy realized. The flat tone carrying the earth-rending news. Then it had been that speech that begins, "Sometimes a mother and a father grow apart . . ." *Grow apart*. Things don't grow apart. They either grow together, or they die.

The street was one-way. A half block ahead, the light went to yellow, but Jimmy kept on at the same speed. It was full red when he went under.

"Is it only when they kill themselves?"

George Leonidas had spoken.

"A lot of Sailors are suicides," Jimmy said, "but some were murdered. Some were accidents."

"I was electrocuted," Machine Shop said from the back, like another track on the stereo. He was wedged, long leg bones and bony arms and all, into the Porsche's jump seat, the little fold-down seats meant to hold bags of groceries or maybe a kid or two. His bent head was stuffed up against the leatherette headliner of the ragtop. It made him look like a giant in a very modern fairy tale.

Jimmy looked up at him in the center rearview mirror.

"A woman threw a plug-in radio into the bathtub with me," Machine Shop said. "I was just taking a bath." There was another millisecond for the corrective voice. "OK, I was with another lady friend . . ."

"All we know, or think we know," Jimmy said to Leonidas (and to himself, for the ten thousandth time), "is that it happens when there is some unfinished business. Maybe *because* there is unfinished business. Nobody knows. You're here as long as you're here. Then you move on."

"Where are you taking me?" George the Lion said.

"Nowhere," Jimmy said. "We're just talking."

He pulled it down into second and took the next right, onto Castro, took it a little faster than he had to.

---

It was Friday night in the Castro. The after-work bar crowd had spilled out onto the street, drinks in hand, some of them. All men, in this block. They'd hang out there for an hour or two, and then the night crowd would start to show. Leonidas, even in his present stricken state, was put off by the scene, men with their arms around each other. He had his window up, but you could still hear the punch-bag sound of the bass speakers in the clubs. Techno and house.

Jimmy took a right, climbed a hill, just like he knew where he was going. There was a park to the right as the road curved around on top of the hill.

Buena Vista Park. So maybe he wasn't lost after all. He stopped. There, below, was Lucy's Victorian apartment building, lights in half the top-floor windows.

Les was in the dining room. He had the Les Paul guitar out of its case, had it on his knee where he sat at the head of the long dining table. The table was mahogany, deep red, shiny, with the point of a white lace cover hanging off each end.

So the borrowed apartment belonged to a lady. It would fit with everything else, another woman putting her arms around the waif. Jimmy wondered who she was.

There was a dim light in the front bedroom, Lucy's room. It said she was there, that she was alive. Like Tinkerbell's little light.

Jimmy got out of the car. Machine Shop took the opportunity to unpack himself from the jump seat. They stood beside the Porsche, left Leonidas where he was, still gripping the bar, even with the car parked.

"I appreciate you doing this," Machine Shop said. "Saying the words. I never been any good at that."

"I was mostly just talking to myself," Jimmy said.

"I hear you. If there's ever anything I can—"

Jimmy cut him off with, "There's a woman in that apartment. That's her brother, in the dining room. Her name is Lucille. Lucy. I don't know what his name is. I call him Les. I need you to watch them, while I'm with him."

"I should be at work," Shop said.

"I have money."

"I don't do it just for the money," Shop said. "It's my witness, in its own way."

"Her name is Lucy," Jimmy said and opened the car door. He went to his pocket and took out a fold of bills. He gave a couple hundred to Machine.

"What am I supposed to do?"

"Don't let her kill herself," Jimmy said.

---

Then they were out of the car, walking, Jimmy and George Leonidas, down on the waterfront. It was the happening part of the night, crowds of tourists, even locals, enjoying the seafood joints and the street dancers and the jugglers and each other. It was Friday night.

"Here," George said, pointing to a corner of one of the parking lots between the trolley tracks and the docks. "This is where I saw her, my Christina. There were no people then, or only three or four. Not all this."

"What time was it?"

"Four o'clock."

"Was she alone?"

"There were two others, a man and a woman. Away from her, but watching her."

"What do you mean, they were watching her?"

"Like I was watching her, like she was mine. Like she belonged with me. They were watching her like that, too."

"What did she look like?"

George Leonidas's hand went toward the pocket over his heart again.

"I meant the one you saw," Jimmy said.

The Greek father took the picture from his pocket anyway. He gave it to Jimmy. "Christina is on the right. She would always be on the right, Melina on the left. She looked like herself."

Jimmy looked at the picture: He expected a yearbook picture, maybe the officers of the high school Greek Club. Or an all-dressed-up-for-the-prom picture: full, frilly dresses, a pair of dorky boys in tuxes between the gorgeous twins. What he got instead was a shot of the teens in one-piece swimsuits, Speedos, one black, one silver, standing with water skis beside the stern of a low-slung powerboat on the shore of some big-acre reservoir somewhere inland, brown hills in the background. Maybe Bethany, looking down on Altamont. The name of the boat was *Zorba*. Their black hair wasn't wigs. It was real. They wore it longer and looser in the picture. And wet and ropey. The sun was dropping.

"I saw *Christina*," the father said. "I saw *her*."

His hands had tightened into fists. At his side. As if he was clutching an iron bar in each one.

Jimmy handed back the picture. It hurt to look at the girls.

"You said she saw you. What did she do?" he asked. "Did she say anything to you?"

The sad Greek face tightened up, especially around the eyes. It was as if someone had sprayed something corrosive at his face.

"What did she say?"

George Leonidas took one of those clenched fists and punched Jimmy right in the face. Just like that.

Jimmy took it. It snapped his head back and knocked him onto his heels, but he took it, and all the surprise that came with it. George the Lion stepped a step nearer, closed up the distance the head shot had knocked between them. Only a second had passed. As Jimmy was bringing a hand up to his jaw, where the first of the pain was pushing its way out past the stunned surface and into the bone at the same time, the little man hit him again. In the face again, in the same place.

This time, Jimmy fell away, as if he'd been "slain in the spirit" on some cable TV evangelist's stage. George came after him, punching him twice in the belly, dull thudding hits that, even as Jimmy fell onto his back, made him think, *Old World*. He was getting an old-world beating, an honorable, manly, *controlled* beating, though the man landing the blows had completely lost it.

They weren't in the most crowded area, but there were people nearby, and they turned to look with the sound of the first couple of hits and whatever sounds Jimmy had made. They stepped closer, the witnesses, but there wasn't any cheering or joviality, the way there is in bad movies. They were seeing it for what it was, a bloody shock.

Leonidas couldn't stop himself.

Jimmy just took it. He barely lifted his hands in defense. He tried to get to his feet, managed only to get to his knees.

Leonidas hesitated. Jimmy's let-me-have-it manner broke the heated spell the Greek was under. He dropped his fists back down to his sides, like he was letting go of something, almost like he was throwing away something with both hands.

Jimmy touched his cheek with the back of his hand. It came away with blood smeared across it. But his mouth wasn't cut, and his eyes still worked. And he knew he didn't hurt any more than the other did.

"I don't understand," George Leonidas said. And said it all.

But he had something else for Jimmy. "That's what she said to me. 'Daddy, I don't understand.'"

# SIX

What Jimmy didn't tell George Leonidas was the most important thing, that last night someone else was on the roof with his girls, someone to whisper a word in their pretty ears, another sort of Sailor. What he didn't tell Leonidas was that there were two kinds of Sailors, two ways to respond to this impossible thing.

It wasn't exactly a fashionable idea these days, but some were Good and some were Bad.

What was that one's name? Jacob. Jason. Jamie. *Jeremy*. Machine Shop had offered up the name when his conscience had prompted him, when the other inside him had cleared its throat. *Jeremy*. There's a villain for you. A skinny kid in a black North Beach beatnik's turtleneck. And cape. A Jeremy.

But why would a Sailor, even a bad Sailor, want two innocents to die, to throw off their own lives? Why would a Sailor, even the darkest, the blackest-souled amongst their kind, climb up on a roof to encourage a suicide?

What would it profit?

Jimmy knew the Greek had already heard enough things he didn't understand, already had enough questions, standing there in the parking lot, on the waterfront. He didn't need to hear the rest of it, not yet. Maybe ever.

"Do you have a wife?" Jimmy said.

George Leonidas nodded. His hands were still throbbing with the flesh-memory of the beating. And hurting themselves, but he was in so much other pain that it didn't register.

"Go sit with her," Jimmy said. "Your wife."

Leonidas nodded.

"Don't tell her any of this, what I said to you," Jimmy said. "It won't help her. She'll believe it even less than you do."

"I tell her everything."

"Then tell her you met a crazy man, who talked crazy," Jimmy said.

"A man who just let me beat him . . ." Leonidas added.

Jimmy looked him right in the eye. "Don't tell her you saw your daughter. Christina. It will only make for more pain. Neither one of you will ever see either one of them again, do you understand that?"

"I understand the words," Leonidas said.

"Believe me," Jimmy said. "Neither one of you will ever see either one of them again. Not in this life."

Leonidas suddenly reached toward him. Jimmy flinched, thinking another blow was coming, but George the Lion just gripped him by the upper arm. "If they are where you say they are, then just tell me they are at peace. Go there and see them and come tell me that."

His grip hurt. "I will," Jimmy said.

If Jimmy had had his own nagging voice of conscience like Machine Shop did, now he would have taken it back. Because there was no way he could do what he said he would do, and Jimmy knew it. There wasn't even any reason to believe both girls were Sailors now, just the one. The other was probably just gone.

"Where can I reach you?" Jimmy said. He knew he'd probably never even try.

Leonidas had business cards in a leather fold-over holder. He handed one over. He was in plumbing supplies. Across the Bay. He put the card holder back in his front pants pocket and nodded at Jimmy and turned and walked away.

Card. Nod. Turn. Walk.

Jimmy watched him go, watched to see if he would look over at the pier where it had happened, Pier 35, where the girls had jumped, where the seams of his world had been rent. But he didn't look over.

Jimmy let him get some distance ahead, then followed him. He didn't exactly know why. He followed Leonidas through the crowds of tourists, who only seemed to have grown in volume and *volume* in the last hour, past the street performers, past everything his daughters had passed the night before, past the last things they had seen in life, across a packed open parking lot to a parking structure, open on the sides, to a dark silver Cadillac DeVille, four or five years old, the last of the "old man" Caddies. He unlocked it and got behind the wheel, started the engine, pulled on the lights, never breaking down, never looking back.

Leonidas had never looked back.

*How do you do that?* Jimmy thought.

He thought it through three Chiantis, a few hours later, sitting in a bar, looking back in spite of himself, remembering more than he wanted to about a very specific time and place. And a person. And *Chianti*. What he was drinking tonight was good wine, but then it was cheap, youthful wine, Chianti out of basket-wrapped bottles, Italian-movie Chianti. *La Dolce Vita.* 8½. Dan Tana's on Santa Monica in L.A. when it was still just a good red-checkered-tablecloth Italian restaurant music business and below-the-line movie people went to. Cheap, youthful. She was the one Lucy had reminded him of, starting back in Saugus Café. Mary.

*Don't look back.*

He was outside with the smokers. At one of those tall tables with tall chairs designed to keep you from ever relaxing.

There Lucy was, right across the street. At a table in front of the Starbucks wannabe in the Haight.

With Machine Shop.

The coffee joint was packed, every table full, inside and out, busier than Jimmy's bar. Lucy and Machine Shop were about the only ones without big Friday night smiles on their faces.

Big surprise, she was a little down.

But Machine Shop was on the job, even if this wasn't exactly what Jimmy had in mind when he told him to look after her. They were like new best friends. They had coffees in front of them. Shop would stir his thoughtfully while she talked, stirring and nodding, just like a gal pal. Then Lucy would stop, get to the end of something, end it with a question. Jimmy could tell even from across the street that her voice raised at the end of the line. Machine Shop would stop stirring, nod a couple of times more, and then say a line or two. He was a good listener, leaning in, eye contact. Once he even reached a hand across the table to pat the back of hers, completely nonsexual. Two pats and out. His posture and performance made Jimmy think *Twelve Step* again. Shop had a sponsor somewhere, probably was a sponsor to somebody else, probably a good one, too.

Jimmy drained his glass. The first step is admitting you're powerless . . .

Across in the coffee bar, a fat guy moved, and Jimmy saw somebody else. Polythene Pam. Alone. She was inside, right on the other side of the window, watching Lucy and Machine Shop, watching them to the exclusion of everything else. She had a little demitasse in front of her, a shot.

A guy came up, stood over her. (There was an empty chair across from her.) He had an espresso of his own, had the cup and saucer on his flat palm, an odd way of presenting it. Maybe he was a waiter somewhere. In L.A., he would have been an actor. He was nice enough looking and expected more from her than he got. She didn't even shake her head no, just gave him a chilly "smile" that ended long before it got to her eyes. Dismissed.

She *did* look good tonight, very tempting, even hotter than out on that sunlit bench in front of the Golden Gate gift shop with Sexy Sadie. Even more mod. Tonight she wore a little plaid skirt, a Scottish schoolgirl's skirt. And a fuzzy sweater. And over-the-ankle Doc Martens.

"She's killer-diller when she's dressed to the hilt . . ." Jimmy sang. He tried to take another drink but found his glass empty.

He thought he had sung it to himself, but apparently it was loud enough for a young woman and her date two tables over to hear. The girl looked at him with some pity.

Time to go. He left a couple of bills on the table, weighted them down with the red glass bowl candle, and exited out the front, all but hopped over the low iron railing just to show anybody watching that he was in complete control of his faculties. He didn't look back to see if the girl had any parting pathos for him.

He found a wedge of shadow, even if it did smell pissy, in the entryway of a storefront next to the Chianti bar. From there he could watch the rest of the play over at the coffee joint. Everyone was still on their marks, Shop and Lucy talking, Pam looking a little put off, stirring her little coffee with a little spoon.

Then he figured it out. The empty chair across from Pam was meant for Lucy. It was a date. Spoiled by Machine Shop.

A band of hippies came past Jimmy, six or seven of them, girls and guys. Central casting. Freaky and fun. Hendrix headbands, striped bell-bottoms, fruit boots. One even clinked finger cymbals. If Disneyland had a Haight-Ashbury section, hippies like these would stroll past, saying things like "What's *happening*, man?" and "Be groovy."

The leader wore a fringey vest, a puffy-sleeved shirt, and a sho-nuff Vandyke. His right-hand girl, who wasn't much older than thirteen, blew Jimmy a kiss. Leader Hippie pulled her back in line. As the troupe moved on, there was a little edge of color to him, but not Sailor blue. Or maybe it was just the streetlight.

When the retro hippies had cleared the frame, over at the coffee bar the little scene was ending. Lucy was standing now. She said another line or two to Machine Shop, and he said something back to her. She smiled, and it looked like it was over, but then she tipped her head toward him and leaned into him for a hug, more her idea than his was the way Jimmy read it. Shop kept watching her as she walked up the sidewalk in the direction of the apartment. When she turned the corner at Central Avenue, a block and a half away, he left his place by the little round table and started after her. He was going to watch her all the way to her door. On the job.

Polythene Pam stood up to go.

––––––––––

People make friends. People run into each other, find out they live a few blocks apart, make a date for coffee and commiseration. It happens all the time.

Or take a ride over into Marin on a beautiful, sunny day, like this morning . . .

Maybe he was seeing things that weren't there. Maybe it was innocent.

He didn't think that for a minute.

Jimmy kept ten cars back. Traffic was light. Last night, he had followed Polythene Pam away from the coffeehouse. She'd split a few minutes after Lucy. She was on foot, too. Pam stayed on one side of Haight Street, and Jimmy tailed her on the other, until she crossed the street in the middle of the block and came across to his side. She took the next right, walked across the wide greenbelt, the Panhandle, the eastern end of Golden Gate Park. There were a few street people out and people who lived in the park, but she never hurried her pace. Or looked back. (Here was another somebody who went through life looking straight ahead. With a purpose.) She turned left on Fell and walked two more short blocks.

To a black house.

The house had two-story columns out front and was painted black. There may have been some red trim here and there that didn't read in the darkness, but the house was *black*. And black lacquer at that. It shined. Pam opened the iron gate and let herself in the outsized front door.

So she lived in the Haight. Innocent? Her house looked like a frat house in New Orleans, like a Goth sorority at Tulane.

Jimmy spent the rest of the night on the street. At dawn, he went home to the Mark for a change of clothes and to pick up the Porsche.

Maybe it was time to introduce himself to Lucy.

He made it back to the Haight just in time to watch the Catholic home for unwed mom-ettes come to life. (It didn't look as if anyone was awake up at Lucy's. He parked up the hill.) They had those girls up at the crack of dawn, scrubbing the sidewalks out front, watering the plants in the planters, scattering some bread crumbs for the birds who lived in the trees in the park behind them. They washed the windows. *All the better to see the bright future ahead.* The nun who acted as boss to the detention detail didn't seem too bad, called all the girls by name, even spoke Spanish to two of them, making them laugh. You never know. They say sometimes you're entertaining angels unaware.

There were some signs of life at Lucy's. Jimmy was *this close* to getting out of the car, to walking down the hill to the front door at 52 Central, when Pam pulled up.

Girls' day out. It was nine, a very civilized hour for an excursion. Pam drove a Land Rover County, dark green, deep dark forest green. She was alone. She parked at the curb, and Lucy came out the front door a second later, a sweatshirt tied around her waist, over sporty pants. Bright, springy, coordinated, Gappy colors. She got in the front seat, and Pam revved the engine and backed up a foot to straighten out the wheels, and away they went. The nun was back in her third-floor window, watching the whole thing with a neutral, preternaturally patient look.

Jimmy wished *he* knew how to do that.

Once across the GG, the Range Rover passed through the tunnel to Marin, under the rainbow painted on its concrete face. There was a second and a third exit for Sausalito, but Pam kept going.

The two women talked all the way. They had the windows down, the sunroof back. Pam had that short, chopped-off hairdo for her jet-black hair, so the wind made her look like she was in the stylist's chair the whole way, getting a new cut blown out. Lucy's hair was longer, was like a scarf out the window when the currents caught it right. Out in the bright, happy light of Marin County, her hair had all kinds of life to it, looked almost red.

They took an exit, east, and rolled along across the top limit of the Bay, through an industrial zone, marine industrial, shoulder-to-shoulder marinas and boat repair bays, all along the curve of the water's edge. Maybe they were taking a boat out. The roadway was elevated a bit. The city could be seen in the distance, white and silver, with the dark hump of Tiburon in the foreground.

Here it was. There was a park, a large greenbelt cleared of trees except at either end, an expanse of green that went all the way down to the water, to the big hauled-in rocks and the six-inch waves whitecapped with foam and the detritus of the Bay. The Range Rover came around on the main highway and pulled into the lot.

From the water, from the south, Tiburon looked like an island at the top of the Bay, but close like this you could see that it was a knob at the end of a peninsula, a knobby knuckle on the end of one of the fingers reaching out into the Bay.

And on the end of the knuckle was another high-backed island. Belvedere. It was like the rich part of Tiburon, only almost all of it was rich.

Jimmy drove on past the park and the parking lot, went another half mile or so down to the ferry dock and the phony picturesque "seaport village" of shops and restaurants. There was a roundabout. Jimmy went around about it.

He came back up and pulled into the lot, parked where he could look out across the expanse of grass, all the way down to the water. He'd had the top down for the ride over. He got out and hoisted it up. He was in the first row of the lot, between two SUVs, hidden, dwarfed. A woman on one side of him was off-loading three boys in turquoise soccer gear, ten or eleven, a Jason and two Seans, and what looked like a hundred pounds of support equipment and a Hammacher Schlemmer collapsible sideline parents' two-place couch with cup holders for the lattes from the back and side of a Ford Expedition long enough to be a gas line all by itself.

Jimmy took a book and a warm Red Bull from his cooler over to a picnic table ten feet from the cars.

Lucy and Pam had spread out a blanket. They sat. Pam had a picnic basket, opened the lid, unpacked something from it. Jimmy thought he saw her looking over at him. Maybe she was more aware than Lucy and Les, more suspicious of the same guy always somehow being around. Maybe she'd realized he'd followed her home last night, to the black house. But he was a hundred yards away from them. Not much for Pam to see. Still, he put his nose in his book. It was *Zen and the Art of Motorcycle Maintenance*.

Lucy was watching the little kids on the field. Beside "the big field" where the Seans and the Jasons would be playing there was a tiny-tots field lined out with little bitsy goals and four-year-olds. Girls. The Purple Unicorns versus Rainbow Ponies, though they didn't defend the goals, and only the dads kept score, so you couldn't really call it *versus*. Half of the girls ran around aimlessly while the other half stood and talked. Two held hands. One was lying on her back in the grass, looking at the fat white clouds, opening and closing her legs and clapping the heels of her rubber cleats, like she was making a snow angel.

Pam put her hand on Lucy's shoulder as Lucy watched the kids. Jimmy had wondered almost from the start if Lucy was pregnant, if that was what was at the bottom of her unhappiness. But wouldn't that be too much of a coincidence, with her landing in a borrowed apartment across the way from a home for unwed mothers? Still, he wondered it again, when he saw the way she watched the kids.

And then along came the other one. Sexy Sadie.

Probably just another coincidence . . .

The three of them seemed to have coordinated their outfits. Pam was wearing white ankle-length pants and a short pink top. Sexy Sadie wore a sea-green skirt, a full Katharine Hepburn skirt, and a cotton blouse with rolled-up sleeves. The three looked like catalog models, especially when Pam and Lucy stood to greet the third and they all touched each other's arms and Sadie kissed Pam.

Jimmy hadn't seen her arrive, Sadie. There was a white '57 T-Bird in the parking lot he hadn't noticed before, but that would be a little too perfect. He was guessing the classic Jag sedan, but it was black and seemed too gloomy for her.

Maybe she had parachuted in, rappelled from a rescue helicopter, because now the crack two-woman sympathy team really sprang into action. Again. The three settled back onto the blanket and began to talk. Serious as serious gets. The light changed. As if the god of weather were part of the plan, had just been waiting for his cue, the cottony clouds at the same time took on some color, dark enough and sudden enough to make the parents on the sidelines of the game look up at the sky.

Lucy, on the other hand, was looking down.

Now she was crying, pulling the sleeve of her sweatshirt over her hand to daub at her eyes.

Sexy Sadie patted her leg.

Polythene Pam stroked her hair.

They were whispering to her, every word hitting some soft, assailable spot.

Jimmy had a thought, that he was watching a murder in slow motion.

# SEVEN

Machine Shop sat on the Market Street streetcar, in one of the side seats, one of the wooden slat benches. For some reason, San Francisco had bought up a half-dozen old New Orleans streetcars, refurbished them, kept the names.

Where was *Desire*?

Shop had all his gear with him, on the rollie. He was in his paint, fully, freshly silver.

"Look like you're moving out," a Chinese man seated across from him said.

"No, jus' headed toward my destination," Shop answered.

"You look like robot on vacation."

"Jus' making my witness," Shop said.

Jimmy was on the bench next to the Chinese man. It was an hour before sundown, not an easy time for him generally, the hour when the shadows tended to cross his soul.

But everybody else was happy. The Chinese man and almost everyone else on board were headed to a Giants game, a night game down at the new ballpark, the replacement for Candlestick, with some company's name crowbarred into its name. The streetcar riders were all decked out in Giants' shirts and jackets and hats, like the oddest, most overweight, most over-the-hill team imaginable.

It reminded Jimmy what a blue-collar town San Francisco was at its heart. There were plenty of the rich here, on Nob Hill, on Russian Hill, here in the City and over in Marin, on Tiburon, down in Hillsborough, but it was a city stocked with robust working men and women and their families. A union town. A proud town. A cohesive town. A public-transit town. A sweating town.

Going to work, just like Machine Shop.

They reached some stop, and the doors opened, front and back, and everybody else stood.

"Who're they playing?" Jimmy said to one kid on his way out, a boy eight or nine.

"Asshat *Dodgers*," the kid said, and got a laugh from the crowd.

Hey kid, at least in L.A. it's still just *Dodger* Stadium.

The streetcar rolled out again, empty except for Shop and Jimmy. Jimmy said, "I didn't mean you had to actually *sit* with Lucy last night."

"Yeah, that wasn't my plan," Machine Shop said. "It just happened."

Machine Shop didn't offer anything more, until he realized Jimmy was waiting for a report.

"She didn't come out of her place for a long time," Shop said. "The boy just played his guitar. I couldn't hear it, but I play a little myself. I believe he's good. I *used* to play, in my previous position." Shop went down a memory trail for a second. Jimmy waited.

"A light came on in the front bedroom about ten forty-five," Shop said. "I guess she was sleeping up until then. A few minutes before eleven, she came out. She was dressed up, kinda nice, but she had on a heavy coat, heavier than what she needed really. Had the collar up. Walked down the hill to Haight. She walked right straight to the corner, to the coffee place. She got a coffee, took it outside, sat down. I was watching from across the street, over there where you were later. She was pitiful. I couldn't stand it, came and sat with her, talked to the girl. She's just a child herself."

Shop exercised his lower face vigorously. "Am I cracking?" he asked.

"No, you look fine."

"I gotta get in character," Shop said.

"When you came up and sat down," Jimmy said, "did you get the idea she was meeting somebody?"

Machine Shop didn't answer for a long beat, staring straight ahead. Then he animated, straightened his spine, pivoted his shiny head robotically, and produced a mechanical sound without moving his lips.

"No," he said, unblinking.

The streetcar rolled on through the Financial District, empty, cold-looking, the wind stirring through it on a Saturday night, and made the big left turn onto the Embarcadero. *I Cover the Waterfront*. A Bay sunset cruise ship, out to the Golden Gate and back, was docked at Pier 39; a line of twenty ugly limos waited at the curb nose to tail, new-style prom haulers, stretched Escalades and Excursions. And a Hummer. The last time Jimmy was in San Francisco, the Embarcadero wasn't a tourist stop. The first time he came to San Francisco, there was still a freeway overhead, running along the curve of the docks and piers. It had been torn down a few years back. The docks had been just docks for all those years before that. Then somebody had gotten the idea tourists would come to the water's edge if they gussied it up a little. Come down to see where a hundred thousand wives and girlfriends said good-bye to a hundred thousand soldiers and sailors headed off to war. That was the scene in Jimmy's head as he looked out the streetcar window at the docks and the piers, *that* high drama, though it was before even his time. A lot of tears shed on these piers.

> *I cover the waterfront, watching the sea*
> *Will the one I love be coming back to me?*

Now it was home to another kind of sailor, off to another kind of war. One of their domains, one of their gathering places here. Every city had its Sailors, if some more than others. Even inland. Kansas City, Chicago. Even Orlando. (Though inland, they still tended to congregate near whatever big water was available.) But the big coastal cities collected the most Sailors, from inland, from all over. From small towns. You didn't like to be alone. You needed reinforcement, whether you were good or bad. (The new initiates straightway found out there were two ways to go.) Buses brought them every day, trains. They didn't much like to fly.

Jimmy saw a bright flash of blue around a young woman in a cluster of people at one of the stops. They were street kids, but not too ragged. One boy had a guitar. Even as the streetcar was pulling out again, with that surprising acceleration, Jimmy heard what he was playing, what they were singing, R.E.M., "Losing my religion . . ." Jimmy turned to look back at them, at the girl. Three of them were Sailors, though *her* blue, the edge of blue around her, was the strongest. So she was the newest, probably, or at least the newest to San Francisco. She had that New look in her eyes. She wore a T-shirt from some Oklahoma barbecue. He hoped that's where she was from. Oklahoma.

Machine Shop was looking back at her, too, at the cluster of Sailors. He mechanically rotated his head to the forward position again.

Jimmy rotated, too. He pulled the photo out of his pocket, the Leonidas girls beside the ski boat. With two days now past since she'd died, Christina would look different, but not completely different. He wouldn't have admitted it if someone had asked him, but he was down here to try to find her. There were things to look for. Sometimes the eyes would be the same, if you got up close enough. Jimmy hadn't known her, never spent any time with her before the dive off the roof. If he had, maybe he'd know her when he saw her. The surest link between the before and the after was gestures, the way you walked, nervous tics, the way you bit your lip, the way you brushed your hair out of your eyes. That was what was left. Maybe you could say that about anybody you remembered.

Jimmy watched Machine Shop do his act for twenty minutes. They'd gotten off two stops after they'd seen the Sailors losing their religion. Shop had been "on" since the Financial District, rolled his rollie down the street-car steps as a robot, held the doors open for a middle-aged white lady as a robot, moved away as a robot, even sidestepped a cluster of pigeons feeding on a spilled bag of popcorn as a robot. He drew a crowd immediately.

Shop's act, at least what Jimmy saw, had two aspects: he interfaced with skeptics, and he danced. The interfacing was simple. They tried to make him laugh. Or get mad, in the case of a pair of blocky twenty-something boys, probably in town on liberty from their shitty East Bay jobs. Those two got right in Shop's face and sneered and said some things, worked in tandem, one on each side of him. In the end, Shop's answer was a perfectly executed 180-degree pivot.

The dancing was basically a robot on *Soul Train* or, when the demographic skewed older, *American Bandstand*. A lot of Ohio Players and Earth Wind & Fire. A little KC & the Sunshine Band, the early years. Jimmy pushed through from the second row and put a twenty in the overturned top hat, up until then empty except for Shop's own prime-the-pump fiver. A couple of others followed Jimmy's suggestion. Machine Shop bowed his appreciation in four mechanical stages.

The sun was gone. Here came the night. Jimmy ended up at the crab stand, where he'd gone that first night. Where he'd met the Sailor crab kid who had middle-managed Machine Shop's beating, apparently for the crime of trying to suggest maybe the twins didn't *have* to jump. In Jimmy's mind, this was Sailor Central. For now anyway.

Crab Boy. There he was in his perfectly white sneakers. The stand was busy, every stool taken, a cloud of steam engulfing the scene. A heat lamp kept the curly fries warm. The light turned the whole steam cloud red. Dante's Crab Stand. The kid recognized Jimmy, jerked his head up in a noncommittal greeting, but never slowed the pace of slinging that Dungeness into those red-and-white paper boats. A sheet of white wax paper, a handful of crab, a white plastic fork, a tear of sourdough bread, a look up at the customer for a nod or a no, and then a wedge of lemon. Or not.

"Gimme one," Jimmy said.

"Aye aye, Cap." There were four orders ahead of him.

"You seen Jeremy?" Jimmy said when a stool came free.

"Who?"

"Jeremy."

"I don't know any Jeremy," the kid said and made the name sound funny. "I just barely know *you*. Who's Jeremy?"

Since they were using lines out of movies, Jimmy had one of his own. "Somebody said look him up," he said.

Crab Boy didn't say anything for all of a minute while he filled orders, then got to Jimmy's.

"Where's your metal nigger friend?" he said.

Jimmy wondered if Crabby was related to the blockhead East Bay boys trying to make Shop crack.

"If he heard you say that, he'd . . . turn the other silver cheek."

The kid put the crab and a cup of horseradish in front of Jimmy. "You want that wine again?"

"A beer. An Anchor Steam."

"You're trying too hard, man," the kid said.

Jimmy waited him out.

"I'm just dicking around with you," Crab Boy said. Two more customers were coming up, a couple. "Jeremy's around somewhere. He usually comes later. What do you want with Jeremy?"

"I have ten grand to give him," Jimmy said. "Or is it twenty?"

"That's good," the kid said. He looked at the newcomer customers, raised his eyebrows, brightened his face a little, his version of, "What'll you have?" The man held up two fingers to order, but a forefinger and thumb. European.

"Where ya from?" the kid asked. "Deux. Due. Dos."

"France," the man said. "Montpellier?"

The kid rattled off three or four lines of French, but it was mostly wrong and more than a little confusing to the French couple. But Crab Boy slung it with feeling. He was already prepping and filling the paper boats.

"Who's next?" Jimmy said, apropos of nothing.

It took the kid out of his crab-slinging rhythm, but he tried not to show it. "What did you say, sir?"

"Who's next?" Jimmy said. *"C'est qui, le prochain? Wer ist an der Reihe? Chi é prossimo?"* he added, for fun.

"Ask Jeremy when you see him," Crab Boy said after another delay that showed the kid was anxious about answering wrong.

Jimmy got up, surrendered his stool to the French lady. He overtipped the kid, which was a way of insulting him, because Jimmy knew he wasn't down here on the waterfront to make a living.

He went trolling for Jeremy.

It didn't make any sense, but he went first to the place where he'd last seen him, the only time he'd seen him, Pier 35. Where the girls had jumped. Tonight, nobody was naked, nobody was dying. But, hey, it was early yet. There was a crowd, gathered around a man with a trained cat act, cats walking a little tightrope, jumping from perch to perch. Then he'd have them walk back and forth across his shoulders to show that they enjoyed it as much as he did. For some reason, the ringmaster narrated the show with a thick French accent, at its thickest when one cat "pretended" not to want to do this tonight, and he had to go to his knees to scold her with a finger in her face. Jimmy turned away when the flaming hoop came out.

"Have you ever *smelled* burned cat hair?" he said to a girl as he was leaving.

She gave him a smile. He had seen her in the crowd. She was alone, maybe twenty, twenty-one. Or sixteen. A blonde. Pink Juicy knits, top and bottom. Cute sneakers. There was something about her eyes . . .

But she wasn't a Sailor. She certainly wasn't Christina Leonidas, unless she'd adjusted to her new state faster than anyone ever before. This girl looked more or less at peace, a place few Sailors ever found.

Jimmy bought a coffee and found a bench where he could sit alone to drink it.

He wasn't alone for long.

Meet Jeremy.

Suddenly, he was right in front of him, apparently dropped right out of the sky onto the bench across from him. Their knees were almost touching. Jimmy would have wondered if it was a gay attempt at a pickup if he hadn't recognized him right away, what with the length of long black coat (was it a cape?) thrown over the knee. Jeremy. And here was his "support staff," close by but not too close, three strong-looking ones ten feet away, sitting on other people's cars. Make that four. There was Red Boots. *Five*, Red Boots's sidekick. Good Lord, they *were* capes. Half of them wore long black capes. With silky rope ties to wrap them at the neck. New Romantics! One of them was one of the men who'd stood over Machine Shop on night one, punching him in the face.

"What's that smell?" Jimmy said.

"You're not in L.A. anymore, Brother," Jeremy said. Projected. Rumbled. He had an unnaturally deep voice, like a DJ, a DJ gone bad. Unless that's redundant. It was the kind of deep, dramatic voice that sounded worked on. Probably in front of a mirror. "*All* the senses can come into play here," he intoned.

"You know, I've noticed that," Jimmy said. "At home, I can't smell anything. Here, it's sea spray and patchouli and steamed crabs and . . . what's that purple flower, out under the Golden Gate?"

Jeremy's face was in the light. He wore a black turtleneck over black gabardine slacks. He liked jewelry. Silver. He was an *old* Sailor. Anyone passing by who didn't know him, or who didn't suspect anything about him, who didn't *know* who/what he really was, would peg him for early forties. That was another thing about them. It wasn't that Sailors didn't age, just that they aged on their own clock and calendar. There wasn't exactly an answer to how old he was, how old any of them were. You might as well just pick a number out of the air. Sometimes a Sailor looked ninety and had died at thirty and been in this state just ten years. Others times, more likely, a guy would look mid-thirties with fifty or sixty New Years on him. Doing the math didn't do you much good. This one had probably been a Sailor since the 1950s. Maybe since the 1930s. At least the '40s. Maybe he'd been down here, this Jeremy, watching the wives and girlfriends saying good-bye in the war. Picture him sidling up to them, insinuating himself into their blues, offering his handkerchief for them to dry their tears. He was a predator. He'd probably be here another hundred years.

He looked like Charlie Watts. But without the happy-go-lucky disposition.

"So it's true?" Jeremy said.

"What's that?" Jimmy said.

"That the Sailors of the north have, what you call it, an identifying scent."

"I think I just meant your cologne," Jimmy said.

"I heard the scent is rather sweet," the other said. He was a familiar type among those on the bad side of the Sailor world, pretensions of sophistication, but a thug.

"I shouldn't have said anything," Jimmy said.

Over by the cars, Red Boots got a message from somewhere, just like the other night, another Sailor running up. There was action somewhere. It didn't seem important enough to involve Jeremy, but Red Boots went away with the runner.

A moment later, Jimmy saw Lucy. Lucy and company actually, Lucy and the two women moving through the crowd fifty yards away.

Jimmy looked away quickly. He didn't need for Jeremy to connect her to him.

"So who *is* next?" Jimmy said.

It was like Jeremy was ready and waiting for the line. No hesitation. "I was hoping *you* knew," he said. "They say you're a somebody down south."

"You ever been down south?"

"Man of the north, tried and true, Brother," he said. He uncrossed his legs and leaned back. He opened his thighs and hustled his balls, rearranging things in that way jocks do. And salesmen, trying to close the deal, man to man.

"What does killing a couple of girls get you?"

Jeremy just took the line like he'd probably take a two-by-four between the eyes. Rock steady. *What else you got?* That's what it meant to be an old Sailor. And this was sure enough a salty dog. Jimmy started wondering if maybe he'd been around for the '06 quake.

"One step forward, two steps back," Jeremy said. "They're in a better place, some would say."

Jimmy had had enough cryptic bullshit to last him awhile. "I believe I'm going to get me some more of that crab," he said.

But, before Jimmy could split, Jeremy suddenly sat up straight and lifted his nose in the air. One of his Watchers across the way perked up a second later, as if he'd gotten the silent signal, too. Suddenly they were all on their feet, Jeremy's crew, looking around in every direction. Like hunting dogs.

And then they were gone, all of them.

A second or two later, the background noise changed. A movie sound engineer could explain it, would know all the layers, would know what had built the previous sound, the ambient resonance of the water, the waves against the pilings of the docks, seabirds on top of that, the traffic near and far, and all the ways the crowds were noising, and would know what had changed.

It wasn't a silence exactly. It was nothing, turned up loud.

Jimmy looked over to the right. Whatever had happened, it was to the east, the Embarcadero.

He found it.

He walked into the back of the crowd. Here was another kind of audience. Jeremy and his men were already there, had already pushed through to the front.

It was a streetcar, stopped dead in its tracks.

It was a body, cleaved into halves.

It was a transit driver standing there with that nothing-I-could-do look.

And that smell in the air, spilled gore.

Jeremy dispatched his men. To Look. It was like the other night, the men circulating through the bands of spectators, staring individuals in the eyes. Looking.

Jimmy moved closer. He couldn't see if it was a man or a woman, old or young.

Of course he thought, *Lucy.* When he'd seen her, with Sadie and Pam, they were heading this way. If they were headed anywhere. They were just strolling. Pam had a drink with a straw, something bright red in clear plastic. Sadie had her arm in Lucy's.

It was a man. Two halves of a man.

Jimmy stepped closer.

The eyes were still open. The upper half was on its side. The lower was on its back. (Had this human being already lost the right to personal pronouns?)

The impact had torn open his pants. He had an erection. Jimmy had heard of it, a final jolt of nerve voltage through the cord, a last rude impulse. A last joke.

"Don't you have a tarp or something?" Jimmy said to the driver.

The driver shook his head. "You don't touch 'em. You just wait."

Then Jimmy saw Lucy in the crowd, across, on the far side of the halved man. She had seen it, and seeing it had changed her face.

But she was moving away, or being moved away, Sadie with her arm around her, Polythene Pam coming along behind them, finishing her drink, cute as a bug.

He went after them, pushed people out of the way to get to them, but they were too far ahead of him.

# EIGHT

He heard the newspaper land on the carpet in the hallway, against the door.

Some call it morning.

He was in the club chair with the drapes open. There was a little blue on the right side of the sky, but it was still dark. He had a glass of vodka in his hand, the glass from the bathroom, but he wasn't drunk. It hadn't done anything for him. He never read the paper anymore. The news always seemed to be something he'd already gotten some other way. But he got up anyway and went to the door.

It was fat. A fat paper. He let the door close against his back standing there and then held the lever and let it close quietly, with just a click. No use waking anybody.

He went back to sit in the chair by the window. He put the paper on the ledge. He'd gone to get it not for the news but in the hope it could renew the sense that the world was still out there, remind him that maybe the world wasn't as small and as empty as it felt right now to him. The cold air from the AC ruffled the edges, made it flutter.

He turned the paper over to the front page.

It was below the fold, but there it was:

**STREETCAR SUICIDE**

With a picture. The body covered.

Things tend to be a little dead at a newspaper on a Saturday night. They'd given the assignment to a reporter, probably somebody young, maybe even an intern, and let him or her do a feature treatment rather than just the hard news. So the first graf wasn't the five W's, but more along the lines of . . .

The weekend revelers and visiting conventioneers in their matching T-shirts who congregated at the edge of the Bay on a Chamber of
Commerce brochure–perfect Saturday night never expected . . .

The dead man was thirty-six years old. It said so, right there in the
seventh paragraph. Jimmy made a point of not letting his eyes linger over
the name.

He snatched up his cell phone and called the first number on the scroll.
His "client."

"A voice from the past," Angel answered.

"And I haven't even said anything yet," Jimmy said.

"You caught me. I was just getting ready for services, just getting in the
shower."

"I forgot it was Sunday."

"It's raining here. Maybe I'll just go stand outside."

"Rain . . ." Jimmy said, thinking about it.

"So what's up?"

"People killing themselves left and right," Jimmy said. "Three since I
got here. And I was right there each time."

"But you didn't have anything to do with it."

"Not so far as I know. If *you* had been here, maybe you could have
talked them out of it."

"It's never me," Angel said. "God through me. I'm just the . . . whatcha
call it. Relay man."

"Lucy's all right," Jimmy said. "As far as I can tell."

"What is she doing up there?"

"I don't know. She's just been acting the tourist. With her brother."

"Her brother?"

"A kid maybe fourteen, fifteen. Plays guitar. Has a kind of retro look, a
porkpie hat. I like him better than her."

"When did he come into the picture?"

"She stopped in Paso Robles for him."

"But she's all right. That's good," Angel said.

"She's dragging me around to see the sights. So far we've been to Sausalito and the Golden Gate, past Alcatraz, over to Tiburon, down to Fisherman's Wharf. All around the Haight."

"What's so funny 'bout peace, love, and understanding?"

"She's made a couple of friends. Girlfriends. They seem to . . . brighten
her spirits."

There wasn't any use in talking about slow-motion murder. It would sound stupid if he said it out loud.

"People like her," Angel said.

"Who is she?" Jimmy asked. "Who is she to you?"

"I like her, too," was the answer, for all it didn't say.

"So what do you want me to do? Kidnap her, bring her home?"

"I don't know," Angel said. "Now I'm worried about *you*. Before, you sounded good, glad to be out of L.A. Now you sound like you're waiting for the other shoe to drop."

"Maybe," Jimmy said. "I'll watch her. I'll call you."

"God bless you," Angel said.

"That's what the panhandler said to me the other day up in Sausalito, when I blew him off," Jimmy said. "I'm not sure he really meant it."

He took a shower, a long shower with the water as hot as it would go. In L.A. you always heard the voices of the water conservation nags when you were in the shower, even when you were reaching for the handle on the toilet. Here, it rained, really rained, and San Francisco was that much closer to the mountains and the snowmelt to start with. They had water. So the shower flowed freely, almost washed away the heaviness in him.

The phone was ringing when he got out. The room phone.

It wasn't even eight o'clock yet.

He let it ring long enough for a wrong number to go away, give up. It kept ringing.

"Hello."

"This is Duncan Groner. The *Chronicle*." It was a cracking voice, an old man's voice, a voice with some *coot* to it. Jimmy assumed the man meant the newspaper, not that he was an oracle. Even before he added, "I'm a reporter."

Something clicked about the odd name. Jimmy walked with the phone over to the window where the thick Sunday paper was. The byline on the *Chron*'s suicide puff piece was Dana Gruber.

"You don't write under the name Dana Gruber, do you?" Jimmy said.

"Holy Mother of God, no," the voice on the phone said.

"The initials are the same."

"That's all. She's a *journalist* . . ." Then, without a breath between the words, he said, "So you were down there last night, too. I understand you were there for all three." It wasn't a question.

"Yeah, I was there."

"I'm doing a follow-up on the Leonidas girls, tying it in. I talked to

George Leonidas. He said talk to you, that you had something to say about it. A different angel."

"Did you say *angel*?"

"I meant *angle*. Sometimes I'm a little dyslexic early in the morning."

"Mr. Leonidas got it wrong. I wouldn't be any help to you."

There was a little pause. "I know you, Brother," the man on the other end of the line said. He didn't say it like the secret Sailor code that it was, more like they were old friends. They weren't. They weren't even new friends. He waited. He expected the silence.

Jimmy said, "I guess I could use some fresh air. Where do you want to meet?"

"How do you feel about church?" the reporter said.

––––––––

Fresh air? It was like being in an auditorium-sized pool hall. It was a ball-room in a hotel on Cathedral Hill. The cigarette smoke burned Jimmy's eyes and constricted his throat from the second he came in. It was like walking into a house afire.

But it *was* church. A pastor, a skinny man with a big, booming voice, was at a pulpit up front on the elevated platform with its white tacked-on pleated skirt. His voice was not just big but had a kind of authority, a kind of weight, a *been there/done that* intensity. He was talking about Peter, *Saint* Peter, and overcoming the past.

Jimmy squinted, looking for his date in the haze.

Duncan Groner was alone in the last row of hotel ballroom armless stackable chairs, against the wall, under an eight-foot-long mural of the completion of the transcontinental railroad, the driving of the golden spike. He had a fat, round, red eraserless pencil stuck over his ear and a long reporter's notebook on the empty seat beside him. And, Jimmy would learn in a second, a buzz on.

The banner strung up behind the preacher said: Western States Roundup Alcoholics Anonymous. Yee-haw.

Groner gave him a wave over, moved his reporter's notebook for him to sit.

"I thought San Francisco had a smoking ban."

"They do," Duncan Groner said. "They cut 'em a little slack. For the conventions. Especially this one." He had a cigarette of his own in his hand, a Player, a thick, unfiltered, English fag, smoked down to the nub.

In his other hand, he had a tall coffee in a paper cup. He swirled it around a couple times and took a sip.

"Thanks for coming, Brother. God loves a cheerful giver." Groner's face matched the gravelly voice, ears a little gnomish, flappable, a bulbous nose, a weak chin, droopy dog eyes. Here was another old Sailor. He looked to be in his sixties, wiry, lanky. He wore loud checked wool pants and a yellow short-sleeved shirt with a press on it. And tan-and-white saddle shoes. He looked like he should be at the horse track with a stingy brim hat pushed back on his head. Or the dog track. "God says the past doesn't matter," he said. He snatched up his notebook and flipped back a page. "Or rather that 'the slate is wiped clean.'" He swirled his coffee again and took another hit. "God doesn't even care if you've inadvertently polluted your shorts at one time or another."

"Even advertently," Jimmy cracked.

"Oh, Mother of God, a free-willer!" Duncan Groner said, loud enough for a woman six rows forward to turn. "Sorry," he said. And lifted his coffee cup to her.

With a surreptitious slip of the fingers, he extracted a brass flask shaped like a kidney from his pants pocket. He kept it at his side, popped open the cap with his thumbnail, tipped it, and poured a dollop into the coffee cup kept down at his side and clipped the cap down again. And then he made the bottle disappear. For this, at least, he had the dexterity of a surgeon. He swirled the coffee again. Jimmy could smell the bourbon. A man twenty rows up turned and looked. Maybe he could he smell it, too.

Groner continued, "You have to accept that there is a Superior Being, a Higher Power, something greater than you." He flipped closed his notebook. "What they don't say is how can you *not* drink once you know *that* little piece of information."

"I believe the answer to that is, *God loves you*," Jimmy said.

"He doesn't know me," Groner said.

The reporter had what he needed for whatever he was writing, so they slipped out, retired to the hotel bar across the lobby. It wasn't even ten yet. The bartender and a busboy went to restocking the bar after the two lone customers had been served, an old-fashioned for Groner and a Virgin Mary for Jimmy.

There wasn't much restocking to do.

"I bet you love *this* convention crowd," Groner said.

The bartender smiled hatefully.

Groner stirred his drink with his finger. "By the way," he began, "George Leonidas isn't buying any of it. No sale." He lifted the drink to toast Jimmy and then all but drained the old-fashioned in the first "sip."

"He thinks you're insane," Groner finished.

"That's usually the intention," Jimmy said. "With third parties."

"Up here, we tend not to even try to explain things to third parties."

"That works, too."

"It never helps."

"No, it never does," Jimmy said.

Jimmy liked him. All Sailors were good liars, if they made it through the first weeks, months, without falling apart. You had to learn fast how to read each other and then trust what your instinct was telling you.

"So who's next?" Jimmy said and bit his stalk of celery in half.

Groner let a half minute go by. "Maybe it's you," he said.

"Or you," Jimmy said.

Groner laughed. "Is it that obvious?"

"What are you going to say about the Leonidas girls?"

"Mother of God, I saw their *room*," Groner said and shook his head. "It was like an explosion in a Dubble Bubble factory. They slept in matching canopy beds. One liked Justin, one liked Clay."

"That was probably last year," Jimmy said.

"They change so fast." The way Groner said the cliché, sour and sincere at the same time, made Jimmy wonder if the grizzled old cynic had been, of all things, a *daddy* once. "George had just bought them both a Kia. Two Kias. They came into the City in Melina's. It was in the covered parking lot across from Pier 41. It had a hundred and eleven miles on it."

"Did you find out why they wanted to die?" Jimmy said.

"You were there," Groner said. "I wasn't. What did you see?"

"In the moment, it was hard to get past the nakedness."

"The assumption was they were loaded, but they weren't. What they had in their stomachs was essentially a Jamba Juice mango smoothie. They'd each had one. One had some Midol in her blood. She was menstruating. Funny, you'd think the two girls would be in sync, but they weren't. There's always a detail like that. Maybe it's why I do this."

Jimmy said, "There hadn't been any signs of depression? High drama?"

"Happy and healthy."

"You said you were 'tying this in.' To what?"

The bartender came past. He pointed at Groner. Groner shook his head, though his glass was empty.

"In the last five days, there have been twenty-six suicides in the City. Usually, there are one or two a day. And more than half of them have been, as you say, the 'high drama' kind. Two off the Golden Gate last night, five minutes apart. Three last week. They usually get one jumper every two or three weeks. People are killing themselves spectacularly all over the city. Not the head-in-the-oven kind, alone in the garage with the Nova." He sucked the bitters-dashed sugar off the cubes at the bottom of his rocks glass.

"That's not what you meant when you said, 'Who's next?' is it?" he said, and looked at Jimmy.

Jimmy didn't answer.

"Why would a Sailor be up there with them, whispering in their ear just before they jumped?" he said instead.

"First I heard of it," the reporter said and almost made it sound like the truth.

Groner changed his mind about that second drink and, while he waited for it, asked Jimmy what had brought him to San Francisco.

Jimmy surprised himself with how much he said. About Lucy and Les. About Angel back home. About the boat ride over to Sausalito. About what he had thought had almost happened on the Golden Gate. About the park on Tiburon. About the two women who always seemed to be hovering.

*It's getting to me,* that's what he was thinking as he heard himself summarize the last days. There was too much death here, and it didn't have anything to do with him, however much they tried to make it be about him, however much he seemed to be right there when the bodies dropped. Sailors had their own kind of agoraphobia and for their own special reasons. They never liked to be too far from the home port. They started getting antsy. Maybe it was time to go home.

"Go to her, this Lucy, talk to her, tell her people are worried about her, take her home," he heard Groner say.

---

The Haight. Lucy wasn't there. And the Skylark was gone. Maybe she'd figured it out on her own. Maybe she'd packed up and was headed south.

But he knew that wasn't true.

He drove across the Golden Gate, blew past the spot where the dropped drinks had splashed into the oncoming traffic, where Lucy had stopped almost in the middle of the bridge, where Les had caught up to her. A couple was handing off their camera to another tourist for a shot of the two of them with the backdrop of the city, their backs against the low rail.

He took the first exit, dropped down into Sausalito. The baby-blue Skylark would be easy to spot, wherever they were, if he got lucky.

He didn't get lucky.

He kept on, stayed on the road that swung around the pinched curve of top of the Bay. It gave him time to practice his speech.

Tiburon. He found them. The Skylark was right there in the parking lot of the picnic place next to the playing fields, in the row of spaces closest to the highway. He couldn't have missed it if he wanted. It was sitting there all alone, like a big sign that said: Here!

So he *had* gotten lucky.

He pulled in and parked, found a place.

He watched them through the windshield of the Porsche. This time Lucy had brought Les with her. There was no sign of the others, the women, the helpmates. It was a sweet little scene. The sky was blue. The water was beautiful.

A little soccer player came running his way, right toward Jimmy. A boy six or seven with his shin guards over his socks, out of uniform, silky baggy pants and mismatched top. He had a set of keys jangling in his hand. Jimmy looked across the field. There weren't any games on. (It was Sunday. They probably didn't have games on Sunday.) But there were two or three boys at some distance and a few parents. (Lucy and Les were close by, but not right next to the parents and kids.) There was a chirp as the Tahoe two spaces away from the Porsche unlocked its doors.

The boy was impatient to get back to the field, to his friends. He yanked opened the passenger-side door and climbed in. Jimmy looked over, saw him rummaging between the Tahoe's front seats.

He came out with a white squeeze bottle of sunblock, slammed the door, was already running back across the field when he aimed the remote behind him and locked the Tahoe. California kids. Or maybe they were like this everywhere now.

As the boy closed in, a woman, who'd had her back turned away, standing, turned. Maybe she'd heard his voice. Maybe the boy had said something, maybe protested about the errand she'd sent him on, interrupting his play. "Here . . ." maybe he'd said, with an impatient edge to his voice. The boy was holding up the sunblock.

She took a few steps toward him, to meet him. She kneeled down.

It was all it took. She was far away, a hundred yards at least. She was across any number of gulfs, of chasms, of distances. Of time and space and reason. On the other side of possibility, across a wide field of coincidence and improbability. But it was all it took, the shape of her. The outline of her.

Her hair in the light.

The flash of white in the luster of her face, the teeth in her smile, the smile in her eyes . . .

As she knelt and finger-painted sunblock under the boy's eyes, across his forehead, and down the line of his nose.

Mary.

# NINE

The same song was playing on a dozen radios, all tuned to KHJ. It was an AM kind of night. The sidewalks were more crowded than the four lanes of the street, and the street was plenty crowded, weekenders in from the suburbs to see how the other half lived, to pretend to be something wilder than what they were. It was the middle of summer. It was an even warmer night than usual, riot weather, but there wasn't any chance of a flare-up among this throng. The word was *mellow*. Moving along on the sidewalk, cruising out of the sound of one radio and then into the zone of the next, was like moving along *inside* the song, like walking with the singer, best friends.

It could have been Polk Street or MacDougal Street or South Beach, or even Fisherman's Wharf, but it was Sunset Boulevard, the Sunset Strip. It was L.A.

It could have been now, but it was 1995.

It could have been a lot of songs, probably should have been "London Calling" or "My Sharona" or even the Carpenters and "We've Only Just Begun," but it was Tom Jones and "It's Not Unusual (To Be Loved by Anyone)." Another big pop lie.

She was with another guy the first time he saw her. *She* was Mary, her name was Mary, though it would take most of the night for him to find that out, to work his way through the jungle of playful protective coloration she threw up, *to break her down* was the way she always put it later when they were telling others about how they met, about that first night.

Jimmy and Mary.

He was with someone else, too. Most nights he was alone, particularly on the Strip. He lived nearby, a little house down below Sunset, below a restaurant everybody was going to at the time, Roy's. (Now it's the site of the House of Blues.) It was dead center in the Strip. It was close enough to the Chateau Marmont to walk over, which Jimmy did all the time.

The girl he was with that night worked as a secretary at a record label.

She liked him more than he liked her. She brought him records, what they called "product." The LPs (they were still making them, along with cassettes and CDs) always had a hole drilled through some corner of the cover, a sign that they were meant for promotion. She'd bring him boxes of them. When she realized she liked him more than he liked her, trying to change that, she started bringing him boxes of "cleans," albums that weren't punched, that could be sold or traded for whatever you wanted. She hadn't figured out that Jimmy was different, different from everyone, and that he didn't care about money. (And, because he didn't care, he had a lot of it or could always get it.) She didn't know he was a Sailor. It was the secret he kept from almost everyone.

The guy Mary was with was a director.

*It's not unusual to be loved by anyone*
*It's not unusual to have fun with anyone*

She was twenty-two; the director was thirty-eight. She was five ten; he was five eight. She was blond. He was blonder. Jimmy and the secretary, who had her arm threaded through his as they walked, were on the north side of Sunset, next to Tower Records. Mary and the director were across the street, going into a sushi place with a bamboo facade and glossy bright red paint around the door, making the entryway look like a garish mouth.

"Do you know her?" the secretary had said to Jimmy, when she saw him looking across the street.

The joke they said later, Jimmy and Mary, each taking a line in the telling of it, was that the director had looked back through the red mouth of that door and said to her, "Do you know him?"

Mary and the director had fought over dinner, and she had ended up walking away from him. From his white Jaguar sedan specifically, with the director standing next to it, sake-drunk, the valet standing there, too. She'd walked away on up Sunset, headed west, pretending to be drunk, too, which she wasn't at all. Jimmy had found her in Gil Turner's, a bright, glass-fronted, classic corner liquor store near the end of the Strip. She was inside, at the counter.

He was alone by then, too, behind the wheel of the only car he had, an oxidized white '68 Cadillac convertible, the punch line to some joke he'd forgotten. The top had long ago been knifed by vandals, so he left it down, at least once summer came. At the time, he thought he was just cruising, but he could admit later he was looking for her.

He parked. She came out. He set off after her. He caught up to her, walked alongside her. She was headed back toward the center of things. He didn't say anything for a half a block. That section of the strip was dead, the block before the Rainbow and The Roxy.

"Let's hear it," she said, when she realized that he was just weird enough to walk along beside her silently, maybe forever. "Your clever first line."

"I don't have one," Jimmy said. "I don't have a clever *last* line, either."

"Thinking ahead, are we?"

She was as tall as he was. And she had on flat shoes, dancer's shoes. Capezios. She was skinny but not a model. She probably wasn't a dancer, either. He thought of asking, but it sounded too much like a pickup line.

"You want these?" she said and offered him an unopened pack of cigarettes, after they'd walked another half block. She was setting the pace, not fast, not slow. Not an escape, not a stroll.

"Luckies," he said.

"I don't smoke," she said. "I felt sorry for the man in the store."

"That's Gil. Himself."

"I felt sorry for Gil."

"He's probably a millionaire," Jimmy said.

"So millionaires aren't worthy of our concern?" she said. Jimmy wondered if she *was* drunk, the way she chose her words. He'd learn soon enough that it was just *her*. Then, at least. The way she was then. She said, "I felt sorry for him because of the look in his eye, because he looked forsaken."

"What's your name?" he said.

"Lucky," she said.

Jimmy pulled the ribbon on the white-and-red pack of smokes and tapped it against the palm of his hand.

"Why do people do that?" she said.

"I don't know, I think it packs the tobacco tighter or something," Jimmy said.

"Or everyone saw someone do it in a movie."

"Are you an actress?" Jimmy said.

"No, you are," she said. "*You* are."

They walked almost as far as Tower Records and the sushi place. Jimmy was prepared to run into the boyfriend again, the director, but that would be overestimating him.

"Let's go somewhere. Where do you want to go?" Jimmy said, standing there on the sidewalk. In 1995.

"San Francisco," she said. "L.A. is bothering me. You're not the Cut Killer, are you?" Lately, since the beginning of summer, there'd been a series of killings, girls' bodies left spread-eagle on road cuts, the sloping gouges into the rock where the highway sliced through. Nine of them.

"Where do you want to go?" Jimmy asked her again, as serious about anything as he'd been in a long, long time.

———————————

Mary wasn't a single mom. She wasn't alone.

*He* came late to the soccer practice or play date or picnic or whatever it was. Sunday afternoon in the park on Tiburon. Her husband. Jimmy saw him drive up in a black BMW X-5. On the phone. He parked and sat there another two minutes, finishing his call. There were two other mothers and a father next to Mary on the sidelines of the playing field. She had her back to the parking lot and didn't see him. She had her eyes on the boy, who was dribbling a ball down the field, or at least making an earnest six-year-old's attempt at dribbling.

*Her* son. It was hard for Jimmy to even think it. He didn't know much about kids but got close guessing the boy's age. He did the math. Everything in him wanted to get closer, to see more, but he knew that Mary would spot him, his shape, his coloration, as easily as he had hers. Or at least that was what he told himself, to keep himself inside the car. To stop himself. He turned the key and started the engine. The sound of the rev made Mary turn to look. It was then that she saw her husband walking toward her across the apron of the field. He wore a dark gray suit, but as he came closer he pulled off the necktie and unbuttoned the collar of the blue shirt. He folded the tie in half and slipped it into his coat pocket. (Who goes into the office on a Sunday? Even for a half day?) He was dark-haired. With a hundred-dollar haircut. He smiled at his wife from ten yards out and then looked away quickly to find the boy on the field, to wave, though the kid wasn't looking.

He came up and kissed Mary, put his hand on her back. Her hair was longer. And darker.

Jimmy drove away out the exit of the lot but turned left on the main road in and stopped on the shoulder. There was a little elevation, to look down on the field, the water behind it, Sausalito behind that. The boy had come over. The father had kneeled down to ruffle his hair. The mother was saying something. A family was laughing.

Jimmy let out the clutch and drove on. Fast and loud.

Very high school.

And what do you call sitting in the dark in a car on a hilly lane on Tibu-ron, on Belvedere, across from a black Craftsman house with a light in the second-floor window and a woman framed there, lifting a boy's T-shirt over his head, his arms raised as if surrendering?

---

Mary kept living in the director's house, though she said it wasn't "living *with* him . . ." In his rented long and low ranch house up at the top of a cul-de-sac in Benedict Canyon. ("Leased," she said. "He always makes me say *leased*.") Whatever it was now, it had been a family's house once, stuck up off in a rustic canyon, three bedrooms, two baths, a kidney-shaped pool, an enormous bank of rock behind it like a wave threatening to break. Now it was all white, inside and out, refrigerator white, and had bizarre white rocks the size of apples and grapefruits scattered across the white gravel of the roof.

"It's like the surface of the moon," Jimmy said the first time he saw it in the daytime.

"I like it," Mary said.

There were four girls living there. They didn't mind being called girls, except for the thirteen-year-old, who was the director's daughter, there for the summer. The others were Mary's friends. The girls. One was a friend from before Mary had moved in with the director; the other had become a friend. April and Michelle and Mary. They'd all three slept with the direc-tor at one time or another.

"You have to move," Jimmy said.

"You're always trying to relocate me," Mary said.

The director was Canadian, pretended to be French. He'd done one movie, limited release. It starred a rock star, and the movie was notably unprofitable, so a few people at the studios and the agencies got the idea the director was hip. So he had that to ride for a few years. But he didn't even have a deal anywhere now and was much angrier inside than anyone knew, even his agent. He'd shot another film with a little money from a horndog Pasadena dentist who liked the idea of the girls in the house up there in Benedict, liked the vodka-in-the-freezer thing, liked the old-school drugs they sometimes brought out for his sake. Everyone else thought *that* part of it was just too eighties. There were a pair of old-fashioned Movi-olas in the bedroom where the director had stashed his daughter. Every once in a while he'd go in to work on it, at least run some film through his hands, but most of the time he went to restaurants and out to parties and meetings when he could get them and looked for the next thing.

"Come live with me," Jimmy said.

It was the morning after they'd made love for the first time, four days after that first night on Sunset. They were at Hugo's, down on Santa Monica, a breakfast, brunch, and lunch place. Everybody else there was doing business.

"I don't even know what you do," she said.

"I don't do anything," he said. "I think about you."

"What did you do before I came along?"

"Think about you."

If anyone was close enough to hear him, hear them, Mary would have made fun of the line. But he meant it.

"Me, too," she said.

He could never tell anyone the things they said to each other.

They spent most of that day together, the day after they'd made love for the first time, rode out to the beach with the Cadillac's ragged ragtop down, out to Paradise Cove to watch the surfers trying to make something happen on a collapsed, glassy day, then ate drippy cheeseburgers at a joint while the red sun flattened out at the horizon. The burger place was on a rise above a south-facing beach, on one of the twists and turns along the line of the coast, and the effect of the right-hand, apparently northern sunset was unsettling, though neither of them noticed it then.

"Everything can change in just a day," she said.

They were riding back into the City, the back way, up and over Mulholland in from the coast, alone on the two-lane blacktop scrolling through the hills. He was watching the way the Caddy's high beams swept the manzanita, let himself think that the light going across the brush was what had released the scent that filled their nostrils. It hadn't rained in two or three months. There was a not-unpleasant dustiness to everything. What did the Eagles sing about in "Hotel California"? The "warm smell of colitas, rising up through the air." He wondered what it was, colitas. It sounded like a plant, like manzanitas.

"Everything can change in an *hour*," Jimmy said. "If it's the wrong hour."

"Or the *right* hour," Mary said. "You're so gloomy."

He left her at the gate of the white house. It wasn't that big a house, but the owners had put in a rolling iron gate and painted it white, too, so the renters, the *leasees*, could say they lived in a gated place in Benedict

Canyon. Jimmy cranked the wheel, the power steering pump complaining, and turned around in the cul-de-sac. He wouldn't go in, didn't want to drop in on that scene again after so good a day, didn't want to have to try to make it all lie down in his head one more time. The director always had a crowd over, standing around the black-bottomed pool, looking down at the lights, drinks in their hands, or joints between their fingers like they were cigarettes. Strangers. New people every time.

In the rearview mirror, Jimmy saw her push the button on the squawk box and wait. She pushed it again.

He wasn't in any hurry to get home. In just a part of a week, she'd gotten him into some new music, new to him. Gloomy Canadian singer-songwriters, as it turned out. She'd made him a tape, two-sided, 120 minutes. So, driving around, killing time, he had Leonard Cohen and the last cigarette from the pack of Lucky Strikes she'd given him that first night. He almost hated to smoke it, but he smoked it, cruising east on Sunset into East L.A. Lately he'd been spending more and more time with his friend Angel, had come back around again, reconnected. Everything seemed to go in circles. Angel was a Sailor who worked on vintage cars, who had a shop downtown, who was also a preacher in a way, a street preacher to gangbangers and their knocked-up girlfriends, to the people almost everybody else wrote off. He went by his apartment, went by the storefront church where Angel spent a lot of time, but never found him. He wanted to talk cars, nothing else. He headed for home.

The phone was ringing when he came in. When he answered it, it was just screaming.

# TEN

He slept. The phone had detonated a couple of times, but he'd slept through it. He sat up. There was a knife-edge of light under the drapes. He'd drawn them when he came back from Tiburon. He'd *slept*. He'd even dreamed. It wasn't that Sailors never slept, but it was rare. They'd sleep an hour or two once a month. But they almost never dreamed. What had he dreamed? Like the rest of us, he couldn't exactly remember. Angel was in it. There was a gathering of some kind, characters moving in from all quarters, in some kind of empty room. It felt ordinary, obvious, pedestrian. The surprise was that Mary wasn't in it.

He ordered breakfast, a big breakfast. He was acting like a Norm all of a sudden. It came, and he ate it. He took a shower and put on a clean shirt. Like it was the first day of the rest of his life.

When he stepped out into the hallway in the hotel, he had to step over the *Chronicle*. If it had been facedown, he wouldn't have stopped, and his day might have gone a different way, but it was faceup, looking right at him, with a headline across half the page:

## THREE GOLDEN GATE SUICIDES
## WITHIN SPAN OF ONE HOUR

"Span." At least someone on the headline desk had a sense of humor about it. Jimmy picked up the paper and tucked it under his arm. He took the elevator straight down to the garage. While he waited for the car, he read the details. The three suicides off the bridge were unrelated. One was a German tourist, a woman. One was a woman in her nineties. (You had to wonder how she got up and over the rail.) The third was an anomaly, a man in his twenties who'd gone off the *west* side of the bridge, the side facing out to sea, something that almost never happened. Maybe he was a sailor. Small *s*.

It made Jimmy go back to the bridge. Maybe he was looking for something to bring him back to the present.

He drove along the Marina, the broad sweep of created land, a former marsh filled in a hundred years ago with '06 earthquake rubble. Now it was as if it had been there all along, another pricey district with its rows of two- and three-story houses, shoulder to shoulder on the left, red-tile roofs and pale ice cream colors, and the expanse of Marina Green and St. Francis Yacht Club to the right. And the Presidio ahead.

And Fort Point, under the southern anchorage of the bridge. Jimmy parked in the lot next to the rocks, the water so close that the cars' windshields would all be grayed out, misted, when the drivers returned. The massive red/orange ironwork of the bridge, this end of it, was overhead. Sometimes you could hear the traffic noise above all the sounds of the Bay. To stand underneath it felt a little like being inside a hollow skyscraper. It also made you see how high it was off the water.

Jimmy walked along the shore on the paved path toward the angular brick fort. It had been built at the beginning of the Civil War, to guard the mouth of the Bay, set there long before the bridge. It was a Monday and still early, and tourist traffic was light. As vacationers' destinations go, Fort Point seemed not to mean much to non-Americans. The crowd, what there was of it, seemed like Kansas people, men in short cargo pants with skinny white legs who looked like they'd been up since four thirty, their portly wives, and kids in Disneyland tees and knit Target shorts the colors of the houses back in the Marina District.

Jimmy knew Fort Point was a gathering place for Sailors. By night anyway. They weren't out now, or at least they wouldn't be expected to be, only the ones looking for trouble.

But George Leonidas was there.

"Hello, sir," Jimmy said, surprising himself with the deference, the formality.

The grieving father, if that's what he was here for, grieving, was sitting on a bench next to the freshly painted guest services restroom. He was wearing the same clothes, but a fresh version of the brown cuffed trousers and the white short-sleeved shirt. And the brown wing tips. He sat with his legs open, his forearms on his knees, one hand wrapped around the fist of the other, as if holding it back from doing what it wanted to do. His eyes were on the water but unfocused. He hadn't seen Jimmy until he spoke. But he didn't seemed surprised to come upon him here. Maybe nothing surprised him anymore. He nodded a greeting, tipped his head up.

When Jimmy got a good look at his eyes, it was hard to think of what to say to him.

"How's your wife doing?"

Leonidas nodded.

"Better than you, I bet," Jimmy said. He didn't mean it harshly, but Leonidas bowed up a little, seemed about ready to come at him, to say something, but didn't. He knew it was true.

Jimmy looked down at him. *I shouldn't have told you,* he thought. He almost said it out loud. *This is what you get, when you tell them. It doesn't make it easier; it makes it harder.* The truth doesn't always set you free. Sometimes it wraps you in a whole new set of chains.

"Why'd you come down here?" Jimmy asked him.

"A kid on the waterfront told me to. Works at one of the crab joints."

"Told you what?"

"That he thought he saw my Selene here."

"Selene."

"Christina," George Leonidas said. "I called her Selene."

He suddenly looked at Jimmy, very directly. "I never saw Melina," he said. "My other girl. Is she the same as . . . as what you said? Like Christina?"

"I don't know. Probably not. Stop thinking about what I told you. Forget me."

Jimmy watched as the Greek's eyes left him, went to the underside of the bridge, out across the bowed line of it toward the center.

"There were three more. Went off the Gate," he said.

"I know," Jimmy said.

"It's not anything I ever thought of. Before," Leonidas said, still looking where he was looking. "I was in the army. In Vietnam. You see people die, and it changes the way you think. You think different. You just want to come home, work hard, have your house."

Jimmy thought of the pink rooms Duncan Groner had described, the girls' rooms.

"One of them was an old lady," Leonidas said. "Ninety."

"Go home," Jimmy said. "Go back over to El Cerrito. Stay away from the City, from places like this."

Leonidas nodded. He got up, still nodding. Jimmy got the sense that something had scared him, something he'd felt in himself, an idea, an impulse. He was grateful to be yanked back to himself. He offered his hand, and Jimmy shook it.

Jimmy watched him walk away, watched him until the Greek was behind the wheel of the Cadillac, in the first slot in the lot. He'd been up all night, the first one there. Jimmy watched until he saw the Caddy's wide hood dip at one corner, when the engine started.

He stayed on the bench for a minute, then made a pass through the fort, walked across the open courtyard, but it was all just sea breezes and sunbeams.

He didn't know what he was looking for anyway.

———

Coroners' offices have less security than you'd think. Jimmy walked in a back door, off the loading dock. He came down one corridor and then another, threaded his way into the interior, following his nose.

He was alone in a roomful of the dead for a good two minutes before anyone came in.

And *she* didn't work there.

"I'm sorry," she said. She was in her late fifties. She was dressed like a businesswoman but in particularly muted colors. Rich, but muted. *Dignified.*

Jimmy just smiled, the it's-all-right smile.

The coroner came in, a deputy coroner. He'd probably heard voices in the room. He was in his thirties and fleshy with heavy glasses that could have been military-issue. He looked like he should be working in a comic-book store somewhere.

He looked at Jimmy first. He seemed to know the woman.

"Can I . . . ?" he asked.

"She was first," Jimmy said. Maybe it would give him time to figure out what he'd come here for.

The man let his eyes linger on Jimmy for another beat, then crossed the room to a steel desk, curved corners, a gray "marble" linoleum top, like an old schoolteacher's desk, or a cop's desk. There were clear plastic bags on top. He found the one he was looking for. It had a number on a tag. He lifted his glasses to read it—so he was nearsighted!—and then went to the wall of body drawers. He pulled one out, pulled away the polythene over the face, put it back, and checked the number on the end of the drawer.

He left it open and looked at the woman. She came over. He nodded at her. The woman pulled down the plastic and looked at the body.

Jimmy slipped out, left them alone. There was something that convinced him she wasn't a family member, but Jimmy couldn't decide who she was. Clergy? She looked too uncertain, too off balance for that. But she also didn't look like she was any stranger to morgues. He was at the water fountain, taking a good long drink, when she came out of the body room. She didn't stop to lean against the wall or anything, didn't twist a hankie in her hand. She wasn't distraught, but she had a tear in her eye. And, with this one, you got the idea those eyes hadn't cried in a while, that her eyes were just a bit too old to tear up easily. Or had seen too much.

Jimmy came out into the parking lot in time to see what she drove, a pearlescent white Infiniti FX45 SUV that was probably almost pink in the right light. She pointed the remote at the door. There was a double click, and she went first to the hatchback and opened it and put the plastic bag there, on the carpet.

He didn't know why exactly, but Jimmy tailed her across town to Russian Hill.

The Infiniti was parked in the stubby driveway of a six-story apartment building, a vintage place, *some* vintage. It had character. He found a place down in the next block and hiked back up the incline. No wonder San Francisco women had such good-looking legs. He was about to go into the first floor—the door was propped open—when he saw something on the door of the Infiniti, letters impossible to read from any real distance. He came closer. They were silver on white. Dignified. Rich. Muted.

What they said was:

### GRACEFUL EXITS
### SENIOR MOVING—ESTATE CLOSURE

In the lobby was an old-fashioned elevator, with a brass arrow to point to the number of the floor. It was pointing at six. The top. As good a bet as any for where the woman had gone. Jimmy pushed the button to bring it down and stepped back. It was slow. It took twenty seconds just to creak down to five.

He leaned against the opposite wall. He'd been smoking all day, since he'd gotten in the Porsche in the basement garage of the Mark, since he'd dropped the metal door of the glove box, looking for his sunglasses, and had seen the pack of cigarettes he'd bought at the little store back down in Paso Robles.

Luckies.

He was snubbing out the cigarette in the sand in the canister ashtray across from the elevator when the Infiniti woman stepped out of a door at the end of the lobby, a door that had been left standing open but that he hadn't noticed.

"Hello," she said. "Again."

"Hi."

"Do you need a minute?"

Jimmy took one, to think what to say. He had been intending to work on his opening lines on the ride up in the elevator, have something worked out before he got to the top floor.

"I know it's difficult," the woman said.

"Unprecedented," Jimmy said.

She smiled and nodded. She'd been misting up again, just like she had in the coroner's office. He could see the teary sparkle in her eye. She turned around and left him there, went back through the door at the end of the lobby, left it open.

When he looked in, it was a small apartment. The door opened into a four-foot-square foyer and then a twelve-foot living room. It was tiny, but it was a deluxe apartment. The building was on the top of the hill, so even on the first floor there was a view, a blue and white pane of color, clear and bright, like a stained glass rendering of a slice of the skyline and the Bay beyond. The woman saw him looking out the window and for some reason got a bit flustered, apologetic.

"I opened the drapes," she said. "She kept it so dark in here."

"It's all right," Jimmy said. "It's a beautiful day."

She crossed to him, a card already in her hand. "Someone said you weren't coming in until this afternoon," she said. "Patricia Hatch."

Jimmy took the card. He convinced himself that he was working, working for some greater good, and just let the lie tell itself.

"Were you her only child?" she said. "No," she immediately corrected, "I'm sorry. A neighbor said she had a daughter here in the City who came to see her often. Who had just moved here?"

Jimmy kept quiet, took in the place. Every inch of wall, every flat surface, was covered with photographs, framed. On the coffee table was an ashtray from The Coconut Grove.

"Oh, I'm so sorry," she corrected again. "You would be *grand*children. I forgot how old she—she was *ninety*."

There was picture after picture of a beautiful, sassy girl, maybe twenty-two. In gowns. In a bathing suit, what they used to call a bather.

"Why were you crying?" Jimmy said, still scanning the pictures. "At the coroner's. And here, before I came in. I mean, in your business you must see the same thing, over and over. Was something different with her?"

The woman stepped closer, with a kind of familiarity, the same familiarity she'd been apologizing for ever since he came in.

"Can I show you my favorite picture?" she said.

"Please," Jimmy said.

"It's this one." It was a publicity shot, the young woman as a chorus girl. She handed it to him. "You see, I was a dancer, too," she said. "A million years ago."

"But not seventy," Jimmy said.

"No."

Jimmy put the picture back on the table.

"The world has changed so much," the woman said.

Jimmy couldn't argue with her there. "I don't have a sister," he said. "You said a woman had been coming by?" He tried to amend his tone, to keep from sounding like he was pushing. "Someone young?"

"That's what they said. A new friend. Maybe she's just someone in the neighborhood," the other said. "Someone like me. Who cared very much for your grandmother. It was good that she had a friend."

She went to her purse and started unpacking. A pad. A gold pen. A phone with a keyboard. A handheld tape recorder. A digital camera. "Timothy from our office will be here in a few minutes. Of course, you can have your own Trusted Witness for the inventory." He heard her capitalize the *T* and the *W*. He thought, *That's what I'd like to be: a Trusted Witness.* Angel was a Trusted Witness. Jimmy knew a few others. "Of course, you can take anything today, before the walk-through," she said.

"I think I'll walk around the block," Jimmy said.

"Of course."

He made another scan of the room. There weren't any pictures anywhere of anyone who looked like a son or a daughter or a grandson or a granddaughter. Or a man friend. Or even the "new friend" she'd made. No friends, neighbors. Nobody. But don't you get used to being alone, being lonely, in ninety years? Don't you get used to outliving everyone, even get used to outliving yourself, at least what you used to be? Your perk? Your spark? The tone of young skin? The beauty, the sex that drew people to you? If she had been sixty, it would have made sense. Or seventy.

At least now he knew how she got her leg up and over the rail on the bridge. She had been a dancer.

"I wonder why I thought I should do this today," Jimmy looked at Patricia Hatch and said.

"Everyone is different," she said.

And he made his exit, graceful or otherwise.

---

The world wasn't neat. The world didn't make sense, at least not moment by moment. Nobody knew that like Jimmy knew it, but still, he tried to neaten it up where he could, even if only in his own head. He made lists. He checked things off.

So, after Russian Hill, he looked into the other two suicides off the Golden Gate, the latest ones.

The German woman apparently was traveling alone, had checked in, alone, to a fairly expensive room at a blue-and-white nautical-themed hotel down on Fisherman's Wharf, a new hotel in an old, old brick building, a former cannery. You could look out every window and see the Buena Vista bar and the cable car turnaround and the water beyond. It didn't look like the kind of place a last-stage depressive would pick for herself. She'd been there three days, had made the rounds of all the sights, had asked the concierge for maps and restaurant picks. She was signed up for a wine country bus tour tomorrow, prepaid. (A *pair* of tickets. Why?) From here, it was on to L.A. for the woman. Alone.

Jimmy talked to a half-dozen guests and hotel staff. It didn't make sense to anybody, but everybody admitted they didn't know much about her, about how she was spending her days and nights. The concierge seemed particularly to feel the loss. The woman was German. Europeans understand that you tip the help at the end of your stay.

So that was two out of the three.

What about Mr. Wrong Side?

He had AIDS. That was the first thing Jimmy learned about him: he was dying of AIDS. It was right there in the paper, a sidebar bylined by Duncan Groner, who apparently owned the suicide beat. Jimmy had stopped for an Irish coffee at a place in North Beach. By night North Beach would be packed with tourists and locals, one of the neighborhoods that satisfied both of them, with good-as-Rome Italian restaurants and bars and hipster bookstores and strip joints. It was three in the afternoon, and the coffee and Irish whisky was good. Up and down in the same cup.

The young man was living in a hospice. Too weak to move out of his bed, they had thought. So he'd had some help. Jimmy didn't really want to follow up on it. He had the address for the hospice. It wasn't far away, four or five streets over. He didn't want to follow it up because the answer to the question of why the young man was dead was too clear. In spite of what he told himself all the time, he didn't like simple, obvious answers. A young man killed himself because he was dying in a slow, bad way. Jimmy wanted it to be something else. He wanted a little mystery. Not a lot, a small mystery, easily blown out, like a candle, by a professional with a modicum of sense, even if he was from out of town and wrapped in the cloak of his own mysteries, dragging around his own chains.

Then again, there was that detail . . .

The man dying of AIDS had to have had some help.

And something else . . .

Most of the day, Red Boots and another had been tailing Jimmy, neither one of them looking all that happy to be up in daylight.

# ELEVEN

He stayed away for as long as he could, which turned out to be a day and a half. It was five thirty. Mary waited behind the wheel of her husband's black BMW X-5, in front of a dance studio on a side street in San Raphael. The light was what they call in the movie world the Golden Hour. Everything looked good at five thirty. She wasn't on the phone. Maybe she was listening to the radio. She had the window down. Jimmy was across the street, in the Porsche. He hadn't been this close to her before. Her hair was a little darker, at least in this light, than it had been back then when it was so blond it was almost white, when sometimes it looked like there were lights inside it, or at least electricity. He remembered the first time he saw her in daylight, walking toward him, away from the director's house up in the canyon, early enough in the morning that no one else was awake.

She put her head back against the headrest. She had one knee up against the door of the car, sitting like a man. She seemed happy, glad to be exactly where she was.

There was a reason Jimmy didn't like the simple, obvious answers. They hurt more.

*She just doesn't love you.*

*You'll never see him again.*

*There is no God.*

*Everyone's afraid at the end.*

*The past is passed.*

*She is happily married now and has a little boy and never thinks of you and is out of your reach forever . . .*

*She's alive; you're dead.*

Suddenly there were little dancers everywhere. The doors must have opened somewhere, sending them out to their parents and nannies.

But they weren't dancers. Mary was parked directly in front of a dance academy, but it was next door to a martial arts dojo, blocked by her car.

Another kind of dance. The boys and girls, six and seven and eight and nine, spilled out in their gis, still all jacked up from the class, half of them kicking the air as they crab-walked across the asphalt, white belts or no belts, calling out things to each other, a happy little assault force.

The boy who was Mary's boy was one of the last to leave. He came out and stood in the angled sunlight just outside the glass door. The dojo had been a retail store of some kind in its previous life. The instructor came out behind the boy, a serious hand resting on his low shoulder. He was a black man with a Navy SEAL's body. Whatever he was saying to the boy, the boy kept nodding. By this age, living where he lived, living like he lived, the kid probably had five coaches in his life. He knew the coach drill.

The teacher dismissed the little warrior with a gentle hand on the back of his head. The black man's palms were so white they almost flashed in the bright, angled light. The boy ran the rest of the way to the SUV, opened the back door, and climbed up and in, buckling himself in and pulling the door closed. The front passenger-side window came down. The sensei leaned in with some words for the mom.

*She is a mother, here, in this life. A wife, a mother.*

*There's your answer, simple as that. No mystery.*

It made Jimmy's chest ache.

He followed them halfway home, halfway back to the hump of Tiburon, but he kept going straight when Mary turned left into the parking lot of a market. He'd had enough *obvious.*

He looked up in the rearview mirror. Had he caught her looking over at the departing Porsche? Following it with her eyes? Maybe he'd been tailgating or maybe she thought he had. He was wearing the blocky Ray-Ban Wayfarers from the glove compartment. That's what he had always worn then. *Then.* Maybe she'd seen him in her rearview mirror.

Maybe she . . .

No, it was something simpler than that. It had to be.

He watched the day die in a place that was almost painfully beautiful, Mount Tam, Tamalpais, one of the world's most scenic overlooks. At least if you loved California, if it spoke to you, the general drama of the coastline, the specific drama of San Francisco. The knob of the mountain was bare but for grass and outcroppings of smooth rock, hundreds of feet above the water, right at the Gate. The bridge was to the right. Though the sky was still full of light, the cars' headlights were all on, on the bridge, three lanes north and three lanes south, as if the curbs were channeling opposing flows of bright lava. Or surging white blood cells.

*Two ways to go,* he thought.

Southbound. He should be southbound. He should get the hell out of there. He turned and looked at the Porsche. With the riotous colors in the sky melting on the classic curves of the fenders, it looked like a model sitting there. The whole picture, and him in it, looked managed, staged, touched up. *A pensive, handsome young man and his automobile, the symbol of his success.* He should finish this cigarette and grind it dead on the ground and get behind the wood-rimmed wheel and turn the key and see the white light leap into the corners of the gauges, see the red-edged needle jump to three-quarters—plenty of gas to get well on down the road—turn the key further, hear the engine go, see the tach leap with the first punch of the gas. Hear and see everything that said *Go!* Everything that said leave the land of the dead before they all started coming to life.

*Go.*

He let the Lucky Strike burn all the way down, pinching it like a jay, staring at the car sitting there. He thought about the day he bought it. The car. He thought about who was with him. He thought about the ninety-year-old lady. He thought about the German tourist, about the wine-country wine she didn't drink that day. He thought about the young man dying of AIDS, until he died stepping off the wrong side of the Golden Gate. Everything he thought was complicated. None of it was self-evident. The voice in his head—the voice of himself, *Jimmy Miles*—was a dozen voices. He was like Machine Shop. But with Shop, at least what was in his head was a debate. With Jimmy, it was ten points of view. Twenty. It was like being in a bus station at midnight listening to crazy people, all of whom think they know you. It was like being in a room with every version of yourself you've ever been, hearing every lying man and boy you've ever been turning on you.

Maybe *that* was the gathering he'd dreamed of that morning.

*Two ways to go.*

He came down off the mountain and went north. To Tiburon.

A few minutes before seven, the babysitter drove up to the big Crafts-man house in a yellow Volkswagen convertible. She looked college age. She parked on a curve just below the house. She got out, locked the car, started toward the gate in the hedge, then remembered something and went back to the bug. A book. In case her boyfriend wasn't home when she called. Mary's husband answered the door, stood there in the frame. White shirt, dark pants, tie around his neck waiting to be tied. He was a good-looking man. Jimmy still didn't know what his name was. He hadn't seen him again since the first time out in the park until now. He had a glass of red wine in his hand. Even from across the street, Jimmy could guess the lines in the joke he made with the young girl about it.

Mary was upstairs in the boy's room. Jimmy didn't know his name yet, either. She was getting him into PJs. Or trying to. He was jumping on the bed, taking advantage of the special circumstances, a weeknight left with a sitter. She caught him in midair on one jump and hugged him with such devotion it might have scared him a little. There must have been a voice they both heard from downstairs, mother and son, because they suddenly looked at each other and made the same funny face and turned for the door. A second later, the light went out.

There were two ways off the tip of Tiburon, two ends of the same road, but one way was more direct than the other. Jimmy couldn't keep himself from making assumptions about Mary's husband, filling the blanks. He didn't seem like the take-the-long-way kind of guy.

Jimmy guessed right; here came the X-5. Somebody had gotten it washed since the late afternoon. With the dark trees of Tiburon behind it on the dark street with its tasteful lighting, it was all black on black, glistening. Everything today looked like an upscale car ad.

Jimmy waited, let them get a ways up the road. He was parked in the lot of a closed gas station. The lights were out except for three moons of backlit white plastic, the signs over the pumps on the three bays.

Self Self Full, they said. Take your pick.

Jimmy was a little underdressed, a suit, no tie, but didn't have any trouble crashing the do in the St. Francis ballroom. It was a fund-raiser for some charity, something with *Heart* in the name. He wasn't on the list. He wrote a thousand-dollar check. Suddenly they knew him. A smiling woman who reminded him of Patricia Hatch from Graceful Exits pinned a red ceramic heart on his lapel.

"Good luck," she said.

"Thank you," Jimmy said. He was looking down at his new lapel jewelry.

"I mean in the auction," she said.

It wasn't hard to blend in, stay concealed. He had put on a black suit that morning and looked like every other man in the room, even the ones who'd thrown on a tux. You had to get close to see that Jimmy's shirt was taupe and that he wasn't wearing socks with the loafers. He hit the hosted bar for a champagne and crème de cassis, which is what everyone else seemed to be drinking, and found a shaggy arica palm to screen him.

Mary and her husband were at one of the front tables. With two other couples. Jimmy was across the broad room, with twenty tables between them, but he thought she looked his way once, fixed her eyes in his direction. But then someone in the foreground waved, and Mary waved back. So much for *I somehow sensed you were there*. She went back to her conversation with the man next to her. They were seated boy/girl.

Jimmy looked at her husband again. He was caught up in a conversation with the woman seated to his right. Or was pretending to be. Who was he? So far, Jimmy had held himself back from thinking too much on it. That was too high school, too. What difference did it make? He hadn't seen Mary in almost ten years. So what if she still looked the same to him? Ten years had passed. She had found someone. What did he think, that she had joined some I-can-never-love-another order? What was that phrase that everyone used now? She had *moved on*.

She flashed a smile to the others at the table and pushed back and stood. She took her clutch bag off the table. She moved toward opened double doors, the exit.

It was risky business, but Jimmy moved out from his blind and started on a line that, if he kept on it, would intersect her path. She stopped to talk to someone. She was only thirty feet away from him. He stopped. If she looked any direction except straight ahead when she finished talking, they'd be face-to-face. It would make for a dramatic scene, if drama was what he wanted.

*So. It's you.*

But she didn't look his way, walked straight out the exit.

He went through another open door into the hallway. He looked for the doorway where she would have come out. There were restrooms there.

Jimmy ducked back into the ballroom, found another potted plant to meld with. And snagged another kir royale from the tray of a passing waiter.

Mary's husband was impatient, maybe even suspicious of where his wife had gone. He kept up his end of the conversation with the woman next to him but still managed to look over at the exit every ten seconds. He did everything but check his watch.

Then he checked his watch. He got up, tossed the napkin in his lap onto the table. Jimmy realized he was older than he'd thought. Older than Mary. She'd be in her early thirties. Her husband was in his mid-forties.

He touched the shoulder of the woman he'd been talking with and said something and started off where he'd been looking all along, toward the exit.

And then she appeared in the doorway. She looked altogether innocent, refreshed, touched-up, relaxed. Until she saw the look on her husband's face, coming toward her.

He smiled but meant something nasty by it.

When he got close enough, she said something to him.

It didn't change the look on his face.

They were stopped beside one of the buffet tables, the dessert table. She said something else to him. Her tone had changed. She walked past him, or tried to. He took her by the wrist to stop her.

She said one word, glaring at him. Jimmy guessed it was probably his name.

He let go of her wrist.

Now it was his turn to say *her* name, as she walked away from him. She kept going.

Maybe it was the light, or that there was a tall ice sculpture behind him, but there was *blue* behind his head and shoulders, a blue edge. *Blue.*

But when Jimmy looked away, at Mary, and then looked back at her husband, the blue was gone.

Was it too late to get *simple* back?

On his way, he looked them up on the seating chart out in the foyer, where he'd laid down his check.

Dr. Marc Hesse and Mary Hesse.

---

When he drove onto the plaza in front of the Mark Hopkins, to leave the Porsche with the valet instead of driving down into the garage himself, Machine Shop was there. Pacing. Scrubbed out of his silver paint.

He had a wild look in his eyes.

It was late. Jimmy was tired. When he got out, left the motor running, Shop was right there.

"Your girl killed herself," he said. "Your Lucy."

# TWELVE

It was too nice a night for it, hot as hell, but clear. Jimmy roared up Benedict Canyon in Beverly Hills in the huffing old Cadillac, fouling the air behind him. It was a cruising car, not a ride-to-the-rescue car. Or whatever it was that he was riding to. In his head he could still hear Mary screaming on the phone. It was uphill all the way, twisting and turning. He stuffed the gas to the floor, and the land yacht shuddered, downshifted itself into first. It was like an old surfer digging hard to get a fat classic long board up and over a wave. Strange, the things you think of when you're thinking everything at once. Jimmy remembered a toast Ronald Reagan used to give, "May the road rise up to meet you . . ." He must not have meant this.

There were headlights way behind him. He was afraid he'd blown past a cop hiding on a side street, but he didn't slow down. He wasn't going to stop.

It *was* a cop. A black-and-white. It overtook him. The cops never even looked over at him.

*We're headed the same place,* Jimmy thought.

The cops' Gran Fury bottomed out on a dip in the road with an ugly sound and a splash of sparks, but the driver never let up.

There were *eight* cop cars under the streetlights at the end of the cul-de-sac, at the end of the road, counting the plain-wraps and the higher-up suits' cars with all the antennae. No press. Yet. Jimmy had gotten the screaming phone call at one ten. It was one twenty-five.

The gate was open for all the coming and going. A uniformed officer stood there, dead center.

"You can't park there."

Jimmy had just stopped the Cadillac in the middle of the street and gotten out. He took a step closer, saw the look on the cop's face. It seemed like a good time to lie.

"My sister lives here," he said.

The cop gave in quickly, too quickly, so quickly it scared Jimmy about what was inside.

"Go on," the cop said. "Just give me the key."

Jimmy didn't know he had it in his hand until he looked down.

The white house was doused in blank light from double floodlight fixtures on the corners of the garage and the far end, by the pool. There was another cop at the front door, after you crossed the driveway. A cop in a suit. The door stood open behind this one. It was a Dutch door, cut sideways across the middle so the top half could open on its own. They made doors like that for families with kids, to keep them in but to let air and light in, too. The two halves weren't lined up, locked together. There was blood around the knob outside but so dark it looked like chocolate. All the shine had gone out of it. What it looked like was shit. The cop in the suit wasn't standing guard; he was working, taking notes. He had twenty years on the officer out in the street, at the gate. He was a detective, a lieutenant.

"You can't go in there," he said, not looking away from whatever he was seeing on the face of the lower half of the door.

"My sister lives here."

Now the cop in the suit looked up at him but still used the same voice. "What's her name?"

It was only then that Jimmy realized how quiet it was, how nothing was coming out from the house. You'd think there'd be voices. Somebody. Something. There was a smell coming from the house he'd never smelled before.

He told him Mary's name.

A bit of the cop's steel shield came down, the slightest softening of his reserve, his self-protective distance. He was relieved.

"She's alive. She's all right. She's in the den." He even put his sentences in the right order, to save Jimmy the pain of even a half second of suspense.

Jimmy shifted, as if to go past him, through the door.

"Don't go in here," the cop said. "Go around."

"Thanks," Jimmy said.

"Better yet . . ." He called over another of the uniformed cops, who stood in front of the closed garage, his hand resting on his holstered revolver, as if something else was going to come out of the night.

"Yessir."

"Go in; if they're done with her, tell her that her brother is here."

The uniformed cop slipped in through the open door without touching it.

"He should have gone around, too," the veteran cop said, going back to the work. "Nobody needs to see that."

Jimmy knew what he meant by it, knew it was a tough guy's way of saying, *You're going to have to take care of your sister.*

Mary came around the corner of the house, but it took a few minutes. She stopped, just stood there in the middle of the driveway, her arms limp.

They let Jimmy take her through the gate, out to the end of the cul-de-sac, to the empty street across from the white house.

It wasn't something she could *tell*. Not yet. He saw that. She was trembling, but then it would stop, and she would be so still he would have shaken her if her eyes were closed. To see if she was alive. She just stood there, her back to the house, her eyes on the opposite ridgetop. It was only now that Jimmy realized where the city was, by the blue-gray edge to the scrub at the top of the hill. As if L.A. itself was a Sailor. It was what she was looking at.

"Which room were you in?" Jimmy said. He put his arm around her. She was as tall as he was, but that night, now, she seemed diminished.

"The study, the office," she said.

Maybe this was the way to let her unburden herself, a piece at a time. He didn't ask another question for a long time, long enough for a helicopter to fly over, coming in from the south, headed for Mulholland or the valley beyond. Jimmy wondered how long it would take for the first news cameras to arrive. He didn't want to be out in the open like this then.

"You were asleep?"

She nodded. She'd gone slack again, still. He dropped his hand from around her waist. She didn't seem to notice.

"David and Michelle were in my room," she said. "Off the hallway. So I went to the other end, to the office to sleep. The couch. I *told* them all this." She said the last imploringly, exasperated.

Then she seemed to remember who he was, who he wasn't.

"I'm sorry."

There were voices from somewhere. They both turned. Shafts of light were projected on the slab of hillside behind the house, sweeping flashlights. The cops were in the slice of concreted "backyard" between the house and the rock. The pool was on the other end of the house. Their voices, indistinct, guttural, masculine, rude, were rebounding off the rock, amplified somehow by the arrangement of things.

"I have to find someplace to go," Mary said, a crack of panic in her voice.

"You're going to stay with me," Jimmy said.

He took her home.

People always think someone should *sleep* when a thing like this happens, that the person *can* sleep. But Jimmy had been through his own version of a world-wrenching blowup. The ground had opened up in front of him once, too. He knew what it meant, knew what you saw when you closed your eyes in those first hours. *Everything can change in an hour, if it's the wrong hour.* So when he got Mary home, he asked her what she wanted to do. The bedroom door was open behind them.

"I guess lie down," she said.

He left her sitting on the bed, sitting in the center of it, with her legs crossed under her. He left the door open halfway. Something else he knew to do.

As he walked away, she came out of the bedroom, went into the bathroom. He listened at the door. He wasn't sure what he was listening for, but thought he should listen. She washed her hands for a long time, with the water on full.

"At first, they put my hands in plastic bags," she had told him before, as they were backing away down the cul-de-sac in the Cadillac. "Then they took them off. They never said why."

In the kitchen, Jimmy took a bottle of water from the icebox, left the door open for the cool and the light. He didn't turn on the overhead, sat at the turquoise Formica table, cracked the seal, and drank it down. He looked out at the lights of the city below his house. The kitchen window was closed. The little house didn't have air-conditioning, or even a wheezing window unit in the bedroom. He didn't know if opening the window would make it cooler or hotter. He reached back into the refrigerator, opened the freezer door, and pulled out an ice tray. He held it upside down over the table and twisted it. The cubes clattered out like dice in a complicated game. He picked up one and sucked it like a Popsicle.

He knew the layout of the house up in Benedict. Two nights ago there'd been a party he didn't want to go to, but went to anyway. It was Thursday night now, so that would have made it a Tuesday. Nobody in that crowd seemed to notice it wasn't the weekend. There were thirty people there, inside/outside, around the pool, a few of them famous, or at least famous somewhere. Recognizable. Actors, musicians. A high-hair metal band, whose look said they hadn't checked in at the record label lately, hadn't gotten the memo, came late and stayed late. Throughout the night they went everywhere together, side by side, in a cluster. Maybe they'd just shot a video that day and were still unnaturally synced. They stayed until the end. Or at least they were still there when Jimmy left.

That night Mary had met him at the door, at that Dutch door, and had kissed him. Other people were in the room, the living room. The girls. Michelle, April. In front of them, Mary had kissed him on both cheeks, Euro style. It had ticked him off. Somehow two kisses were less than one. He didn't see much of her for the next hours. He spent the first half of the night alone out by the black-bottomed pool, posing for a Hockney, a drink in hand, staring down at the reflective surface, maybe waiting for a coyote to come down out of the brush to drink. The rest of that night he spent in the office, the "study," though the director wasn't the type to study much of anything. He ended up being alone there, too. It was tucked away, off the master.

So he knew the rooms. He knew the layout. Stage right, stage left. The long hallway with its blank walls, where the director would have hung his awards if he had any. (That Tuesday night, he was off with some woman agent in his bedroom. Having sex would have been the least vulgar thing they could have been doing.) At one end of the hall was the living room, opening to a dining room and the kitchen, all opening onto the pool. At the other end of the hall were the bedrooms, two next to each other on the right, the "kids' rooms," the master at the end on the left, across the back of the house, with French doors to the concrete area behind the house, where the cops toward the middle of the night had focused their attention.

So he knew the layout.

Jimmy tried to put it together. Maybe *make it up* would be more accurate. He tried different scenarios, different entry points for the killer, different paths through the house. Different orders to the deaths. Who was first?

Then he realized something. The coroner's vans had never come the whole time he was there.

He was moving the melting ice around on the Formica tabletop. There was a siren somewhere down the hill or ripping across on Sunset, above the house. Maybe that was what had triggered the realization about the body wagons.

He had been on the scene for two or three hours, and no coroner's van had arrived.

What did that mean?

Jimmy and Mary stayed inside for the next three days. The scene had very little drama, only quiet talking, talk about nothing at all, about music, about the neighbor's cat who, even though Jimmy's kitchen window was twenty feet off the ground, came twice a day to tightrope-walk across the sill. Three days. Three days that way. Just the two of them. Angel brought in food sometimes. They drank a little. Mary started reading a book, something on the bookshelf left over from high school for Jimmy. The first day, in the first hours of pink light coming over the city, he had unhooked the television so neither one of them had to see the pictures from the news helicopters of the desecrated bodies spread-eagled on three road cuts in three disparate parts of the county. The director, Michelle, April.

# THIRTEEN

*There are rules; we just don't know what they are.*

That was Angel's line. Over the years, he'd said it ten different ways to Jimmy. He'd said it the first night, when he'd found Jimmy on the street in Hollywood, standing across from the Chateau Marmont, in the crowd watching the ambulance, when he'd seen in his eyes whatever it is they see. Angel had spent the first three days with him. *First Days.* Angel had been the one who walked him through the first blue moon, though they didn't have a name for that person, that role. Hand-holder? You were lucky if you had one, if you weren't going through it all completely on your own, that first blue moon (and the ones after it), when some of the Sailors were called home, when some of them left whatever *this* was for whatever was next.

Everyone should have someone saying, "There are rules; we just don't know what they are." Whether it's true or not.

They were riding north on the 5, Jimmy and Angel, just now climbing up out of the San Fernando Valley.

It was night, when you think of the past.

"You should have took the cutoff, the Fourteen," Angel said. They were in Jimmy's Cadillac.

Jimmy didn't say anything.

"We should have took my car or something," Angel said.

"I wanted to go this way. Same difference. I was thinking of Saugus, the speedway," Jimmy said. "I'll cut across there." The top was down, but it wasn't too loud to talk. Mary's tape of Leonard Cohen and Joni Mitchell and Neil Young and Buffy Sainte-Marie was in the deck, down low, barely audible. Jimmy had been listening to it so much lately, it was full volume in his head, in his soul. Mary was back at his place. "Maybe I'll come up here this weekend, get her out of the city."

"She like cars?" Angel said.

"I doubt it. She doesn't have one."

"I didn't think *you* liked it, when you and me come up here."

"I liked it. What's not to like? It's loud and cheap and smoky and they run into each other."

"She's going to be all right," Angel said, because Mary was what they were really talking about, thinking about.

They'd already driven past five or six road cuts. Out here, where the highway opened up a little and the subdivisions of blunt, ugly houses only came along every two or three miles, the cuts were immense, great sloped gashes. Geology classes from UCLA took field trips up here. Field geology. Jimmy had seen something on TV about it once. It was a way to see what was under the surface, what primal sedimentary or metamorphic or igneous superstructure was there all along under ten feet of topsoil. Faults and folds. Layers of history. Shifting tectonic plates, north and south coming into collision. Jimmy remembered the professor's line. A road cut is like an *autopsy* on the earth.

"I mean, there was no connection to *her*, on her own," Angel said, when Jimmy didn't say anything. "She was just there. Wrong place, wrong time."

These days Mary was in that state of mind that said, *Why me? Why did I survive?* Jimmy, selfishly, without any evidence to point to, in his own mind had come up with the idea that she was spared because he loved her, because they loved each other. Jimmy and Mary. There was your reason.

They rolled on north, cut back east at Saugus, by Bouquet Junction into Placerita Canyon to the 14 and north again, past the great shoved-up plates of Vasquez Rocks off to the left, where so many sci-fi movies and Westerns had been filmed. For its otherworldliness, its sense of the edge, the frontier. A moon a bit past half side-lit the scene. Every time you saw Vasquez Rocks, especially by night, it looked weirder than your memory of it.

There was the long, easy climb up the grade. The Caddy was purring, running steady. At eighty-five. The forced march up Benedict Canyon the other night must have done it some good, blown out the pipes. Or put the fear of God into it.

"You should let me fix this up for you," Angel said.

"I like it the way it is," Jimmy said.

"It runs all right, but it looks sad. Does it even have a top?"

"It has one. It's ripped up."

Angel put his hand up to surf the wind. With the elevation, the air had gotten a little cooler, but not much.

"Here we go," Angel said, as they blew under the green rectangle of a sign. "Nine more miles."

"Nothing happens *fast* out here, does it?" Jimmy said.

"They get rattlesnakes in their garages," Angel said. "That can get fast on you."

Then they were cruising down one of the wide streets in a subdivision this side of Palmdale. It was three a.m. by then and real dead. The highway was a mile behind them, but if they'd pulled over and killed the engine they could have heard it, even over the sound of all the air conditioners, the steady river-sound of the cars, the interspersed basso profundo of the semis headed the back way toward the Central Valley, Bakersfield, and points beyond.

It was house after house, shoulder to shoulder, all the same color, at least under the moonlight, big stucco boxes, blank yards. L.A. was forty miles south. Some commute.

The motion-detector lights over each garage clicked on as they passed.

"You better have the number right," Jimmy said. "I mean, it's not like he can say, 'I'm in the white house with the little lawn boy out front.'"

"Watch it, Brother."

"This is a long way from L.A.," Jimmy said.

"Lot of cops live up here."

It was something he'd said, the cop at the door at the murder house, a beat after he'd let Jimmy know Mary was alive, that she was all right, that she was in the den. "It passed over her," he'd said. Angel had made a few calls, confirmed it. The detective was a Sailor. *Passed over* was their way of saying *spared*, though it meant something completely different. A good number of Sailors were cops, just like others were EMTs and emergency room doctors, people up all night anyway. They all took care of each other, like they took care of the new ones, stunned on sidewalks or beaches or beside overturned cars, in the first minutes of their new "lives." A Sailor tended not to say no to another Sailor, unless one or the other was one of the bad ones. (Who took care of each other in their own ways.)

And this was where he lived, the vet cop who wasn't as tough as he meant to be, in one of these big, ugly houses, a house he had probably tried to talk his ex-wife into taking.

"What is it? What's the number?"

"One one eight five two. Should be on the left side."

Jimmy looked up in the rearview mirror. The cop was standing in his unadorned front yard.

"Should be three houses back," Jimmy said.

The cop's name was Dill.

This was Dill's "day" off. He put a paper plate of Oreos and a gallon jug of whole milk and two glasses on the dining room table. He already had a glass of his own going. Cookies and milk. Sailors tended to eat exactly what they wanted, when they wanted. It could just as easily have been a bowl of raw Vidalia onions. Or ice cubes.

"They have their rules," Dill was saying. "They scrub the bodies. They shave the pubic hair. They always position the bodies faceup, head up. They close the eyes."

He'd put the Oreos right on top of *The Case*. He lifted the paper plate to pass it to Angel, and the face of a dead girl looked up at them, a close-up, outdoors. Full sunlight. Very white, white bordering blue. Jimmy and Angel recognized her from the news. She was the first of the dead. The first victim in what came to be called the Road Cut Killings, from two months ago, early in the summer.

"It's always high on the cut. Maximum light. Facing east usually."

"*They*," Jimmy said. "You said *they*."

The cop nodded.

"So the paper, the TV has it wrong," Angel said. "Road Cut *Killer*."

"The papers and the TV have their own version of it," Dill said. "It's always that way. Personally, I treat reporters like they could just as well be the ones who did it. But that's just me. Long and short, they know about one-tenth what we know."

"How many have there been?" Jimmy said. "How many dead?"

"These three made thirteen."

Angel started to say something.

"Eleven that were in the papers," Dill finished.

"Who were the others?" Jimmy asked.

"A couple in Encino. They never made it out onto a cut. They were left in their house, in their bed."

The dining room table was covered with pictures, official pictures, and official documents and newspaper clippings, but only a few of those. The pics were hard to take. They were full color. It was the nineties. They were in color. With the old black-and-white, you could trick yourself into thinking it was a still from a bad movie. What this looked like was meat on rock. Angel shuddered involuntarily. He grabbed the handle of the jug of milk, poured himself half a glass, like it was whisky in a cowboy bar.

When Angel lifted the jug, there was Mary's picture.

Jimmy saw it.

Dill saw him looking at it. "No reason for her to be there," the cop said.

As it is with cops, the way they talk, there were a couple of ways you could take it.

"Your girlfriend," he added.

Jimmy nodded. He wondered just how early the cop had figured out that Mary wasn't his sister.

He picked up the picture of her. It was one the cops had taken that night, before he got there, inside, Mary standing in front of a white paneled wall in the study with her hands down at her side. It made her look so helpless. Small.

"How many of them are there?" Jimmy said, looking at her.

"I say two. Some think three. One detective thinks it's two men and a woman they share. But she's a woman. The detective."

What the cop did next was hard to take, even with the skewed view of the world Jimmy and Angel had, worse in a way than looking at the photographs, because what he did was walk them through every case. Starting at the beginning.

And it really meant *walking*, walking in behind the killers, a step behind them, seeing what they saw. It was almost like your feet stuck to the floor, made that bloody kissing noise. He started with victim one, at the beginning of the summer. He would pick up each photo and hold it through the telling. The setup for each story was the entry. The approach to the victim was Act Two. The killing was the climax, the body on the road cut the denouement. He would hold the picture and begin, each time, with a line like, "They parked on a street just below . . ." He might as well have started each line with a personal pronoun. And present tense.

*We come in from the garage . . .*

*We walk down the hallway . . .*

Jimmy looked up at the ceiling. There was a galvanized metal plate over an electrical box dead center above their heads. Chandeliers get repossessed? Or divvied up in divorce proceedings? Or maybe the couple had never gotten around to buying one. Angel said Detective Dill had been divorced a year. He'd married a woman with a kid, a boy, a teenager, but it had only lasted two years. There weren't any other details. There's hardly ever any story to it when a cop gets divorced, if what a story is, is something with at least a little surprise in it. Dill hadn't been a Sailor for a long time, four or five years, a lot less than Jimmy, an eternity less than Angel. Maybe what broke up the family was the truth, when he finally got around to telling it. Maybe at this selfsame table. Probably at this hour.

When Jimmy looked at Dill again, he could see the very faintest edge of blue around his head and shoulders. Very weak. Maybe he was a good man, but he was a weak Sailor, putting in his hours but mostly just waiting for release. Some blue moon to sail away.

"The French doors across the back of the house were never locked. They were probably open, with the heat. There was a shorted-out circuit breaker in the AC unit on the ground, mid-house. Either it had been out previously or they shorted it. There's a possibility one or both of them came earlier in the day to prepare the way. No one was home for two hours midafternoon. There were exterior lights, blue, but they weren't on. The lead put a hand, his right hand, high on the right-hand door of the double doors, and opened it, or opened it further. It opened out . . ."

Suddenly Jimmy was back in the scene. The episodic tale of the summer of murders had come round to the leased white house at the end of the cul-de-sac. To *him*. Not that he hadn't heard every word of the telling of the other killings, every detail, every footstep, every clicking drop of the blood onto every floor.

"They wore gloves," Dill said. "There were no prints left anywhere. And rubber-soled shoes. Converse."

Jimmy started filling in the details. He thought, *Mary stirred on the couch in the study* . . .

"Like the other times, they killed together, two together," Dill was saying. "The lead put his hand over the girl's mouth, the girl in bed in the master bedroom, and the second then choked her with both hands. Smoothly, with a strong, steady grip, tighter and tighter, but not enough to break any bones. This was Michelle Gandy. She struggled, broke two toes on her right foot, either on the footboard of the bed or striking one of the two on either side of her."

*Did Mary hear something? Did her eyes open?*

"They left her, for now," Dill continued. "The master bedroom opened onto the long hallway. One started through the doorway first. They apparently hadn't made any noise that had alerted the others in the house. They looked back." Dill looked over his shoulder. "The French doors were wide open, letting in whatever sounds out in the night there were, possibly masking any of the sounds of violence."

Jimmy thought, *Mary closed her eyes. It was nothing.*

"The man, David Fifthian, never woke up," Dill said next. "He was alone in the first small bedroom off the hallway. On his stomach. He was killed the same way, though facedown. Feathers were found all the way into his lungs, from the comforter, from trying to pull in what air he could. Both of them handled his neck." Dill made his two hands into an open circle. "One pair of hands on top of the other. He wore just a V-neck sweater. He had had sexual relations in the bed in the master bedroom and then left his partner there to come to this room. They wrapped his ankles with a leather belt from a pair of trousers on the floor near the door and used it as a strap to pull him off the bed and out into the hallway, once he was dead."

*Stay asleep,* Jimmy thought, as if he was standing over Mary.

"The third, April . . ."

Jimmy wanted to make him stop. What he wanted was to take Mary out of there, lift her off the couch, out of Dill's narration, before one more thing happened. He wanted to cut her out of the story, let all this happen to strangers, with no connection to him.

"...April Joules. She was awake. Reading. In the second small bedroom. She couldn't have heard them. She was in a chair, beside a table with a gooseneck lamp, beside an open window."

Jimmy remembered something he should have remembered before. He interrupted, "Was his daughter there?"

It was the only interruption. Dill shook his head. "Vancouver."

It made Jimmy realize how little he and Mary had said about the whole thing over the three days, how little he had asked or she had offered.

"Because April Joules was awake, they stabbed her in the chest," Dill finished. "There was a different blood pattern."

Jimmy looked across at Angel. He had his head bowed. His lips were moving, mumbling a prayer. Or a curse.

"All of the bodies then were dragged into the living room for the desecration, and the body of at least one, probably the man, was dragged out the front door. The bodies of the women were likely packaged and carried out."

*Did the wind blow the door shut? Once they'd left? Is that what woke her? Is that what brought Mary out into it, too late, or exactly late enough?*

When it was finished, they talked a little more, about each other. "How are you doing?" was a question Sailors asked each other frequently, and it meant more than to the rest of us. And then, in the empty foyer, behind the closed front door, they formed a circle and held hands, like a prayer circle, only they didn't bow their heads but rather looked straight at each other, a scene someone from the outside world would never have understood.

Jimmy dropped Angel off at home in Silver Lake. It was six in the morning by then. Some of Angel's neighbors were breaking the day, loading tools into their trucks. (They couldn't leave the trucks loaded on the streets all night.) They'd gotten used to seeing Jimmy in the old Cadillac, Angel's friend. A couple of them waved. They were even used to them being out all night together. They probably thought they were just partying.

Mary wasn't in the house when Jimmy got back.

The light was full then, bright and hot, coming in through the east-facing windows. He looked for her in every room. He looked in the closets. He looked under the bed, feeling foolish on top of his sense of panic. He tried to tell himself maybe she'd gone for a walk, gone to a friend's.

He circled the base of the house, calling her name.

She was in the storage room beneath the kitchen. She was covered with dirt. There was no floor. She cowered in the corner, in a jail of rakes and hoes and shovels. In as much dark as she could find.

"They came back after me," she said before he could say anything.

He got her out of the corner and held her. He said the words to calm her, to dismiss it, the way men do to women.

She pulled away from him.

"They were here," she said. "They came an hour after you left. There were two of them. They wore black. Black pants and coats and black sneakers . . ."

# FOURTEEN

It became Jimmy's first case.

He got up that morning and moved Mary to another house, a friend of Angel's down so deep into Latino territory that it'd be next to impossible for anybody who wasn't Latino to get to her.

Now it was noon, and he was headed west on Sunset, west all the way out to Temescal Canyon.

He had "looked into things" for people before, tracked down a lost soul here or there for Angel or for some other Sailor or friend. Or friend of a friend. He had tailed people, to make sure they were all right. To make sure they had made it home, made it back to a safe place. He had tucked in his share of desperate, hurting people, sat up all night with people who needed someone there to keep them from falling apart. Others, he had "looked into" to see just how bad they were. To confirm that here was someone for an innocent, a friend, a Sailor to steer clear of.

But this was something new. Something closer, with higher stakes.

The first of the Road Cut Killings had come in a cabin out at the end of a tight, twisting road, a road that all but turned into a footpath as it climbed higher into the hills. The farther you went, the narrower it got, like a capillary. Temescal, Benedict. Maybe there was a canyon connection. It was a one-bedroom cabin. She was young. An actress. Or would-be. Like everybody else, she'd been in a few commercials, was up for a pilot or a continuing role on an episodic. Or at least that's what she'd probably told the folks back home. Maybe there was a Hollywood connection, but that was too easy. Everyone was connected to Hollywood. Jimmy had spent nearly the entirety of his existence here. From time to time he had to remind himself that dry cleaners and hot dog stands and churches in other parts of the country didn't brag on the famous people they served. Some places weren't about the show. Some people just *watched* movies and television shows.

There was a bleached-out plastic For Rent sign out front stapled to an oak, as if anyone could just happen by the place. Word must have gotten out. There had been no takers in three months. Jimmy parked the Cadillac, turned off the engine and the music with it.

There was a cicada somewhere, with that high-tension sound, like a rattler on crank. He left the driver's door open, stood in place, turned a full circle. You could see the rooftop of another cabin halfway up the side of another canyon across the way, but that was it. Nothing else that had anything of a human stamp on it. Hard to believe the towers of Century City were three or four miles from here, in the air anyway. It was a good place to kill somebody.

"Hello?" he said, louder than he'd intended.

There was a little yodel slapback from the other hillside, but nothing else, not even a dog barking back at him. As he started toward the cabin, he stopped to pick up a straight length of branch dropped out of one of the oaks. What was he going to do with a stick? Use it the way a kid uses a stick to poke a dead thing? To make sure? He was more spooked than he'd thought he'd be. Detective Dill had done too good a job at painting a picture of what had gone down inside.

He tried the knob on the front door. It was locked. The door was baby blue with hand-painted flowers, years old. Temescal had been a favorite hippie canyon in the '70s. Hippies and bikers. After that, it was rich Hollywood types, weekenders, weed smokers. Who told themselves their new jobs hadn't changed them. *It* hadn't changed them. Then they got bored, and the drive was too much trouble. (*It* won.) And the next wave moved in, whatever it was. That the actress lived up here told Jimmy she'd probably come from someplace real and missed it, *real* like trees and birds that go to sleep and shut up when the sun goes down. Real like mice. And mud daubers.

Real like dying of old age. With your clothes on. With your heart still on the inside of your body.

There was a back door to the cabin, but it was locked, a dead bolt and a clasp and padlock to boot. New locks, a little late. Jimmy found a loose window, old rippled glass, and was just about to get it forced open when it decided to shatter instead. He reached in, unlatched it, pushed it up, and crawled through. And it wasn't until he was inside, standing in the cabin's one bedroom, that he saw that he'd cut himself, cut his hand, badly enough to bleed all over his T-shirt, where he'd scratched himself on his shoulder. He looked down at the floor. There was a puddle like a rose petal under where his hand hung down.

He didn't learn anything in Temescal Canyon. Or at least nothing that clicked into place at the time, anything that meant anything to him then.

So he went to the movies.

The Vista. They showed foreign films and American classics, double bills that didn't seem at first to belong together. This week it was *The Searchers* and *The Road Warrior*. It was a Monday night. He was all but alone in the place, just three or four film buffs sitting in their favorite seats, and the kid from behind the popcorn counter who was a film buff, too, who knew so much about movies that it crowded out the unimportant stuff like human relations and the future. Jimmy sat dead center, two-thirds of the way back. The four hours of screen murder and mayhem for some reason felt like a nice, long, warm, cleansing shower.

Not that he didn't keep thinking about the Temescal Canyon girl. He hoped she wasn't the kind of aspiring actress who just wanted to be famous. He had stood in her living room. The cabin really only had one main room, with the kitchen against one wall, and the bedroom and bathroom. (It was like the low-ceilinged cabin in *The Searchers* John Wayne kept coming back to, without an answer.) Jimmy had stood there, in the middle of that front room. It was sad. It was easier to get inside the actress's head than the killers'. She was only twenty-four, but Jimmy's mother was twenty-one when she became a star. A star. Miss Temescal, or Miss Wherever She'd Come From, was only twenty-four but must have wondered if she was already too late.

And, as it turned out, she was.

The bathroom had a big old porcelain tub with claw-and-ball feet. Jimmy had crawled into it. From it, you could see up the hillside out a high, sideways window. Up there was a firebreak cut into the scrub brush, a gap to stop the flames from eating up and over the crest line. In fire season, the manzanita and scrub ground cover got a new name: *fuel*. Detective Dill had told Jimmy and Angel where the young woman was killed, the bedroom, but he had said they didn't know the particulars, or not all of them. And not the beginning of the slaughter, the horror. Maybe she had been here, taking a bath. Candles? Maybe she'd pushed open the window to let in the smell of the trumpet vine that curled up over the back of the cabin. Had she heard something? The hills would be filled with coyotes. She would have gotten used to them right away, heard their yipping and seen them for the dogs they were. Had she heard something else? A car coming up the hill? There were no tracks, just the tracks of her Jeep CJ-7. Had they come down on foot on the firebreak? They pulled casts of the Converse shoe prints from behind the cabin, from under the window where Jimmy had come in. The cops knew from the beginning this was going to be bad. And showy. Her brown heart had been left on the counter beside an antique tortoiseshell comb and a burned-down candle.

He left twenty minutes into *The Road Warrior*. The rescue motif had got to him. And the burnout in the two heroes' eyes.

Jimmy drove by the house in East L.A. that held Mary. He didn't stop. He'd had the feeling someone was following him earlier in the day, and it still hung over him. Two of Angel's men were out front, leaning against the fender of a glossy lowrider. They knew him, raised their beers in salute. Or to tell him she was OK. There was a light in the third-floor window. It was an apartment building. He wasn't sure, but he told himself that the light was her. That she was reading.

The next to die, after the actress, was inland, Ontario, out halfway to Palm Springs. It was a good thing he liked to drive, had nowhere else to be. And the third was south, halfway to Orange County, a teenager on the streets, a girl in the hard-core surf scene, down in Redondo.

An actress.

A middle-aged man, a fifth-grade teacher.

A street girl.

White.

Black.

Filipino.

It was a triangle, if that mattered. On a map. West, east, south. The cop Dill had said that the beginning and the end, the old alpha and omega, was always *motive*. The job was to find the logic. What you were looking for was the obvious.

Four, five, six. Seven, eight, nine.

No more triangle. The murder scenes were all over the place.

The surfer girl was the youngest, seventeen. The oldest was ninety, snatched from his bed in a convalescent hospital in Long Beach.

Eight women, five men.

Then there was the couple in Encino, the ones who didn't make it onto the official list, into the papers, onto the TV. (The cops liked to keep a card or two facedown.) The scene was out in the Valley, a house south of Ventura Boulevard, a quarter-way up into the hills, in a neighborhood of big houses but close together, which is maybe why the couple never ended up on a road cut, were left there in the house where they were eviscerated.

Jimmy came in from the back, came in across the golf course. He stopped fifty feet out. The house was Moderne. Most of the rear of it was glass, floor-to-ceiling, tinted black squares tucked under the flat roof. It was three in the morning. The man had been a television writer, hour cop shows when what they wanted was hour cop shows, true-crime woman-in-jeopardy movies of the week when *their* time came around, shifting as easily as he'd gone from Mercedes to Lexuses. Or would it be *Lexi*? When the long-form writing work ended, nothing much else came his way, but he had money in the bank and this house, for which he'd paid seventy-six thousand dollars. His wife sold real estate. Jimmy wondered if her agency was handling the house. There was a For Sale sign in the backyard, aimed toward the water hazard. Apparently no buyers for this one yet, either.

He was about to move closer to the house when a light snapped on. Jimmy jumped, though he was still fifty feet out. The windows weren't covered, no drapes or shades, or they were pulled open. The light had come on in what was the den. It was a table lamp. No one was visible. Jimmy waited. Maybe the light was on a timer. But set to snap on at three a.m.?

Then an overweight kid stepped into the frame of the interior doorway. He just stood there, looking into the big, wide room, as if he was uncertain about stepping in. He wasn't a kid exactly, except in L.A. showbiz terms. He was probably in his late thirties. He wasn't overweight exactly either, just fleshy. In L.A. showbiz terms. He was barefoot and wore silky running pants, a white T-shirt.

The light went out. Jimmy waited.

The light came on in the kitchen. There was the fridge, a stainless steel side-by-side Sub-Zero. Jimmy expected the kid to come in, go over, open it, look in, the way people do in the middle of the night. But he stayed standing in the doorway again, this time with his hand still hovering over the wall switch. The rooms were all bare, stripped down, hyper clean. Open House clean. *Show* ready. The light went out.

Now the kid picked up the pace. He went from room to room, light on, a beat, light off. He was like a scared little boy or girl looking for the source of the out-of-place noise he'd heard, home alone, hoping there'd be reassurance at the end of the search, when he'd checked everywhere.

Jimmy knew what it was. He had run through this routine himself. It wasn't about what was *there*, under the bed or in the shadows in the closet. It was about what was missing. Jimmy called it the I-can't-believe-it dance, though he threw an obscenity in the middle.

*They're gone.*

The light came on upstairs, in the upper right-hand corner of the house, where there was a balcony. It went out. Ten seconds later it came on again. This time the kid stepped in, left the doorway, crossed the room, and stood at the foot of a king-sized bed. The bed where they'd been found, in that horrible configuration. (Jimmy had seen the picture, could see it too clearly still.) He just stood there.

This was the second part of the story.

The first part was the actual loss of the thirteen human lives. The reality of what they did in life, their jobs, their work, what they filled their days with. And the potential. What the writers at the papers and the TV stations like to call "the hopes and dreams." Maybe she would have been a star. He might have been Teacher of the Year. She didn't get to see her daughter graduate from preschool. Maybe they would have made a movie remake of one of his TV shows.

But the second part of the story was the subplot, the story of those who'd been left. Left in pieces. Left not understanding much of anything anymore. Left with your heart ripped out, too, or at least a deadweight in your chest. Left in a foreign country where somehow you don't speak the language and the people don't like you. Left with pictures you can't look at. Left with songs you can't stand to hear anymore.

Left to stand in his parents' bedroom, "house-sitting" in his own life.

Jimmy ended the night, or at least the night ended around him, standing outside another house, standing at the foot of the Chateau Marmont on Sunset, his eyes on the penthouse and the railing.

# FIFTEEN

"Where's your little doggy?"

It took Jimmy a second to hear the spite in her voice. She was in her sixties, maybe seventies, and stood an arm's length away from him with her feet apart and her hands on her hips, as if braced against a wind or on the pitching deck of a ship. She wore all black, a dress, a sweater, a shawl over that. Old Country. He was on the sidewalk across the street from a pricey condo building in Brentwood, a four-story taupe job with black trim, black wrought iron around the windows.

The seventh of the dead. A twenty-year-old woman.

"I don't have a dog."

"Today you don't," the woman said. "The other nights you did."

"Must have been somebody else," Jimmy said. What he didn't say was that, generally speaking, dogs don't like Sailors.

"I *saw* you," the woman said. She pointed her finger at him.

Jimmy just let her go on to her next line.

"I think it's revolting, you coming around here, over and over," she said. "Let the dead bury the dead."

Jimmy decided to take a shot with her. Maybe there was something here. "I don't even like dogs," he said.

She tilted her head.

Jimmy pressed on. "I think they're a menace, fouling people's yards with their feces. Snarling, snapping. Urinating willy-nilly."

She liked the sound of this. "It wasn't you?" she said.

"Not if the person had a dog," Jimmy said.

"I don't like dogs," she said.

"I'm like you, then," he said. "You live in the neighborhood?" Jimmy asked.

"Right behind you," she said. Right behind him was a cute little Spanish-style bungalow. Covered with tile. From top to bottom, side to side. Ceramic tile, blue and white and green and yellow, every inch of the face of the house, every surface, and out into the yard, up and over fountains and benches and from the front steps to the street on a curving sidewalk. Tile. If it had had a pattern, it would have been a mosaic, but there was no pattern to it. It was a crazy-quilt house.

Jimmy hadn't really looked at it when he'd parked the car and gotten out, his eyes on the condo, checking the number.

"Damn," he said now, scanning the tile house. He tried to add a flip to it, to make it sound like he meant it admiringly.

"You're as bad as him," she said.

"How so?"

"Coming out here, drooling over this. The death of that poor girl."

"I was just going for a walk . . ."

"No, you weren't. You were rubbernecking. Or worse. Let the dead bury—"

"I *am* the dead," Jimmy said.

She took a step back.

He let her wonder for a minute.

"I write television scripts," he said. He named a show with a creepy attitude, then tried to look as much like Rod Serling as possible. He tossed his head in the direction of the condo. "I thought this might make a good episode."

"But you'd change the names," she said. There was something plaintive about the way she said it.

"So you knew her?"

The woman shook her head. She pointed toward an arched-top picture window on the front of her house, a table, a chair, a Tiffany lamp there. "I sit there. I would see her come and go, out of the underground parking. She never walked anywhere."

"What did he look like?"

"Who?"

"The one you thought was me."

"Like you. But with motorcycle boots."

He knew he wasn't going to get much else out of her. The "colorful" have their limits as information sources.

"How many times did you see him?"

"Three nights. Just standing there, where you are."

"When?"

"The night after it happened. And then the next night. And then a week later."

"Did you ever talk to him?"

"Are you going to use him in your story, too?"

"I don't know."

"Not with that dog, I wouldn't talk to him. That was the idea. The idea of the dog. To keep you back. To scare you."

"What kind of dog was it?"

"Some black kind, the kind you don't even see until it shows its teeth."

There was steady west-side traffic up and down Barrington the whole time they stood there talking. Brentwood had its gentle hills, curving streets, all very easy. If you had the money. The tile house was one of the last of the single homes left on this stretch of Barrington. The rest were condominiums. She probably didn't even know that the developers called her a holdout.

A car stopped in the middle of the street right in front of them. A Bentley, a ten-year-old Bentley. Black. Waiting for oncoming traffic to clear before it turned left. It made the turn. The window came down as the driver stopped in the driveway beside a keypad switch on a post. A hand came out and tapped a code onto the keys. A hand with a Rolex. The iron gate of the car park rose in recognition.

"That's him," the neighbor lady said. "Her father."

The Bentley went down the sloping drive. The gate closed.

The woman turned to go. "You can stand out here and embarrass yourself all you want," she said, hard-ass again. "Don't think I don't know who you are. Boots or no boots, dog or no dog." She walked away up her tiled walk, which looked from this distance like walking on broken glass.

Twenty minutes later, the Bentley came back up out of the building. The window was coming up.

You didn't have to see any more of the man at the wheel behind the black-tinted glass to know who he was. He was everywhere, or his face was. Looking down from billboards, on the sides and backs of buses. And always with a single word across his chest, over his heart: *trust*. The dead girl's father was Mike Roberts. Of Channel 8. Now he'd gone white-haired and slipped from the network wholly owned and operated down to an independent station, but he'd brought half of his viewers with him, and whatever the ratings were or weren't, he was still *The Anchorman* in Los Angeles for anyone who'd been here longer than five years. For the new arrivals, he must have seemed like *El Presidente* or *El Jefe* or *The Pakhan*, staring down at his people from every rentable, printable surface.

He was no pretty boy. He had a face like a marine, or a movie star playing a marine. And they *did* trust him. He was the one who went out and stood in the rain for the rest of them, hillsides sliding in the b.g., the one who raced in a panel van on the crest line in Angeles Forest with the flames "leaping across the highway, Trish!" for the sake of the safe at home in their living rooms. Even if all that was years ago.

When his little girl was still a little girl.

But her name wasn't Roberts. It was Weinstein. Rachel. And as far as Jimmy knew nobody had ever connected the daughter to the father. At least there wasn't anything in any of the newspaper clips Dill had given him. It wasn't public knowledge. Another card facedown. She'd been seventh in line.

Jimmy thought back. The coverage had ramped up about then. Maybe that was why: one of their own had been taken. *If it can happen to us . . .*

Along about then was when the people of the city really started feeling threatened. He/they were out there.

Who was next?

Jimmy was following him, following the Bentley. Roberts took Sunset all the way in from Brentwood into Hollywood. The Action Eight studios were in a block-long, solid white Greek Revival curiosity on Sunset, the old Warner studio, where Warner Brothers had started, where *The Jazz Singer* had been shot a thousand years ago. *Mammy!* The Bentley slowed at the gate, and the window came down so the anchorman could chat up the guard, who obviously knew the car, who already had the crossing arm up. The biggest billboard of all was over the studios.

*Trust.*

Rachel Weinstein had been dead two months. Jimmy wondered who or what Mike Roberts trusted now.

He had pulled to the curb across the street. Jimmy didn't know why he'd followed him. He stayed there an hour, waiting for an answer. All he got for his trouble was a glimpse of the Bentley behind the gates in the parking lot. A young man came out, opened the unlocked trunk, removed a white cardboard box, something not too heavy. The kid, the intern, was trying to balance it on one leg so he could reach up and close the trunk when the guard from the gatehouse came running over to assist.

Maybe the anchorman had given his girl his Emmys and now was getting them back. Prick a famous man, and does he not bleed?

Jimmy ended the day back in Encino, Encino by daylight this time. He parked the Cadillac across from the television writer's long, low house. He didn't know what he was looking for here, either. He was still new to this.

On the For Sale sign out front there was a radio frequency, a lightning bolt logo that explained it. The Realtors had a new trick. Jimmy tuned it in on the car radio. It was a two-minute commercial for "the property." Which, it turned out, was spectacularly more valuable even than it appeared. Or at least priced that way. It was a woman's voice, warm as the smell of fresh-baked cookies, probably another actor doing this to pay the bills, waiting for that big break. Music played in the background, George Winston, if Jimmy knew his New Age tone poems. He shut it off just as she was getting to the square footage of the "bonus room" and got out.

He stood there on the sidewalk across the street for five minutes, just stood there. He could almost hear the screams from out here, through the tinted, double-glazed glass. Is that what he wanted? Is that what he was looking for? Is that why he'd come back? Is that what he was waiting for? For it to get *real*?

He heard a sharp sound behind him, metal scraping on something, and turned. It was a gardener with a grass rake raking the lawn next to a concrete driveway, hitting it every third or fourth stroke, his eyes down. He was a South American, hard to say what country. A few years back, they were all "Mexicans"; people thought that, but they weren't, many of them. There were Salvadorans, Guatemalans, Costa Ricans. It also was hard to say how old the man was. He wore clean khakis and had a red kerchief knotted around his neck. Put him in a suit on a telenovela, and you'd realize how handsome he was.

"Amigo," Jimmy said.

The tile house lady in Brentwood may have stepped back from Jimmy when he spoke, but this man *jumped* back. Five feet. With a scared-to-death look, an I-know-you look. He backed over a rosebush, lifted his rake, and turned the handle sideways, as if he was going to make the sign of the cross with it. From the reaction, Jimmy might as well been a monster, out in broad daylight.

A monster the gardener had seen standing there before.

The man kept looking around, as if looking for the black dog . . .

———————

Angel picked up Jimmy in front of his house. In a primer-red Porsche Cabriolet with no top, just the metal birdcage frame folded back without any cloth over it. It was a '64. A 356C. It had already been lowered a bit, lost all the chrome, the radio antenna frenched in, but in a way that didn't look wrong. The seats were bare-bones, but they'd already been rebuilt, too, had a Tijuana border-crossing five-dollar blanket thrown over them.

The engine had a perfect sound to it. It had gotten the first dollars.

"Whose car is this?"

"Nobody's," Angel said. "Mine. Yours. I'm just doing it for myself, for the glory of God."

"Jesus is gonna love it," Jimmy said.

For now, they were headed nowhere. On Western Avenue, south. It was what they did instead of talking on the phone. It was ten thirty or so. A weeknight. There wasn't much traffic.

Angel took Jimmy's Jesus line with a smile. He always did. He was content in his belief and easygoing about others' disbelief. It worried him, made some part of him sad, but he repeated the same line ten times a day, usually out loud: "It's in God's hands." There was so much doom around him, he had to pick his battles. *Let go, let God* was another one, another line he repeated.

"Let me ask you something," Jimmy said. "'Let the dead bury the dead.' What's that about?"

"It's in Matthew."

"Yeah, I know. I looked it up. I thought it was Shakespeare."

"What do you think it's about?"

"I think it's *harsh*, is what I think. You read the story. Jesus is heading out, some guy wants to follow him but says first he has to go take care of his father's funeral. And Jesus says, 'Let the dead bury the dead.'"

"I used to think it was about *us*," Angel said. "Back about a hundred New Years ago . . ." That was what they called the increments of time since they'd become Sailors, since it'd happened to them, since they'd crossed over to death's other kingdom: New Days, New Weeks, New Years . . . Angel Figueroa had been a Sailor almost seventy years. But looked mid-thirties, in his white T-shirt and baggy starched jeans, and long, hipster-straight-back black hair.

"I mean, I thought, here we are, we were the dead, walking around, here was a job for us."

"What does it mean?" Jimmy pressed.

"Jesus was a rebel leader." Angel always said Jesus like the gringos, not *Hay-soos*, at least when talking to white men. "It was the beginning of things. He was starting the revolution. Jesus *was* the revolution. 'Follow me and become fishers of men,' he said when he was talking to fishermen. He meets you where you are."

"So what did he mean by it?"

"You sound like you're mad at him."

"What did he mean?" Jimmy said, harder. He was looking away, looking at the whores on opposite corners of an intersection they blew past. If you didn't slow down, they didn't even look like *people*. They just looked like sex. Sex and money.

Bad sex and dirty money.

Angel was nothing if not patient. "'Let the dead bury the dead.' All that matters is what happens now. Next. There's no purpose in the past."

Jimmy let a block go by. "But *you're* the guy who restores old cars," he said.

"I don't restore anything," the other said quickly. "I make something new out of the old. *Too* new for some."

Angel shifted gears, literally and figuratively. "Are we looking for something? Somebody?"

"Yeah, somebody who looks like me," Jimmy said. He told Angel the story of the tile-house woman in Brentwood and then the yard man in Encino.

"He got a name?"

"Three or four or five. I just call him Handsome."

They drove around the rest of the night, looking where they knew to look, looking for trouble, but they didn't find him, the man who maybe looked like Jimmy, the man in black with the black dog.

They didn't find him the next night, either.

Or the next day. Or the day after that.

But they found him.

Or at least they found his den.

It was six o'clock. They came walking down the alleyway between two brick buildings in a "neighborhood" of shit-hole apartments and rooms by the week in the shadow of downtown. And not one of those *romantic* shadows of downtown where painters rent lofts and documentarians make movies of each other and the beautiful poor. Angel's body shop was five blocks away, so he'd met Jimmy here. Six o'clock. Anywhere else in L.A. that would have meant the light was pretty, but down here the shadows had won the battle between light and dark a half hour ago. Here the Golden Hour only meant you couldn't quite see.

What Jimmy had was an address, a location, a home base for the man with the black dog, the man who'd shown up at eight of the murder sites, from what Jimmy had learned. Who'd just stood there across the street, whichever street it was, the day after. And sometimes the next. Reliving it? Funny word for it. In the end, after a few days, Jimmy found somebody who knew somebody who knew something. So a few words, an idea, maybe even a lie, had led Jimmy to this alleyway. Maybe to the man.

But what did he know about detective work? He'd heard a line once, about art, about sculpture. About a sculptor known for his enormous, very realistic sculptures of horses. He had been asked how he could do it, his technique. "It's simple," the sculptor had said, "I just chip away everything that doesn't look like a horse." What did Jimmy know about detective work? Nothing, except to go everywhere he could go, cut away everything it wasn't, until a shape emerged. What did he know, except that almost everything was a mystery and that what was most true about a thing you usually didn't see until it was too late.

"Which floor?" Angel said. He was stopped, looking up at the side of the brick building at the end of the alley. It was six floors, old arched windows bricked in years ago, covered by a picture of something, signage. If it was one of those romantic alleyways in a documentary about the poor, the old sign would have been a fading picture of an orange tree with a lush, fading, green Promised Land behind it. What it was instead was a man in a bowler hat wearing a truss.

"My guy didn't say," Jimmy said. "Just that this was his squat, that he slept in the daytime. Or at least people only seemed to see him at night."

So they went inside. The first floor of the brick building was open from side to side, with posts, with high windows with arched tops, with unfinished, worn wood on the deck. It had been a factory. Jimmy and Angel crossed to a pile of rubble in the middle of things. Angel picked through it and found a length of hardwood, like a table leg. Maybe it had been a furniture factory. Or a coffin factory. He gripped it by the skinny end.

"You look like a caveman," Jimmy said.

To tell the truth, both of them were spooked. They'd bought into the hysteria. They'd been carrying it around, a gnawing unease, both of them, for six days. Since the killings up in Benedict. There hadn't been any more murders since the director and the two women, but that had only increased the apprehension somehow. The whole town's apprehension.

They went upstairs. The staircase was wooden but strong.

There wasn't any dust in the center of the treads. Somebody had been coming and going.

"You should have called that cop Dill," Angel said.

"He was gone," Jimmy said. "Out."

"I got his cell somewhere."

"We're here, we might as well go on up."

"I wasn't saying don't go up," Angel said defensively.

The second floor and the third floor were open side to side like the ground floor. Open and empty. The light was all but gone. Now they had to put their hands on the railing to feel their way up.

But there was light above. Golden light.

They came out of the stairwell onto the fourth floor. It was wide and empty, too, but across it there was a single tall window bringing in a sharp-edged quadrilateral of gold light.

They moved toward it. There was a heap of clothes, a bedroll.

And a body.

He was on his side, the upper quarter of his head smashed in from a blow that could have been inflicted by a club like the one still in Angel's hand. Angel looked down at it, as if he was thinking the same thing.

Angel said, "He doesn't look anything like you."

"It's not him," Jimmy said. A moment passed that wasn't as long as it seemed. "It's the guy who sent me down here, from out in Van Nuys."

There was dog shit everywhere.

---

On the drive home, Jimmy and Angel saw people standing outside an electronics store, looking in at the bank of TVs. Same thing at another store down the street.

The radios in all the cars around them weren't playing music. It was just talking. All talk.

It was like the end of the world. Or the beginning. The people they passed on the sidewalks and the people in the cars around them seemed to be, if not happy, lightened. The Porsche had a hole in the dash where the radio used to be or Jimmy and Angel would have tuned in the news themselves.

Jimmy went straight to the television when he walked in the door of his house.

Mary was there, startling him, coming out of the bedroom.

She let the TV tell him. They'd caught the killers, black Converse high-tops, bone saws, leather gloves, in an apartment in North Hollywood.

Two Russian brothers.

Neither one of whom looked anything at all like Jimmy.

# SIXTEEN

"Your girl killed herself."

In Jimmy's state of mind, with where he'd just been, what he'd just seen, *who* he'd seen, Mary and her husband, it took him a second to think which girl.

But he figured it out. And the guilt started.

"Get in," Jimmy said.

From the circle out in front of the Mark Hopkins the two of them went across the city to the scene of the thing, the place where she'd done it. And then to the morgue. In that order, Jimmy delaying the latter as long as possible. It was Machine Shop who'd said, when Jimmy showed some hesitation, that they *had* to go see the body, to be sure it was really her, be sure that Shop had gotten it right, though it had happened almost right in front of him down at the waterfront. Plus, Shop had a friend who worked nights in the coroner's office, a Sailor.

They'd already hauled the crumpled car away, the little baby-blue Sky-lark. Bad for business. They'd already hosed off the blood. The car hadn't caught fire—when Lucy had driven it at fifty or sixty into the concrete face of Pier 35, the same blank building where the Leonidas girls had jumped.

"There was nobody with her, right?" Jimmy said to Shop, standing there next to the circles of oil and transmission fluid and the white blanket of the powdery flame-killer SFFD had sprayed down just in case. Atop the engine gunk was pebbly absorbent, what at the old Saugus Speedway they used to call "kitty litter." They'd be back later that night to sweep that up.

"No, nobody," Shop said.

"Where were you?"

"Over there," Shop said and pointed to the corner of a parking lot. "Working. It was all just getting going. Where were you?"

Jimmy didn't answer that question. He looked from the end of the story in front of him back over his shoulder to the beginning, at least this last chapter of Lucy's story. She had come on a straight shot down the Embarcadero. There was a curve in the wide boulevard but not enough to make her slow. It wouldn't be hard to get up to speed. Pedal down, go. It's the long skinny one on the right. You don't want to be going too slow, embarrass yourself.

"Was she thrown out?"

Machine Shop just nodded. Jimmy remembered the scene in front of the store down in Paso Robles, how she hadn't put on her seat belt.

It was rocking Jimmy, standing there. Everybody knows how they'd kill themselves, if it came to that. What sad, sorry method they'd pick from the list. This right here was the way Jimmy had thought of, from the time he was a kid. And just about every time he came up on a freeway overpass abutment. Speed meets an unmovable object.

"It was a sweet little car," he said. "Too bad."

Shop didn't have anything to say to that. He wasn't into cars, not the way Jimmy was, not the way Los Angelenos were. (Who was?) Now wasn't the time to bring that up, that old north/south row.

"She didn't suffer," Shop said. One of those things you say.

Jimmy scanned the flat face of the pier building. Pour-and-fill concrete. Probably three feet thick, given its age. Barely a scratch.

You could throw any number of little sad girls at it and not make a dent.

"Let's get to that morgue," Jimmy said.

Turned out she hit face-first. But there was that baby-blue dress, the one she'd been wearing the first time he saw her, in the café in Saugus, the dress that made him think of Mary. There wasn't much blue left, stained as it was. He wondered what her purpose was, putting it on again, for her last scene, for the end. Or maybe she hadn't had a purpose. Maybe he was the only one who saw purpose everywhere. Seeing the dress again made his skin crawl.

"Maybe you can start looking for her brother," Jimmy said to Machine Shop as the coroner's assistant drew the sheet back over Lucy, like a magician trying again when the trick didn't work. "Go by the apartment first, but he hasn't been there for a couple of days, as far as I could see. Maybe he doesn't even know what happened to her. I don't know if he was close by or what. I hope not. I don't know *who* was there."

"What are you going to do?" Machine Shop said.

Jimmy turned away. "Try to get this smell out of my clothes," he said.

The coroner's assistant said, "There's no paperwork yet. You want a prep?" His name was Hugh. A Sailor.

"What do you mean?"

"Any family?"

"I don't know," Jimmy said.

"Normally, when we get the word from the family, if they're out of town, we just bag 'em for chilled shipping."

"I don't know," Jimmy said again. It was getting to be the thing he thought and said more than anything else.

"Because I could do a prep," Hugh said. "On my own. In case there's any viewing or anything. Here. I mean, this isn't a funeral home, but—"

"Sure," Jimmy said. "Why not? Make her look good. Do what you can."

He was thinking of Angel.

---

They call it *nightside*. The second shift at the newspaper. The business offices are closed, but the guts of the paper are churning. It's the time of day when it all looks most like you'd expect a newspaper shop to look. Maybe no chain-smoking, green-shade-wearing editors anymore, shouting "Get me rewrite!" to the copy boy, not even any clattering typewriters these days, but busy, purposeful, noisy, even dramatic. That was nightside at the *Chronicle*. There was work to do. In the morning there would be San Franciscans waiting to be pulled back into their communal lives by the slap of the paper on the driveway, on the doorstep, on the plush green cut pile carpet of the Mark Hopkins.

Like the coroner's office, the *Chron* by night was surprisingly wide open as far as security went. It wasn't midnight yet. Maybe the bomb-throwers came around later. Jimmy parked the Porsche on the street, on Mission Street, and came in one of the workers' entrances. The first floor was where the presses were, where the pressmen wore square hats folded out of newsprint, at least the old-timers, what was left of them. Jimmy came in as if he belonged there, and nobody stopped him.

Duncan Groner wasn't in the city room. They said he was in the library, what they used to call the morgue. (Back at the coroner's, did they call it the library now?) Once Jimmy had gotten up to editorial, he had run into a few questions. He talked his line, spoke Groner's name. He got an escort, a kid. Good thing, because the library was in the windowless bowels of the place. He never would have found it on his own. There were big leather couches. Groner was asleep on one, flat on his back, his hands over his sternum, fingers laced. He looked like he was positioned to go down the chute at a water park. Only he was snoring. The kind of snoring that comes with exclamation marks at the end of each declining sentence. One terminating snort was loud enough to wake him. His eyes popped full open.

"How long have you been there?"

"Just walked in," Jimmy said.

"I've been *sleeping* lately," Groner said, sitting up. "Odd."

Jimmy didn't say anything.

"Have *you*?" Groner said.

"As a matter of fact, yes."

"And *wanting to* other times when I'm unable."

"It must be spring," Jimmy said.

"That's it," Groner said. "Spring." He extracted his flask from his trouser pocket and popped the cap and took a boy-oh-howdy. "Spring in September."

"I don't get any blue from you," Jimmy said, looking down on him on the couch. "Same with a lot of the Sailors here. Some do, some don't."

"I probably extinguished it," Groner said and raised his bottle to finish the thought.

"A clean-cut kid down on the waterfront working at a crab stand . . . A pair of thug boys I saw beating another Sailor, my first night in town . . ."

"I've always heard the azure edge was stronger down your way," Groner said. "More visible. Readable."

"I never heard that," Jimmy said.

"Funny, you don't look bluish," Groner said. Before his nap he had taken off his shoes, placed them side by side on the carpet next to the couch. He retrieved them, slipped them on. When he went to tie the laces, his fingers were uncooperative, a little shaky. You couldn't tell if it was age or alcohol.

He must have noticed being noticed. "'Sure, I'm a old gnawed bone now,'" he said in a rangy voice, "'but don't you boys think the spirit is gone. I'm all set to shoulder a pickax and shovel anytime somebody's willing to share expenses.' Now there's a movie. *The Treasure of the Sierra Madre*. Why don't you make them like that anymore down there in Lost Angeles?"

"I don't make movies."

"I meant the collective, editorial *you*."

"So why are all these people killing themselves?" Jimmy said. He was still standing over the other.

Groner leaned back on the couch. "If you ask me, a better question is why not?"

Jimmy waited him out.

"I guess the ten of them this morning prompted this," Groner said.

*Ten?*

"And then there was another one tonight," Groner finished. "But the overnight ones were the headline. It's a helluva story, I have to admit. Dayside got it, unfortunately."

"The one tonight was the girl I told you about," Jimmy said.

Groner heard that and knocked off some of the "colorful character" show.

"The girl I was supposed to be watching out for."

"We didn't have a name for her."

"Lucy," Jimmy said. "Her name was Lucille. I didn't know her last name."

"Hers was one of the better ones, actually," Groner said. "Very public." In the next breath, he said, "I was considerably less . . . *entertaining* myself."

You never asked a Sailor how they'd died. You waited for them to say it, if you cared to know one way or another. Jimmy didn't usually care. He had found out early that it never really added much to his understanding of another Sailor man or woman, so he never asked. Some people needed to tell you. If they decided to tell you, you listened. Or at least stood there and let them empty the bucket.

"A bullet to the brain, which I thought at the time was the source of my gloom," Groner said. "Small caliber. A little chrome-plated Colt .25 automatic. I thought I was minimizing the mess. I had no surviving family, so I guess my concern was for the sensibilities of what we now call 'the first responders.' I didn't know then how quickly they become dulled to the offal."

"What year?" Jimmy said, surprising himself.

"Nineteen twenty-two," Groner said. "So I didn't even have the excuse of the crash, Black Friday. It was a Black *Tuesday*, actually. I was fifty-one."

"What are the overall suicide numbers now? How many total?"

"Aha, you're looking for a reason! For your Lucy's act of negation."

"Is there anything that ties them together?"

"United only in death . . . Twenty-eight Romeos and nineteen Juliets.

Which is unusual, the ratio, the high number of women. Usually the men far outpace the women. As whites do blacks. Hispanics are moving up on the outside rail. Asian women, almost never. Asian men, after the age of sixty. Before sixty, they lag behind almost everyone, hari-kari, seppuku in popular entertainment aside. They're spread all over the city, which is something of a surprise."

"What about suicide contagion?" Jimmy asked.

Duncan Groner wasn't the sort to raise an eyebrow in surprise, but *something* registered on his face. And it took him a beat before he spoke, as if things had to be aligned in his head. Or realigned.

"You *are* engaged in the subject," he said.

"Well?"

"Even as we speak, I'm sure great committees are meeting, with the wringing of Great Hands," Groner said. And here he paused with intent. "A number of the suicides now appear to be in response to the earlier ones, to the publicity. In response to, as you say, 'the contagion,' a wonderfully melodramatic phrase."

Suicide contagion wasn't the result of some recent research on Jimmy's part. He'd run into it before.

"Copycats."

"Not exactly," Groner said. "More like, *Now I see that life is maybe not so sacrosanct after all.* With people hurling it at the fronts of buildings and such." He stood and put a hand on Jimmy's shoulder and said, "Something we in the brotherhood have known for some time."

Jimmy looked at the bony, skeletal hand on his shoulder.

"I'm off work," Groner said. "Rested and refreshed. Let's go pretend it's happy hour. I know a place where Sailors drink free. And freely."

# SEVENTEEN

The people of San Francisco didn't *look* like they all wanted to die. Of course it was morning and, if the sun wasn't exactly shining, it was up there somewhere on the far side of the "marine layer." Jimmy was walking. Marina Green. They didn't *look* suicidal. They didn't look like the creeping cloud of death had o'ertaken them. The people of San Francisco looked like they wanted to play tennis, at least the ones standing at the back of the open hatch of the Porsche Cayenne all in white, in the parking lot of the private waterfront tennis club. They looked like they were thinking ahead to dinner, the ones coming out of the Safeway with a bag of groceries in each arm, a stick of French bread sticking out of one, just like in the movies. They looked like they wanted to go to work, the ones going past him in their cars all fresh and clean in their laundered starched shirts, in their ties, with their suit jackets folded lengthwise at the collar, like a butterfly, and laid over the back of the empty passenger seats beside them.

Die? They looked like they wanted to jog in matching outfits, earbuds in their ears. Then meet for brunch. They looked like they'd just had their teeth bleached and wanted everybody to see 'em. They looked like they wanted to sail the bay in forty-footers, loop around Alcatraz, out and back under the Golden Gate, the kids up front with their legs over the side. They looked like death was the furthest thing from their minds.

An old familiar feeling came over Jimmy, that *I'm here all alone* feeling. He had his own kind of hope, but he didn't have it this morning.

When he made it back to where he'd parked the car there was a white flyer tucked under the wiper, white with a rainbow. A free concert on the Panhandle in Golden Gate Park. Three or four bands, food, holistic healers . . . Just like the last thirty-some years hadn't happened. Over the rainbow, it said: Celebrate Life!

*OK!*

Midmorning. The Haight was just coming alive. The sun had broken

through. Down at the corner on Central, down the hill from Lucy's, the
white-haired, ponytailed man who lived over the wine store with his black-
tongued dog was out on the side of his place with a hose, watering a color-
coordinated square of flowers around the base of a sapling staked out in the
tilted sidewalk. The chow sat on the stoop in another of his old-man poses.

The ponytailed man made a point of not looking up when Jimmy
parked the Porsche against the curb halfway up the hill, halfway between
the corner and the Victorian apartment.

The nonlook made Jimmy go up to him. Or, rather, down.

"How's it going?"

"Good morning," the man said. He kept watering, kept his eyes on the
stream as if he had to watch it or it would all go wrong.

"The woman who was staying on the top floor, up at the corner . . ."
Jimmy began. The man nodded, nodded in a way that said he knew what
Jimmy was going to say next.

"So you know she's dead?"

The man nodded again. Jimmy got the idea somehow that this one
had known more death than most, maybe even more suicides. But he still
watered flowers.

"I was looking for the boy," Jimmy said.

The man shook his head.

"Her brother."

Nothing.

"You haven't seen him?"

The man shook his head again.

Jimmy decided to see if he could blow things wide open. "I'm an investigator. From L.A. I followed her here."

At least now the man looked at him.

"I was supposed to keep her safe, keep an eye on her, anyway."

"Nothing you could do," the other said.

Jimmy saw him look up the street. Machine Shop was standing on the
corner next to the apartment, on the corner across from the Catholic Home.

Jimmy thanked the man with a wave. The man said *No problem* with
a lift of his head. The rain from the garden hose kept falling on the petu-
nias, which by now must have been screaming for help.

Jimmy climbed back up to the corner. "You got leaves in your hair,"
Jimmy said to Machine Shop.

"I slept up there, in the park," Shop said. Then he heard what he'd said.
*Slept.* "I've been sleeping lately. Funny."

"Why up there? You got a place, right?"

"I thought the kid might have gone up into the park," Shop said. "You know, when you can't stand to be around the other person's stuff . . ."

Jimmy knew.

"Actually, I used to live up in here."

"In Buena Vista Park?"

"Sometimes," Shop said. "First Days. First Month."

Maybe Machine Shop was about to tell the rest of his story, after the part about the plug-in radio landing in his bathtub.

But Shop stopped short. "So what are we going to do?"

Jimmy looked up at the apartment. "You sure he's not up there?"

"I pushed the button. I heard it ringing. I tried last night, this morning. There was one light burning all night, in the hallway. He's not up there."

"Well then, let's break in," Jimmy said.

There was a way around the back of the apartment building, up a little alleyway where they stored the garbage cans, behind a white lattice-work shield. They really *were* fixing up the Haight. Even the alleys looked healthy.

"How many times you done this?" Jimmy said, when they were standing in the middle of the living room.

"I've done it. Seeing what's in the icebox, that's what creeps me out," Shop said. "Or a half an apple, on the table."

"Like the people at Pompeii," Jimmy said.

"Pompeii. I used to put that shit on my hair," Shop said, which was another way of saying, *Can we talk about something else?* He walked off toward the bedroom.

There were two toothbrushes in a Coke glass on the back of the white old-style pedestal porcelain sink. Hygiene, right up to the end. For Lucy, anyway. The boy had left his behind, wherever he'd gone. Jimmy had to find him. He had a special worry for the people left behind. The faucet was dripping, slow, three seconds apart. With the kind of sound that yanks you out of bed at midnight, that a Sailor can hear when nobody else does, day or night, anywhere. Anything like a clock.

Jimmy tightened it down. And then stood there until the last drop formed and fell.

"The Wind Cries Mary," Shop said behind him.

Jimmy felt like he'd been stuck in the chest.

"What? What did you say?"

Machine Shop held up a square bar coaster. And then, in the other hand, five more, all the same. "Your boy's been hanging at The Wind Cries Mary, a guitar joint over in the Fillmore. He had these all laid out on a little table beside his bed."

*The Wind Cries Mary.* Doesn't it though.

———————

It said "Open @ Eight" on the door of the club, but ten was probably more likely. It was painted purple, a box that had expanded into the windowless box beside it. An expressionistic suggestion of a Fender Stratocaster stretched in broken neon across the face of it, like a poor man's Hard Rock Café. A marquee spelled out the name of the guitar slinger of the moment, if the moment was ten years ago. Or twenty. One-night stands. A different player for the next three nights. Maybe the place looked better at night.

Jimmy parked at the curb out front, and he and Shop got out. They split up to circle the club and check out the alleyways. They met up again in back. Nothing, though there were a couple of street people living around the trash bins.

"I don't like to think about him, just being out there somewhere," Shop said. "It's not good."

They were about to get back into the Porsche.

"Wait a minute," Jimmy said.

He had seen a face, a part of a face. A young face, in the window of a liquor store across the street and down a couple of numbers.

A kid in a hat.

Jimmy crossed between a speeding bus and lagging truck and made it into the liquor store in time to see the form of the kid duck into a hallway in back, between the coolers. (He was wearing a *knit* hat.) The boy went through a door and slammed it behind him but it banged back open, and Jimmy went after him.

"Hey!" a hard voice said behind him. "What the—"

The kid had run into a storage room. There was another door out, on the back. The room was stacked to the ceiling with cases of booze. The gaps between the towers were more the kid's size than Jimmy's size, and the boy threaded the needle, ten feet ahead of his pursuer, and got his hand on the knob of what looked like an exit.

"It's all right," Jimmy said. "Wait."

The exit door opened. Light blew in. Jimmy found his own way through the boxes and ran outside.

He caught the kid in the paved space behind the store.

It was somebody else's little brother.

"*What?*" the boy said, that way only fifteen-year-olds can. "What?"

"Sorry," Jimmy said to the kid.

He didn't know what to say to the clerk with the shotgun standing in the doorway, the gun held down low and braced against his hip like he knew what it was.

When they all settled down, Jimmy apologized, said he was looking for his brother.

"You forgot what your brother looks like?" the clerk said.

# EIGHTEEN

Sailors never flew, unless drugged and bound and gagged, so Angel came north on the train. The Coast Starlight. Two of his guys had dropped him off at Union Station in downtown L.A. Then it was across through the San Fernando Valley, coming out at Oxnard, then up the coastline on into the Central Valley, sunset about Salinas, in the dining car if you were in the mood, then rolling miles of dark fields, just enough time to think of all the things you should have done differently since ninth grade. The Starlight left SoCal midmorning and made it into Oakland after nine.

When Jimmy drove up out in front of the station, Angel was standing there. The train had gotten in early.

Then they were crossing the Bay Bridge back toward the City.

"How did she get in touch with you?" Jimmy said. It was almost the first thing he said to Angel.

"What do you mean?"

"How did you know she was in trouble?"

"Lucy never got in touch with me," Angel said. "A friend of hers come to me."

"And said what?" Jimmy said.

Jimmy's tone had some accusation in it, but Angel didn't let himself react to it. He knew what it was, what was behind it. Guilt. Jimmy's anger at himself. Angel cut people a lot of slack.

"It was one of Lucille's girlfriends, a girl I didn't really know but who knew about me," Angel said.

"Knew what about you?"

Jimmy had two hands gripping the wheel. He noticed them, his hands, as the Porsche rolled under another pole light on the bridge, as the orange light flared in the cockpit and he got a shot of the taut skin across his knuckles.

"I just meant—" Jimmy started.

"I *loved* her," Angel said, cool and calm. "But where's that gonna go? She was young. I'm old and a Sailor on top of that. Or, I'm a Sailor and old on top of *that*. You know how that works." The last was as much a rebuke of Jimmy (and his own past, his own history with women) as Angel would offer in this story. "So I never told her right to her face. I was 'her friend,' helping her out when I could, talking to her when some guy did her wrong one way or another. This girl, Mariel, she knew that, the last part, that I cared about Lucy."

Jimmy stared at the backs of his hands, willing some of the tenseness out of them. He stared until one relented and let itself drop off the wheel onto the leather-wrapped shifter knob.

"I even introduced her to the last guy," Angel said. "Guy I stripped and cleaned the Skylark for."

"So what happened, after the other girl came to you?" Jimmy asked. "I'm just trying to start at the beginning."

"I know what you're trying to do," Angel said. He reached to the floor between his knees for his leather gym bag. He unzipped it and took out a pint of Courvoisier. Jimmy had smelled the sweet stink on Angel when he'd embraced him on the concrete in the front of the station in Oakland. Angel never drank at home. Too many of the people around him, the boys and men he was trying to help, had drink and drug problems. Things were confused enough for them. He never offered the bottle to Jimmy. Angel unscrewed the cap and took a sip. "You're trying to start at the beginning. You're trying to *find* the beginning." He had a little edge to his voice. He took a second hit.

"I'm sorry," Jimmy said. It had a kind of all-purpose quality to it.

They rode in silence for half a minute, crossed Yerba Buena Island in the middle of the two halves of the bridge. It was like a fist of rock in the middle of the Bay.

When they went through the tunnel, there were no cars close around them in the lanes going into San Francisco. The Porsche engine sounded a good rumble.

"Love that tuned exhaust," Angel said. "L.A. Symphonic." He screwed the metal cap back on the cognac and dropped it into his bag.

"*Lil' Bitch*," Jimmy said. It was what Angel had named the car when it had been reborn in his shop back in L.A. years ago. James Dean's Porsche 550 Spyder was named *Lil' Bastard*. Jimmy and Angel never said the name to anybody else.

Out the tunnel, off to the right across the slate water, was Alcatraz. And, dark at its side, Angel Island.

"There's your island," Jimmy said.

"Yeah, I wonder if they'd let me camp out," Angel said.

"I got a room for you," Jimmy said.

"So after I got the call from Mariel," Angel said, "I went all crazy-like and drove over there, right then, that night. I took this old piece of shit car of my neighbor's so Lucy wouldn't look out the window and know it was me. I parked up the hill a little bit, but I could see everything. She was in her front room. She has this house." He paused. Jimmy knew Angel was adjusting the tenses in his head. *Has* to *had*. Or trying to.

"It's all right," Jimmy said. "I don't need to know any more."

"She was sitting right in the front window, where I could see her, like a picture in a frame," Angel said. "Like she was waiting for me. But, of course, she was waiting for this guy. To come back. Or just, I don't know, waiting for things to get better again for her."

"Yeah, I saw that look," Jimmy said.

"She just sat there."

"So when was that?"

"The night before she left. To come up here. Last week. The Skylark was parked out front of her house, and I was on the other side of the street. She shouldn't have left it out like that, where people could see it."

"You talk to the boyfriend?" Jimmy said.

"The dead don't talk," Angel said. Then he said, the way he always did, one of his jokes, "Oh, yeah, I forgot, sometimes they do."

"He was a gangbanger?"

"Yeah. But he was just out with his sister, down in San Diego, leaving SeaWorld, in the parking lot, when they hit him. Friend of mine down in Diego said it was another gang."

"When was that?"

"I don't know, sometime. A week before she left to come up here."

"She was waiting for him to come back to her. But he was already dead, and she knew it."

"Well, you know how that is, don't you? Holding out hope."

"You didn't go to him before? To find out what the problem was between them, what broke them up?"

"Never thought of it. I guess, inside, I was glad about it. That they broke up." Angel looked at Jimmy. "So I feel it, too," he said. "Responsible. Guilty. Like I could have done something. Should have." He looked out at the lights of the City to the right flashing through the bars of the railing, the curve of the waterfront, the Embarcadero. "And that don't make any more sense than *you* feeling the same thing."

Jimmy wondered if Angel knew he was looking at where it had happened.

"What about her brother?" Angel said.

"He's out there somewhere. I don't know where."

"I didn't know she had a brother, until you told me," Angel said. "She never talked about him."

Jimmy told him about The Wind Cries Mary.

"So we find him," Angel said. "Bring him in, get him home."

Jimmy had gotten Angel a room next door to his at the Mark.

"I'd rather sleep in a ten-dollar-a-night place, down around Market," Angel said, standing in the middle of the room with Jimmy and a bellhop.

"You gotta get out more, bud," Jimmy said. "The ten-dollar-a-night places are forty now."

"*Sixty*, I believe, sir," the bellman said.

"I was going to say *five*," Angel said and tossed his leather bag on the turned-down bed. And Jimmy tipped the boy.

By then it was eleven thirty. They came downstairs again. They'd left the Porsche in front of the hotel.

"I guess you can't do *that* down in the Tenderloin," Angel said.

They went across town to The Wind Cries Mary. It was about all they had to run with when it came to finding Les Paul. (Finding him and then getting out of San Francisco, while they still could?) He wasn't there. They sat through the second half of a set by a doodling jazz player who played too many notes. For Jimmy's ear, anyway. There were three or four *other* Les Pauls there. They were hanging around the front when Jimmy and Angel pulled up, kids fifteen or sixteen, a couple of them with guitars in cases. And it was a school night, too. The doorman seemed to have been hired for the flat look on his face and the size of his biceps, especially when his arms were folded across his chest. But at least one kid had made it in. He stood in the back next to the door in and out of the kitchen. The mesmerized look on the boy's face made Jimmy think maybe he was missing something when it came to the jazzbo onstage with the fat hollow body. But none of the boys was *their* Les Paul.

The star of the night came on, a black player with a scarred Strat that looked like it had already been on the road ten years by the time

Hendrix was joining the army. And the player was older than his guitar. Jimmy wondered what the man looked like in daylight, out front under the stage light. Maybe he never saw daylight. He was out there with just a bass player and a drummer, both white. The bass player was in his twenties, the drummer a chewed-up-and-spat-out rocker with dyed black hair, maybe a wig. The band played almost nothing, just stood back, literally, figuratively, while the man went where he went. For most of an hour, an idiot in the crowd called out the name of a song, *the* song, the one the Rolling Stones had "discovered" and covered and hit with. And everybody else before the Stones and after. When the player finally got to it, the idiot shouted, *"Hoo!"* for a half minute until Jimmy threw a wadded napkin at the back of his head and told him to shut up.

The guitar player managed an impossible thing: he somehow went back to the original ache, the initiating heartbreak behind the song, however many years ago it was. His guitar had a baby picture laminated onto the front of it. The mother of his new baby couldn't even have been born when the *other* she broke his heart, but the way he played and sang, the wound sounded fresh, still sore to the touch.

"Let's go," Jimmy said when the song was done.

He had told Angel about Les Paul and about The Wind Cries Mary, but she was the only Mary Jimmy told Angel about that night.

# NINETEEN

The night Lucy had died and Jimmy had ended up in the library at the *Chron* with Duncan Groner, they'd talked Sailors, suicides, and San Francisco.

But Jimmy hadn't left it at that. At the end, as they were walking out to go get that drink, Jimmy spoke her name, almost as if it was just an afterthought.

Mary Hesse.

Or rather, he spoke *his* name, Dr. Marc Hesse.

There was a beat. "Don't personally know him," Groner said.

He plopped down into an armless roll-around chair and rolled over to one of the terminals. His two index fingers went to work, typing hunt-and-peck at a furious speed, more peck than hunt. He hit *Enter* with his elbow, to be funny.

"There used to be black steel file cabinets in here, wall to wall, floor to ceiling," he said. "Mother of God, I miss them. Now you put in a name and you end up with pictures of some gentleman servicing his wife in Quito, Ecuador."

The screen filled up in front of him. Text and pictures. But fully clothed.

"Cardiologist," Groner said first. "Who is he to you?"

Now it was Jimmy's turn to hesitate, to shove aside all the words that were gathering around the truth. To come up with the right lie.

"Something I'm working on," was the one he settled on. It was true in its own way. He'd been working on the idea of Mary over all the years since they'd been together, trying to tame it in his head. Trying to get over it.

"I thought what you were working on was a sad little Mexican girl who came up here and killed herself," Groner said.

"It goes where it goes," Jimmy said. He was looking past Groner to the image of Hesse on the screen, a color shot of the doctor in another tuxedo at another charity event. Or maybe the same tuxedo. Jimmy couldn't help but see a cold, unpleasant look in the other's eye, in the shape of his face, in the reluctance of the muscles around his mouth to gentle into anything remotely like a real smile. That face said, *I can do anything I want to you.* To Jimmy, anyway.

"Cardiologists are cold bastards," Groner said, like he was inside Jimmy's head. Maybe the San Francisco Sailors had come up with some powers their brothers to the south had missed out on, like mind reading.

Another screen full of information replaced the first.

"Not much about his years back East," Groner said, reading. "Sketchy. A liberal arts college in central Florida, then Duke for med school. He's thirty-eight, one kid."

Jimmy held himself back from asking what he really wanted to know. About Mary. *Her* past. What she had been doing since their time together in L.A.

"He's on boards, professional and philanthropic, *loves* stray animals apparently, believes in neutering, plays tennis." The bony index fingers went to work again. "Oh, this is rich. He's a Mormon. So that means he has a year's worth of food and water in the basement of the nine-bedroom house in Hillsborough."

Jimmy waited.

"He has a house on Tiburon, too," Groner said, reading. "And probably a cabin up in Sebastopol, where he dances naked in a fern-ringed redwood glen with a secret assemblage of men at solstice."

Groner spun in the chair to look at Jimmy. "His wife is beautiful," he said after a long beat. Then he looked back at the screen.

"Mary," Groner said. "He doesn't deserve her. Maybe none of us do."

Jimmy took the reporter's obvious, immediate dislike of Marc Hesse as an act of friendship, though Groner couldn't know why Jimmy hated him.

"Any chance he's a Sailor?"

Groner shook his head and said, "I'd know."

And then they'd gone off into the night for that drink.

Hesse had offices downtown, in a building across from the TransAmerica Pyramid.

Midmorning, Jimmy was standing out front. Groner had called him at the Mark with the address. Hesse had just moved from previous digs. This new place wasn't even listed yet.

Jimmy knew enough about movies to know it was the building with the "florist's shop" on the ground floor where Dirty Harry had faced down somebody, said something sharp while the punk was left to stare into the holey end of the .44 magnum. It wasn't *Dirty Harry* itself or even *Magnum Force*. It wasn't "You have to ask yourself, do I feel lucky?" or "Go ahead, make my day." The movie was probably *Sudden Impact*, and the line wasn't good enough to get remembered, the way it was with sequels.

He should have been off with Angel, looking for Les Paul. He hadn't even knocked on Angel's door when he left the Mark.

Jimmy rode up in the elevator. He felt lucky.

He didn't know what his intentions were, what the plan was. What was he going to do, slap Hesse in the face with a glove? Challenge him to a duel? *Go ahead, make my midmorning.*

It never came to that. The doctor was in surgery.

The waiting room was empty. Everything was perfect. The magazines were unmussed, in neat stacks. Unread. Even the sports magazines. Even the swimsuit issue. Everything had a new smell to it. The receptionist was cute, didn't have a drop of blood on her. She was a little flirty, maybe bored with a long, slow morning. Or it could have been that everybody who came in was old and pale and short of breath. Jimmy's breath was just fine.

The art on the walls was original. Oils. One canvas pulled Jimmy closer. It was of a boat entering a harbor, a black-and-white sloop, a storm behind it like a giant with a puffed-out chest. The painting even had a name: *In Time*. It wasn't pretty, as pictures went. It went right up to the edge of pretty, stopped just short; *art* that way, not decoration or entertainment. Jimmy wondered why a doctor, a cardiologist, would choose it for the eyes of those waiting. *We found the blockage just in time? You're safe here?*

It made Jimmy want to eat a steak, drink a martini, *Celebrate Life!* with the new hippies in the Haight. What he remembered of it.

It made him want to hold Mary.

"Bye," the flirty receptionist said to his back.

---

A call to Groner on the run got him the name of the hospital where Hesse was. Under the hood of some poor bastard. Valve job.

Groner kept the info coming, a second call. He told Jimmy to look for a deep dark red, big-dog Mercedes, a CLS500.

"A color called Bordeaux Metallic."

"Sounds delicious," Jimmy said. "Fruity, but not casky, I hope. But how am I going to find out what row he's parked in?"

Jimmy was already at the hospital, in the corner of the lot. He was making a joke.

"Where are you?" Groner said.

Jimmy told him.

"Look straight ahead, on the right," Groner said. "Under the carport."

"Now you're starting to creep me out," Jimmy said.

"I can see through walls, across town, but only if the conditions are exactly right," Groner said. "A friend works there, in the ER. I just called her. Hesse's name is on a parking place."

"Your friend a Sailor?"

"Yes."

"So you're sure Hesse isn't a Sailor."

"I would say no," Groner said.

"Would you say any more?"

"I've never heard of him, never heard anybody speak of him," Groner said. "Remember, I've been here a very long time. And then there's the boy."

"Yeah," Jimmy said.

Sailors were sterile. Some cosmic safeguard. Or joke.

"Of course, the boy is six. Hesse could have fathered him Before."

"Yeah."

"But then why would they so resemble each other? You haven't seen the boy. I'm sitting here looking at a picture of him."

Of course Jimmy had seen him. The boy didn't look anything like Mary, but Jimmy wondered if he'd just thought that because he liked that idea, because it made the reality of the situation a little less painful for him. So the boy looked like his father.

"I have work to do," Groner said. "People to bury, mysteries to demystify. Good luck. With whatever it is you're doing." And he was gone.

Hesse didn't appear for two hours, two hours before he got into the bulbous new Mercedes and backed out of a reserved parking place. (His name wasn't on it.) The hospital was the medical center at UCSF. On Divisadero.

He came back toward downtown. He disappeared into the Sequoia Club on Hyde, the private club, pulled up in front, left the Mercedes with a valet. He stayed inside for a half hour and came out into the afternoon looking fresh, clean shirt, pressed suit. Came out under the SC's arched doorway, under the letters cut into the stone . . .

**GREAT GEARS TURN**

Hesse then drove west on Geary, through the Richmond District, out to Fourteenth Avenue, where he turned right, headed north. He stayed

with it as Fourteenth turned into California 1 in a tunnel of tall old trees,
a corridor of mystic greens and almost black browns that kept closing in
tighter until it burst open into the Presidio, then onto the Golden Gate.
Dr. Hesse was headed home.

Jimmy stayed right behind the Mercedes on the bridge until he realized how close he was following. It was borderline road rage. He eased off,
let a BMW motorcycle and an Accord pulling a U-Haul trailer pass him
and then tuck back in, so he had a wall between him and the Mercedes.
A cool-down zone was another way to look at it.

Jimmy had a *What am I doing?* moment. He hadn't learned anything
so far, nothing except that Marc Hesse was fairly young, fairly good-
looking. Rich, clean. A member of society in good standing. Belonging
to all the right clubs. Paying rent, fixing heart valves. Buying good art.
Friendly when it came to the little people. He'd waved to a pair of nurses
coming in as he was leaving the hospital. So what if they only tentatively
lifted their hands, as if they didn't exactly recognize him? It was the
thought that counted.

A wearer of Italian suits.

A brand-name shopper when it came to cars.

A neuterer of strays.

A *giver.* What else?

Oh yeah, not sterile.

Alive, not dead. Living a life with the one woman who had shown
Jimmy what love could look like, when it finally came round to you.

Jimmy yanked the wheel right, took the exit for Sausalito. It was just
about the last self-protective instinct he'd have for a good, long time.

# TWENTY

You know you've got it bad when you start lying to your friends. About her. About you. About *it*. Or just leaving it unsaid, which is another way to lie. Jimmy was on the same bench as before in the little pocket park on the north end of Sausalito, when he had been tailing Lucy and Les Paul four or five days ago. But he wasn't thinking about them. He was looking, through the trees, past the red-and-white ferry boats, one coming in/one going out, past the sailboats in the marina, across the water to the knob of Tiburon. The tip of it was shaped like a turtle. Maybe that's what *tiburon* meant. There was a light chop on the water, a little wind. Sitting there, he was wondering why he hadn't told Angel straight out about seeing Mary. About the hole seeing her again had pulled him into. Angel knew more of the story of Jimmy and Mary than anybody, knew it from all angles. Start to finish, beginning to end.

Maybe he'd tell him now. Because Angel was walking across the grass toward him.

"He's here somewhere," Angel said from ten feet out. "We lost him. He came in on the boat."

Les Paul.

"What are *you* doing here?" Angel said.

"Just out riding around," Jimmy said.

"Come on, let's go find him."

Jimmy didn't move off the bench. Angel looked at him.

"*Maria, mi Maria, esta aqui,*" Jimmy said. *Mary, my Mary, is here.* He'd gone to Spanish without thinking about it, but it made sense. The Spanish Jimmy knew he learned from Angel, back in those L.A. days.

"Where?" Angel said.

"There. Tiburon." He lifted a finger to point at the arched back of land across the way.

"That's bad," Angel said.

"She's married. Has a little boy."

"You talked to her?"

Jimmy shook his head.

Now Machine Shop was walking toward them across the grass.

"That's bad," Angel said again. "Bad for you, bad for us."

"He's down here," Shop said. "I found him."

Jimmy got up.

Les was in a bar. And he had a beer in front of him.

"Doesn't anybody check IDs in this town?" Jimmy said. They were in the doorway. The bar was open in the front with French doors that slid aside, and open on the back to the water. Heavy, dark, carved curving wood, a stained glass skylight. It was about as Sausalito a bar as there could be. The boy was alone at a round table with his back to them, across the half-filled room. With his beer.

"Let's get him," Angel said.

"Wait," Jimmy said.

There was a drink next to Les's beer glass. A pretty pink cosmo in a martini glass. Down a sip.

"Did he have somebody with him before?" Jimmy said.

"Not when I saw him," Shop said. "He was just sitting there by himself, looking out at the water."

Jimmy saw her, saw *somebody*. Moving away. The restrooms were in the corner. *A flash of white*.

They waited a moment, to let her come back, but she never did.

"Come on," Jimmy said, and they started in.

The boy probably heard Jimmy's voice. He got some signal, maybe just instinct, and turned.

He didn't stop to think. He ran like hell, bolted away from the table so fast and rough it knocked over the beer glass. Ran like an underage teen in a bar.

They'd say later they'd forgotten how fast a teenage kid can be, how much go a boy has. He went out the back. For a second, Jimmy thought Les had jumped in the water, right into the Bay, but there were sailboats and houseboats moored all along the back sides of the bars and restaurants, and Les Paul leapt from one rocking deck to the next, broad-jumping, scissoring over rails and deck chairs like a middle school record holder. *Running for his life* is what you'd call it if you saw it.

He got away from the men. It was never even close.

Jimmy went back into the bar, straight into the ladies' room. It was empty.

Or at least there was nobody in a white dress.

----

Other people seemed to take comfort in the circularity of things, how things doubled back, repeated, came round again, but Jimmy hated it, had always hated it, that fact of physics or metaphysics or the cosmos or whatever it was. He wanted something new to happen, something unprecedented, instead of the same old thing recycling itself. And the same people.

At least that's what he told himself, sitting there behind the wheel of the Porsche in the parking lot of the waterfront park out on Tiburon.

*Again.*

What he told himself was that he was there because it was where he'd seen the woman in the white dress. But he knew why he was really there.

He had his own kind of hope. That afternoon, scanning the park, he had too much of it.

The cosmos made him wait two hours.

Mary walked across the grass from the parking lot. Today she and the boy had ridden their bikes over, had come in from the south on a bike path, the boy on a terminally cute scaled-down ten-speed, probably titanium, probably a thousand bucks' worth. The bikes were just left in a rack. Not even locked. Mary walked with a tall coffee in her hand, a stainless steel Thermos cup. The boy had a net sack with his soccer gear thrown over his shoulder. It was a good life. This is what stay-at-home mom meant for the wife and son of a San Francisco cardiologist.

Mary spread out a blanket, while the boy kicked a ball around. She looked over at the car, the Porsche. The top was up. With the sun sliding down in back of the water behind her, there had to be glare on the windshield. Jimmy knew she couldn't see in, couldn't see him. So why did she keep looking over? Did she remember the car? Why did she just stare, stare off at nothing, as if someone was reading an old, familiar story to her?

The soccer ball rolled over to the blanket, to pull her back from wherever she'd gone, from whatever had taken her away. She threw it back to the kid.

Jimmy realized he'd made a point of *not* learning the boy's name. That night in the newspaper library Groner could have dug it up, on the registry of whatever pricey preschool the boy had gone to, the team list of his little soccer crew, his bike registration. Groner knew it now, had to.

*"What's his name?"* Easy question.

The boy was kicking the ball and going after it, getting in front of it, playing all of the game in his head. Jimmy remembered the way he used to do the same thing with baseball when he was seven or eight, remembered how he'd throw the ball up and hit it and run the bases, even if they were just his mother's magazines laid out in the backyard, run until he'd switch sides and go after the ball in the outfield, throw it into the air again and catch it and throw it home.

He let his mind slip out of gear, let himself pretend that he'd just pulled up, that she was expecting him, that this was one of those moments where you stop yourself. *Stop and smell the roses.* Where you hold back a second and look at the other out there on the grass, unguarded, waiting for you, and you think, *She loves me.* Before she sees you and puts on whatever face that calls for.

Mary was staring at the car again.

He waited until she looked away again and then started the engine and backed up and drove away.

But not far enough.

Today was the day when he was going to meet Mary face-to-face, and he knew it. He just didn't know where.

He drove into the village of Tiburon, the little loop of shops and restaurants at the end of the road that went out to the top of the peninsula, by Belvedere, out at the water. He parked in plain sight, lending a hand to Fate. He didn't put any money in the parking meter, whatever that meant.

He drank a beer, out on the deck behind a place. There were hardly any men anywhere, just pretty women, most of them young. Married. In tennis clothes, in white jeans. Drinking white wine. There was an imposing view, the ferry docks, the expanse of water, Alcatraz and Angel Island, the cityscape behind, all with an impossible depth of field.

He'd ditched Angel and Machine Shop back in Sausalito. He thought of all the things he *should* be doing. He thought of the weight of what he knew was coming next.

But not enough.

"Are you ready for another?" a voice said.

The waitress looked like one of the Tiburon wives, minus the BMW X-5 and the tennis togs and the portfolio. And the cardiologist.

"I don't know," Jimmy answered honestly. His glass was still half full. Or was it half empty?

He drained it before the next wave of sarcasm rolled in.

---

*"Let go, let God,"* Angel was always saying.

*Surrender to the Force, Luke.*

"Any port in a storm," Jimmy said aloud as he walked up the street in the village toward the Porsche, with the second beer in him, with the edge off. Everything was a little soft-focus.

*Give up, that'll make it happen. Things happen when you stop trying to make them happen.*

*Just do it.*

"So that's what I want," Jimmy said to himself, stepped from word to word with a rhythm that matched his footfalls on the sidewalk. *"Another man's wife. A little boy's mother. Amen."*

"Jimmy," Mary said.

She was sitting on the steps in front of a shop right beside the nose of the Porsche, the Porsche with the parking ticket flapping in the breeze. The shop was closed. It was a place that sold pillows, all of them shades of yellow, from what you could see in the window. It had a cute name.

She stood.

He meant to be prepared with an opening line. He knew he'd remember it, whatever he said, whether she did or not. He knew he'd probably regret it, whatever it was.

She was more self-assured. Or maybe it was that it was her town.

"You always wanted us to come to San Francisco," she said. "I never knew why."

"And we never did," he said.

*Are you ready for another?*

"It's a kinder place than L.A.," Jimmy said. "Maybe that was it. I knew you'd like it. But, you know, back then I thought and did a lot of things for no reason at all."

She sat back down on the steps, straightening the skirt of her dress, pulling it tight across her backside just as she sat. All the women were wearing skirts and dresses. Maybe it was just San Francisco. Or they were dressed the way he liked because it was his fantasy. In her skirt, on the blanket in the park, Mary had looked like Lucy. Or like the girl in foreground in the Wyeth painting, *Christina's World*, with her legs stretched out to the side. Mary used to like that painting, had a print of it on her wall, the one everyone liked, but that didn't diminish it for her. Jimmy wondered if she remembered how they used to talk about whether she was crippled or not.

He sat beside her. She'd left him space. They were tucked away, with a low hedge on either side of them. *Out of view,* he thought.

"You still have your car," she said.

"You saw me, in the park," Jimmy said.

"Yeah. I mean, I didn't know it was you."

"You always did like the car more than me."

"That's not true," she said. It made him remember something about her, something she did, turning back a smart-ass answer with directness. By being straight.

She was still looking at the car in front of them and not at him. There wasn't much traffic, but she turned her face aside or looked down whenever a car did pass. She didn't want to be seen. She couldn't. She wasn't going to sit there forever, he knew that. He knew she was thinking of something besides him.

"You saw my little boy," she said.

*Don't say his name,* Jimmy thought.

She didn't.

He realized that she'd taken the boy home before she came looking for him. She'd changed her shoes, left her bicycle somewhere. Was her car close by? Had she walked back into the village? Did she have a nanny? Had she taken the boy somewhere else?

He was looking at the side of her face. This close, he could see how changed she was. She had aged a little but not much, a little around the eyes. But she had changed in other ways. He wondered if he would have recognized her right away if he'd seen her up close first, instead of across the park. Maybe she'd had some plastic surgery done. She was married to a doctor, after all.

"You look good," he said.

She let her hand touch his, the edge of it. It was as much as he'd get, but it was *her* touch, unchanged. It was just enough to mess him up good.

A clot of clouds went over the sun. She stood, brushed off the back of her skirt, as if she'd been sitting in a pile of leaves.

She was about to say something when Jimmy said, "It's still so strong."

It was the only line he spoke all afternoon that he didn't rethink later, that was naked and true.

Even if it didn't stop her from walking away.

# TWENTY-ONE

Turn the page, things change.

Since the day of the ten suicides, spread all over the city, a dark meanness had rolled into town, a jittery *Now what?* that everyone felt. Ten plus Lucy. They were back down on the waterfront, Jimmy and Angel, coming around the Embarcadero in the Porsche. If he was home in L.A., Jimmy would know how to describe it, that dark sense hanging over everything. And how to duck it. In Los Angeles it would manifest itself in freeway gunplay, "cutoff shootings," boys on overpasses blowing out windshields with fist-size nuts stolen from job sites. It'd be the dry winds they called Santa Anas, ushering in "homicide summer," "earthquake weather," baseball bat attacks at kids' games in the parks. It'd be fistfights at gas stations, gang dustups at Magic Mountain.

Here it had its own style. You felt it in the waves of nervous energy that came off the knots of men standing around the piers. Each cluster of Sailors, out here almost all of them men, would turn and look at the Porsche as it rolled past. Put a fire in a barrel in the middle of them and it'd look like the old newsreels of the Depression. Waiting for something to happen, for whatever was next, *wanting* it, even if everybody knew it would probably be worse.

"Man, look at this," Jimmy said.

"It's been getting strange back home, too," Angel said. "Everybody's got the jitterbugs."

Jimmy hadn't thought about L.A. in a while, not the L.A. of the present. And he'd stopped wanting to run there. He wanted to be here now.

"Who was the last one Lucy talked to?" Angel said. They were driving through a corridor of waterfront Sailors now, waiting for them to part like herd animals on a Land Rover safari. The men opened a path. They seemed to be a polite lot, for beasts. Almost intentional. It was after two in the morning. Another hour or two, they'd have the world to themselves.

"Did you try to find out?" Angel pressed when Jimmy didn't say anything.
"No."

"When was the last time you saw her?"

Jimmy felt like he was in the dean of boys' office. Or a cop station.

Then he remembered. "Down here," he said. "The night of one of the suicides. A guy stepped in front of a streetcar."

"Did you ever talk to her, face-to-face?"

"No."

"Machine Shop said he talked to her, had a cup with her one night."

"I was across the street," Jimmy said defensively.

"He said she was a real talker," Angel said. "Baring her soul." He was quiet for a minute. "She was never that way with me, just said something when it needed to be said, not even then most of the time. She was real sweet."

*What do you want me to say?* Jimmy was thinking.

The Sailors were packed in tight around the car now. And not so fast to move out of the way. Angel saw where they were. Pier 35, where Lucy had died.

"I don't need to *see* it," Angel said.

"Shop called, thought he saw Les Paul down here. With the woman in the white dress."

"She was with Lucy, the last time you saw her?"

"Yeah. And another woman. Short black hair."

Les Paul. Sexy Sadie. Polythene Pam. The Leonidas girls. Truth was, Jimmy was looking for everybody.

*Anybody* except Mary.

---

Turn the page, you got another day. Whether you wanted one or not. Duncan Groner had had his own way of bringing Jimmy back to the case, of pressing his fingers down on the fiery Braille again, of dragging him back across the bridge from Marin to San Francisco.

"Page A-6," Groner had said, a wake-up call at the hotel, though Jimmy had never turned toward the bed that night. "The *Chronicle*, All the News That's Fit for Fools."

It was a full page of faces. The dead. The suicides.

"Some friends of yours . . ." Groner said.

Jimmy opened the newspaper standing in the doorway to the suite, and there they were, all the suicides, in clean rows with their names under-

neath, way too much like a high school yearbook. He'd expected something else, the latest edition of *the present* maybe, not the past.

What he'd expected was something about Mary. Or her husband.

The accompanying copy was bylined. Duncan Groner apparently
had become the go-to guy for self-murder. There wasn't much "story" to
the layout, one long graf in which the reporter laid out the terms: San
Francisco proper usually had eight to ten suicide deaths a month. (The
Golden Gate had its own segregated stats, *two a month* since the plain-
clothes patrollers had been instated, "blending in" with the despairing.)
Since the first of September, all told there'd been forty-eight suicides,
*successful suicides* was the term, bringing to mind dozens more with *half-*
slashed wrists, with only a *half* bottle of pills to be suctioned out in the
ER, jumpers off one-story roofs, shooters firing starter's pistols at their
temples. Groner ended the lead-in with a few sentences of behind-the-
scenes stuff, the disclosure that the editors "vociferously debated" the
"dangers" of "publicizing" the suicides (of telling the truth, in other words),
for fear that the "suggestible" in San Francisco might think the unthinkable, and act on it, join the club. Even if the initiation ceremony was a tad
severe.

Faces. Hairstyles, forced smiles. The retoucher's craft. Lives smoothed
out, flattened onto cheap pulp paper, tamed in black and white, gussied
up. There was the old lady, the ninety-year-old chorus girl. The young
man with AIDS. The German tourist. All the pictures shaved off years,
decades in some cases. Now the AIDS man from the hospice was outdoors, resurrected into a brighter yesterday, coastal cliffs behind him, his
perfect thick hair wild in the wind up off the water, a white smile on his
face that made you wish you could see the cutoff person at his shoulder,
the man, Jimmy guessed, who'd gone through the drawer of pictures to
pick this one. There were the Greek twins. There they *all* were.

"What exactly are we looking for?" Angel said.

"*New*," Jimmy said. It was a vulgar term.

Some of the Sailors, the more dramatic ones, used the word *aboard*
when they were talking about new Sailors: a new Sailor was "aboard." New
meant "new meat."

"You don't think Lucy's down here, do you?" Angel said. For Angel, the
whole thing had more than enough drama on its own, he didn't go seeking
more in language.

Lucy *could* be down here, Lucy as a Sailor. A lot of them were suicides,
*successful* suicides. The murdered were another contingent, especially among

the darkest of the Sailors, the ones who liked the shadows. The rest had died in accidents. But a loose definition of the term. More than a few had been the ill "misdiagnosed" into this state. Before their time.

Everybody had their own unfinished business, even if none of them knew exactly what it was.

Jimmy had only glanced at her picture in the *Chron*, Lucy's picture. A portrait from a few years after high school. From Sears? Kmart? Old enough and fuzzy enough almost to be someone else. (He wondered where they'd gotten it. From family in Paso Robles?) He didn't look at it long because in the picture Lucy looked a little like Mary. Not the hair, but . . . Why hadn't he seen it before? (Or had he? He'd flashed on *something* in the café down in Saugus.) More likely, it was some trippy side effect brought on by the acid of his guilt. He was supposed to save Lucy, and Lucy *wasn't* saved.

"Did you see the pictures of all of them? In the paper?" Jimmy said. "They had a picture of Lucy."

Angel shook his head. "I got my own pictures of her."

The Sailors were blocking the way now. Jimmy thought about a tap on the horn. Maybe in San Francisco they wouldn't kill you for it.

Then he saw the Sailor right in front of him, across the hood. This one was very tall. He was black, but light-skinned. He had spotted skin, looked particularly African.

And he carried a staff, a wooden rod taller than he was.

Jimmy and Angel looked at each other.

"Let my people go," Angel said.

But this Moses wasn't there to part anything, not yet anyway. He just stared at Jimmy and Angel. The other Sailors seemed to press in closer, surround the car. Moses stayed where he was, in front of the hood, one of the Porsche's chrome sissy bar bumpers against his leg. Against his calf. That was how tall he was.

"I guess this is the valet parking," Jimmy said, and turned off the engine.

They both opened their doors at the same time, pushing back the men on the side, and got out.

There didn't seem to be any women Sailors down here. It was a rough-looking crowd.

"They're going to mess with the car," Angel said.

"Maybe not," Jimmy said. "Maybe they'll cut a couple of out-of-towners some slack."

"It's not going to be here when we get back," Angel said.

The man with the staff had started away. Jimmy and Angel set out after him, figuring that was the plan. Somebody's plan.

There were hundreds of them down there. Something about the gathering, the whole scene, felt ceremonial. The general agitation in the air, in the San Francisco night, seemed to have found a focal point.

But they were all silent. Like obedient spectators for a play.

"Maybe we should do this tomorrow," Angel said.

"This isn't something *we're* doing," Jimmy said. Now the San Francisco Sailors were moving the two outsiders along. Jimmy and Angel were just going with the flow. There wasn't any resisting, no use. It felt inevitable, whatever it was.

Jimmy lost sight of the tall African.

One of the grimmest-looking Sailors got right in Jimmy's face. "We fell away," he hissed at Jimmy. Or at least that's what Jimmy thought he said.

Jimmy tried to get past him. The man said his line again.

This time Jimmy heard it right. "We follow Wayne," the man was saying.

The others around him joined in. "We follow Wayne . . ."

"Good for you," Angel said. "I follow Jesus."

A brutish Sailor shoved him. Angel shoved back. "Step off."

"We serve the Russian!" one of the few women said defiantly.

"Look," Jimmy said.

Just in time. The tall black man with the staff was waiting next to a door in the front of one of the waterfront warehouses. Jimmy and Angel and their escorts had crossed two hundred yards of pavement. The Sailors had closed in behind them. Wherever the Porsche was, it was swallowed up.

The door on the front of the warehouse was closed.

Jimmy walked to it. He expected it to open. It didn't.

"Knock," Moses said.

Jimmy went along with the gag.

Even before the door opened, Jimmy and Angel heard it. Wailing, spacey guitar. Live. They'd found Les Paul.

He played real good.

# TWENTY-TWO

Through the doorway, there was a corridor. There was a nobody dressed all in black. They followed him. There was nothing on the walls, nothing on the floor. After a few yards, another door, with a raised threshold, like a hatch, like the mouth of a trap. From here on, the walls seemed cold, slippery. Not that Jimmy or Angel were reaching out to touch them. Everything from the door on in was painted black. Or, if not black, some deep red.

The crying guitar got louder.

They stepped over another threshold and found themselves in a space three levels high, a single room a hundred feet from end to end. They still couldn't spot Les, but the sound had a location now, the far end of the big, hollow room. The chamber was lit by gaslights positioned along the side, flamboyant brass curves, feminine shapes, clear glass globes. And real flame, not some electric update. Now they could see that the walls were metal. Iron or steel. There didn't seem to be any windows, but there were drapes, red velvet, to match what furniture there was, preposterous curvy Victorian divans and claw-foot mahogany tables atop thick rugs, like the great rooms halfway down the coast at San Simeon or, farther down, in Hollywood, in Charles Foster Kane's Xanadu. Somebody had a flair for the dramatic.

The room was a great jam room. Some combination of the slick walls and the baffles created by the yards of pleated velvet made the guitar notes swoop around the room like a special-effects ghost. Like the ghost of Jimi himself, because what the boy was playing was soaring and free-form. A sound to match, to fill the plush void of the space.

"There," Angel said.

Lucy's baby brother was on a second-level landing, behind an iron railing, beside a lowboy Fender amp with a red-glowing jewel light on its face. He had his eyes open as he played but wasn't looking at anything, certainly not at them. Jimmy realized he had never gotten the kid's real name. The kid had on his black porkpie hat from that first day up in Paso Robles. He still looked fourteen, even if he sounded ninety-nine.

Then they weren't alone anymore.

It was Jeremy. Cape-wearing Jeremy. All-in-black Jeremy, who whispered in your ear and told you to jump.

He came in from offstage, stage right, walked with an ivory-headed cane, looking, in that setting, like a turn-of-the-century opium dealer who pimped on the side. But without the happy-go-lucky disposition.

But it turned out this wasn't *his* play, Jeremy's. He was just a supporting character. He greeted Jimmy, "met" Angel, which meant he saw him and nodded in his direction. Les reached the end of his jam, let the last of it sustain for twenty or thirty seconds, then killed it off with a last strike at the strings.

"Cool," Jeremy said.

The kid started sketching out something else, heading off elsewhere, a new set of chords and changes.

Everyone seemed to know what they were doing there, everyone except Jimmy and Angel.

Someone else was coming, footsteps on the hard floor. Was the floor metal, too?

"Whitehead," MC Jeremy said to Jimmy and Angel a second before the man himself appeared.

Whitehead.

He looked to be in his sixties, thin but with weight to him. The skin on his face was tight and smooth, his hair silver, buzz-cut. His eyes were pure black at the center, at least looked so here, on this stage. He wore a suit that fell the way expensive suits fall, a politician's suit, the color of coal, black or blue, depending on where the light was. He seemed to hesitate under one of the flickering gas wall lamps, his hands folded in front of him, as if to let Jimmy and Angel get the full effect. Jimmy knew the type, the kind of man who liked to think a person would remember forever the first time he saw him. The tip of his third finger on his right hand was gone, from the knuckle out. He wore an onyx ring, to draw attention to it.

A shudder went through the room, strong enough to make the boy up top stop playing. It was as if someone had backed a truck into the side of the warehouse.

Jimmy wondered if it was a quake, though it was already over if it was. He looked at Angel. Angel had spread his feet apart, for balance.

Les Paul started playing again, rolling with the punches.

Whitehead turned to an intercom on the wall behind him, a Bakelite and brass device as out of the past as the rest of the furnishings. He depressed a switch and spoke into a conical mouthpiece.

Jimmy realized that what was coming up his legs was not the after-effects of the shake but a low, regular vibration in the floor itself, as if there was a generator in the next room. Whoever's place this was, you got the idea they were off the Pacific Gas and Electric grid.

Angel leaned in a little closer to Jimmy. "Let's just see if we can get the kid and go. I don't get this."

There was another shudder, the floor shifting under them.

"Sit, please," Whitehead came closer and said. "You'll be more comfortable."

There was a smell, a new scent, heavier than the sickly sweet perfume of the two men, the marker of the Sailors of the north. This was a thicker smell, a pungency that rode a little lower in the air. *Diesel.*

In the same moment Jimmy put a name to it, there was a sense of move-ment. And the floor under their feet became *the deck*, the walls around them *the bulkheads*, the doors *hatches.*

They had cast off.

Les Paul played on.

"I exhausted part of my youth in Los Angeles," Whitehead began as he stepped toward a wing chair in the center of the room. He sat and crossed his legs at the knee. The nobody who'd ushered them in, *aboard*, crossed to his master's side with a silver tray, a snifter of something golden. Noth-ing was offered to Jimmy and Angel.

Jimmy dropped down onto one of the couches, stretched out his arms along the top of the back, right at home. He looked up at the dark recesses of the rumbling chamber.

"Great gears turn," Jimmy said.

It was sufficient to make Whitehead turn his black eyes toward his impudent guest.

"What does that *mean*, anyway?" Jimmy said, trying to sound like a teenager.

Whitehead ignored the distraction, the question. Angel was still standing.

"Sit, please," Whitehead said. And then, after the comma, "Mr. Figueroa."

Angel picked a chair.

The pitch of the vibration changed. Things stilled for a moment; then there was a stronger tremble, and the room's equilibrium shifted. The rocking was polite.

Whitehead began again, said his first line again, "I exhausted part of my youth in Los Angeles," with just the hint of irritation at having to repeat it. It made it seem as rehearsed as it was, as thought-out. It made what came next feel like a politician's stump speech. Too repeated, probably not true. "I had been in the Brotherhood—we still called it that then—two or three years. San Francisco was exhausted for me. Gratefully, I say only temporarily." He wasn't drinking his drink, hadn't even lifted it to his nose to admire, just palmed it like the prop it was.

Jimmy wished he had it. He thought of a line to interject into the proceedings, to throw the other off balance, but decided instead to rear back on the couch, be cool. Let the man empty his bucket.

"I was alone. On the train, of course." Whitehead looked at Angel. "The Coast *Day*light. Of course, this was before the Coast Starlight, years before." He waited. When Angel nodded, Whitehead's eyes released him.

"I remember coming into Union Station at sunset. I remember the sound of it, the echo. I came outside, into that very striking Los Angeles sunset panorama. Spectacular. I was met at the station by a man, an actor whose name you would recognize, who of course was a Sailor, too. I admit I was a little starstruck. I had seen so many of his movies. And not all of them on the late show, I have to admit. He was waiting, parked at the curb in—"

Jimmy held up a finger, pointed at the air. "Jefferson Airplane," he said. Les Paul was working allusions to a few classics into the set.

Whitehead put some steel in his voice. "I met Red Steadman that trip, that very night, as a matter of fact," he said.

The name wiped the joke off Jimmy's face. Walter E. C. "Red" Steadman was the leader of the Sailors to the south. He and Jimmy had had their clashes over the years. The young man and the old man. If they had made any kind of peace, it was an uneasy one.

Whitehead enjoyed the moment. And the next even more. "Of course, I was something of an emissary. Steadman wasn't receiving *me*, Wayne Whitehead, but rather the one I represented, whose card I carried in my vest pocket."

He tapped his heart.

And then he spoke the name.

The night, the drama, the episode dutifully had followed the principle of rising action, starting with Black Moses out on the pier parking lot with his rod and his staff, who led them to Jeremy. Then Jeremy led them to Whitehead—and Whitehead, in speech at any rate, to the unnamed famous actor and then, "that very night," to Steadman, untitled leader of the Southern California Sailors.

And then, by nothing more than the utterance of his name, to the man himself. It was designed to take Jimmy and Angel to the top of the mountain, let them see the view.

And how far there was to fall.

"The Brotherhood—we still called it that then—was a different animal in those days," Wayne Whitehead continued, his voice now confident, steady, impressive, as if he knew he'd already met the most important of his objectives. "Everyone knew everyone, or at least acted in that spirit. We looked each other in the eye. We *measured* each other. I wouldn't say we trusted each other, but there was understanding. Cooperation, after a fashion."

"We just want to get our people out of here," Jimmy said. "The ones who are still alive. Actually, all we want is the kid up there, Johnny Guitar. We get him and we go home. It's actually simple."

"Just the boy?" Whitehead said. "Really?"

He knew about Mary. Jimmy could feel it.

"I've been back to Los Angeles many times . . ." Whitehead said, starting down a new line.

Jimmy stood. "How about we all go up top?"

He looked at Jeremy to see if he got the joke: the warehouse building they'd first entered was the selfsame one the Leonidas girls had dived off, Pier 35. Where Lucy had met her end, too.

"Get a little fresh air, see the city lights? Maybe we're cruising past Alcatraz. Angel gets seasick, I'm just telling you."

"I was there in Los Angeles for the murders, in the nineties," the host said, bringing it all back home.

It wiped another smile off Jimmy's face.

"And, of course, the aftermath," Whitehead said. "That was the last time, actually. And the first time I heard *your* name."

Jimmy was still standing.

"I'm nobody," he said.

"Those who know you best say otherwise," Whitehead said.

There was a bump. They'd arrived back at the mooring, back at the wharf. The little play was over. At least the first act.

The nobody Sailor made ready, stepping over to open the hatch.

Whitehead stayed in his chair. He made a little church out of his hands, looked at them over his nine fingertips.

They weren't back at the waterfront, or at least not Fisherman's Wharf. When they went through the last door, they were somewhere else, stepping out of another warehouse building with its back against another pier. There were ships all around, but it was dark, *past* dark. The ships looked to be old navy ships being stripped for salvage and old freighters, some of them navy gray, too, some black, some rust red, all dead-seeming, under a blurred navy gray half moon.

"Where are we?" Angel said.

"Go ask Alice," Jimmy said.

Then *they* started to emerge. Forms, shadows coalescing into human forms. People. There were scores of them, coming in from all quarters. A show of strength. Or *need*, because they all had looks of expectation on their faces. Anticipation, hope, fear. Waiting.

*Who's next?*

Jimmy and Angel had left Whitehead and Jeremy behind them in the hold of the ship, had just followed the nobody out.

But now Whitehead was standing right behind Jimmy, seeing what he saw.

"They know who you are," he said, just loudly enough for Jimmy to hear. "You have a reputation."

There began a reverberation coming up from the gathered, a vibration like the engine on the boat, low and indistinct. They were saying something over and again. It was like the noise they call for from a crowd of extras in a movie, vague mumbling that sounds like a hundred conversations but is really only a few words repeated. The same words. With the crowd of them, it was oddly melodious.

It got clearer as they synced up. "We follow Wayne . . ."

Whitehead stepped around Jimmy and waded into their midst.

Jeremy had come out from the ship, too, with his long cape draped over his arm. Now he came forward and, hoping at least some in the crowd were watching *him*, unfurled it and let it fall over his shoulders. These San Franciscans liked their Romanticism, if that's what it was. Jeremy stood with his hands on his hips but still looked like what he was, a sidekick, a right-hand man.

Jimmy was watching Whitehead and his congregation. "Funny, I wouldn't take him for a people person," he said to Jeremy, who seemed to like the line.

"Thought maybe you'd want to know: The Greek girls, what's left of them, are down here," Jeremy said.

"They're both Sailors?"

"Double down, I say," Jeremy said. "Whenever you can."

Now it was Jimmy who went into the crowd, into the wake closing behind Whitehead.

"Where are you going?" Angel called after him.

Jimmy kept going and didn't answer his friend.

Jeremy turned and grinned at Angel, a look Angel didn't get at all.

# TWENTY-THREE

Two girls were holding hands. It was a start.

Jimmy found them down by the piers, walking apart from the others. One of them kept looking over her shoulder at him. She smiled, in fact. The girls wore matching clothes, long blue dresses out of some cheap goods. It looked rough to the skin and the color uneven, as if hand-dyed. It made Jimmy think of cult clothes, pretty hippie girls on a commune, flowers in their hair but a dreary, frightened servitude in their hearts, following the master. (The trick was to not want to be the master.)

"Wait," Jimmy said when the one turned to look at him again.

She waited, held back her sister.

When he got closer, he saw how young they were. With Sailors the new form matched the old, at least in age and usually in size. From a distance, or in a photograph, one might pass for his or her former self, except to the eyes of a close loved one, to whom the new person always looked like a stranger.

It wasn't a logical thing. The Sailor way was a ball of mystery, surrounded by a hundred miles of fog. There was a famous fog in the Central Valley, starting south of Bakersfield on Old 99 when you came up from L.A., Thule fog, so thick it looked like dishwater. Whenever Jimmy drove through it, or up to it (you couldn't drive through it at its worst), he thought, *This is what it's like to be a Sailor.* A sailor at the wheel of his boat.

"Hi," the girls said together. They weren't twins in this domain, but they looked alike.

"Hi," Jimmy said.

They seemed so trusting, so open. Unafraid, now that they had each other. They also seemed to know who he was. He wondered why, what they'd been told about him.

They were *New.* It was all over them. Jimmy had already decided they probably weren't the Greek girls, the reborn Leonidas twins. He just had a feeling about them. The fog. He was about to ask them, gently, about themselves, when they just smiled again, or at least the one of them did, and they walked away.

*Down the rabbit hole again . . .*

Jimmy followed them into a room in an old military building, World War II–era, wooden, with brown linoleum floors. One of those buildings built fast, when the world was coming apart on two fronts. It had a ten-foot ceiling, exposed rafters, all very intentional. There were windows along both sides, but they were covered with blackout cloths, just like in the war. It was an officers' mess, with a long table.

An odd one, because the table was set with candelabra and a table-cloth. And a meal on silver serving plates.

The chairs were filled with women. The two sisters were seated on either side of a woman who looked a little French, with short-cropped hair. They stopped talking and eating when he stepped in, then went back to it. They were different ages, but there was something in their faces, all of the women, something about their pale skin, that made Jimmy think of the Procol Harum line about the sixteen vestal virgins leaving for the coast. (And, although his eyes were open, they might just as well have been closed.) It was a little like a scene from a dream, like a memory of an event that never took place.

A couple of the women looked familiar. It took him a second to real-ize that some voice in his head was telling him that two or three of them resembled women out of his past. *That* dream. At his right, closest to him, was a dark-haired beauty who reminded him of a woman from a year or so ago in his life, a "client" who'd become much more before it was over. And next to her was a girl who instantly made him think of a girl he'd fallen hard for when he was just a kid, maybe the last real love before he'd become a Sailor. (Maybe they'd slipped him something on the boat.) Right in front of him was a punky-looking girl with silver hair. *Eighties Girl.* She stuck out her tongue at him. Jimmy almost laughed. He'd accepted the trippiness of the scene, was going with it.

Then he realized the short-haired woman at the other end of the table looked a little like his mother. He didn't exactly want to dwell on that.

There was an open place at the table. Was it meant for him? There was a glass of wine there. He decided now would be a good time to drink half of it.

It wasn't all women. Machine Shop was there. Shop had dressed for the occasion, whatever the occasion was, a maroon suit that could have been sewn from the remnants of the velvet hanging on Whitehead's vessel. Put him in a plush red Al Green suit and the seventies really came out. Shop hadn't even noticed Jimmy. He was totally into the women around him, full shuck and jive, a bit of the old "And how are you fine ladies this evening?" When his eyes met Jimmy's, he looked embarrassed, guilty, caught. He was supposed to meet Jimmy at the Wharf.

"Sorry, man," Shop said.

"Yeah, I was looking for you up there."

"And now you're here."

"How'd *you* get here?" Jimmy said.

"They brought me in a limousine," Shop said.

Jimmy guessed that all this was part of Whitehead's master plan, whatever it was.

Then he saw Mary. Or rather "Mary."

At the far end of the table. If the lights were up, she probably wouldn't have looked a thing like Mary. Not the twenty-two-year-old Mary Jimmy had met on Sunset Strip in 1995, not the woman now, out in Tiburon. But the hair was close, the face the same shape. She was wearing a dress that made Jimmy remember the one Lucy had been wearing there at the start. But that was all right, too; all of them were getting tangled up in each other's stories in his head.

He took his wine over to her. Nobody paid him much mind. He stood over her.

She looked up at him, stopped whatever conversation she was having. This close, she didn't look like Mary at all.

"Come sit by me," Jimmy said to her. "There's a seat down there by me." He sounded drunker than he was.

"You're always trying to relocate me," the Mary *almost* lookalike said. Or Jimmy thought she did.

# TWENTY-FOUR

"I still see them," Mary said.

She had just said it, blank-faced, sitting there in her white slipcovered armless chair, the light of a cream candle dancing on her face. They were in a restaurant on the Sunset Strip. Le Dome.

Back then it was the kind of place Jimmy wouldn't have sought out on his own. A little rich, a little too hushed. He'd go if someone else suggested it, but it was too snow-white and *round* for him.

Mary had picked the place. "I want to talk to you about something," she had said.

He had assumed it was one of those girl talks about commitment, about "moving to the next level." In a way it was. But he was way ahead of her, ready to relocate to any level she named. He loved her, simple and sure.

But what she had said in Le Dome was, "I still see them."

"It's over," he said. He knew what she meant.

"I know," she said. "I know it's *supposed* to be over. I know everything you know, everything everybody else knows. They arrested two brothers. Russian brothers. There is all the evidence against them. I don't care. I *still* see them."

"Where?"

Jimmy leaned closer. Everybody knew about Le Dome. The arch of the smooth, plastered ceiling meant the sound bounced around in funny ways. Conversations ended up where they weren't meant to go. Jimmy had been there one night, late, alone, stood up by someone, and heard more than he wanted to about the problems in the marriage of a fading television star and his young wife all the way across the room. He was worried about who else was hearing Mary. The place was almost full.

"I was on Melrose," Mary said. "Two of them were following me. In the middle of the afternoon."

He didn't say anything.

"I told you when I met you I was crazy," she said.

"What did they look like?" Jimmy said.

"Just like before," she said. "Black on black. Sneakers. Black jeans. Black T-shirts. One of them was maybe one of the ones who came to your house after me."

"What did they do?"

"They just followed me. I'd go in one store and when I came out, they were waiting, hanging back two stores up the street."

"Why did you want to come *here* to talk about this?"

"I didn't want to fall apart. I feel like I've been doing that lately anyway. I wanted to be out. Among the living."

Jimmy asked her if she'd been thinking much about the others in the house up in Benedict. Whom she'd survived.

"Yes."

He reached across the white linen to her. "It's over," he said. "They caught the two men. They were the ones. The killings stopped."

"No, they didn't," she said. "They *didn't*."

There'd been a copycat murder two weeks after the Russian brothers had been arrested.

"I have friends who are cops, Mary."

"Yeah," she said. "Why is that?"

He didn't have a quick answer for her.

Wait a second or two and that *is* your answer.

"Why is that?" she said. "You're a record producer."

Remember, they were both young. It was a time, and they were an age, when *what you do* could be a very roomy jacket. And you could have three or four of them on the rack by the door. Pick one. Nobody checked the label, as long as it looked good on you. He was a "record producer" working on a demo for a band in the Valley anytime they got some money together, and sometimes when they didn't. She was an "actress." Or was it "singer"?

"I know people from lots of different . . . areas," Jimmy said. "It's an L.A. thing. I'm just saying: The cops are convinced they got the people who did the murders. All of the murders."

"Why did you go downtown that day?"

"What day?"

He knew exactly the day she meant. In the scene they were playing out in the restaurant that night, Jimmy had been behind Mary from the start. Running to catch up.

She just waited him out.

"Angel had heard about somebody else who could have been responsible, involved in the killings. We were downtown checking it out."

He should have stopped there.

Instead, he made a joke. "Going to see a man about a dog."

Mary said, right back at him, "There was a man with a dog, all in black and a black dog. *I* saw a man with a dog."

It was like laying down the first card in her hand.

"Twice," she said. "I saw him twice."

There was the second card.

"Where?" Jimmy said.

"The first time in daylight, when I went back up to the house in Benedict."

"When? You went back up to the house? Why?"

"Last week. Sunday."

The third and fourth cards.

"Why did you go up there?"

"I don't know," she said. "I was just thinking about it. Too much. I just wanted to see it again."

He was shaking his head. "You shouldn't go up there. Or you should have told me. I would have taken you."

"Always riding to the rescue," she said. "That's my Jim."

"When was the second time you saw him?" Jimmy said.

"A couple of nights ago," Mary said. "In the yard." She meant *his* yard, *their* yard. "You were gone somewhere."

The fifth card.

She had ordered a glass of red wine after they'd cleared away their dinner plates, but she hadn't touched it until now. "I was feeling . . . desperate," she said, drawing the wine to her. "I was feeling . . . pushed into a corner. He was just standing there, down the slope from the house, with that black dog, looking up at me in the kitchen window, as if waiting for me to *do* something."

She tasted the wine. "I don't like it that you have a gun," she said. "And I especially don't like it that you left it where I could find it."

He held his question. About her, about the gun, about what she had been considering that day. He held his question. And, he realized later, held his breath, too, the same as if he had walked in on her in that moment, holding the gun, precisely at the time in her life when she didn't need to find a gun.

"I put it away," Mary said. "In the hall closet, under all those books, in the back. Tell me you'll get rid of it. I don't want to see it again. Not when I'm going through this kind of shit, feeling this."

Jimmy didn't have a gun.

---

Two days later there was another copycat killing, another heart ripped out, another body spread-eagle on another road cut, and a secondary wave of panic in the L.A. basin. There wouldn't be any more, but it was enough.

This time, the killing seemed to trigger suicides, a half-dozen of them. "Panic suicides," the article in the *Times* called them. Maybe they'd happened before, in the first wave of killings, the *real* killings, but it hadn't been reported.

There was another term they used, official psychologists, to describe what they were afraid of, if reason didn't prevail.

*Suicide contagion.*

If reason didn't prevail. As if reason ever prevails.

---

Jimmy moved the two of them up to a house at the edge of Angeles Forest, high in the rocks and woods above Altadena. A house with a pool. The owner was a Sailor friend of Angel's; Jimmy didn't know him. The owner called it a "cabin," but it had three bedrooms and was behind gates, though the back of the property was open, open to the woods and the rocks behind it. It was all the way at the end of its own road. The view from the window over the kitchen sink was of Mount Baldy.

It helped. Mary felt better. Safer.

She assumed Jimmy didn't believe her, didn't believe that the Cut Killers could still be out there, looking in people's windows. Or tying up loose ends, whatever it was that they were doing. Killing again. Maybe he *did* believe her. She didn't know what he was thinking. She got up each morning and made a big breakfast, the kind of breakfast her mother used to make for her father, eggs and bacon and fresh orange juice and pancakes or waffles. She'd found a waffle iron in the cabinets. (There wasn't a phone, but there was a waffle iron.) She'd eat everything she'd made. Jimmy had trouble keeping up with her. He'd make the runs down to the store. She would make the lists, apparently having decided to cook her way through every one of her mother's recipes, as best she could remember them.

He came "home" one day, and she'd painted "Good Day Sunshine . . ." with clear red fingernail polish on the kitchen window.

Without ever deciding to, without ever talking about what should happen next, they stayed in "the cabin" like that for two weeks straight, Mary never leaving the house and grounds, and Jimmy only leaving to make the supply runs. And to make a few calls. There was no TV. What they had for entertainment was each other and a few board games, cards, and a beautiful old tube Zenith stereo with three-foot-high stained cherry speakers and a cabinet full of old LPs.

All day Mary played *The White Album* over and over.

----

She came out from the kitchen, the dinner dishes done.

"Honey, I'm home," she said.

"That's supposed be my line, Lucy," Jimmy said.

"I'm more *June*, June Cleaver." She crossed to him. He was in a chair, an old man's recliner, reading. There was a cabinet of *Popular Science* magazines. From thirty years back.

"I was just reading about the future," Jimmy said. "We're all going to have personal helicopters by nineteen eighty."

"Nineteen eighty! It sounds so futuristic . . . I was *seven* in 1980. I was born in 1973. When were *you* born?"

He had made a pitcher of martinis. He had found the glasses and everything behind a little bar, the kind covered in black pleat-and-tuck leatherette. He'd delivered one to her in the kitchen while she was cleaning up. Now she took a sip of his. First, she kissed him. He could smell the gin on her breath.

*When were you born?*

"I don't think June and Ward Cleaver were drinkers," he said, letting her question evaporate.

She plopped down into his lap. "Sure they were. The Beav drove them to it."

He kissed her.

After a second, she said, "I love you," and said it in a way that made him think she wasn't used to saying it. He thought that, even after the voice in his head ridiculed him for it.

"I love you, too," he said.

"I feel safe," she said. "I feel safe."

"Nobody knows we're here. In the middle of nowhere."

"It's like we're lost," she said, against his neck. "Or is it *saved*? Can you be lost and saved at the same time?"

"I'll ask Angel."

She jumped up. "Check this out!"

She was like a girl again, more girlish than before. Than when they met. She went over to the stereo on the bookcase. She turned on the amp. The speakers thumped, then buzzed up to attention.

"I figured this out, how to do it, all by myself this afternoon," she said.

She took hold of the mechanical control on the side of the turntable and shifted it out of gear. "You put it between forty-five and thirty-three and a third . . ."

She took *The White Album* off the shelf. She unsheathed one of the disks, checked the label.

"Wait," she said, to herself.

She reengaged the speed control lever. When it got up to speed, she put the needle down. After a second of click and sputter, it began.

"Revolution No. 9."

She waited until it came to the refrain, "Number nine . . . number nine . . . number nine . . ."

"OK," she said. "Got it? Now . . ."

She disengaged the speed lever again, slipped it into neutral. Then she put her finger in the center, on one side of the label, right on the bright green apple, and turned it backward, counterclockwise.

"I didn't know you could actually do this," she said over the wobbly, warpy backward noises, music for aliens.

"All right, I hear it, stop," Jimmy said, with an edge to his voice she didn't understand. And a *sadness* she couldn't understand.

"Not yet," she said. She was still spinning the record backward with her finger, coaxing the guttural discord out of the vinyl, trying to keep the rhythm, what there was of it.

Jimmy sank into himself.

She reached the place in the "song" where the announcer spoke, said his syllables over and over atop the orchestral noises, atop Beethoven's Ninth or strings tuning or whatever it was.

"Turn me on, dead man . . . Turn me on, dead man . . . Turn me on, dead man . . ."

She turned her face to him. She looked like a teenager, so happy in the moment. "It's one of the clues! 'Paul is dead.' Remember?"

*Turn me on, Deadman.*

He went outside, out onto the deck, beside the pool. The bleached-out water was just a step down from a huge rock that jutted out of the side of the hill, looked like a natural pool that way, in that "California perfect" way. A dragonfly skimmed the surface, like something out of a future war.

The windows were open. The music came out after him. Mary had flipped the record, and now she played the side over and over, Disk 2, Side 1, lifting the needle over "Helter Skelter" each time "Sexy Sadie" ended.

# TWENTY-FIVE

This time on the night run over the desert mountains north on the 5 to his new cop friend, Jimmy was alone. Angel was elsewhere. L.A. was panicky again. The suicide toll was climbing. And there were frayed nerves in the Sailor world, too, a generalized high anxiety that meant Angel had home calls to make, hands to hold, people to talk down off the ledge. It was what Angel did.

Nobody seemed to know what it was. Sailors were just wound up tight, waiting for something. Looking for somebody who could change things or even bring back the old status quo, when things were straight. Maybe they'd caught the same bug that was testing the nerves of the rest of L.A., driving even the Norms to start thinking the unthinkable.

Angel had handed him the key to the "new" Porsche, the '64 Cabriolet with no top, primer red, halfway to restoration. No top, no leather on the seats, a metal floor, but with the motor *there*, twenty foot-pounds past tight.

"I got a ticket on the way up," Jimmy said, when he dropped into a lawn chair in Detective Dill's backyard.

"The down side of Boiling Point Ridge?"

"Bingo."

"Rookie," the cop said. "Fish in a barrel, man."

They had walked straight through the house from the front door. The divorced cop hadn't done a bunch of decorating since the last time. Dill lagged behind a beat, then came out after Jimmy onto the patio with two bottles of beer and a brown leather briefcase. He handed one Negra Modelo to Jimmy and held out the neck of his for a clank.

"You know, Boiling Point's actually a town a mile or two from here," Dill said. "What's left of it. They could have named the subdivision Boiling Point Estates or some such, but they didn't. I don't know why."

"Well, I'm not a marketing person," Jimmy said.

"So what do you want to know?" the cop said in one of his other voices, a cop voice. "What else?"

Jimmy told him everything Mary had told him.

The question was: Had they really caught the killers? Or could they still be out there? Could they be somebody else?

Dill opened the briefcase. He flipped through some papers, but when he spoke it wasn't as if he was having to look at anything to refresh his memory. "They had knives and saws, including a Czech-made, Russian Army–issue bayonet, with blood and tissue, matches to victims one, seven, and eleven. Cleaned with paint thinner, but not enough. The girl up in Temescal Canyon. The schoolteacher out in Riverside, the woman but not the man. The old lady Jehovah's Witness in Santa Monica."

He handed Jimmy a police photo, color. A power tool.

"Milwaukee Sawzall. Cordless, so they could take it with them. A number fourteen drywall blade. Blood and organ tissue from the last victim on the blade."

Dill dealt out another photo. It was of a section of floor, kitchen floor from the looks of the linoleum, ripped up, a hidey-hole space between the floor joints exposed. And a tin box with the lid ajar.

"New blades, used blades," Dill went on. "Victims four, five, nine, and ten."

"How noisy is a Sawzall?"

"They never had to worry about noise."

"The news just said *saw*. Nobody said anything about power tools."

"There's always what's real and what's *news*. It's the way we play it. One advantage we keep."

Dill handed Jimmy some photocopies. "Receipt from the Sherman Way Home Depot for the Sawzall with the signature of one of the Russian brothers. Receipt from Home Depot for blades, the other brother. A second battery pack, the first brother again. The tin box is what a kind of Russian cookie comes in. They call them biscuits. The receipt is from a Russian specialty store in Glendale. They taste like they were baked under Khrushchev, but what do I know?"

"Why didn't they confess?" Jimmy said, handing the pictures back. "With all this against them."

"They usually do," Dill said. "I don't know. They got a famous lawyer. Early. They went quiet . . ."

"What do you have on the copycats?"

"Not as much, but enough. Whoever it is—and it's the same person both times—he's missing some of the details."

"Which means he isn't inside," Jimmy said, forgetting in the moment whose backyard he was in.

"Cops wouldn't kill like this," the vet detective said. "Cops like to *save* people. Even bad cops. Bad cops do things like kill the wives of dirty bookstore owners for five hundred bucks and all the videos they can carry. But even then, they think they're performing a service for society. Say what you want about those of us who are Jehovah's Witnesses, nobody thinks we should have our hearts cut out and left on the side of the road." The last was the cop's idea of a joke. He wasn't a Witness.

Dill sat back. "What's it say on the car door?"

"To protect and serve."

"That's right," the other said. "There's no *inside* in this one. These two are all the way *outside*. You can see it in their eyes. I don't know who the copycats might be, but the Russians are locked-down bad guys."

The cop saw what was on Jimmy's face, saw the way he was sitting, the way he had lined up the photos and photocopies on the low white plastic Costco table. Jimmy looked like a lawyer who wished he'd drawn a different case.

"But . . . but . . . but . . . But what?" Detective Dill said.

"What if the people killing now are the real ones? What if these Russian brothers were made up, set up?"

"Come here," Dill said, halfway out of the chair already.

Jimmy followed Dill into his bedroom. High angled ceiling, a ceiling fan on high, sounding frantic. Not much else. There was a king-sized bed with a pressed wood headboard and just a white sheet stretched tight across the mattress. And a single pillow.

Across from the bed was a tall dresser with a Costco TV/VCR combination on it, nineteen-inch. It opened its mouth and took the unlabeled VHS tape from Dill's hand.

Jimmy stood there. They both stood there, holding their beers, glad to have them once it started.

The Russian brothers had seen a few too many movies. Or too much "reality TV." Somehow they'd gotten the idea that what they were doing would make a good show, even if no one could ever see it. Or maybe some part of them wanted to make sure they'd be convicted, when the time came. Wanted it *certain*, that would be another theory.

Their shooting style favored the extreme close-up.

---

The cop and Jimmy Miles stood out in the front yard beside the Porsche at the curb. It was almost three in the morning.

"Sprinklers are going to come on in a minute here," Dill said.

"When do you work next?"

"Six. Third shift."

"So what should I do?" Jimmy said. "About this girl."

"Your sister."

"Got any ideas?" Jimmy said.

"You moved?"

Jimmy told him a limited version of where he'd gone.

"Stay there," Dill said. "There is more shit hidden in Angeles Forest than even God knows. Stay up there. Let her forget about it, or at least file it away. Kill your TV. Let the panic blow over. It'll come to trial."

Jimmy nodded. The scene felt so empty, so *desert*, it was hard to remember there were a couple of thousand others sleeping all around them. Norms.

"In my experience, people—and by 'people' I mean 'women'—are always afraid of the wrong things. Afraid when they shouldn't be, not afraid when they should be. Of course, when I said that to my wife one time, when we were out with some friends, she said, 'What I'm afraid of is twenty-odd more years of that rich of bullshit.' So there's that."

"What about the men?"

"They're afraid of everything," Dill said. "At least the ones I have any respect for."

It was still hot. The streetlights staggered down the streets in the sub-division were the yellow/orange kind, the kind that gave everything that sickly look city planners seem to prefer. Even the Porsche looked tired, out-of-date, sad, there in the driveway.

Jimmy was staring at something out in the road, something four or five feet long, stretched out, like a strip of shredded tire or something. There was another a few feet away.

"Those are rattlers," Dill said. "They like the heat soaked up in the asphalt all day. I used to run over them but then I . . ." He trailed off. "Live and let live. Some time of year, I forget when, they shed their skins. You find them under the bushes and hedges and shit. They look like the rubbers in the parking lots out at the beach."

Jimmy said, "Got any idea what's up with Sailors these days?" Dill hadn't been a Sailor all that long as these things went, four or five years, but he'd been on the streets as a cop a lot of years before that. One thing Sailors all did, the good and the bad ones, was respect experience.

"I was hoping you'd tell me," the cop said. "*I've* never seen it like this. People I trust say they haven't seen anything like this for a lot of years."

"Since when? When was the last time?"

"When the man stepped up, the Passing. Fifty years ago."

Jimmy dug in his pocket for the loose key to the Porsche.

"I know your man in black with the dog," Dill said.

It stopped Jimmy.

"They call him Kingman. For Kingman, Arizona. Bad town for a Sailor."

"He's a Sailor?"

"*Old* salt. Made his way out here twenty years ago."

"But he has a dog."

"I don't get it, either," Dill said. "Maybe it's the one dog in the world that likes us. Maybe it's a *Sailor* dog, something new. I hate new."

---

"What time is it?" Mary said when she felt him move in against her in bed.

"After midnight," Jimmy said.

"It was after midnight when I went to bed."

"That was the last song on the radio, coming up the road. 'After Midnight.'"

She made a sound like a laugh. "Don't wake me up," she said, dreamy.

# TWENTY-SIX

There was a place called the Pipe in Long Beach. Jimmy waited until late afternoon before he rode down out of Angeles Forest. There wasn't much use in going in earlier.

He figured he'd start at the sea, out on the edge, and work his way inland, looking for Kingman.

Just because. Because the son of a bitch had stood in his yard, looking up at his troubled girl in the kitchen window.

Because maybe he'd planted a gun in Jimmy's house, where Mary could find it.

Just because.

There was still a little light left in the sky. It was pretty, the last light of the day, the light of surrender, as night moved in. The light was pretty, but nothing else was. The Pipe was wetlands, soggy marsh littered with what floats, whatever is cast aside and floats. Sailors, a certain kind of them, lived down here in the hulls of beached boats, boats on their sides, demasted sailboats and the rusting iron skin of a trawler. The "leaders" would be there, the dominant ones. There was a chance Kingman would be among them.

There were different kinds of Sailors, different levels. *Ranks* wouldn't be the right term, because it would imply they were linked in service to some mission. In the end, Sailors were all just dealing with themselves, in it for themselves, trying to make sense of it. Even Jimmy Miles. Even Angel Figueroa.

But there was a kind of Sailor easy to spot: Walkers. Everybody said there were more of them in Los Angeles than almost any other city. Go figure, the one place where *nobody* walked. They'd lost all hope, given up, gone slack, checked out of the whole world of Good or Bad, and were a real danger because of it. The Pipe was always thick with them. Down here they tended to stand around fires, hard as it was to keep them going with everything wet, staring into the flames as if waiting for the fiery face of a god to appear, to tell them at last what to do.

"I'm looking for Kingman," he said, to anybody who would let their eyes meet his.

Jimmy didn't like doing this alone, but he hadn't been able to find Angel. He called him. He kept calling him. Angel's phone rang and rang. And he wasn't in his usual haunts. His men didn't know where he was, just that someone had come for him at noon.

There were a lot of ragged-looking Sailors down at the Pipe, shaking their heads *no*. But no Kingman, no black dog.

Jimmy cruised through Hollywood, down a back alleyway in the shadow of the Hotel Roosevelt, another gathering place for Sailors. The alleyway, not the hotel, which had gotten almost toney again. He was driving the Porsche. Angel had thrown a race-tuned exhaust on it. In the canyon of buildings, it provided a rolling thunder effect that made the men and the few women who were down here turn and look. He parked and got out.

Up close, the men looked like they were all on speed. Full-on jittery. Dilated pupils. Moving hands. It was what Angel had been talking about, the *jitterbugs* in the Sailor world.

"Who are you, Brother? What do you hear?" one of the men said before Jimmy could even get out of the car.

Two other men gathered closer, in anticipation of an answer.

No Kingman.

Jimmy drove by his house, stopped out on the street but didn't turn off the motor. One of Angel's men was staying there, in case anybody showed up who wasn't on the guest list. After a moment, some fingers came around the corner of the heavy drapes in the window in the front room, moved them a half inch.

"Water the plants out front, bud," he said, letting out the clutch to pull away. "They're looking a little brown."

The Sailors downtown that night were the worst off.

Same as it ever was.

Jimmy didn't come down here unless he had to. The downtown Sailor scene had a certain drama to it that he tried to avoid. And so far he had avoided it, except for the couple of times they had dragged him into it, into the arch ceremonial bullshit they reveled in. Their headquarters was an "abandoned" courtroom with its high soiled marble walls on the top floor of the old Hall of Justice building. On Spring Street.

Jimmy kept going right on past it. Even sped up a little.

He went in on foot. His hands were sweaty. It was a funky neighbor-hood. Sixth Street. He'd done what he could, put the Porsche right across from Cole's, a street-level, five-steps-down antique saloon with a bloodred mahogany bar and booths carved with the initials of traveling salesmen and USC frat boys from the thirties. But it was a Wednesday night and early yet, not even ten, and Cole's was still dead. The Porsche looked wide-eyed as he walked away from it.

He came east two blocks. He'd been down here enough to know it wasn't as dangerous as it looked. Most of the people whose eyes met yours weren't thinking what you thought they were, didn't want your watch, weren't trying to guess which pocket you kept your cash in, weren't draw-ing lots for your garments. The dangerous ones you probably never saw coming. Street people were mostly just people on a street.

He stopped in front of the hollow, dead building where he and Angel had climbed the stairs and found what they thought was the "home" of the man with the black dog, and the body of the North Hollywood street person who'd directed Jimmy there.

The House of Kingman.

The homemade video Dill had shown to Jimmy to close the deal with him had had the opposite effect. It had blown the deal apart, and just when Jimmy had the pen in hand, too, hovering over the long sideways line with his name under it. It didn't happen right away, not even on the ride home. It came later that night, or maybe came the same hour dawn came to the house in Angeles Forest, while Mary still slept beside him.

Jimmy knew something about movies. His mother was a star. His father was a director. There was a screening room in the house Jimmy was born into. A studio nanny pushed him around the Fox lot in a French perambulator. All of his parents' friends, and all of their enemies, were in the business: actors, directors, shooters, composers, editors.

*Editors.* What was missing were the two-shots. There were no shots of either one of the brothers and a victim in the same frame. The shot list: A brother alone. A victim alone, usually in close. A wide shot, pulling out, a brother looking down at the floor. An extreme close-up of an incision. Sometimes the brother would be looking at the camera, sometimes wav-ing it off. Sometimes there'd be a smile, a kind of sour smile that gave off a sex vibe. Naughty. There was one shot of blood on hands, in close. Hold-ing a gutting knife. *Someone's* hands.

There were no two-shots.

Jimmy was circling the base of the building, outside. The House of

Kingman. You could walk all the way around it, alleys on the sides and on the back, Sixth Street out front. He and Angel had come in from the back. Jimmy headed that way. He didn't think Kingman would still be there, but maybe there'd be somebody else inside who knew something. Or maybe there was some value to standing again over the spot where they'd found the body.

Where Jimmy had had to look at the face of someone who'd died because of him.

It was dark ahead. The light on the corner of the building was out. A black, dead bulb. (Shouldn't that be the ultimate version of a *stop*light?) But Jimmy had a light in his hand, his own light, a foot-and-a-half-long Maglite he'd thrown onto the other seat of the Porsche when he left the cabin to drive down into whatever was supposed to happen next. Half light, half club, a cop flashlight.

He came around the corner with the light. Somebody scurried away at the other corner of the back of the building.

There was a flash of blue.

"Brother!" Jimmy called out.

The door was closed. A metal fire door. Jimmy watched his hand reach out toward it.

A shoe crunching glass. A sound effect.

Behind him. He spun around.

The shape had already stopped. It spoke.

"Knock knock," Dill said.

Jimmy felt the way a Rhodesian Ridgeback looks, bowed up.

"Come on," the cop said, stepping forward out into a little more light. "There's nobody in there. Certainly not Kingman."

He turned and walked back up the alley toward Sixth. "Come on, let's get in out of the rain," Dill said. It hadn't rained in three months. Jimmy fell in behind him.

A black-on-black LAPD detective's Crown Vic was on the street.

"Get in," Dill said and got behind the wheel. Jimmy got in up front. He left his door open out onto the sidewalk. Cop cars don't have automatic dome lights. Nothing dings or talks.

"You been busy tonight," Dill said. "Forget about Kingman. I shouldn't have said anything."

Jimmy thought a second before he did it, but he began to spit out his doubts about the videotape. He only got two sentences in when Dill leaned forward and started the engine.

Jimmy closed his door, and they pulled away.

"I have the Porsche up here on the street," he said.

"It'll be taken care of," Dill said.

It was about the last thing Dill said as they drove across downtown to the 101 north. Traffic was light. Dill slid straight over to the inside lane and stayed there, rolled up to seventy, seventy-five.

All the way to Universal City. Maybe he was going to take Jimmy on the *Psycho* ride, take him in through the midnight VIP gate, buy him a churro.

They drove east on North Glenoaks Boulevard. And pulled into a motel, an old-style, single-story, U-shaped motor court.

A dark motel. With the sign off. Not even a No Vacancy.

A man dressed in LAPD blues but without a badge on his chest, stripped of anything that shined or named, stepped out of the office. On Dill's side of the car. Jimmy looked to his right and saw another cop next to the ice machine with a pistol in his hand, down at his side. They both wore body armor vests.

Jimmy liked drama as much as the next guy, but . . .

"What's this?"

"The Federovs."

"Here?"

"Live and in color."

"So who's in the special cells they built down at Terminal Island?"

"Russians all look alike," Dill said. "Actually, the Federov brothers aren't Russians. They're Ukrainians. That's one of the things that honks them off. So I make sure and call them Russians."

By then, they were out of the car and walking toward the back of the U. Another guard stood in front of the door to a unit.

They'd ripped out the partitions between three or four units across the back of the motel, taken them down to the studs, and pulled out the ceiling up to the rafters. They'd sprayed what was left of the framing flat black. The cage that held the two brothers was dead center in the space, built out of gate and handrail iron and metal mesh. And painted black. They'd left the motel carpet on the floor, the bathroom in the corner. The carpet was dirty green. Another guard was fussing over a coffeemaker in the corner, in what remained of a kitchenette.

The brothers were playing chess at a Formica table. They didn't look up until the door opened again, and the guard stepped outside for a second, on some signal from Dill.

"I brought a friend of yours to visit," Dill said. "He thinks you're being framed."

"Yah," one of the brothers said, the younger one, the bigger one. Everybody knew all about them.

"He *loves* Russians," Dill said.

"He's right," the other brother said. "Innocent. Not guilty."

"Leave us alone!" the first bellowed.

"Go ahead," Dill said to Jimmy. "Look them in the eye. You tell me."

"Yah!" the first brother said. "Innocent!"

And then he laughed.

When Jimmy came out, there was the Porsche, waiting for him. It was such a Sailor thing to do.

Jimmy opened the door.

"So. You all right, Brother?" Dill said, right behind him. "Did you see what you needed to see?

"Yeah," Jimmy said. And he almost meant it.

What did he know about cracking a case?

Or even about guilt or innocence?

———————

When Jimmy made it to the gate at the end of the long private road up in Angeles Forest, he yanked up the parking brake and killed the headlights but left the motor running. He got out. The gate wasn't automatic. There wasn't a remote control. In fact, he'd locked the gate when he left, a length of chain and a padlock. He unlocked it, shoved it open. He stood there a moment in the open gateway. After being in the city and then in the traffic, it all looked really dark. He thought he heard something out in the trees. The woods were thick all around him. He listened for the sound, but it didn't repeat.

He'd had enough of noises, enough of suspicions.

Mary was in a deep sleep, but a gentle one. In the bedroom. With just a low light on beside the chair. She'd felt safe enough to turn out all the lights in the rest of the house and go to sleep in the bedroom. He pulled the wool Pendleton Indian striped blanket up over her shoulder, to send her even deeper into that peace.

He was about to sit in the chair at the end of the bed, to read away what was left of the night, when he heard their footsteps on the deck.

Loud. There was no intention to be quiet. Loud enough to make Mary stir.

He leaned over her, awakened her the rest of the way.

"Get in the closet," he said when her eyes came open.

There was a sliding door from the living room out to the deck, to the pool. He could see them out there as he crossed the room.

Six of them.

He opened the door and stepped out.

He had already recognized one of the shapes: Angel. Detective Dill was next to Angel. Even in the dim light, Jimmy could see that Dill had an embarrassed look on his face. It was harder to say what the look on Angel's face meant.

The blue edge around them was vibrant, all of them. This was official business.

Angel waited for Jimmy to look at him directly. When Jimmy did, Angel's face said, *It's all right.*

Whether it was or not.

The other men were less . . . conflicted.

There was a round man, cartoonishly large, Orson Welles–size. And in a suit with a vest, like some Daddy Warbucks. They were in a semicircle, facing him, like a tribunal. Next to the fat man was a man who had *cop* written all over him, but *ranking officer*. Next to him was a man, not small, not big, who didn't give off much.

And then there was the biggest man.

Who wore a hat. Whose face, save the eyes, was covered by a wool scarf, like this was London. Who even wore gloves, gray doeskin, lest his hands somehow give him away.

It was Walter E. C. "Red" Steadman, who in a way was their king. It was the first time Jimmy had ever been face-to-face with him.

It turned out Steadman was just there for the visual effect. And the scent of almost ultimate power he gave off. Steadman nodded to the non-descript man, who delivered the word.

"You are not incorrect in your conclusions," the mouthpiece said, "but this matter suits our larger purposes at this particular point in time."

A hoot owl picked now to hoot. *"Who?"*

"And now it's over," the nondescript man finished. "Your part in it, at any rate. It is over. Do you understand?"

He said the last with a surprising kindness.

"What about the threats?" Jimmy said.

"There were no threats," the high-rank cop said.

Red Steadman looked at the ranking cop to silence him. Jimmy noticed that Steadman didn't move his neck, as if he'd been injured somewhere along the line. Or as if he was very old. The "chief" wouldn't speak again.

"*Who?*" the owl said again.

"It's over," the mouthpiece said. "Anything that happens now will not happen to you."

Jimmy looked like he was about to jump in with something.

"Or to yours," the man added.

"Why are the two Russians going along with it?" Jimmy said. "Just curious."

No one thought it was necessary to answer.

"You should, in the morning, go back to your house," the mouthpiece finished. "Stop trying to see the bigger picture. Just live for yourself, for as long as you are here."

It was a line Sailors told each other, the last phrase anyway.

The nondescript man turned to Angel. "And you, too. Bless you, Brother."

Jimmy wouldn't let it go. "Why do Sailors want people murdered, and other people, Norms, panicked, killing themselves? Why do you want all these people to die?"

Jimmy was looking Steadman in the eye when he said it.

This time, there wasn't any thought any of them would answer. Their eyes had moved to the house behind him.

Mary stood in the open doorway.

She ran out of the house and past them.

Jimmy came after her. "Mary!"

It was steep, it was downhill, it was dangerous. And the woods had gotten even darker.

# TWENTY-SEVEN

There is an angry, ugly rhythm to an argument. You don't have to hear the actual words; the sounds are enough. They're like blows in a fight. Three or four jabbing syllables and then the louder thud of the knockout punch. But the other isn't knocked out. Not yet. It's never over that quickly, no early-round knockdowns. There's always more. You rephrase. You repeat. Redundancy is a given. You aren't judged on grammar, maybe on the number of fricatives and glottal stops. The percussion. Or the footwork, the angry, ugly dance of it. There's a reason arguments end in violence, in hurled glassware, in slammed doors, in slaps, in gunshots. Punctuation is everything.

Dr. Marc Hesse slammed the bedroom door on his way out, and Mrs. Mary Hesse came to the window and looked out at the night, tears running down her cheeks like commas.

Jimmy was across the street but fifty yards away, close enough to hear the angry, ugly sounds but not to see those tears. So maybe he just filled in the blanks, seeing what he wanted, what he needed to see. Just enough to hate Hesse.

The other night in front of the Victorian apartment house, with the Greek father and Machine Shop packed into the Porsche, Jimmy had remembered the ride with his own father when he was ten or eleven, when his father told him he and Jimmy's mother were divorcing, that speech that begins, "Sometimes a mother and a father grow apart . . ." Jimmy remembered something else. When he was sixteen, he told his mother what his father had said that night, and what she had said back to Jimmy was, *"Les chaînes de mariage sont si lourdes qu'il faut deux pour les porter. Et parfois trois."* They were in a car, too, the huge white Chrysler 400 that was her last car, top down, somewhere in Hollywood. "The chains of matrimony are so heavy it takes two to carry them. And sometimes three."

The garage door came up. The Mercedes's red taillights and white backup lights flared, and the SUV charged out, the automatic radio antenna extending so fast it dragged across the last of the garage door hurrying to get out of the way. Mary stood witness in the upstairs window, in the master suite, over the garage. It was a big window, with true divides, beveled leaded glass, black frames dividing her into eight-by-tens.

Jimmy hated him for making her cry, for bringing her to the window to watch him go. He hated him.

Given what he was about to do, it was a useful emotion.

A sound made Mary turn toward the door. A woman stepped into the bedroom, a young woman wearing a dark suit, a uniform of some kind. A nanny? They spoke. Something was determined. Mary came out of the house a few minutes later, a sweater over her shoulders. Jimmy stepped back into the deeper shadows. The street they lived on, Alcatraz Lane, went two ways down the hill. She started off to the right, toward San Francisco, toward the view rustling through the gaps in the evergreens. Jimmy went the other way. All the streets out on the point of Tiburon emptied down onto the drive that circled the tip of the peninsula and led to the village.

Mary walked along the fronts of the shops and restaurants. It was eight or nine. The shops were closed, the restaurants busy. With the indoor smoking ban, every place now had tall stools and tables out front, where the happiest people seemed to gather. Or at least the loudest. Jimmy was a hundred yards behind her, coming up the same side of the street. He saw her look over at them, the happy, loud people. She kept on walking.

There was a compact marina just past the traffic roundabout and the heart of the village. She walked out to the end of a dock. It should have gotten cooler out on the dock, with the wind off the water, but somehow it felt warmer. Maybe it was just Jimmy. The air smelled fresher here than on the other side of the Bay.

Mary stood there with her back to him. There was the sound of the wind, the sound of the boat tackle banging against itself, but still, she had to have heard his footsteps on the planks, coming toward her. Didn't she? But she didn't turn. She must have known it was him. At last. Again.

When he was five feet away, she turned.

He stopped.

There was a moment. The sliver of a moon over her shoulder clicked into a new phase.

"What are you doing here?" she said.

He didn't say anything, let her make up her own answer.

"This isn't a good night," she began, as vague as that.

He crossed the last few feet between them. Could be she moved at least a step closer to him. He put his arms around her and drew her in. There was some exotic perfume behind her ear, somewhere on her, that he almost knew, though not from their time together. Not from the past, at least not *their* past.

He waited. And then he kissed her.

He hadn't kissed anyone in months. When it's that way, you could forget how smooth lips were, how warm. How unlike any other skin.

"Besides that," she said. Her voice had changed into something more comfortable. "What are you doing here? San Francisco."

Jimmy wished she'd asked something else, almost anything else. He wished he had it in him to lie. "Angel had a friend," he said. He noticed the tense. "A girl, a girlfriend maybe. She had just broken up with somebody else, came up here. She was kind of messed up. I was keeping an eye on her."

Mary waited.

"She killed herself," Jimmy said. "Down on Fisherman's Wharf."

"That's sad," Mary said. "That's sad." It was something else he had remembered about her, the way she repeated lines sometimes. She pulled away from him, turned back toward the water, the lights across. It was as if the word about Lucy had broken her will about something. "There have been so many of them lately. It's all people are talking about."

After a moment, she said, "That's something I never thought of. As bad as it ever got."

Jimmy knew that wasn't true. "Let's get a drink," he said.

She turned to him. "We can't do that," she said.

"We'll go somewhere. I have the car."

She looked at him a long time, judging him, he thought, and wondered on what count. How. Was she judging him for *then*, or for now?

"Come on," she said, and started past him up the dock.

They walked over to the last pier. There were three fingers of docks and slips. Jimmy just followed her lead. Halfway there, he took her hand, but she let go after only a few seconds, a few steps. He sensed she was angry, but also sensed that it wasn't entirely focused. It was a rising anger looking for something to form around, something to be about. Something to beat her fist against.

She walked out to the end of the last dock. It was where the big sailboats were, thirty-footers and up.

One of them had her name on it.

*Queen Mary.*

The cockpit was open, uncovered. It was a Swan, a beautiful Swan, a forty-five footer. She climbed over the lifeline and into the cockpit. There didn't look to be any live-aboards in the boats in the neighborhood, but there were voices from somewhere close. Voices over the water, that sound. Jimmy looked until he found them, two or three guys in the cockpit of a Hunter 38 out near the head of the next pier, the glow of a cigar or two and the good smell of it winging over. Here behind the curve of the little bay there was barely any wind. Jimmy stepped over the lifeline onto the boat.

Mary was unlocking the cabin. She slid the panel door up and out of the way and stepped down. After a minute, she reappeared with a bottle of wine and two glasses. Plastic glasses, but stemware, a nice shape. Boat drinks.

"I drink a lot of wine now," she said and handed him the bottle and a corkscrew to open it with. She plopped down in the seat beside the wheel and pulled her legs up and wrapped her arms around them. All the years that had passed since they'd been together in L.A. blew away.

Jimmy opened the wine. When it popped, there was a response from the guys on the boat across the way. Maybe, "Cheers!"

"I don't know them," Mary said. "They came in a few days ago, sailing down the coast, I think."

Jimmy got that she was also saying, *I wouldn't be here if I knew them.*

But at least she seemed to have lost the anger. "You know what you said yesterday?" she said. "About how it was still so strong?"

He gave her a glass, found a place to stow the bottle, and sat beside her. He didn't know if it was a question she meant for him to answer or not.

She seemed to finish her own thought by drinking half of the glass of wine. Punctuation.

She took his hand now. He brought their hands up and kissed the back of hers, something he never would have done if anyone could have seen. He was different when they were together. Always.

He tasted the wine. It was a rich Chianti.

"Are you cold?" she said.

"No."

"People from L.A. are always cold up here, always talking about it."

"I hate L.A.," Jimmy said. He didn't mean it.

"That's not true."

"I'm never going back."

She surprised him by taking him seriously, like the girl she used to be.

It was something else she used to do, something else that made her different from all the rest.

"You know, it never stopped for me," he said.

The sailing-down-the-coast guys laughed loud and rough at something.

Mary moved away from him just enough for him to notice. He followed her eyes. She was looking at the dots of house lights out on the point, above the village, or maybe she was reacting to the intrusion of the guys on the other dock.

"Is the boat yours or his?"

"Mine. He never comes down. He bought it, but he forgets it's even here."

There was another laugh from the men across the way, as if her last line was the punch line to the one about the cardiologist and his restless young wife.

Jimmy stood. He put his wineglass in the teak holder next to the wheel and went forward.

Mary thought he was going to say something to the other sailors. "Jimmy," she said.

But then she saw him kick off his slip-on shoes.

The *Queen Mary*, this *Queen Mary*, was stern-out, its back to the Bay. Jimmy stepped off the boat onto the dock with the balance of a dancer, already getting into the rhythm. He unhitched the bowline with a twirling figure eight, like a cowboy with a lariat. He stepped back onto the boat and curled the line in a circle on the deck, one-handed, another trick. He lifted the white fenders up and over the rail as he came aft and undid the second sheet and the stopper line. He put his foot against the dock and gave it a gentle push. The planks, the cap of the piling backed away.

Mary just watched him through all this. There seemed to be pleasure in it for her, whether it was because of a memory or just the pleasure for women that comes when men finally act. And become themselves, or at least what they think of as themselves. She took the key out of her sweater pocket, a single key on a chain with a fat marshmallow float. She held it out to him. He put it in the ignition and turned it over a click, but not enough to start the engine. He snapped on the nav lights.

He hoisted the main while the stern was still coming around, the boat sliding away from the dock, all from his one push. When she was around, with the sail still just coming up, it caught wind, and the boat started forward across the flat marina water splattered with reflected lights.

It was all pretty slick as moves go, slick and quiet, no engine, and when Jimmy sailed by the men aboard the Hunter on the other dock, they tapped their beer bottles against the rub rail in approval.

Mary went below. She was gone a minute. When she came back to the cockpit, she had on full weather gear, jacket and pants. Everything but a nor'wester hat.

Jimmy had gotten them out past the tip of Belevedere Island already, headed toward the Golden Gate, Sausalito off to the right.

"So, we're making a passage," he said, about her change of clothes. "Hawaii."

"Catalina," she said. That's where they used to sail.

She settled back in beside him. He was standing behind the wheel, one hand down to steer. The sail began to luff a little. Without thinking about it, Mary leaned forward and pulled in the sheet looped around the winch and cleated it.

"Who's sailing this boat?" Jimmy said.

"You are, sir," she said.

And then they didn't say anything for thirty minutes.

Not a word.

Not a memory, not a question.

Not a promise, not a hope, not a regret, though their heads must have been filled with all of those things.

Night sailing. Jimmy didn't know anything like it, anything that combined the serenity, the mysticism, the calm, with that underlying sense of danger, that sense of things that *could* go bump in the night. There was the bright fire of the City to his left, the rust red arc of the bridge ahead, and, beyond it, a kind of darkness not duplicated anywhere else, only over water. There it was, all of it, wide-screen. The wind was light, but there was enough of it to raise some chop, to occasionally throw up a burst of spray, like a handful of confetti. Everything was warmer than Jimmy would have expected it to be. Maybe it was the tide, the famous tide that caught the Alcatraz escapees all those years ago. So the cops said, anyway. The Bay seemed empty. Maybe it was just a trick of the mind. Jimmy wondered when it was most crowded.

He also wondered what would happen if he just kept going.

He stayed on the same track until just shy of the Golden Gate when he came about. It was then that Mary came up beside him at the wheel. She reached across him, put her hands over his. He thought first that it was a tender gesture, but then he realized she wanted the helm. He pulled his hands out from under hers.

She changed his course. She changed his trim on the sail. The boat immediately picked up speed, moved more cleanly through the water. He found his Chianti and sat with his back to the cabin, sailing backward so he could look at her, with the lights behind her, almost like a corona. It was something else he remembered about her, the way she didn't just sit there, even when she was just sitting there. She was always moving. It was like each moment made him replace some soft-focus sense of her from memory with the reality of her. Of Mary. Now what was before him was vivid and strong and undeniable. Here.

He wanted to give her whatever she wanted.

He had *that* feeling.

Jimmy followed her eyes, looked over his shoulder. Ahead there was a large fishing trawler, halfway across the Bay, heading out from Oakland probably, ablaze with deck lights, covered with fast-moving shapes, crew, draped with nets on cranes. It was still a half mile away but bearing down, an intersecting course, insistent enough, big enough, to stir something in the blood.

Mary kept her hand on the wheel as she dug in the cabinet under the seat and came out with a yellow-and-black battery lantern. She pointed it up at the sail, not turning it on until it was aimed away from their eyes, to preserve their night vision.

The sail sprang into whiteness, tall as a billboard.

"Let them see us," she said.

Even from a third of a mile out, they heard the change in the pitch of the other's engines. A big thing had yielded.

On the lee of Alcatraz, the wind slacked. Mary eased the boat up into it, to catch what she could. Jimmy tried to suss which cluster of lights ahead was Tiburon, the marina, the restaurants. He thought she was turning for home.

But he was wrong.

She reached forward and started the engine, waited to see that it caught, then started forward to drop the main. Jimmy reached over to steady the wheel, though it was steady enough on its own. He could tell that she was used to sailing alone, even a boat this big. She stood by the boom on the foredeck, atop the cabin, pleating the sail, left right left, as it collapsed onto itself, then looping and tying the stays when it was down. She came back to the helm, pushed the throttle forward a little.

She powered out from under the sweep of the light on Alcatraz, out of its reach, then across a sudden section of chop.

To Angel Island.

It was black, had a mountain in the center of it, was fifty times the size of Alcatraz. Mary steered to the windward side but cruised on past the cove where the overnighters were moored and the campers gone ashore.

She found their own blank section of water. She steered into the wind and cut the engine back to idle. The last of the momentum spent itself. The boat drifted its last foot. They stopped. She listened. They were alone.

"You want to drop an anchor?" Jimmy asked.

"Yeah," she said.

He went forward and let down the anchor, hand over hand, because it was quieter than the electric winch.

She backed up the boat until the hook set. She shut off the engine.

When he came back to the cockpit, she was drinking the last of her glass of wine.

"You were smoking when I saw you in the park," she said, so quiet he could hardly hear her, right next to her.

He sat beside her. She put her head back.

"I bought a pack of Lucky Strikes, on the road, on the way up here," he said. "Something made me think of you. And Luckies. That first night on the Strip."

He didn't tell her about all the other times something made him think of her these last few days.

"I wondered what you would remember."

"The house up above Altadena, in Angeles Forest," he said.

"I would hope you'd remember better times," she said.

*Not the end of it,* Jimmy thought. *Everything before.*

"That isn't what I remembered about you and me on the way up here, but . . ." He stopped himself. "What do you remember?" he said.

"The way we were together," Mary said. "What we were like. The way people always said we were exactly the same, just alike, and we weren't at all, but there was something when we were together that made it seem that way. That made me better."

"Do you want the rest of the wine?" he said.

She shook her head. Chianti. It was what they always drank. Then. His first night in San Francisco, his unnamed, unseen admirer had bought him a glass in the bar on Columbus. Another thing that sent him down this road, aimed him toward this. Could it have been her? Could she have seen him then? Why wouldn't she say so now?

He leaned over her. He could feel the heat coming off of her. He

remembered pulling the blanket up across her shoulders as she slept in
the cabin above Altadena. The last seconds . . . The last seconds before it
all changed, before she saw just enough of who he was, who he really was,
to rend things. *Forever*, he thought, *until now*. He put his hand on the side
of her neck. He could feel her carotid, her pulse. His wrist was against the
cold knife of the tab of the zipper.

He pulled it down, the zipper. It made a sound like a murmur.

She lifted her back for him.

His hand moved across her breastbone, found another pulse. She wasn't
wearing anything under the weather gear.

They moved from the cockpit to the forward cabin. Inside. The physi-
cal part was as good as it had always been. Unthinking, natural, confident,
unequivocal. The expected and the surprising at the same time. It had
always been that way with them, even when they were on the run in L.A.
and scared, up in the Angeles Forest, maybe especially then.

The intervening years, gone. At least in this.

When it was over, they talked, or Mary talked and Jimmy listened. He
listened to her and studied her face in the indefinite light, while the boat
rocked, like a car alone on a good night road. (Was it only the light of the
City, coming across the water?) Her face. She'd changed more than he'd
thought. How could it be otherwise? Years had passed. And she wasn't
like him. He had to keep reminding himself of that. Of course time would
change her. The shape of her face was the same, but her eyes seemed
stiffened, the line of her nose drawn straighter. He thought again she'd
probably had some preemptive cutting and sewing, the kind doctors' wives
get. He wanted to reach out to touch her cheek but held back.

She was talkative. She seemed caught up in purpose. That was something new. Before, after sex, in the L.A. days, she'd been soft, conforming,
quiet but not sullen, a perfect definition of *easy*. Making love then seemed
to take her out of the world. Tonight it seemed to have set her up to want
something more from it.

That, he didn't understand.

"I want us to be together," she said to him.

Mary left the cabin, went aft, naked.

She looked back at him. And then just stepped off the stern. It made
the smallest of sounds, the water receiving her.

He couldn't help but think about the suicides.

He stood looking down at her, standing on the aft deck.

"Come on," she said. He was naked, too.

He knew why she'd gone into the water, that she had to wash the sex off of her before she went home, exchange its scent for some other, for something innocent. Salt for salt.

He had understood that much.

———————

Mary's nanny, or whatever she was, stood at the head of the dock, waiting for them as they walked away from *Queen Mary*. Her suit, in this setting, seemed almost nautical, a first mate's uniform. She was almost at attention.

She pulled Mary close and said something. Mary turned and cast Jimmy a complicated look and then started away, with the young woman falling in behind her, leaving him there.

# TWENTY-EIGHT

A white rose in a vase filled with milk.

It was waiting for Jimmy on the table in front of the bay window in the living room of the hotel suite when he came back from Tiburon. At midnight.

The thorns hadn't been trimmed.

It felt equal parts threat and seduction.

Jimmy called downstairs for the bellman.

"What is this?"

The bellman squirmed, once he was standing there before it. "I don't know, sir?" he said.

"You didn't bring it up?"

"No, sir?"

"The bellman before you?"

"No, sir?"

"Stop turning everything into a question," Jimmy said. "I'm confused enough."

"Yes, sir. No, sir, I didn't bring it up. And I've been here since . . . yesterday. Someone called in sick."

Its scent filled the room. You couldn't avoid it.

"Do you want me to take it away, sir?"

"No, I like it," Jimmy said.

"Yes, sir," the boy said. "It's very . . . white."

"You don't have to understand something to enjoy it."

"No, sir."

Jimmy gave him a twenty. The bellman started for the door.

"You were here all day, all night? Is that what you said?"

The bellman stopped. "Yes, sir."

"Anybody leave any messages for me?"

"No, sir. Not that I know of."

"My friend in the room next door, have you seen him?"

"No, sir."

"When you go back down, see if anybody called."

"There were no messages. I was at the desk."

"Thanks." Jimmy gave him another twenty. He turned for the bedroom, to change clothes.

"I believe they came up from the kitchen, sir," the bell said, when it looked like the scene was over.

"What came up from the kitchen?"

"The flowers. I didn't actually see them, but I understand they had their own delivery persons. For all of them."

"Other people got these?"

"Yes, sir. The men on the sixteenth floor. Above you. From L.A."

Jimmy had half talked himself into the idea that the flower had come from Mary.

He took a shower. A midnight shower. He was going to go look for Angel. He felt bad about the way he'd left him the last time he'd seen him, never even looked back as he walked away from him down on the docks on the second stretch of waterfront, the old navy base or whatever it was. When Jimmy had followed the two cute girls into the mess hall full of women.

Over the downpour of the shower, he heard a thud, the outside door slamming closed. It shook the wall. He listened, but there wasn't anything else. He turned off the water.

He'd left the bathroom door standing open, the door into the bedroom. He wrapped a robe around himself and came out.

The door to the living room was open. There was Angel.

Angel stood looking at the rose.

"What's this shit?" Angel said, feeling Jimmy's presence behind him.

"I thought maybe you'd know," Jimmy said.

"Did *she* send it?" Angel was changed. He turned with a look on his face Jimmy had never seen before. He looked like he'd been beat up. And left ready to dish some out.

Angel didn't look like Angel.

"I'm sorry I left you back down there, at the navy base, or whatever it was," Jimmy said. After the scene with the women in the dining hall, he'd looked for Angel but couldn't find him.

"Is that what you're sorry for?"

Jimmy didn't say anything.

Angel advanced on him, shoved him. "Is that what you're sorry for?" he said again.

"What happened? Where have you been?"

Angel pushed him again. Jimmy stayed on his feet.

"You go chasing after *her*, and Lucy dies!"

It hit Jimmy like an iron bar, hurt all the more because Angel had waited so long to throw it in Jimmy's face. Jimmy didn't say anything, didn't try to counterpunch. Because Angel was right. Once Jimmy had seen Mary, everything else had fallen away. He had wrapped himself in the past from then on, walked those streets again, not these. He had looked for her, not for Lucy. He worried about her, not Lucy. Before long Lucy had her new best friends whispering in her ear, and he was glad. Let *them* take care of her. He had stood by and watched a slow-motion murder. Was it only in that moment, standing there in his hotel room, that he was able to admit what was obvious, that the two women were agents of . . . Of *what*? Of something that wanted death.

And that he had stood by and watched it, like it was slow-motion crash test footage, projected drive-in style onto the end of a building. Onto Pier 35.

"Tell me what you know," Angel said. "About Lucy. What happened to her?" Angel was shorter than Jimmy, but somehow now he loomed over him. "All of it." His fists were still clenched at his sides.

So Jimmy told him.

He told him all of it. About the first day, about Sexy Sadie and then Polythene Pam outside the Golden Gate gift shop, felt foolish using the nicknames, but what else was he going to say? The woman in the yellow dress, matching purse? The cutie in the too-short skirt and Doc Martens? He could have taken the trouble that first day to find out their names, but he was content calling them Beatles names, from *The White Album*. Because that was the trip he was on. He told Angel the real deal on the two women, how they'd started out looking like helpmates for Lucy, sympathetic ears, but then transmuted into something else. Into the opposite. (He left out the part about not figuring it out in time.) He told Angel about the last night when he had seen Lucy with the two of them, down at Fisherman's Wharf, the night the man had been cleaved in two by the streetcar. On the suicide list, it would have been number . . . *What was it?* He even told Angel about the second time he'd tailed Lucy and the women to the grass out on Tiburon, how he never looked over at Lucy again once he'd seen Mary and her boy playing fifty yards away.

That day.

---

They were in the Porsche, Jimmy and Angel, just driving, a loop around the fingerprint of the City, the perimeter, then into the center, driving nowhere, until most of Lucy's story had been told. It was after two.

Angel had lost his anger, or buried it. "The radio is better here," he said. "Why is that?"

"Everything is better," Jimmy said. "I think that every time I come here."

"Then, after a while, you start missing L.A."

"I start missing L.A."

"Everything is too *free* here, that's the problem," Angel said.

Jimmy looked over at him.

"Everything comes too easy," Angel said. "Back home, you have to *earn* everything. Work for it, fight for it. A lungful of good air, a piece of shade, something green. Somebody nice. Here it's like they just give it to you."

Jimmy had told Angel everything about Lucy, everything he had, even about the day in the waterfront park when it was Lucy and the women and Mary. But he hadn't said anything about *Queen Mary*, about the night sail, about where he'd been just a few hours ago.

He was still trying to figure out what it meant.

Jimmy stopped at the top of a hill. It was the rise above the Victorian on Central. He hadn't realized he was headed here until he turned the last corner, looping around little Buena Vista Park. He was on autopilot.

"This is the apartment," he said. "Lucy's."

Angel got out of the car, gently closed the door behind him. He looked across at the top-floor windows. There was a light on. In the living room.

"Who's in it now?"

"I don't know," Jimmy said. "It belongs to a lady two doors down the street. Or she manages it. Lucy got the key from her. And the combination to the alarm, which Lucy never set again. I never talked to the woman, the landlady, never found out what the connection to Lucy was. The light's probably just on a timer or something."

A single table lamp burned in the foyer of the Catholic Home, a light that seemed to say, *We're here, anytime.* Jimmy wondered if it was true, if the door was unlocked, if they'd come if you rang, even now, at two in the morning.

"Across the street that's some kind of home for pregnant girls."

Angel turned to look at the home, but not for long. A two-second look.

Angel had seen enough. He got back in.

Jimmy rolled on down the street, not even starting the engine. Quiet. He stopped at the corner. Haight and Central. He looked left.

"There's a guy, white hair, ponytail, lives above the store."

"Yeah?" Angel said, looking over.

"If I was back home, I'd think he was a Sailor. The kind that watches everything. Reports in."

"Yeah."

"Except he's got a dog, kind with the black tongue."

"You never know," Angel said, uninterested.

Jimmy turned left on Haight Street, drove by the coffee place where Lucy had had her "date" with Machine Shop. While Polythene Pam watched. Jimmy spotted the culty girls again, the "sisters" who held hands, the wispy-dress girls from the other night down at the shipyard. Tonight they were hanging with the central casting hippies, the Sailor hippies, at the mouth of an alley. The leader with the Vandyke, Shakespeare in his pointed shoes and his bells, gave them the old *I know you* smile as they passed.

"He may be a Brother," Angel said. "Hippie Boy. Something about him."

Jimmy looked up in the mirror. One of the sisters was watching him go with an imploring look. Jimmy wondered why.

"Sailors are all acting hinky up here, too," Angel said.

"Yeah."

They drove by the black house a few blocks over, down on the Panhandle. Jimmy pulled to the curb.

"What's this?" Angel said. "Besides about the weirdest house I ever saw."

"One of the girls I told you about who hung out with Lucy lives here. Pam. Or at least I tracked her back here."

"It's *black*, right?"

"Yeah, I came back in daytime, hoping it was purple."

So they made the loop, hit the highlights, did the tour. The Lucy tour. The apartment on Central, the coffee place, the black house. They'd already cruised by the place where she'd died, Fisherman's Wharf, Pier 35. It was what Jimmy should have done the first night when Angel came in on the Amtrak Coast Starlight, would have if it wasn't for his mind being elsewhere.

They had the top down on the Porsche. They kept hearing sirens. Echoing. In a city built on hills, sound moves curiously. They stopped at a blind intersection, hearing the wail. Both of them looked left, but then it came in from the right, two city ambulances, racing west, nose to tail.

Jimmy took Van Ness and then Mason and drove out along the water to Fort Point, not because Lucy had ever been there but because he'd run out of places to go.

Except for the morgue. Which was where Jimmy already knew he would end the chapter.

Fort Point. A cop stopped them in the parking lot before they even made it close to the redbrick fort, raising a hand. He was just standing there, no car, nothing. His uniform wasn't even all there. He looked as if he'd come over from home on his bicycle. Extra duty.

"What's up?" Jimmy said.

"Private party," the cop said.

It was a quarter mile away, whatever it was. At the far end of the parking lot under the rumbling undercarriage of the bridge there were a couple of buses, curved metallic shapes catching the light. You couldn't see much of anything else from here. A few knots of people.

The officer leaned over and looked into the interior of the car, just enough for Jimmy to catch the scent on him, the marker. A Sailor cop.

"What year is this?" the cop said. "Sixty-five, sixty-six?"

"Sixty-four," Jimmy said. "Three fifty-six C. The first 911s came along in sixty-six."

"Sweet."

"We'll just turn around," Jimmy said, and eased forward.

"Have a nice night," the cop said.

But instead of turning around, Jimmy went straight. Gunned it. Charged toward the far end of the lot like it was a gymkhana in a shopping center parking lot. The cop shook his head but didn't run after them, didn't unholster his service piece, didn't even radio ahead.

"Guy just flipped me off," Jimmy said, watching in the rearview.

Sitting there were two old-style streamline buses, one in front of the other. Polished aluminum. Without markings. People were disembarking, orderly, in line, joining those who'd already stepped off.

Blue people.

"Those are Chick Warren's buses," Angel said. "Tito Nava did the roll and pleat on the seats. They're tricked out. Blue lights in the headliners."

"They're all L.A. Sailors," Angel said. "What are *they* doing here?"

Another group watched the new arrivals, from a distance, standing together, silent. Not blue, most of them, but on fire in their own way. San Francisco Sailors.

"Field trip, I don't know," Jimmy said. "It doesn't involve us."

He popped the clutch and roared out of there. The SFPD cop stepped out of their way with a sweeping gesture, like a wiseass matador.

––––––––––––

There was a helicopter overhead, a news helo.

There was a line of ambulances, like a parade, lights spinning, splashing light onto the buildings that surrounded it. There were already spectators on the sidewalks.

The morgue.

"What's this?" Angel said.

"I got a call," Jimmy said. "They're shipping Lucy's body out in the morning. To Paso Robles."

It was Angel's turn to look like he'd been struck between the eyes.

Jimmy said, "But I don't know what all this is."

He parked, got out. Angel took a minute in the front seat, alone, then got out, too.

"Maybe you don't want to do this," Jimmy said.

Angel just shook his head.

"She'll be dressed up and everything," Jimmy said. "A guy here took care of her. A friend of Shop's."

They had to walk past the line of ambulances. There were five or six of them, waiting, engines running, lights rotating like idling helicopter blades. Every thirty seconds, the news copter came round again with that thudding Vietnam sound. It hurt the head. It felt like being inside a lawn mower.

Duncan Groner was on the loading dock. When they got closer, up to the ambulance at the head of the line, they could see the first of the bodies.

Wrapped in white, like mummies. Head to toe.

Groner waved to Jimmy. The old reporter was trying for cool and collected, but the story had him excited. The lights from all the ambulances made him look like he'd been doused in blood, standing there.

"What happened?" Jimmy said.

"*Eighteen*," Groner said. "Eighteen of them."

"What happened?"

"A cult," Groner said. "Over on Fulton Street. They have a house, a four-story Victorian, five bedrooms, four to a room. A flying saucer–tethering pylon on the roof, everything inside painted white, like John and Yoko."

A wrapped body was rolled past and through the double doors. A wheel on the gurney squeaked. The body was small.

"The youngest was sixteen, the oldest twenty-eight, except for their maximum leader. He'll be bringing up the rear. He and his lovely assistant, Rita."

"Suicides?" Jimmy said.

"Drink the Kool-Aid," Groner said. "The cosmos awaits."

Jimmy looked at the spectators across the street, saw a familiar face or two. When he turned back, Angel wasn't there.

"What are you doing here?" Groner said, but Jimmy was already headed inside.

The latest suicides had brought out the senior coroners. And deputy coroners and body probers and morticians and, already, politicians in suits. Angel stood in the middle of them, lost.

The late-shift Sailor mortician named Hugh was there, Machine Shop's buddy. He and Jimmy saw each other. Hugh raised his hand, high, like a kid in class. Jimmy led Angel over to him.

"It's kind of wack here, but I already had her out," Hugh said. "I put her in the D Room."

Angel had a freaked-out look in his eyes.

"Come on," Jimmy said. "Then we'll get out of here."

There was a commotion behind them, at the pneumatic doors, which kept trying to close but never got a break. Another body had come in on a gurney. This one wasn't skinny, but he, too, was wrapped like a mummy. And tight, as if this was some ultimate spa treatment. Some final reduction. The cult's leader. Groner walked alongside, enjoying all this more than was becoming. Rolling in immediately behind the fat man was, just a guess, Rita. Whose wrap could not fully blunt her curves.

As Jimmy and Angel walked down the hallway, away from the action, the volume came down.

From the many to the one.

The black linoleum was shined to an absurd pitch, the way it is in prisons, that shine that can only come from people with all the time in the world. It was like walking on obsidian in some Egyptian temple.

Here was the D Room.

The door was closed but unlocked. The lights were on. It was the barest room in the world. The room at the end of the world.

She was covered. On a wooden table.

Propped against her hip was a hand-lettered index card with her name and *vitals*, if that was the word.

Somebody had taken a calligraphy class.

*Lucille Estella María Valdez*

Her elbow stuck out from under the covering. Her sleeve. White satin. She was dressed in white satin now. At least Jimmy wouldn't have to look at that baby-blue dress again.

There was motion beside him, Angel crossing himself.

It was Angel who peeled down the covering sheet.

And it was Angel who said, after a second, there at the end of the world, "That's not her."

# TWENTY-NINE

Think *dark. Darker.*

Who did this? What exactly happened?

When a big question was thrown in Jimmy's face, his usual first response was to look for the answer in Coincidence. *Shit happens*, wasn't that the bumper sticker? You find out something wasn't at all the way you thought it was, and you're scrambling to make sense of it. And you think, *Coincidence.* You think that if you pull back a little bit, go over all the pieces, see this leading to that leading to this and this, you'll see that it was coincidence, chance, the roll of the bones that made it happen. That made this particular shit happen.

So some other Lucy-looking girl with a 1978 baby-blue Buick Skylark convertible just happened to plow into the flat face of Pier 35 right around the time the real Lucy, Lucille Estella Maria Valdez of Paso Robles, was getting suicidal?

What's next?

*Think dark.* When *Coincidence* isn't the answer, look next for a human explanation. Skullduggery. Conspiracy. Men in shadows pulling strings for dark purposes. Jimmy Miles probably had a lower opinion of the human animal than most people, men in or out of shadows, pulling strings or dancing on the ends of them, but it didn't wash. Why? How? Who? For what purpose? If this wasn't Lucy, the Lucy he'd followed here all the way from her house in L.A., who was it? *Why* wasn't it Lucy? Who would it profit? How would they do it?

Coincidence. Conspiracy.

Too many questions, you went to *Cosmic.* Some cosmic Somebody is working out His (or Her) will, moving chess pieces on a whole other plane. You only thought that was Lucy you were seeing on the slab in the morgue in the baby-blue dress, her face smashed in. It was just a trick of the gods, a bit in a skit that amuses them ever so slightly. Part of the plan. What they wanted you to see and think about and act upon, for some reason. There was a time when Jimmy's mother went religious, Angelus Temple religious. Jimmy was ten or eleven. She dragged him down there with her to Echo Park for three-hour Sunday services for the half year it lasted. He remembered some of the songs, the old rawboned hillbilly hymns. One of them said,

> Farther along we'll know all about it,
> Farther along we'll understand why.

But Jimmy didn't have the luxury of waiting for it all to make sense later. This was way too here and now. And human. On *this* plane.

Think *darker*. Darker than dark.

Who set this up? Why? Who would it profit? What would he gain?

"Look, you're sure?" Jimmy said. "I mean—"

"She looks a little like her," Angel said. "But not enough." He pointed at her face, with two fingers together, almost touching her forehead and then her cheek. It was a gesture that looked like he was blessing the girl. "Her eyes, her nose. It's not her. This one's older, for one thing. Ten years, maybe. She's also more mestizo. She's also probably Salvadoran. Lucy was Mexican."

Jimmy hadn't really looked at the girl on the table until now. And now when he looked at her . . . But how could you know? What do you go by? She'd gone into the wall face-first. Her skull had been smashed. Who knew what mortician skills Hugh had. Maybe he just wasn't any good at this. It *didn't* look like Lucy. But what did Jimmy know? How close had he ever really been to her? Ten feet away in the café in Saugus?

"This is somebody else," Angel said. "Lucy is still alive out there somewhere. I know it . . ."

Jimmy covered the body. The face.

"So who's this Hugh?" Angel said. "The one who sent us down here."

Jimmy knew what Angel meant. Start at what's right in front of you and backtrack. Go from man to man to man until it started making sense. New sense.

"He's a Sailor," Jimmy said.

"Yeah, I know. I got that. That can mean a couple of things."

"Friend of Machine Shop's. He works nights here."

Angel said, "So lay it out for me."

"Machine Shop was right there, Pier 35," Jimmy said. "He didn't see it happen, but he was on the scene right after, saw them load the body. She was wearing the blue dress."

"Did *anybody* actually see it happen?"

"I don't know. I guess. It must have been crowded down there."

"Then what?"

"They brought her here. Shop and me came here, after we'd gone back down to the waterfront together."

"And this girl is the one you saw that night? That same night. Here."

"Her face was crushed in," Jimmy said. "I don't know."

Angel said, "I never *knew* Lucy was dead. You know what I mean? I never felt it."

The intensity was still there, but his anger was gone. And Jimmy knew why.

"She's alive out there somewhere," Angel said. "Her and her brother."

---

Angel wasn't even three feet from the car when he put a Sailor on his back in the parking lot with a single shot to the face. Angel wasn't that big, so a good part of what knocked the man down was just surprise.

"Sorry," Angel said. "Don't come at me like that."

They were on Fisherman's Wharf. It was three in the morning. The tourists were long gone, but there were two or three hundred Sailors between the Porsche and the warehouse building. And no Black Moses to part the Red Sea this time.

Whatever tension, noise that had been in the air before, it had been cranked up a few notches. The waterfront Sailors saw Jimmy and Angel for what they were, two guys looking for trouble, or for something on the other side of trouble, and most of them backed out of the way.

But not the guard at the door. It was Red Boots, the blond, pouty Billy Idol in the peacoat and navy watch cap who'd tailed Jimmy his first night in town.

"Hold up there, mate," he said, putting a hand on Jimmy's chest.

Jimmy slammed his face into the metal door, something of an over-reaction.

But effective. It knocked the door ajar.

Jimmy and Angel came down the same corridor as before, but this time it opened out onto a dock, inside the huge, unlit warehouse space.

They got their first look at the exterior of the ship.

It was painted black, or some dark color that looked black in this gloom. It was big, a refitted oceangoing trawler. With its three-deck-high square windowless cabin, it came off looking like a missile cruiser.

"What's the difference between a boat and a ship?" Angel said.

"This is a ship," Jimmy said.

There was a gangway that was level with the dock, a double-wide hatch at the end of it on the other side. It was probably where they'd been led in the other night for their audience with Wayne Whitehead. Jimmy snatched up a three-foot wrench propped against a mooring winch and went aboard, Angel behind him.

Nobody home.

And no bent guitar notes sustaining in the air.

The oil lamps on the walls burned. Just enough light to illumine the oval, black marble-topped table in the center of the room and the white rose in the vase of milk.

Jimmy gripped the wrench a little tighter.

He yelled. "Hey!"

They waited.

"We should have took him that night, instead of playing whatever game that was," Angel said. He meant Les Paul.

When they came out through the hatch again, they weren't alone. Twenty or thirty of the Sailors from outside had come into the warehouse. They were still not saying a word, quiet enough to make it creepy.

Just staring at the two out-of-towners.

Jimmy shifted the wrench to the other hand, but they weren't any threat.

"We follow Wayne," one of them said without much behind it. A few of the others gave him a look.

They were staring at Jimmy as if he was somebody. As if his reputation had preceded him. As far as Jimmy knew, he didn't have a reputation. Not here.

"Go," he said.

Surprisingly, they went.

Maybe it was the wrench.

"Come on," he said to Angel. "We'll go south, to the shipyards where we were before. It was where all the women were."

"She's not dead," Angel said. He said it in an odd way, different from before.

"Maybe he's there," Jimmy answered. "Maybe he's looking for her there."

Angel was looking into the shadows.

"What?" Jimmy said.

Angel waited a second, still looking into the shadows, then said, "We know she's not dead, son. Where is she?"

There was a rope locker on the dock. "Come on out, it's all right," Angel said. "We're the good guys. We just want to find her, too, get you guys home."

There was a scurrying rat sound, and the kid exploded up out of the plywood bin. Angel charged in, crossed twenty feet in two seconds, but it was only fast enough to catch an ankle.

"I'm Angel, man, Lucy's friend!"

But the ankle was slick, wet from sweat. The boy escaped Angel's grip but fell hard, on his face, onto the dock. He didn't stop moving. He jumped to his feet and made it another ten yards before Angel was even sure he wasn't still holding him.

"Stop! Come on, man!" Angel said. "You gotta stay with us! We know she's still alive!"

The kid turned with a look of hurt and confusion and anger and suspicion all at once, but only slowed for a second.

And then he was out, through an open door at the far end of the long room, lost into the night again.

When Jimmy and Angel came out of the warehouse building, things had changed yet again. The numbers had swelled. It looked and felt and even smelled like the exercise yard at a prison.

Familiar faces. Some of the L.A. Sailors had come calling, had come over from Fort Point. Some of the roughest ones. Angel knew most of their names. Jimmy knew to stay away from them. The ranks of the San Francisco Sailors had grown. There was a face-off going on, maybe just starting. Some of them, on both sides, had weapons in hand, clubs, lengths of chain, or heavy marine rope. There was an ugly sound in the air, ugly anticipation, like the sound in the auditorium before a heavyweight fight.

But then it stopped. When they saw Jimmy and Angel.

They followed them with their eyes.

Or was it just Jimmy?

They split open a path before him. *Yea, though I walk through the parking lot of the shadow of death . . .*

A woman they'd seen earlier stepped in front of Jimmy again and said her line again. *"We serve the Russian . . ."*

"I don't know what that means," Jimmy said.

To answer, she pointed. Across the skyline, the winking cityscape behind them, like a backdrop in a play.

"I don't understand," Jimmy said again. She was right in his face.

She kept pointing. Now he saw it. Maybe. Was that what she wanted him to see?

A violet light atop one of the hills, brighter than anything around it, brighter than there was an immediate explanation for. It burned with the intensity of an airport runway light.

*Violet.*

The Porsche had been left unmolested.

Jimmy got in the car, but Angel didn't.

"I'm going to stay down here," he said after a second. "In case Lucy's here. In case the kid pops out again. Maybe he'll lead me to her."

"We should stay together," Jimmy said. "Until we understand more of this, what this is about."

Angel shook his head. "I don't care what it's about," he said. He set out back toward the waterfront and all the Sailors.

———

Jimmy crossed the empty foyer of the Mark.

There it was again. *Hope.* It was all over Angel. He was walking with it like it was his new best friend. Jimmy hadn't run after Les Paul because he wouldn't have known what to say to him if he caught him. He saw the look on the boy's face when Angel had said his sister was alive.

The kid knew she was dead. He knew. He was her brother. He knew.

And now Jimmy was back to knowing it, too. Lucy was dead. Angel had talked himself into something.

Angel had hope. Sometimes it gives you perfect vision, sometimes it blinds you.

It all made Jimmy's head hurt. It made him want to lie down. *Sleep.* He looked over at the first-floor sitting room as he went past, the big pink divans. He had tried all night, through all the death and death talk, through the gathering storm, not to think about Mary, to keep it in some safe spot, the way when something is really good you don't want to connect it to the world, you don't want to dirty it, you want to leave it where it is, perfect. He wanted to let a day or two go by, to think on all of it. To think of her. Of them. He wanted it to be waiting for him, whenever he got through with this, whatever this was.

The last thing he wanted was to see her again now.

But there she was.

Mary stood in the corner of the sitting room. The far corner. She had

changed her clothes from what she wore on the dock, the last time he saw
her. She was wearing black pants and a long coat, a coat that seemed too
heavy for the night, for the season. She looked severe.

"What's the matter?" he said.

She took his hand but then let it go a second later, self-conscious. Even
if there was no one there to see anything.

"Can I stay with you?" she said. It was a line she'd never said to him.

But if she wanted rescue, she came to the right guy.

He didn't ask any questions. He took her hand and led her away, across
the lobby, toward the elevator.

They got in. He didn't want her to say anything else. He didn't want to
know what it was. At least not out here, not now.

But she said it anyway. "He knows about you," she said, as the elevator
doors closed.

Jimmy just pushed the button for the fifteenth floor.

"When I came home—"

Before anything happened, the doors opened again, as if he'd pushed
the wrong button.

Four men. In dark suits.

The biggest one was Red Steadman. Walter E. C. "Red" Steadman.
He flashed blue, strong blue. It made Jimmy take a step back and take
Mary with him, though he knew she wouldn't have seen what he saw. The
blue.

*Steadman.* From the deck behind the house in Angeles Forest that
night. From other nights.

At Steadman's side was a portly man with a briefcase in hand, a short
man as far around as he was tall. (Who had also been on the deck that
night.) On the other side was an average man of average size. He wore a
hat, or carried it in his hand, a gentleman, if one out of another time. He
nodded to Jimmy, all polite, familiar. As if they were all just fellow guests of
the Mark. The fourth was a thug of some kind, but a well-dressed one.

They stepped forward into the elevator. The thug made it one too many.
The average man flicked his hand, and the thug stepped out again. The
doors closed.

It was Steadman who reached across and pushed the button for the
sixteenth floor.

"We're just above you," he said.

Jimmy had let go of Mary's hand, but he could feel her trembling beside
him. Staring straight ahead.

Steadman seemed to catch the scent of her perfume but never looked at her directly.

"Did you get your flowers?" Steadman said. He slowly turned to look at Jimmy. "Did we *all* get them?"

Jimmy shrugged.

"Interesting gesture," Steadman said, looking forward again. "What do we think of it?"

"I don't think anything."

"Must be . . . new management," Steadman said.

It was a long few silent seconds before the doors opened again. At fifteen. The men moved aside to let Jimmy and Mary out.

Steadman was standing next to the polished brass wall of the elevator, so Jimmy had two views of the last look he gave them before the doors closed.

Mary was still trembling, standing at the door to Jimmy's suite while he found the key. He wasn't sure she'd recognized Steadman. Them. She'd never actually seen Steadman's face on the deck that night. That night, he was wrapped in a scarf and wearing a hat, his face covered. Even his hands. Maybe she had gotten it just from his shape, from his vibe, from the dark richness of his suit. Maybe she remembered the fat man. And the other, the nondescript man with his hat in his hand, the mouthpiece. He'd been there that night, too.

All she really needed to get from seeing them was that Jimmy was the same thing now that he had been then, the same impossible thing. Whatever name they called themselves. She didn't have to see a flash of blue to know that.

He opened the door, and she went in ahead of him, not looking back.

She never said a word about the men. Or of the coded, elliptical talk of flowers, of "gestures" and "new management."

Or of her husband.

She went to bed. They went to bed together but didn't make love again. They didn't talk about the future or about the past. Jimmy just put his arm around her until she went to sleep. He stared at the ceiling, not ever realizing that she wasn't asleep at all.

# THIRTY

They had words and she left.

What they said to each other didn't matter. What it was really about was the impossibility of the two of them. What they both knew. Morning reality.

Jimmy asked her where she was going. What he meant was, *Are you going back to him?* Mary didn't answer.

She wasn't even ten feet away, out of Jimmy's reach, before he knew that she wasn't angry—she was scared. And very alone.

———————

Almost any time's a good time to meet when you hardly ever sleep. Jimmy had called Duncan Groner. Now they were in the all-night restaurant on Columbus. At five in the morning.

Jimmy asked for and got a glass of Chianti. And a couple of poached eggs.

Groner was sticking to black coffee.

"So is she dead or what?"

"I never met the lady," Groner said.

Jimmy had told him everything about Lucy. Everything.

"You were there, at the scene. You wrote the obit. Tell me what it was like. Take me through it."

Groner said, "Did *you* ever think of going out that way, behind the wheel? Or maybe you did go out that way . . ."

"When did you get there? To the waterfront."

"Twenty minutes after it happened. I was home. I live in Colma."

"Was the body still in the car?"

"She wasn't wearing a seat belt."

"Was the body *on* the car? In front of the car? Under the car?"

"Now *that* would violate a basic law of motion," Groner said. "And be a justifiable cause for suspicion."

"Help me," Jimmy said. He drank about a third of his breakfast wine. A businessman at the next table gave him a look.

"There wasn't anybody around in the immediate vicinity when the car hit the wall," Groner said. "Somebody could have rammed the car into the wall, run from the scene, while some other somebodies—it would take more than one—deposited the body there. Oh. And cast some blood around. A good deal, actually. I don't know where they would have had this body stowed beforehand. What are you thinking, in the ambulance?"

"I'm not thinking anything," Jimmy said.

"Here's another scenario," Groner said. "The car was operated by remote control. The girl, Miss Nobody, was already dead. A body. Yet full of blood, like a ripe pomegranate, ready to burst."

"I guess sarcasm is something you use every day in your line of work," Jimmy said.

"Yes, it is. And on the weekends. Even sitting alone in my little backyard."

"How about this?" Jimmy said. "Somebody talked another girl into killing herself, put the idea in her head and put her behind the wheel?"

There was a several-second delay before Groner laughed, a lag Jimmy would think about later, would try to calibrate.

"Yeah, crazy," Jimmy said. "What's next?"

"How about this?" Groner said. "Dr. Hesse is a Sailor."

Jimmy had to remember to breathe.

"You said he wasn't when I asked you."

"I believe I said I wouldn't think so," Groner said. "I'm afraid I made the mistake of assuming something didn't exist because I hadn't heard of it."

"Where is he on the local organizational chart?"

"Not on it, as far as I can tell. Though he may have pretensions. Just lives the good life. Wink wink."

"How long has he been a Sailor?"

"Years. Thirty?"

Groner studied Jimmy's face. Jimmy was chewing on the inside of his cheek.

"So I guess the boy, who looks just like Hesse, is adopted," Groner continued. "Or he was hers from some previous dead end. I don't know, maybe Hesse put the kid under a knife to make him look more like 'Daddy.'"

"How did you find out?"

"People were asking about you," Groner said. "I in turn asked about those people. You go back up the line."

"When? When did my name come up?"

"For me, the first question about you came a few days ago, just when the girl died. Your Lucy."

Jimmy waited for the rest.

"But the Jimmy Miles File had already been pulled. He'd made inquiries of others before it got around to me. Or I surely would have alerted you."

"He."

"Hesse."

"When? When did Hesse start asking about me?"

"That's what I don't understand," Groner said. "A month ago. Before you came north. Great gears turn."

He put a little drama in his voice. "So maybe *he's* the mind reader, the prognosticator."

A minute earlier, a pair of men had walked by the restaurant, and one of them had looked in, looked only at Groner. Jimmy wasn't sure Groner had noticed.

But Groner noticed now, when the two men came in the front door, shoulder to shoulder, wide enough to block the exit of the businessman.

"I believe *you'll* be getting the check," Groner said, with a little shake in his voice.

Jimmy got up defensively.

"It's all right," Groner said, getting to his feet, too. "It's nice to be noticed."

"Who do they work for?" Jimmy said.

"Oh, could be any number of people," Groner said. "These days."

The men took a step closer, like starting a sentence.

Groner raised his open hands in surrender. He had spotted two more of the same subspecies on the sidewalk out front. And a car.

Jimmy just watched it go down. They hustled Groner out and into the back of the car.

At least it wasn't Hesse's big wine-red Mercedes.

———————

*Then it became visible . . .*

Jimmy stopped the car, driving westbound on Haight. The nouveaux hippies were bopping down the street. He'd just passed them. It was minutes after sunset. Haight at Ashbury.

They were flashing red auras, faint to Jimmy's eye, but unmistakable.

"Are you seeing that?"

Machine Shop looked back over his shoulder at the hippies. "Uh-huh, *red*," he said.

"I never saw it before," Jimmy said.

"It's the moon. Or all this *meshugas*. All this *activity*."

"What about the moon?" Jimmy said.

"We're goin' into a new moon. Man, you don't know much, for being a emissary from the south and all. Everybody's different—San Francisco is different from L.A. You're blue, we're red. Blue sometimes but red sometimes, too, when the moon goes into a certain phase. You and me together will make purple. The world's a rainbow, man."

"Let's walk," Jimmy said.

"You're the one driving . . ." Shop said.

The two of them had been cruising for hours in fairly aimless loops. Not that Machine Shop was complaining. Jimmy had gone by Shop's Tenderloin hotel around noon, talked him out of going to work down on the waterfront. Jimmy needed the company, needed someone around him, beside him, someone from the time before everything started doubling back onto itself. A week ago seemed like a long time now.

Angel had never come back to the Mark.

"Maybe I need a night off. Sometimes I wonder if that silver paint is bad for you," Shop had said as they were getting into the Porsche.

They made the run up across the Golden Gate to Marin. Past the house on Alcatraz Lane out on Tiburon. It was buttoned up, the black shutters closed. Jimmy drove around the circle in the village, then past the marina. The Swan, *Queen Mary*, was at the dock, a cover over the cockpit now, the mainsail sheathed. The cruise-down-the-coast guys in the Hunter 38 were long gone. Jimmy was beginning to wish he had made friends with them and gone along. Nothing was much simpler than a boat on the ocean, out of sight of land.

He took the 280 south out of the city to Hillsborough, a community of gated homes big enough to look Euro rich. He'd tried to reach Groner all day on the phone, at work and on his cell, but he never answered. He needed another address for Hesse. He pulled into a little branch library and dug into a city directory. There was nothing listed. But there Hesse was, in an old number of the local weekly, a picture in a backyard in a black short-sleeved shirt and tan linen shorts, a fund-raiser for a preschool, though there wasn't any mention of Little Marc and no pictures of his smiling, supportive wife.

And no mention at all of the undead.

The article didn't let slip a street address but referred three times to "Butternut Drive" and even ". . . at the end of Butternut Drive . . ." As they cruised by the numbers, single- and double-digit and nothing more, Jimmy asked Machine Shop what he knew about Hesse.

Nothing, it turned out.

"I move around at the *bottom*," was the way Shop put it.

They found the house. The circular driveway was clean and clear, right up to the four-car garage. It didn't look lived in, but that seemed to be the idea with all the homes on Butternut Drive. Show houses.

Machine Shop didn't ask any questions, not a one all day, seemed content to just be along for the ride. They stopped for lunch at a sawdust-floor burger joint next to Stanford, a bit on down the peninsula, and then came back up on the 101 into the City. With the working stiffs.

They made one last stop, the building downtown where Hesse's office was. Jimmy stayed in the car at the curb in a loading zone, let Shop ride the elevator up.

"It's closed, locked," Shop said when he came back down.

Which didn't seem exactly right.

Night fell. Jimmy found a place to park on Haight, and he and Shop set out. They walked up one side of Haight Street eight or ten blocks and then crossed and came down the other. It was a midweek night but the tourists were out anyway. Jimmy and Shop came past the nouveaux hippies again, face-on this time. Nobody seemed to be in any hurry to get anywhere. More laid-back than the sixties, actually. The leader, with his Vandyke beard, who had seemed a little hostile to Jimmy before, this time put his hands together and bowed.

"I know you, Brother," he said self-consciously, stiffly, the way you greet a foreigner with a phrase not your own.

"Right," Jimmy said. "Hola."

There was a flash of red from Shakespeare.

The young sisters were in the back of the group.

"Can I talk to him?" the one with the imploring eyes pressed forward and said. Her sister tried to hold her back.

"Of course," the leader said. "If he is willing."

"Hi," Jimmy said to the girl. She looked about fourteen.

There was a stiff moment, and then the hippie leader said, "We'll dig you later, Babygirl. We'll be at The 'Choke."

And he led his merry band away up Haight. Babygirl's sister looked back at her, not happy.

"I'm going to get a tea," Machine Shop said, when he picked up that Babygirl was still hanging back, with him there.

"Got any idea what The 'Choke is?" Jimmy said.

"Yeah, down the street. That's where I'll be."

When Shop was gone, the girl leaned against the wall, took refuge beside a rainspout pipe. She said, "He calls me that, Babygirl, or Cry Baby Cry," she said.

Jimmy was about to say something.

"But my name is Christina," she said. "Christina Leonidas?"

Everything's a question. Maybe everybody's name is a question.

"Are you doing OK?" Jimmy said.

"My dad calls me Selene," she said.

"Yeah, I know. He told me."

He heard a breath, or an unformed word, catch in her throat. The perfect word, that explained everything.

"He'll be all right," Jimmy said. "I'm watching him."

"I thought I saw him the other night."

Jimmy nodded.

"No, I mean . . . again. Out at the Yards."

"You mean the Point, Fort Point," Jimmy corrected.

"No, the Yards. Where we saw you. Down south. I mean, I thought I saw him, but—"

"That's your sister, right?" Jimmy interrupted. "That's Melina?"

Christina nodded. Cry Baby Cry nodded.

"She's . . . different from me," she said. "She has all these 'friends.' I just feel like going home." She looked at him directly. "I know I can't, so don't even."

"I wasn't going to say it," Jimmy said.

"I mean, I know how it is. Sorta."

"Where are you staying?"

"We were in this apartment place, down in North Beach, with these really nice people, you know . . . Sailors. But then Melina said things were changing, that something big was going to happen now, that we had to move, to be with the right people."

"So where are you now?"

"With these people, the hippies. But we go back down to the Yards a lot, too. Where the women are, where The Lady is. Sometimes. That's how I knew about you."

"The Lady."

"That's what she told us to call her. She is so nice. She even let us go to her house."

Jimmy decided to break the rule.

"Why did you jump off the roof? What was going on that night?"

She flushed red, so bright and so sudden it was as if she'd expelled vaporized blood into the air around her head and shoulders.

"It's so stupid, I don't know," she said. "We were just hanging out with this guy Jeremy. We were just having fun. He knew all about everything. It was fun. I guess we were drinking, but it wasn't that. Suddenly, we were both so *sad*. We were like crying and everything. And Jeremy was crying with us."

"Stay away from him," Jimmy said.

"Well I know that now," she said, with a little fight in her voice that made Jimmy want to hold her.

"The Lady knows who I am?" he said.

"Of course," she said. "I told you . . ."

"You mean from the other night. At the Yards."

He was remembering that moment when he first saw her, the woman with the short-cropped hair, when he thought she looked like a version of his mother.

"From before that."

"What did she say about me?"

"Just that you were a good person. Someone who understood stuff. Someone to follow. And that was why you had been brought here."

"To the Yards?"

"I guess."

Click. A fragment of light appeared in the angled space between the tops of two buildings across the street, a lamp, a flame, a mirror behind the trees, that hadn't been there a second ago. And a rustling sound at the same time, though there couldn't be any real connection. Jimmy followed her eyes to it. It was the moon. What there was of it.

"Do you know what Selene means?" she said. "In Greek?" She didn't wait for him. "It means *moon*. When I tell people that now, they think it is so cool."

He walked her down the street to The 'Choke, a coffeehouse. A coffeehouse for real, not like the Starbucks wannabe. Yesterday's coffeehouse, not today's. Jimmy didn't tarry. Once he saw the hippies, saw Christina's hard-eyed sister, once he had delivered her back to them safe and sound, he bought a pack of American Spirit smokes and then came back out the front.

And into the shadows across the street.

Machine Shop was already there.

"What are you doing out here?" Jimmy said, lighting up.

"I can't take too many people inside a place," Shop said.

"Too bad, since you're an entertainer," Jimmy said, his eyes across the street at The 'Choke.

"It's limited me," Shop said.

After a few minutes, the group came out en masse. Shakespeare bade the Leonidas sisters adieu, standing there on the sidewalk, kissed his fingertips and then touched each of them on the forehead. The girls got on the first eastbound bus that galloped up. The lights on the bus were bright, and the sisters squinted as they made their way down the aisle to the wide seat across the back. Christina saw Jimmy through the window and waved. Jimmy waved back.

"Youngest Sailors I ever saw," Machine Shop said. "The two of them."

"I was seventeen," Jimmy said and started away.

The remaining hippies, two girls and two guys and their leader, had taken a left, heading away up Ashbury.

Jimmy and Machine Shop followed them, on foot, across Oak to Fell, across the Panhandle.

To the black house, where the band let themselves in.

# THIRTY-ONE

"I have to be back before dark," Mary said.

She drove a car Jimmy hadn't seen before, a two-seater Mercedes convertible. Early seventies and perfect. Light silver, the color of a knife. The road was in the country, with a nice gentle back and forth to it, through a valley where they grew flowers, mile after mile, color by color, in strict, clean rows. It was like being led by the hand across a color chart. It was like driving through a rainbow, only the colors were harder. Even to the two of them, even in the moment, it felt like a dream. With that same sense that it had to end, and probably abruptly.

Mary had called the Mark and told him where to meet her, a corner away from Nob Hill. She told him to take the cable car and where to get off. She had called at eight that morning. Something made him think she'd just dropped her boy off at school. They took the 280 out of town, the same way Jimmy and Machine Shop had headed south the day before, and then along the reservoir lakes, lakes to the right, the moneyed communities to the left. He watched to see if she looked over at Hillsborough, in the direction of Butternut Drive. She didn't. Another ten miles, and she veered off right onto San Mateo Road, the road up and over the ridge of mountains between the Bay and the peninsula towns and the coast.

"I have to be back before dark."

She didn't give a reason. He could come up with three or four on his own, and he didn't want to think about any of them. He certainly wasn't going to ask her why. He just looked at her, what the wind was doing to her hair, the shifting light to her eyes.

"I never rode in a car with you, you driving," he said.

She didn't say anything.

The fields of flowers ended, and the road came out at Half Moon Bay. It was a Thursday. There wasn't much traffic, local or otherwise, through the main strip of town. Half Moon had been there awhile, had some character, some Western to it. It also had that nobody-will-know-us-here feel.

They went to the beach, parked, and walked down onto the sand. The waves were gentle. And empty. Pillar Point was to the right, a confusion of sailboat masts and The Breakwater. Even that had an unpeopled look to it.

The two of them had a way of not talking in settings like this, a history of *un*pregnant silence. Back when they were first together they would go out to the beach at Malibu or Paradise Cove or up into the mountains or out to some alluvial plain in Joshua Tree and just be there, side by side, no pressure to talk, no impulse to frame things with words. It was one of the first pop-up signs that told Jimmy he loved her, when he realized that she didn't need to say anything, especially in those situations when anything either one of them might have said would probably be weak. Or just wrong.

But he spoke now.

"This is where Mavericks is, right? The big waves."

She pointed straight out. "In the winter months, December. A half mile out past the point. It's tow-in surfing. I don't even know what you can see from here. They go out in boats, on Jet Skis. The waves are forty, fifty feet."

The calm in front of them suddenly seemed like something else that could end abruptly. She took his hand. She looked up the beach in one direction. Someone with a dog was coming, too far away to even tell if it was a man or woman, throwing something to send the dog out ahead.

"Are you afraid of him?" Jimmy said. He meant her husband, Hesse.

She didn't have a quick answer. Or a defiant one, which surprised him.

She pulled him to her. "I'm glad you're here," she said. Was that the answer?

"What did he say? When you were arguing?"

"This isn't about him," she said. "In the end."

"Of all the city parks in all the towns in the world, I walk onto yours," Jimmy said, holding her.

She wasn't going to let him throw movie lines at her. "L.A. is only a few hundred miles away," she said. "We would have run into each other again eventually."

"You knew where I was; I didn't know where you were."

"You're the one who used to talk about Fate all the time," she said. They still held each other. It didn't sound as harsh coming out of her mouth as the words would look on a page. Or would seem, remembered. "You were the one who always said that we were meant to be together."

"We were young."

"What are we now?" she said.

"Together," Jimmy said.

He wanted to say one more line. He wanted to ask her why she went into the arms of a Sailor, why she married a Sailor. Was it possible she didn't know about Hesse? Even he didn't believe in a Fate that blind. Or blinding.

She seemed to sense how close he was to asking the real question about her husband.

"Come on," she said. "There's a motel up the way. I called ahead."

The man with the dog had reached them. Mary didn't look his way, but Jimmy did. The man didn't want their eyes to meet, put all his attention on the dog.

"Rex!" the man yelled and threw the stick again.

Mary was looking up at the sun. Or maybe she was gauging the time left by the position of the faint curl of daylight moon.

———————

They made it back before dark, time to spare. In time.

In time for Jimmy to be waiting at dusk for Hesse to exit the medical center. To tail him. Maybe in time for Mary to pick up the kid and make it home and shower and change into evening clothes for a reconciliatory dinner with her husband someplace nice in the City, because Hesse never went home. He drove from the UCSF med center to the Sequoia Club to get cleaned up, emerged a half hour later in a slick suit for a dinner date.

Only the doctor met someone else for dinner. A *woman not his wife* is the phrase.

Great gears turn. And not-so-great ones, too.

Jimmy had seen all the detective movies, so he knew, Jake Gittes and *Chinatown* aside, no self-respecting investigator did divorce work. The money wasn't any good, the hours blew, and the customers were never satisfied at the end of the thing, were more likely to hate *you* more for telling the truth than the guilty party for living the lie. When he started "looking into things" for people, formally and informally, for money or, more often, for his own private reasons, he knew what he *wasn't* going to do. He wasn't going to follow husbands to dinner dates. But here he was.

Why was it always husbands? Because husbands tried to pull it off in town. Women at least had the sense to go out of town. Out to some sleepy little beach town for instance. On a Thursday afternoon.

Jimmy didn't have any reason to think Hesse had identified the Porsche, so he'd only stayed two car lengths behind the corpuscular red Mercedes as it left the Sequoia Club. He had the top up, but that was because it felt like rain, the air thickening, clouds descending onto the hills of San Francisco like a stage curtain dropping. He was working. He had half a pack of the American Spirits left. Angel's pint of Courvoisier was in the glove box if he needed it. There was good music on the radio. He'd made love hours ago in a motel at the beach with the only woman he cared about, still had her scent on him. Life was confusing, but it was good. A wave bigger than Mavericks might be building a thousand miles offshore, but it wasn't here yet.

Hesse and the woman met at the restaurant. Separate cars, meet out front. They'd picked a restaurant on top of a high-rise with glass elevators on the outside of the building, right downtown. Maybe they thought it would look like some kind of business meeting, on the up-and-up. Sophisticates in a sophisticated city. The woman wore a stylish hat, a two-hundred-dollar version of a skateboarder's sock hat. Nothing sexier than that.

They left their cars, rode up together.

Somebody else was there. The man who'd been on the Half Moon Bay beach with the dog was there, too. Minus Rex.

Jimmy waited a beat, dodged the dog man, rode on up after them.

Their first courses arrived.

She had her head bare now. It was the short-haired woman Jimmy had identified as The Lady, the Sailor the New Leonidas girl had talked about, the one from the mess hall with the candelabra who'd reminded him a little, but not all the way, of a young Teresa Miles.

There didn't seem to be much passion to the thing. But, just as Jimmy thought that, Hesse reached across the table to touch her hand, to make some point. They *almost* looked like lovers. She drank. He didn't. The view of the city was lovely behind them. It was a very businesslike date. Jimmy remembered Groner's line about cardiologists and their cold, cold hearts. And Hesse a Mormon on top.

Jimmy was almost enjoying it, watching them, a great position at the bar, a gin to make it look right.

Then The Lady said something, and he said something back. And the lovebirds flashed red. Mauve, actually. And he remembered the twisted-together threads of story that had brought him here, that had twisted tighter with this.

A half hour later, Hesse and the woman were coming down in one elevator, and Jimmy was in the other. They were a bit ahead in the race for the street level.

While they waited for their cars, they stood close and talked. She even touched his hand.

Jimmy watched from the Porsche.

Hesse kissed her lightly. She pulled him back for another, this one with a little more intent behind it. She walked to her car, and he walked to his. He didn't look back at her. She didn't look back at him. The two cars pulled away, the red Mercedes and a silver Prius. The Mercedes with a refined roar, the Prius with an electric hum.

So what did it mean? Jimmy had seen the San Francisco movie called *The Conversation*, too, knew lovers' talk was code, that there was always something else being said, that it could look like one thing but be something else.

But it sure looked like unfaithfulness, betrayal. Or maybe Jimmy was just hoping to dirty up his rival.

He saw movement across the street. It was the man with the dog from the beach, coming out of the shadows, on the phone, with a little hurry in his step. Out at Half Moon Bay, Jimmy had decided that he worked for Hesse, was tailing Mary, Mary and the new man in her life. Now, he didn't know what to think.

He started the Porsche and pulled forward.

Dog Man walked four blocks, fast, with Jimmy lagging behind in the Porsche. The man stayed on the phone.

He went down a side street.

Jimmy drove by and looped back. Mary's black SUV was parked down the alley, and the man was at the driver's-side window.

He finished reporting in. He nodded. He walked away from her.

She sat there a minute, then left her car, walked away toward the waterfront.

# THIRTY-TWO

He had left so many hanging out there.

Angel.

Machine Shop.

Les Paul.

George Leonidas. His daughters.

Duncan Groner.

Maybe even Lucy.

Now Mary.

And with the wave building, big enough to cover them all.

He parked the Porsche on Battery and walked down to the Wharf. He was looking for Mary. But he was looking for Angel, too. For any of the rest of them, *all* of them. Unfinished business. It was as if they were all Sailors now. Left hanging until it was finished. Or until *It* was finished with them.

On Fisherman's Wharf, things were Balkanized. Territorialized. Any Thursday night tourists left were clearing out, looking over their shoulders as they split for higher ground.

Because tonight the waterfront was all Sailors. Sailors from the south. San Francisco Sailors. Blue. Red.

The blues were around the restaurants and bars to the west. The reds were gathering to the east, closer to the piers. The docks for the Alcatraz boats were dead center between them. There were further divisions within the two nations, subsets, breakout groups of fifty or a hundred Sailors formed around some leader. Or wannabe leader. There were a thousand Sailors all counted. It felt like the floor of a political convention, minus the signs on staffs. They weren't needed. They knew who they were, and any who didn't, didn't care, didn't care where they stood as long as someone else objected, as long as someone else claimed it as theirs, wanted to push and shove for it.

Whitehead moved among the crowd.

Steadman and his crew.

Jimmy thought he saw Hesse.

He saw Sexy Sadie and Polythene Pam, but just a glimpse, not even enough to tell if they were with the Sailors or in among the last of the escaping Norms.

He'd see them again.

He jumped onto the top of a Dumpster to see over the heads of the others, looking for Angel. In seconds, dozens of Sailors gathered around him. He knew some of them. L.A. Sailors. Some good, some bad. A kid named Drew he'd taken off the streets himself two years back, a nurse, an L.A. cop in street clothes. S.F. Sailors. Two of the women from the Yards, who'd been at the long table. Eighties Girl. There was Angelina, the first-night Columbus Street bartender who he'd wanted to go home and curl up with after seeing the suicides on the docks, who gave him the glass of Chianti from his secret admirer. So she was a Sailor.

But the rest of them were strangers to him.

Jimmy heard his name. Then he heard his name repeated, passed from one Sailor to another, from one to the others around him, and others drawing in. A whisper at first, then openly. He'd never heard his name repeated by a crowd. Who had?

The kid Drew raised his hand to wave.

Jimmy jumped down and tried to get away from it. They only pressed in closer. It started to rain. Soft, steady. Nobody seemed to notice. Jimmy only managed to move another few feet.

Suddenly the kid Drew was pushed up against him.

"Hey, bud."

"Hey," Jimmy said.

"How ya been?"

"I'm looking for Angel."

"Haven't seen him," Drew said. "He's here?"

"Somewhere. Why are you even here?"

"I don't know," the kid said and smiled about it. "I just went with everybody else. The bus up was a trip."

"Be careful," Jimmy said.

"Dude, what's the light about? Up there."

Through the rain, the violet light on one of the city hills was still burning. Steady, iconic, cloud-piercing.

"I don't know," Jimmy said.

"It's *Russian* Hill," a man beside Drew said.

"What does that mean?" Drew said.

The man put a hand on the kid's shoulder and started talking to him, leading him away, putting the word on him. *Some* word. Jimmy tried to move, but a new set had discovered him, crowding in, crowding him, whoever they thought he was. With the soft rain, now it felt like a rock concert, without the music, without the mud. With what was already in the air, more Altamont than Woodstock.

A hand seized him by the wrist. Jimmy looked down. A silver hand.

He found the face. Under the silver top hat.

"She's over here," Machine Shop said.

Shop pushed and shoved, cleared a path, like a bodyguard. Now the crowd really had something to look at.

Jimmy and Shop made it to a place between two dockside buildings, a space that seemed to be guarded by two or three of Jeremy's crew. They stepped aside when they saw Machine Shop coming and Jimmy behind him.

"I saw him over in here about ten minutes ago," Machine Shop said.

"You said *she*."

"No, I said he."

"Who?"

*"Angel,"* Shop said. "That's who you're looking for, right?" The rain was beading down his face and hands, off his painted skin, huge rolling drops of it. He looked like he was sweating like a runner, or crying great tears. "I maybe saw those girls, too," he said. "The ones from last night, who hold hands." It sounded suspicious. It sounded too much like, *Whatever you want, I got it.* Something, or someone, had gotten to Shop. Gone was the verbal tic that characterized him, the self-correction. Everything he said tonight he said once and stuck by it. He was on message. It felt wrong.

"What's the matter with you?" Jimmy said. "You're acting like you're high."

"I haven't been high since 1976. Gerald Ford."

"So where's Angel? Did you talk to him?"

"He said everything was cool. He was looking for you. To tell you. You stay here; I'll go get him and bring him here."

This was beginning to feel like a trap.

"Go back to work, man," Jimmy said, shaking his head.

He'd had enough. He started toward the wall of people on the other side of Jeremy's boys, disappeared into it.

Behind him, Machine Shop said, "Yeah, you're right, I got to get back over to Pier 41."

Jimmy was finished with the Wharf, but it wasn't finished with him. As he pushed his way through the edgy throng, he caught sight again of Sadie and Pam.

One and one, on a bench, on either side of a woman who looked like she needed a couple of friends.

On either side of Mary.

Jimmy tried to get through the sea of Sailors, but they seemed to have something else in mind for him, and he was taken away by it and lost sight of Mary and the women, forced to watch the three of them get smaller and smaller, like the victims of a shipwreck drifting away.

And, in the end, the ocean spat him out elsewhere.

He walked back up to Battery Street. He got in the Porsche and fired it up. He didn't know where he was going.

He didn't get *any*where.

A black Bentley Arnage rolled out of an alley to block his path.

Groner had only gotten a Lincoln Town Car when they came for him.

---

It was another house that looked black, but it was probably just the rain. It was large, four stories, a blockish gingerbread Victorian but done in dark colors, greens and browns and black, with gold edging where it counted. A slate roof.

It was a man's house, you could see from the curb.

The Bentley waited in the stub of a driveway. Jimmy looked out the rain-streaked window at the Goth house. All that was missing were bolts of lightning. Maybe he was supposed to get out. Nobody had said the first word to him. Or to each other. There was a driver and the best-looking muscle Jimmy had ever seen.

A garage door opened on its own, and the house swallowed the Bentley.

The elevator was an ornate cage, black and gold wrought iron. And small. And slow. They'd deposited Jimmy in it and stepped back. It felt a little like carrying out a sentence.

Another man in another black suit was waiting at the other end, with his hands folded in front of him like a funeral director. He made Jimmy remember the woman from Graceful Exits in the ninety-year-old chorus girl's living room.

The room had the same air of the dead to it.

The attendant stepped away into nothing.

Jimmy was worried about Mary, adrift out there, but was afraid to give himself over to it.

"I know that light switch is around here someplace," he said.

There was a rough laugh from the deeper darkness across the room.

"You're young," a voice said.

"Only here," Jimmy said. "Everywhere else, I'm old. When I'm around kids, I correct their grammar."

Jimmy had come in out of a dark, rainy night, physically and emotionally, but it was darker still here. His eyes began to adjust from what, in retrospect, was the blinding brilliance of the elevator. There were a few candles. On tables. They had a scent he'd never caught before, the best candles in the world, from some country Jimmy guessed he'd never visit.

He began to make out the man's shape. The face came last. He was in a wheelchair, a wood and wicker chair. He was a bigger man than his voice suggested. And he'd been even bigger before. A diminished man. Chest sunken, arms gone thin. A man from *then*.

The room began to establish itself. It was large, what once was called a drawing room. There were boxed beams on the ceiling. The floors were dark wood and uncovered. There wasn't much furniture, so the chair could roll without obstructions. There was a large picture window, but the man wasn't beside it. The window was uncovered. There was the waterfront far below, a grid of lights looking like a bed of embers.

Mary was down there somewhere. The other night, down at the Yards, that roomful of women had reminded him of the women he'd known. There was something else about the women in his life: He'd thought he was rescuing each one, one way or another. It was what he did, or tried to do. Save them. More than a few of them threw it in his face on their way out the door.

Now Jimmy could see the man. His hair was white. And full. His head was tipped back against the headrest, until he realized Jimmy was looking at him. He was dressed in dark silk, a jacket or robe. His legs were uncrossed. His feet were bare. His leathery hands were out to the ends of the armrests, as if the chair was a throne. He wore a ring with a red stone. The ring seemed loose enough to fall off.

"Who's next?" Jimmy said. To break the ice.

"That's why we're all here, isn't it?" the man said. "Do you understand the particulars of the process?"

"I don't even understand what you just said."

"Step closer. I'm having some difficulty getting a sense of you," the man said. He took several breaths. Labored. But then seemed to find himself again. "I don't automatically assume that's a bad thing."

Jimmy stayed where he was. "I've got things I could be doing. Why am I here? Why did you have me brought here?"

"You don't know."

"I don't know."

*"Mene, mene, tekel, uparsin,"* the man said. Under the circumstances, with this stagecraft, with the rain running down the outside of the picture window like anointing oil, it was a bit chilling.

Jimmy said, "'You have been weighed in the balances and found wanting.' Daniel interpreting the words that appeared on King Belshazzar's palace walls."

The man seemed impressed. "Are you a Jew?"

"No. My parents were both in the movie business, if that counts."

"A Christian?"

"No. So somebody has found me wanting? Is that why I'm here? Who? Found wanting for what?"

"Actually I was talking to myself, about myself," the man said. He hesitated for another couple of rough breaths, to force a little more oxygen into the blood. "The three words were *three* messages. *Mene.* God has numbered the days of your reign and brought it to an end. *Tekel.* You have been weighed on the scales and been found wanting. *Uparsin.* Your kingdom is divided and given to your enemies."

Before the man spoke again, he waited almost a full minute, long enough for Jimmy to hear a clock ticking somewhere.

"So," the other said, "you see it *is* about me. Though I stopped believing in God a hundred years ago. Took from him his uppercase *G.* Corrected *his* grammar, you might say. Come closer, boy. Young Mr. Miles."

"Who are your enemies?" Jimmy said. "Wayne Whitehead? Red Steadman? Hesse? Marc Hesse?"

"Who?"

"Who else then? The Lady? Who's next?"

"Soon enough it will be beyond me. All that is certain is that this kingdom will outlive me. And *someone* will be king." He shifted in his chair, uneasy, restless. "Come closer, I still can't see you. My eyes . . . Everything is going away. What can I say about you if I can't even see you, son?"

"So is that what the business down at the Wharf was about, people looking at me as if I was somebody?"

The man took the question as rhetorical.

"I'm not up for your job," Jimmy said. "It's a joke somebody's playing. I'm not built for it. I don't lead, I don't follow."

The man reached down and unlatched the brake on the chair.

"Take me over to the window," he said.

Jimmy stepped behind him and wheeled him twenty feet across the room to the window. A reflection of the two of them rolled out of the night sky to meet them.

"Help me stand, James."

There was rustling in the wings. The attendant had never left.

"Go away!"

The rustling quieted.

"Help me."

Jimmy reached around him in the chair with both arms to the small of his back. His body was dry. He didn't hold much heat. Jimmy lifted him to his feet. His hip popped. He felt to Jimmy like he weighed less than a heavy winter coat on a hanger.

The man took a second to steady. He tightened his dressing gown around himself modestly, around his straight hips, over his bony white legs, over the knobs of his knees.

"They said you came north on a mission of mercy, a favor for a friend," he said, standing there at the glass, a shaky pile of sticks. "A favor for another Sailor." He drew in another labored breath. "There was a time when a sentimental gesture like that would have impressed me."

"Well, it all pretty much went bad," Jimmy said. "My 'mission of mercy.' So I'm with you."

There was another dry, rasping laugh. "You remind me of myself," the other said. "A hundred years ago, when I was foolish."

"Thanks," Jimmy said. "I guess."

"Ah yes!" the man said suddenly. His focus had shifted, his depth of field.

The rain had lifted. Some hand had moved aside the clouds. There was Alcatraz, alone amid a range of black like the electrified capitol of a dark, dead, desert country.

With that nothing moon overhead.

# THIRTY-THREE

The Bentley boys deposited Jimmy back where they'd found him and whispered away up the rain-slick street.

He drove over a couple of blocks. Mary's SUV was gone.

He took a minute. What he hoped was that the dog man from the beach had found Mary down on the waterfront, gotten her home, and calmed her down. And then he had come back for the car.

Hope. It came and went. And was always ridiculous, if you stared hard enough at it.

He put the Porsche in gear, but before he could pull out, there was thunder. Familiar thunder.

*L.A. thunder.*

Coming at Jimmy from the far end of Battery was a lowrider. But not just any lowrider: a lowered and sectioned '56 Mercury, white over midnight metalflake blue.

Angel's lowered and sectioned '56.

He parked nose to nose with the Porsche, but ten yards out, killed the headlights. There were two heads in the frame of the windshield. There was some talk between the two, or Angel talked and the other nodded. And waited.

Angel got out. Jimmy got out.

"You all right?" Angel said.

"Yeah."

Jimmy waited for an explanation, but wasn't going to wait for long.

"I went back to L.A.," Angel said. "Twelve-hour turnaround. I've been driving around, looking for you. I just saw Machine Shop down on the waterfront. He said you were somewhere around here. Said to tell you he was sorry, for some reason. It's crazy down there."

Jimmy was looking at the Mercury. At the girl in the front seat. Angel looked back at her, too.

"Get ready for something heavy," Angel said.

He walked back to the car, to the passenger side, and opened the door. The woman got out. She was wearing a full skirt, like a fifties girl. She had dark hair. She straightened her skirt. She looked as if she'd like to be almost anywhere else.

Angel walked her forward. She was in her twenties.

"This is Lucy," he said. "Lucy Valdez."

She looked scared. She looked guilty. She looked away. She looked like nobody had had to make up the part about her being sad.

"Tell him," Angel said to her. "It's all right, he's cool."

"I couldn't see how anyone would get hurt," Lucy Valdez said. She had almost no accent. L.A. raised. L.A. Unified School District. "I tried to think it through. I couldn't see how anyone would get hurt by it."

Jimmy wanted to hit her. He knew he wouldn't, couldn't, knew his anger had other targets. One of them the man in the mirror.

"They come to her," Angel said. "A guy."

"Let her tell it," Jimmy said.

Lucy took a step back, a step that put her halfway behind Angel.

"A man called me, from up here," she said. *Lucy* said. "But he didn't say where he was. The phone said four-one-five. He said, 'A man will come see you.' He said that when the other man came, he would tell me what it was, the details. And how I would be paid."

Jimmy said, "Do you have a brother?"

The girl shook her head and started to cry.

Jimmy turned his back on them and walked away, halfway up the block.

Angel came after him.

Jimmy turned.

"They gave her five grand," Angel said. "The guy who came down to L.A. did. All she had to do was be there at her house that one night, the night I saw her in the window from the street, and be out of there at two that next morning. The guy would take things over from there. And she had to leave the keys to the Skylark."

"Who was the girl I was following?"

"A friend of Lucy's. From an acting class she took. They asked her if she had a friend."

"What did they tell her it was about?" Jimmy said.

Angel didn't want to say the next word. "Me."

"How?"

"They told her that some men wanted me in San Francisco."

"They thought *you'd* tail her? It doesn't make sense. Like you didn't know what she looked like?"

"They knew I'd send somebody, one of my guys or somebody, and then I'd come up here eventually."

"When the bait was *dead*," Jimmy said.

"She didn't think that far," Angel said. "She's just a kid. She's *convicted*, man. She knows she did wrong. I found her still out at her cousin's in Duarte. She can't even go home. She can't stand to be there."

"You have enemies here?"

"I didn't think so until now."

Jimmy turned and started back toward the cars, with a sense of purpose that sent Angel after him. "What are you doing?"

Lucy backed up when she saw Jimmy coming, the look on his face.

He grabbed her by the wrist. "Come on," he said, already pulling her up the street, toward the waterfront. "We're going to find the man you met with. You're going to point the finger at him. Lucky for us, seems like everybody's here . . ."

"Maybe he isn't even a Sailor," Angel said.

"It's a start," Jimmy said.

"I never said anybody was in the navy," Lucy said.

"Shut up," Jimmy said.

———

They *were* all there. It was like a living mug book of Sailor suspects.

Jimmy still had Lucy by the arm. Angel was on the other side of her.

Things had gotten even rougher. It was all in boldface now. The segregation had only become more pronounced, the lines drawn clearer. Each knot of Sailors had a speaker at its center, only most of them weren't speaking, just on display, like a dictator on his palace balcony with his arms outstretched to receive the love of the people. But it wasn't love exactly. For some, it was fear. Or that crash at the intersection of admiration and fear that is respect.

Fights were breaking out everywhere. There was Steadman, with the L.A. Sailors around him, bad and good, and a few converts from the north. And a few undecideds, whatever that meant in this context. They'd brought one of the tricked-out buses over from Fort Point, positioned it in the middle of the parking lot. Steadman stood atop it. On the polished, curved aluminum of the bus like that, he looked like Howard Hughes on the wing of a plane. He looked like what he had been in life, an airplane man.

Jimmy didn't imagine that Steadman was behind bringing him or Angel north, but he still made Lucy look at his face and at the faces of his men. The fat man was beside the bus. The hat man was there. And Steadman's muscles, L.A. handlers, one named Boney M and a particularly singular-minded little man they called Perversito.

Lucy just kept shaking her head no at each face Jimmy made her judge. She was scared. She was still crying. She wasn't a Sailor. It was hard to take this in, in one big dose. And she was just a kid.

They came upon Hesse. With him it was hard to tell if he was a focal point, a point of attention, or just another lieutenant moving through the crowd. Maybe he was looking for a crowd, waiting for one to gather around him.

Jimmy dragged Lucy right up to him.

Hesse didn't know who Jimmy was. Or didn't betray it if he did.

"No," Lucy said. "That's not who came to see me. I don't know him. Please. It wasn't even—"

"Shut up."

They pressed on, eastward, leaving a perplexed Hesse behind.

There were groups Jimmy hadn't seen before, with men in the middle he'd never seen, either. There were News everywhere. They were the ones with the stunned looks, the ones with roaring red auras. The ones who shuffled from place to place, waiting for things to start making sense.

"The suicides," Angel said.

"What?" Jimmy said.

"A lot of them are probably these suicides. Somebody trying to run up the numbers."

"When did you start caring about the leadership?"

"I care about it when it touches innocence."

They'd made it to Pier 35, Whitehead's home base. Wayne Whitehead himself stood on top of the face of the building tonight, like the Leonidas girls a million years ago. Last weekend. Only he wasn't naked.

He wore a white suit with a white rose in the lapel.

Jimmy pushed through to the front. Whitehead looked down on him. He raised a hand in greeting.

"Does he think we're his guys now?" Angel said.

"I don't know; I don't care," Jimmy said.

He knew Whitehead wouldn't have made the trip to L.A. to meet with Lucy. He turned her so that she faced Jeremy, scarred Old Salt Jeremy, who stood in his cape at the door into the warehouse, where the ship was.

"*Him,*" Jimmy said. "Do you recognize him?"

She shook her head. "I told you—"

"I know what you told me."

As Jimmy took her by the wrist again, to lead her away, Lucy said, "She looked a little like *her*. But not really."

She.

Lucy pointed to a girl beside Jeremy. It was the nobody who'd ushered Jimmy and Angel into Whitehead's hold, aboard the ship in the warehouse. That night, she wore a navy watch cap and peacoat. They hadn't even noticed she was a girl.

"Just the hair," Lucy finished.

"You said it was a man."

"It was. On the phone."

"You said another man came to see you in L.A."

"The first man said it would be a man, but a *woman* came to see me." Lucy touched her own hair. "She had short hair, like a man."

The Lady.

It took awhile, but Jimmy found her, near where Hesse had been. Hesse was gone, and the short-haired woman was in his place. (Or maybe *he* had been in *her* place.) She wore the same clothes from the date with the doctor. The Lady.

"That's her," Lucy said.

"Who is she?" Angel said to Jimmy, lost.

Jimmy didn't have a quick answer for him. "She was down at the shipyards that night. She's a leader. She wanted to meet me. Or at least she wanted something."

"So what does this mean?"

"I means it's about me, not you. They did this to bring *me* up here, not you."

"Why?"

"I don't know."

The short-haired woman was talking to a cluster of women Sailors, some familiar from the Yards. When one turned his way, she was Christina Leonidas. This was about as far away as you could get from where she and her sister had jumped that night.

*Selene*, her father called her.

Jimmy looked up at the sliver of moon. The clouds were gone.

The woman finished her pitch, or whatever it was. She put her hands on the shoulders of the women around her, smiled, then stepped away a few feet to another group.

But something caught her eye.

Just as it caught a hundred eyes.

People pointed. Across the way, up the hill.

The violet light. It grew brighter and brighter.

When everyone was looking at it, it began to pulse.

In, out . . . Here, away . . .

And then it stopped.

They waited. It never returned.

Some began to cry. Some dropped to their knees.

When Jimmy looked for the woman with the short-cropped, mannish hair, she was moving away through the frozen crowd, the only one in motion.

# THIRTY-FOUR

The Lady led Jimmy to the Haight. In her silver Prius.

He didn't have any trouble keeping up. He'd left Angel and Lucy behind at the waterfront, left them and the others and almost everything else behind, left the gathered Sailors to cry and wonder what was next, for those so inclined. There wasn't any traffic. Anywhere. It was as if the city had gotten the word: Tonight belongs to Others.

She parked in front of The 'Choke.

And the stories started to knit themselves together. The way broken bones are said to. And scar tissue.

She got out of the Prius in a hurry and didn't lock it. She went into The 'Choke. Jimmy went past the coffeehouse and turned around and came back up on the other side of the street, stopping three storefronts away. He could use a cup of coffee. He already knew he was only hours away from the end, whatever it was.

The violet light of the story had begun to pulse.

He didn't know exactly what he expected to find in The 'Choke, but what he found was Mary.

They were all working on her. Or at least they were all around her. She was in the center of the group, with her hands around a cup of tea or something. The hippie with the Vandyke and his people, Sexy Sadie and Polythene Pam, they were all there, listening to what Mary was saying and nodding. She had that end-of-a-long-day look but smiled more than you would expect, but the kind of wistful smile that admits defeat. That wants the day to end, whether there's another one after it or not.

The Lady stood by, five feet away, almost at attention.

Mary finished what she was saying, and Sadie and Pam stood and leaned over her and hugged her, that way women do, draping themselves over the other. *I understand.*

Mary saw Jimmy.

He just stood there in the doorway. As if he was in charge, as if *he* was going to determine what happened next.

As if he could save her.

When the others saw him, they closed the circle around Mary, made her disappear. Like bodyguards. Like magic. They were already in motion, leading her away, out the other entrance, the one on Ashbury.

Jimmy went after them. "Don't go with them," he said.

He saw her eyes in the middle of them.

And then they were gone. All of them. They were already crossing the Panhandle at Ashbury, the whole merry band of them. And not waiting for the light. He went after them.

Beatles music was in the air.

*With every mistake, we must surely be learning.*

Maybe, maybe not.

So this was the black house. Inside.

They had left the door open. He had the idea they never locked it. There probably wasn't even a key.

The living room, the first room in the front of the house, had twenty-foot ceilings and red velvet drapes, Persian rugs on the floor. Mahogany furniture, a wall covered with prints of birds, in different-sized frames, gold frames. There were velvet pillows everywhere and a collection of hats on pegs on another wall.

It was a woman's house. Or *women's*.

He kept expecting to be jumped. Maybe hippies never attack. Next to the living room was a dining room, with a twelve-foot table. Fresh flowers. The kitchen was done in white octagonal tile with a strip of black around the backsplash, looked a little institutional, but on the glass of the window over the double sinks some hand had painted "Good Day Sunshine . . ." in clear acrylic, yellows and blues.

The Beatles' music was coming from the back of the house somewhere. It only made clearer to Jimmy that they were gone already, that they'd run in here and then out the back, to buy time. The sound somehow said empty house.

*I don't know why nobody told you how to unfold your love.*
*I don't know how someone controlled you.*

He found the CD player. There was a den in the back of the house. Painted purple, semigloss. The speakers were built into the ceiling, made it sound like God was listening to *The White Album.*

Jimmy eyed the stairs, thinking maybe they were still in the house, upstairs. But then there was a mechanical sound, from the anteroom outside the den.

An elevator stood open. It was integrated into the dark woodwork. He hadn't noticed it before when he came through. It wasn't standing open before. There didn't seem to be a call button for it. He stepped in. He could smell Mary's perfume, floating above the patchouli of the hippies.

There were three buttons. He went with Up.

But it had other ideas. As soon as he'd stepped into it, the elevator had started to make noises, motors and levers. Not-so-great gears turn, too. It went down. One floor. It stopped, but the doors didn't open. Jimmy pushed the bottom button, and it continued. A light over the door pulsed, a soft light behind a circle of ivory, that seemed to be measuring time and not distance. If it *was* distance, it felt like ten floors. It stopped, roughly.

It opened onto a ten-foot-square room, a room hewn out of rock. With an arched opening to the right, a tunnel leading away.

In the tunnel there were train tracks and a shiny electrical contact centered overhead. It was small.

*OK, I'll bite,* he thought, and started down the tunnel.

He could stand upright but thought to keep his head and hands away from the power line. There were lights on the wall every fifty feet, gaslights refitted with clear incandescent bulbs.

He walked a half mile. It stayed level. It was dry. He would have thought it would be damp, wondered how they did it. He came through a section with a great rumbling nearby, vibrating gear sounds from the other side of the rock. (A cable car barn?) Near the end, there was an intersection with a larger tunnel, this one tiled, a look from another age, a hint of Le Métro. It all seemed automatic, as transportation networks go. There was a light, red/green, at the intersection.

It shined green, so he kept going.

There was a sound behind him. He turned just as an open train car stopped inches away from running him down. It was simple, inelegant, an open box on wheels, eight feet long. A Sailor manned the helm, standing in the rear, like a gondolier. His face wore no expression. Back home, this kind of Sailor was called a Walker. It was a good job for a Walker.

He rode a good distance in the second tunnel, was brought into a room. The tunnel and cart and driver continued on beyond it. He stepped out. The conveyance stayed put.

It was a waiting room. There was a pair of empty wingback chairs.

And three doors.

One opened, saving Jimmy from any test of character or intuition. It was the dog man. "Here," he said, "this way," and held the door open. Jimmy just put one foot in front of the other.

---

They came out into a room, a room where everybody had a purpose. People came and went, carrying things. Most of the people Jimmy didn't recognize, but the hippies were there and some of the women from the Yards. There was an air of imminent departure, the train leaving the station. Another train, another station. Jimmy looked for a clock, but there wasn't one.

Duncan Groner came through carrying a wooden box, what could have been a case of booze. He came out of one doorway and headed toward another.

"You still here?" Groner said, didn't wait for an answer.

The woman with the short-cropped hair and that French look was right at the center of things. The Lady. She'd changed her clothes. Now she wore a dark business suit, blue almost to black, with a waist-length jacket, a straight skirt, a white collar, heels. Like a stewardess on the *Titanic*, if they'd had them.

There was something familiar about the outfit. Then Jimmy remembered the nanny that night on the dock. This was the officers' version of the suit she wore.

The woman gave Jimmy a pleasant smile.

Christina Leonidas came through. She seemed happy, excited, energized, the way schoolgirls are when they're working on a project. Putting on a play, a fashion show, a fund-raiser.

"Did you see her yet?" she said. "The Lady?"

"The Lady" was still standing there, maintaining the same smile, standing by. So Jimmy didn't get it.

"The Queen?" Christina said. "She told us to call her The Lady, or even just Mary, but everyone calls her that, The Queen. *Queen Mary*," she said and giggled.

And there was a flash of red, like a wink.

Jimmy's heart fell through a hundred floors.

"She prefers just Mary," the woman in the suit said to Christina.

Then she turned to Jimmy. "She's in the drawing room."

# THIRTY-FIVE

She stood facing him when he came in. The woman in the suit had deposited him on the other side of the door and then clicked away in her heels.

The room was lit up bright, the way a child puts on all the lights when a night turns scary, when questions threaten to overtake everything. There were deep green drapes, a heavy weave, closed across whatever windows there were. Two of the four walls were covered with dark books, floor to ceiling. There wasn't much furniture, and the wooden floors were bare, polished to a shine that made it look like the two of them, Jimmy and Mary, were standing on water, looking at each other across a gulf.

She stayed where she was.

Jimmy stepped in through the doorway but nothing more. For now.

"I don't know if you knew or not, but The Man is gone," Mary said.

"Yeah, I don't get that," Jimmy said. "Explain it to me."

She smoothed out the front of her dress, or dried the palms of her hands on it, if they were damp. She had changed clothes, too, from what she was wearing at The 'Choke, when she was being "consoled," or he thought she was. Now she was in a gray suit, with a long coat over a long skirt. It was a little odd, high-collared, a little Eva Perón–theatrical.

"There must be other things you want me to explain first," she said.

"You started with that." He heard the edge in his voice.

"Help me," she said.

And suddenly she was Mary again. He almost crossed to her. But he didn't. He remembered that one of the things that had landed him here, wherever this was, was his predilection for riding to the rescue. Or thinking he could.

"You know, that's what The Man said to me," Jimmy said. "*Help me.* He wanted me to get him on his feet, give him a last look at his dimming empire."

Mary turned her back on Jimmy and reached into the drapes and found

the cord and yanked them open. She had her own anger. It was closer to
the surface than either one of them thought.

It was the picture window.

It was the drawing room.

It was the house on Russian Hill.

Jimmy felt stupid for not figuring it out before now.

Still with her back to him, Mary said, "I'll explain it to you. He's gone.
Crossed over. Released. The special exception for Sailors with years of service.
The grace of God. A time and a place. That's all I know about it. That's all *he*
knew, all he understood about it. That leaders sometimes are given a gift."

"Turn around, let me see you," Jimmy said.

She turned. She let him stare at her. She knew that right now she was
two women to him. She was giving him a chance to try to fit one woman
onto the other.

"I understand how you feel," she said.

"Do you?" he said.

She walked to him. Her hand rose to touch his face, but she stopped
it on its way.

She said, "I remember standing in some trees in the middle of the
night, in the clothes I had been sleeping in. I remember a man telling me,
when he finally got around to it, that he was not what he seemed. That he
was something that nobody was, that *couldn't be* as far as I knew."

"All right," Jimmy said.

"I remember six men in a semicircle on a deck, one of them with his
face covered with a gray wool scarf, and it a warm night, too."

"All right, I get it."

"No, you don't. You only get part of it, Jimmy."

She didn't sound angry anymore.

"We're even," he said.

Her face fell. "Is that what you think this is? Something as small and
as far away as that?"

The flywheel in his head was spinning so fast it felt like it could come
apart. He was trying to *see* it, how this had happened, how he had come
to be in this room. He was making lists in his head, drawing diagrams,
schematics. He was trying to piece it together. He was trying to re-create
the wiring, get it together to where, when he threw the switch, the circuit
completed and the light came on.

*The call to Lucy.*

*The stop in Saugus.*

*The trip north.*

*The Beatles in the glove box, the CD he never remembered buying.*

*The way the fake Lucy looked, dressed, cried. Died.*

Mary walked past a table, brushed her fingers across what must have been a switch. All the lights in the room went out at once.

He couldn't see anything. He heard her walk away from him, toward the window.

His eyes adjusted. What he saw first was a dull red glow, her shoulders and the reflection of their line in the glass of the window.

Until that moment, he wasn't sure. Wasn't sure she was a Sailor. It pressed down on him, the knowledge. The fact of it.

He said, "Is that your house, in the Haight? The black house?"

"Yes."

"Why are you here, in The Man's house?" he said. "You seem right at home."

"For the last six years, I worked with Martin. One of the ones who worked for him, but one of his favorites. He never left this house. Everything came to him."

"Why did you marry a Sailor?"

"I want you to be with me," she said, there in the dark.

"Why did you marry a Sailor?" he said again.

"I want us to be together."

"Why did you marry a Sailor?"

This time, she let the clock in the other room play a little fill. "I didn't," she said. "Hesse is just someone I work with. I'm not married."

Jimmy's heart dropped another hundred floors.

"I knew me being married would draw you closer," she said, "not push you away. Would make you want me more. Especially with the kind of man Hesse is."

"What about *your boy*? Where'd you get him?"

"He's mine. Jamie. He's mine. He's *mine*. I'm his mommy, and that's where we live, Tiburon."

She found her softest voice. "Come here," she said.

He stayed where he was. He felt like the pile of sticks The Man was.

"Come here, Jimmy."

He crossed to her. There, behind her, was the City, the Bay. A ship was leaving, out under the Gate.

"How did you die?" Jimmy said, that question they alone can ask. And usually never do.

"I took pills."

"You always hated drugs."

"I know."

"Why did you do it? What made you? Why did you want to die?"

She took his hand. "To reach *you*," she said.

He pulled away his hand. "A girl died, Mary."

"I know," she said. "But that wasn't because of me."

"It wasn't?"

"That was part of someone else's plan," she said. "I didn't order it. I wouldn't have. I had what I wanted. You were here."

"She was a human being."

Mary could have stopped then. But she didn't stop. "Heartbroken girls die every day," she said.

The low clouds and high fog had cleared altogether. The City, the world, was all spread out before them, like a board game.

"Look at us," she said. She meant their reflection in the window, red by blue. Red. Blue. It was like there were four of them.

He was looking past them, at a judging sky.

"I want us to be together," she said again. "We'll do everything together." A sentence for each of the two Marys.

# THIRTY-SIX

The last boat over.

Jimmy liked the idea of that. It matched what he was feeling. He was on one of the piers, leaning against the stub of a piling, smoking the last of the American Spirits. He had left Mary in the house on Russian Hill, blew off all of them up there, and the sense of purpose they rode in on. They didn't have to show him out. He knew the way. He walked over a block and came down to the waterfront on the cable car, on the Hyde Street line, the last run of the night. The car was almost empty, just Jimmy and a Chinese man who looked a hundred years old. It was after two by the time he made it back down to Fisherman's Wharf. The Sailors had had it to themselves all night and had trashed it good. The tourists were all still instinctively hanging back, waiting in their hotel rooms until this particular unearthly storm passed. Most of the Sailors had already cleared out, made the crossing to Alcatraz. The ones left milling around, asking questions of each other, of anyone who'd half listen, were the lost ones. The uncertain ones. The undecideds. The ones even more conflicted than Jimmy. Walkers, most of them, with the faintest red or blue auras of all.

He watched the coming and going. Whitehead's strange black ship made four trips over and back just while Jimmy was standing there, taking aboard anybody who wanted a ride over, north or south, friend or foe, before it was too late. The name was on the stern. *White Rose*.

He turned and looked at Alcatraz, the turtle shape of it, the sweep of the light. *In Time*. Wasn't that the name of the painting in Hesse's office? The sailboat making it into port just ahead of the black storm, just in time. If Hesse *was* a doctor.

*How could you hope to be with someone if you started with a lie?* With a host of lies, interlaced, one feeding off another after a while. As soon as he thought it, he heard Mary's answer: *You started with a lie. You started* us *with a lie.* She was right, he had lied to her from the first minute. The first word he spoke to her was probably a lie.

He remembered it. "Let's hear your clever first line," she had said, on the sidewalk on Sunset Strip.

"I don't have one," he had said. *I . . . I* was a lie. He didn't exist, not in the way she knew.

"I don't have a clever *last* line, either," he had said. At least that wasn't a lie.

He threw away the tailings of the cigarette and got on board the black ship. Jimmy was the only passenger, the last of the night to go over.

---

Alcatraz.

Every city, every society of Sailors had its place. The Place. When they met all together, for whatever ceremonial necessities, they met there. In L.A., it was aboard the *Queen Mary*. Here, it was Alcatraz. There were always enough Sailors in high places in any city to give their brothers and sisters some space. To facilitate. Sailor cops and Sailor firemen would be there to direct Norms away, to declare the glare of lights or the cars or the lines of people filing into a public place hours past midnight "nothing" or "a private party."

Sailors covered the island. As the black ship angled in to bump against the dock, Jimmy saw them. Everywhere. The hundreds, the overflow from the main gathering inside the prison. Whoever was in charge had sure enough fired up the place with blazing lights. It was so bright, so *alive,* there were bound to be calls in the morning to the *Chronicle.* Groner would probably take them.

The local Sailors still thought Jimmy was somebody. As he came off the ship, they stepped out of his way, cleared a path across the dock and up the Z of the ramp, to the big prison buildings on the cap of the rock.

Up top, there was really only one big building. It was two or three hundred feet long, two-thirds as wide, tall, with thick walls angling in. Like a fort. Like a prison. Like a structure used to test bombs. The walls were a cream color in the daytime, and peeling under the almost constant salt wind, but at night they just looked gray. There were support buildings down the slope and out on the point, but they didn't matter, just the big building. There was a concrete and grass yard in front, the front facing San Francisco, and another, all concrete, on the back corner, facing Tiburon.

The light of the lighthouse swept around like a scythe.

Jimmy ducked it, went through the crowd and inside.

They called the main cell block Broadway. It was two tiers high, "oft-photographed." The factions of Sailors had divvied up the space the way they'd divided up the parking lots over at the Wharf. But most of them seemed to be thinking outside the box. Any box. Half were drunk, the other half high, high either from pills or pot (or acid, this being San Francisco), or just from the unsettling mix of order and chaos. Like a prison.

Or maybe it was the cold that had them jumping. It was freezing. Beyond the main cell block was the cafeteria, tables long ago ripped out, but not the clunky apparatus in the ceiling where they could spray out gas in the old days, "to quell a disturbance." Some of them spilled over into that.

On the back wall of the main cell block was the gunrail, a balcony of sorts on the dividing wall. One end of it was against a high, barred window. A man was posted there, looking out the window, looking up at the sky. At intervals, he would broadcast a number. And then repeat it. Wherever he'd started with it, he was down, or up, to thirteen.

Jimmy heard a few more repetitions of his Christian name.

Sailor men and women *dressed* for occasions like this, usually arch versions of whatever they wore living. Whatever that was. The parade down to the docks hours past midnight must have been a sight for any insomniac Kansans peeking around the hotel curtains. There were men in bowlers, men in stevedore caps, men in those slanted knit caps union organizers fancy. Men in oversized Vietnam cammies. Among the women, there were festive Mae Wests and Marilyns and Jackie O.'s. And too many hippie chicks, who probably still had daddies out there somewhere wondering what had happened. A couple walked around wearing real Mae Wests, inflated life vests, glow sticks glowing. Most of the Sailors wore black armbands, but it wasn't a grim scene. What it felt like was a nightclub, a disco minus the music, a meat market in some urban deconstructed space with a cynical name like Regrets. And a rope to keep the wrong ones out.

None of the principals were in sight, not on the floor. There was probably a VIP lounge somewhere.

Security wasn't perfect. A few Norms made it in. There was Les Paul, walking around wide-eyed, with his guitar case and his stingy-brim hat, with a bottle of beer in his hand.

Jimmy saw Angel. Angel had spotted Les Paul, too. He made it over to the kid even before Jimmy did.

"What are you doing here?" Jimmy said to Les.

"He thought it would be interesting," Angel said. "Maybe he'll write a paper about it for school."

"There's a boat out there, you should go get on it," Jimmy said to the boy. "You don't need to see this."

Les Paul put the beer on the floor and started away.

"I talked to him for a long time," Angel said. "I explained it. Sort of. You know how it is."

"She was his sister? For real?"

"Yeah. I just told him his sister was mixed up in something. He always wanted to come to San Francisco. It'll be hard to get him home." Angel scanned the heads. "Machine Shop is somewhere. With that Jeremy, in with those people. He's gone over or something."

"Yeah, he had a lot of back and forth in him," Jimmy said.

"Are you all right?" Angel said.

"I don't know what I am."

Angel was used to lines like that from Jimmy. "Did you find out what it was? Who wanted you here, why?"

"Yeah, I did," Jimmy said. And stopped right there.

They had found a small space next to a cell wall where there weren't others pressing in on them, but now somebody touched Jimmy.

Mary. Mary looking like Mary Magdalene in a hooded cloak, a cassock, though fashionistas probably called it something else. It was black, closed in around her face. One minute she was Mary Magdalene, the next Death in *The Seventh Seal*.

Angel saw her, saw the edge of red light.

It took a lot to surprise Angel. He wasn't surprised. He stepped away.

Jimmy dropped a little of his attitude. "Have you ever been to one of these?" he said. "A little of it goes a long way."

"Can we go somewhere, talk?" Mary said.

"No," Jimmy said. But then he said, "I'm going to go. I don't care about this. Look, when this is over, maybe—"

The man at the window said, "Nine. Nine."

"*Number Nine*," Jimmy quoted. He opened the curtains over Mary's face. "Turn me on, Deadman," he said.

"Jimmy . . ."

"Come with me," he said.

People around them began to recognize her.

"Mary! It's Mary . . ."

It drove her away.

Or maybe it was the Watcher at the window, whose excitement was growing.

"Eight. Eight!"

She looked at him, then went away. Jimmy watched her go, the way people crowded around her, reached out to touch her. He didn't know if he'd ever see her again. If he could. Or if he wanted to.

The clotting crowd pressed in around him. He might have waited too long to escape.

"Seven! Seven!"

"That's bullshit," a voice beside him said. Jimmy turned. It was somebody he didn't know. The man was looking up at the town crier on the gunrail. "He doesn't know shit," the man said. "You can't call phases of the moon by the minute. It's bullshit. *They'll* call it. When the time comes. Just like they'll call the results."

He wore black, head to toe. Right down to the motorcycle boots.

"But I guess some people like that hocus-pocus," he said.

He had a good blue glow on. He offered his hand to Jimmy. There was a studded leather band around it.

"Kingman," he said. "Like Arizona, only farther out."

Jimmy didn't think they looked at all alike.

Kingman had others behind him. They now moved in a pack around Jimmy, closed in intentionally. A semicircle. It was the junior members of the L.A. board of directors. Boney M, Perversito. Even the fat man.

Two industrial floodlights on stanchions popped on, aimed at the center of the gunrail.

"You need to remember who your friends are," Kingman leaned close and hissed into Jimmy's ear.

"You're not my friends," Jimmy said.

"Yeah, that's what I meant," Kingman said.

The door at the far end of the gunrail, the end away from the window, opened.

Whitehead was the first through it.

"Five," the window man said. *"Five!"*

"Shut up!" Kingman yelled at the window man. Some of the crowd laughed. The window man gripped the railing with both hands.

On they came. The candidates.

What followed the appearance of each man onto the gunrail, into the spotlights, shouldn't be called applause, certainly not cheering. But it had a sound, a Sailor-specific sound, something that came out of the back of the mouth, halfway down the throat. Like the huzzahs in the House of Commons. Affirmative grumbling. The vocals were accompanied by the sound of shuffling feet, like walking in place. It was how they registered their respect.

Whitehead got a good reception. Jeremy stood on a bench under the gunrail and scanned the crowd, mentally taking names of any who thought otherwise.

Then it was Steadman. He was so big he had to duck to come through the doorway.

The L.A. contingent responded. And a few of the reds.

There wasn't ever going to be a vote; that wasn't the way it worked. But for now it seemed even between the two men, Whitehead and Steadman.

*"The Next!"* Kingman shouted out. "Steadman!"

The feet shuffled louder. Then a rhythm came out of it. And the rhythm turned into stomping.

Led by the black motorcycle boots.

Jeremy glared at Kingman and the SoCal Sailors.

"What?" Kingman said, glaring back at Jeremy. *"What!"*

Jeremy seized one of the floodlights and turned it on Kingman. Jimmy was caught in the glare, too.

But the crowd's attention wasn't diverted for long.

Because now Whitehead turned toward the door.

To present Mary. In her hood.

Mary Magdalene. Death Mary. A surprise candidate.

*"Queen Mary!"* a woman shouted. Men joined her.

Jimmy fell the rest of the way. Facedown.

He knew she was known. He knew she had her friends. He didn't know that she was poised to rule them, insofar as any of them allowed themselves to be ruled. He thought she had brought him here because she loved him.

She had brought him here to share a throne.

Christina Leonidas had seen Jimmy in the spotlight and now had squeezed in next to him.

"Can a woman be The Next?" she said.

The question was answered when Whitehead handed Mary a white rose.

"I yield," Whitehead said. And bowed at the waist.

The crowd grumbled their approval.

News joined in, lifting all-too-trusting eyes to the hooded figure on the balcony, the moment's Juliet.

"Your enemies watch you, learn from you," Kingman said to Jimmy.

"Red Steadman taught me that. Look at all these News. Fresh dead. They got all this from us. From the Cut thing. Run up the numbers, freak everybody out. But it's not over yet."

Mary looked down at Jimmy, in the other spotlight.

Kingman leaned even closer to him, to make it personal, to make it like a dirty joke, and said into his ear, "I stood over her, man, up in that white house up in Benedict Canyon, had the bloody, dripping knife in my hand. And something stopped me." He laughed the ugliest laugh of all, an ugly breath blown in Jimmy's ear. "Now here we all are . . ."

"One," the now-chastised lookout said. "One."

But it wasn't over. Jeremy shifted the other spotlight from Mary and Whitehead to Steadman.

Steadman moved to the rail.

He looked like a king.

Battling rumbling began, a war of voices and marching feet. The prison seemed to quake with it. Maybe the walls of Alcatraz would crumble with the collective fear and anger and hunger.

Who would it be?

Steadman or Mary?

Jimmy had had enough. He wanted a door. He saw Angel. Angel waved him over. He was along the side. Jimmy started toward him.

"Wait," Mary called down. "Wait."

Her voice stilled the crowd. Completely. In a second.

The light was still on him. Jimmy Miles. The waning crescent moon was now in the frame of the barred window. The hour of decision. Steadman looked defeated, one way or another. A few voices called out Jimmy's name. A few more.

Mary dropped Whitehead's rose, held out her hand to him. To *him*.

Jimmy looked up at her and said, loud enough for any of them to hear, "Whose idea was all the killing?"

Just when it was starting to get romantic.

---

He came down the Z to the docks, to where one of the red-and-white ferries idled. A crewman leaned on the rail with a hand spotlight, teasing the fish.

Jimmy stopped and turned before he got on board. He could hear them, up the hill, receiving their queen. In his head, he could see her there, and suspected he always would, for whatever years he had left to serve.

# THIRTY-SEVEN

They left the top down all the way, even when they ran through a little rain south of Salinas. The kid had his porkpie hat on. The guitar was covered.

Life was good.

"Where'd you get that hat?" Jimmy said over the wind.

"It was my dad's," Les Paul said. "It was in the closet."

"Where's he?"

"Down in L.A. someplace."

The kid wasn't in any hurry to get home. You could feel it coming from him. Going home felt like a sentence.

Jimmy came off the 101 into the middle of Paso Robles. Angel and Lucy were behind them in the Mercury. Jimmy slowed, let him come up alongside.

"Take the 46," Jimmy said. Angel nodded and sped ahead.

Jimmy turned off to the right. He knew where the kid lived, a few blocks ahead, a street over from the main drag where the little store was. But he didn't go there yet.

He drove up into the brown hills a mile off the highway. There was a hundred-year-old oak with free shade underneath it. Jimmy parked.

He popped the rear deck on the Porsche and checked the oil, to have something to do.

"All that stuff you saw, forget it," he said, his head over the engine. It crackled like a fire.

Les was looking to see if he could see the ocean from here.

"I never been up here," he said.

"It's nothing for you to think about the rest of your life," Jimmy said, standing, closing the hood. "It's not something a guy needs to know. It's not even real. A lot of it. They just make stuff up."

The kid turned. "I don't want to forget it. I want to use it. In my music."

It made Jimmy want to cry. Something did.

"What's your name, anyway?"

"Johnny," the kid said.

---

Angel had found his own shade tree, at the roadside twist of stainless steel memorializing James Dean. On 46 just before it meets 41. Lucy was just coming out of the little café with a Coke to go.

Jimmy was flying along at a hundred when he came up on them. He pulled it down into fourth and braked just enough to skid into the dirt lot in front of the memorial.

But Angel saw him coming. He already had the door of the Mercury open for Lucy, and she got in, and Angel roared out of there ahead of Jimmy, letting the speed slam the door closed.